THE DEADLIEST
OPTION

BY ANNETTE MEYERS

The Big Killing
Tender Death

BANTAM BOOKS

NEW YORK • TORONTO • LONDON • SYDNEY • AUCKLAND

Annette Meyers

THE
DEADLIEST
OPTION

THE DEADLIEST OPTION*
A Bantam Book / May 1991

Library of Congress Cataloging-in-Publication Data
Meyers, Annette.
  The deadliest option / by Annette Meyers.
    p.   cm.
  ISBN 0-553-07187-4
  I. Title.
PS3563.E889D44   1991
813'.54—dc20   90-48246
                                                      CIP

Published simultaneously in the United States and Canada

PRINTED IN THE UNITED STATES OF AMERICA
BVG   0 9 8 7 6 5 4 3 2 1

THIS ONE IS FOR "THE GIRLS":

Rita, Dorothy, Anne, Goldie,
and Annette

My thanks to William Dvorine, M.D., Shirley Herz, Michael Levy, M.D., Linda Ray, Philip Rinaldi, Cathi Rosso, Chris Tomasino, Howard Weiss, Victor Gotbaum, Kathy Schrier. Marty, always. And Kate Miciak, the best.

"I was raised to know the difference between right and wrong. I knew it wasn't right not to tell the truth about those things. But I didn't know it was unlawful."

OLIVER L. NORTH

"The secret of success is getting the money out of their pockets into ours."

XENIA SMITH
Partner, Smith and Wetzon

O N E

"Over my dead body!"

This verbal explosion was followed by a thump of such force that the gold-leafed mirror shook, as if someone were being shoved into the wall behind it. Wetzon's eyes widened as her reflected image undulated in the glass; her body jerked back, for it seemed as if the argument would burst into the ladies' room where she had come to fix her face. The scuffle—or whatever it was—was coming from the men's room next door. Another loud thud and angry voices. Then an ominous quiet.

The mirror covered the wall almost completely so that there was not one bare space to which she could put her curious ear. Frustrated, she watched her reflection wrinkle into a frown. "Curiosity killed the cat," she told it.

The door opened and a woman in a red, off-the-shoulder taffeta gown came in. Janet Barnes. Wife of Goldie Barnes, the Lion of Wall Street, chairman of Luwisher Brothers, and honoree of this evening's dinner. A huge red bow covered Janet's ample right bosom and most of her right arm. She swept past Wetzon to the stalls.

The loud voices and the scuffling started up again suddenly, subsiding into a low rumble from a new voice.

Hastily, Wetzon picked up her tiny silk clutch purse and escaped.

Dead cat or not, she had to see who they were. She knew almost everyone here tonight; the argument had to be between people she knew.

She parked herself unobtrusively behind a wide, pink marble column and watched the door to the men's room, hoping she hadn't missed whoever they were. *Nosy, Wetzon,* she said to herself, grinning. She was rewarded almost immediately by the appearance of the old man himself, Goldie Barnes, emerging from the men's room, his face florid with anger, chest heaving under his pleated white dress shirt. At his heels was Neil Munchen, Goldie's protégé, who ran the telemarketing— the fancy name for cold calling—floor for Luwisher Brothers. Neil had what looked like a faint reddish welt on his cheekbone. They walked off in the opposite direction from Wetzon's column, toward the grand ballroom.

She was trying to decide whether to move up behind them, when out of the men's room came Christopher Gorham, manager of the other retail floor at Luwisher Brothers and Wetzon's date for the evening; John Hoffritz, managing director, to whom Chris and Neil reported, known to the brokers as "Search"; and Destry Bird, third in line, not so affectionately known as "Destroy."

How infinitely curious. There had been some kind of pow-wow in the men's room and whatever had ensued was not very nice. The three men, like three penguins in dinner jackets, paused in front of the door. Wetzon inched around the column, dying to know what was being said. Then, as if it were one of those circus cars with all the clowns, the men's room door opened and yet one figure more emerged—a man like a walrus, fat and waddly, his black bow tie askew. Someone she didn't know. As if they'd been waiting for him, the penguins opened their huddle to include the walrus. Curiouser and curiouser.

"Sweetie pie, there you are!"

Damnation. Depend on Smith to barge in, interrupt her eavesdropping, and even call attention to it.

"What are you doing hiding behind that column?"

The three penguins snapped to attention, guarded eyes in frozen faces, and the walrus faded into gray as Smith captured Wetzon's hand and pulled her from behind the pink marble column into full view.

T W O

"Where on earth did you disappear to?"

Xenia Smith, tall, slim, and glowing in her burnished gold Carolyne Roehm gown, was the other half of Smith and Wetzon, the executive search and management consulting firm that the two women had started six years earlier. "Don't you know you should never leave an attractive man like Chris Gorham?"

Had she not noticed Chris in the group outside the men's room? Obviously not.

"Actually," Wetzon said, tongue in cheek, "I've been following Chris around so that other women can't get at him. Now you've ruined everything. Didn't you just see him come out of the men's room?"

Smith shot her a puzzled look. "I really wouldn't do that if I were you, Wetzon. People will think there's something wrong with you, and they'd be right."

"Oh, please, Smith, it was a joke. I'm not interested in Chris—" Oh, why bother? Wetzon sighed and let Smith tow her back to the ballroom. What was the use of arguing with Smith? She never listened and always thought she knew better. Smith would never accept the fact that Wetzon had a serious relationship with Silvestri, the NYPD detective Wetzon had met three years before, after Barry Stark was murdered.

"Besides, you're going to miss everything. Goldie's announced that he wants to say a few words before dinner."

"I've already missed the most interesting event of the evening, thanks ever so," Wetzon grumbled.

She and Smith threaded their way through the crowd of men and women in evening clothes also intent on getting seated. It looked like a convention of tuxedos and Carolyne Roehm dresses, and here she was in her basic black silk.

"The Street is getting to be a regular grubby UN, with all these multicolored faces, though I did see Ellie Kaplan talking to a rather attractive Chinaman at the bar." Smith's comment was an over-the-shoulder throwaway.

"Nice gams," hot breath whispered in Wetzon's ear. A hand brushed her derriere and stayed a bit too long to be accidental. Smith was ahead of her and didn't hear or see her latest main man, Jake Donahue, make his customary pass at Wetzon.

"Get lost, Jake," she hissed, swerving, dislodging his hand.

"Oh, Jake." Smith had turned and spotted him. He was hard to miss—big and beefy, red-haired, with intense blue eyes.

Another oddity. Donahue had some kind of interest in Luwisher Brothers, or he wouldn't be here tonight. With her high cheekbones, olive skin, and almond eyes, Smith was a veritable femme fatale. She had men falling all over her, so it never ceased to amaze Wetzon that she had gotten involved with Jake Donahue, the slimebag who had defrauded investors, fessed up to the government, named names, and had his knuckles rapped lightly by a few months in tennis camp where cooperative white collar criminals served their time.

Oh, Jake Donahue was attractive all right, in the same way all powerful men are attractive. But to Wetzon, he oozed greed. And greed was destroying the brokerage industry that she knew and loved.

They got back to their tables just as the first course, baby shrimp *en croûte*, was being served by waiters in black tuxedos. *Who are the keepers and who are the inmates?* Wetzon wondered, and a giggle rose up in her throat.

"I thought Goldie was going to talk." She elbowed Smith, who was sitting at the next table.

"*Shsh.*"

She looked over at the head table. It was hard to see beyond the lavish floral arrangement. Luwisher Brothers was going all out with this retirement dinner in honor of their chairman, one of the last of the Street's grand old men.

The chair beside her was empty and she looked around for Chris Gorham. She had first met Chris when he was an ambitious young broker at Merrill Lynch, had kept up with him when he became an assistant manager at Drexel. His rapid rise to a management position with Luwisher Brothers had come as no surprise to Wetzon. He now could have equity in a firm because Luwisher Brothers was one of the last of the pure play partnerships left on the Street. If he made partner—and he was in line to—the stock that came with the title would guarantee that should the firm be bought out or go public, Chris would become a multimillionaire overnight. He had it all—except his home life was in tatters. Six weeks ago his wife had taken the three kids and gone home to Charleston for an extended visit.

When he'd asked Wetzon to come with him to tonight's banquet, she had been flattered, and interested in seeing what these inside, self-congratulatory celebrations were like. And besides, it was good for business, as Smith always said.

She spotted him. Back to Wetzon, he was leaning over the head table, apparently trying to get Goldie Barnes's attention. Everyone was trying to talk to Goldie Barnes, it seemed, for he was almost blocked from Wetzon's view by hovering members of the firm.

Goldie was part of the second establishment (if you considered the Morgans, the Schiffs, the Lehmans, and the Loebs and their ilk as the first establishment) on the Street, which included Sandy Weill, who was the inspiration for Shearson; the late Sy Lewis, the Bear of Bear Stearns; Nate Gancher of Oppenheimer; and Don Regan, who had brought Merrill Lynch into the twentieth century and come acropper in the Reagan White House. They were all men who had grabbed the ball from the private, white-shoe club of the old Wall Street and had run with it. They had pushed their way in, aggressively, and the change in trading style, the heavy volume leading to operations snafus, and finally the financial fall-out in the seventies, paved the way for them to take over leadership on the Street.

The changeover that had begun in the late forties, after the war, reached a crescendo in 1981, when Sandy Weill sold Shearson Hammill, Hayden Stone, Faulkner, Dawkins & Sullivan, Loeb Rhoades, Hornblower Weeks, Noyes & Trask to American Express.

At the head table, the walrus Wetzon had seen outside the men's room was seating himself next to Goldie Barnes, watching Chris's every gesture with a bland expression and sharp eyes. His lips moved, but Wetzon found her view thwarted by an enormous pink peony that was part of the table's floral decoration. Standing between Goldie and the fat man was Ellie Kaplan, Luwisher Brothers's biggest producer. Ellie's prematurely gray hair, blow-dried into a thick fringe, spilled over her face. She was wearing a long, glittery silver dress with a scoop of a neckline that hinted at rather than revealed cleavage. Goldie reached up and patted Ellie's cheek. She had been the first woman broker hired by Luwisher Brothers, and Goldie had sponsored her. Ellie turned to the fat man, her lips curled; she seemed to be saying something derisive. The fat man removed a nasal inhalator from an inside pocket and breathed into it, one nostril at a time, ignoring Ellie. When she backed away from the table, Hoffritz and Bird quickly took her place. Hoffritz, with his slimy smile, pushed the drinks away from the table edge and leaned into Goldie. Bird put his arm around Goldie's shoulder. Goldie shook it off.

So now the old order was changing again. Goldie Barnes had put the fusty, dusty, century-old Luwisher Brothers on the map as a contender for the big trading dollars in equities. He was a legend, and scuttlebutt on the Street was that Search and Destroy were forcing him out.

Wetzon looked over at Smith's table. Smith was talking animatedly with an attractive white-haired man who looked a lot like Felix Rohatyn. Leave it to Smith to find the one man in the financial world Wetzon considered sexy.

Back at the head table, Goldie had shifted in his seat so that now Wetzon had a clear view. He was a giant in a tailor-made tux with a great shock of sun-streaked, white-blond hair, combed straight back like a mane. He looked every bit the Golden Lion, the name by which he was known on the Street, and not at all his acknowledged sixty-five years. Goldie got to his feet and was leaning across the table, a glass of bourbon in his hand, as he spoke to Chris Gorham. As she watched, she saw Chris stiffen, as if from a shock. The Lion shook his mane. A small smile played havoc with his jowly face and ended, rather like the MGM lion's, in a growl.

The grossly fat man next to the Lion seemed to be immensely amused by the exchange. Goldie set his glass down. Chris made a sweeping gesture with his arm, as if to punctuate what he was saying, and knocked over several glasses, including Goldie's bourbon and a water goblet. The fat man heaved himself up, but not before he'd gotten splashed with some of the water.

In the confusion, John Hoffritz and Destry Bird appeared and took their seats at the head table, while Chris, anxious and apologetic, signaled to a waiter, who came and mopped up the flood with a linen napkin.

Goldie sat down again and lifted a glass to his lips. He looked over at his wife who sat talking with Alton Pinkus, a member of the board of directors of Luwisher Brothers and a former executive with the AFL-CIO. Janet Barnes had a deep crease between her eyes and she was gesturing vigorously with her fork.

Ellie Kaplan finished her somewhat agitated conversation with a waiter whose back was to Wetzon, and slipped into her seat at the table almost at the same moment Chris yanked his chair back and sat down next to Wetzon. Chris was visibly upset; probably because Neil Munchen was seated at Goldie's table.

"Something wrong?" Wetzon skewered a tiny shrimp. How strange and tense the atmosphere in the ballroom had gotten.

Chris started to speak but was interrupted by the sound of cutlery on a glass. Everyone turned to the head table.

Goldie Barnes took a healthy swallow from his glass of bourbon and followed it with a drink of water from the goblet in front of him. He slowly rose from his chair, a peculiar half-smile on his face.

"My friends, it truly grieves me to spoil your little celebration—" He stopped and coughed and looked up at the ceiling with its famous crystal chandeliers. Surely a joke was coming. The Lion, it was said, had a great sense of humor.

Wetzon's eyes were diverted by a muffled moan to her right. Chris sat hunched down, neck into shoulders, his head bowed.

Someone gasped.

Wetzon looked back at Goldie Barnes. His arms were flailing.

Chris's head spun around; he jumped to his feet.

Someone cried, "Goldie!"

"No!"

"Oh, my God!"

"Help him, somebody!"

The entire room rose almost as one. Goldie's hands clawed at his throat. He was choking, gagging, making horrible noises. His face went from red to blue. He seemed to be dancing. With one final spastic movement, he pitched over onto the head table, amid glasses and plates. The floral arrangement flew to the floor. Diners scattered.

The table rocked violently, then crashed to the floor under the dead weight of Goldie Barnes.

THREE

The afternoon sun streamed through the open French doors and the heady scents of summer wafted into the room, tickling Wetzon's nose. She sat with her feet on her desk, eyelids drooping, struggling to concentrate on Goldie Barnes's extensive obituary in *The New York Times*.

"Dishyonotherwashashon?" Smith's mouth was packed full of Fig Newtons.

"Kindly translate that for me." Wetzon looked up over the edge of the newspaper at her partner, who had the unmitigated gall to look as if she'd had eight hours of restful sleep and was perky and full of energy.

"Did-you-know-he-had-a-son?"

"Who?"

"Why are you being so obtuse? Goldie Barnes, of course. Who else?"

"No, I didn't." She skimmed the obituary. "Here it is. 'Survivors . . . Janet Barnes . . . Goldman Barnes, II.' . . . Hey, he's with L.L. Rosenkind. Isn't that interesting?"

"Fathers and sons," Smith said knowingly.

Wetzon nodded, half listening to Smith and half listening to the smooth way B.B.—their assistant, Bailey Balaban—was handling a cold call. He was getting really adept, zeroing in on some good prospects for Wetzon to follow up.

"It was cardiac arrest."

"I think I heard he had severe asthma—oxygen tank everywhere he went, that kind of thing."

The phone rang once, twice, a third time. Wetzon reached for it. "Smith and Wetzon."

"What do we have B.B. for?" Smith grumbled.

Wetzon put her hand over the receiver. "He's in the middle of a cold call."

"Hi, Wetzon, it's Sharon."

"Do we have a Harold Alpert here?" Smith's question was loud and rhetorical.

"Hi, Sharon, I've been trying to catch up with you." Wetzon shook her head at Smith and swung her feet off the desk, swept the newspapers to the floor, and rifled through suspect sheets until she came up with Sharon Murphy's.

"Sharon Murphy?" Smith mouthed.

Wetzon gave her a thumbs-up signal.

Harold Alpert appeared in the doorway, looking nervous and apprehensive. It was almost four years now since Harold had started with Smith and Wetzon as a summer intern, general factotum, and cold caller. They had made him a junior associate, but on the condition that he also back up B.B. when it got busy. Smith rose and waved Harold out into the garden.

"I think I'm ready to talk to people now, Wetzon." Sharon had a husky, sultry voice that was an immensely successful sales tool—she could get people to listen to her. "Things are just awful here . . . I guess you've heard."

"Heard what?" Wetzon had heard there had been major defections in that branch office. It was a shame that she hadn't had her hand in some of it. But you couldn't be everywhere, and she had stopped beating herself up about it. No matter how good you were, some potential candidates always slipped through the cracks.

"Well, I don't like to say too much—I think they're taping our calls—but we've lost three really big producers here in the last six months, and Wally is suddenly taking managing the office very seriously."

"If he doesn't, he's going to lose the office. The Street is full of managers looking for offices." Since the Crash in October of 1987, the absorption of Hutton by Shearson, the sale of the retail division by

Drexel, Pru-Bache's purchase of Thomson McKinnon's retail operation, and Drexel's spectacular bankruptcy, the retail industry had shrunk considerably; managers had become a dime a dozen, and the firms could be—and were—increasingly particular. The major problem was that a great many of the managers were second-rate, couldn't motivate, couldn't recruit, and couldn't close—that is, get a broker to commit to join. It was the continuing nightmare of a headhunter to have perfect candidates lined up and have the manager unable to write the ticket.

"Morale is horrible. Wally took me to lunch—to talk about my progress, he said, after ignoring me for the three years I've been here—and then all he did was talk about himself, how hard it is to keep everyone happy."

"Let's see . . . you finished last year at three-fifty thou. What do you have in for the first five months this year?"

"Two-fifty."

"Well, of course he's going to take you to lunch. He should have taken you to Lutèce."

"That cheap bastard. We went to the deli around the corner. He couldn't get into Lutèce anyway. I don't know, Wetzon. Just to go to another wire house—I don't know. I think I need a very aggressive cold calling atmosphere, and I want upfront. I'm not going without money."

"You could go to Luwisher Brothers—get into a cold calling set-up. Neil Munchen runs a good program with all the support and leads you can handle. But they don't do upfront deals."

"And they're downtown. I just bought an apartment on Fifty-ninth Street. I want to walk to work. Taking the subway downtown every day will make me crazy. I'll end up spending a fortune on cabs; besides, my therapist is uptown."

"Okay, why not talk to Dayne Becker and Loeb Dawkins? You'll get the deal you want and maybe you can factor in your own cold caller."

"Oh, God, all right. Set me up before I chicken out. Do one this Wednesday about five and the other next Wednesday. Midtown. And not with the Dayne Becker manager you set me up with last year. I didn't like him. He was too laid-back."

"Yes, you're right. He is. There's a super young manager on Fifty-fourth and Fifth. You'll like him."

Wetzon hung up as Harold shuffled past her desk, eyes downcast, and returned to his tiny cubbyhole in their outer office. They had talked him into shaving off his beard, so he didn't look like an Orthodox rabbi anymore, but with his mustache and his horn-rimmed glasses and his slouch, he was a dead ringer for Groucho Marx. She smothered a grin.

"Well?" Smith stood in the doorway to the garden.

"She wants an aggressive atmosphere and upfront."

"They never know what they want, Wetzon. You should never listen to them. Just tell them."

"Where did you go last night?" Wetzon was not about to let Smith get on her kick of how brokers constantly took advantage of her. "I looked for you after—"

Smith smiled a little cat smile. "Jake knows Janet Barnes from way back. Did you know she's a Fingerhut?" She was scrutinizing her face in a hand mirror and plucked out a stray eyebrow hair.

"The liquor dynasty? No kidding."

"They probably got all that booze last night wholesale." Smith put the mirror and her tweezers in her desk drawer. "Maybe I'll call her and offer my condolences. I knew Goldie fairly well. . . ." Her voice trailed off.

She's scheming, Wetzon thought, watching Smith's mind work, *click, click, click. She's thinking about whether Janet Barnes could be useful in some weird way.* Smith was determined to be part of New York's social scene, and now that she was seeing Jake Donahue, she just might make it. Jake was a conjurer when it came to connections.

Wetzon took her jacket off and hooked it on the back of her chair. "Janet is probably in good hands with family and friends, Smith. And you hardly knew Goldie at all. Perhaps a note from both of us—"

Smith cut her off with a curt, "I'll take care of it." She hummed something under her breath. "You know, Wetzon, you're getting to be a regular little black cloud." She wrinkled her fine nose and gave Wetzon a hard look. "Do you realize people keep dropping like flies all around you?" She adjusted the silk scarf at her throat.

"Do you really think so?" Wetzon tried to keep her tone light, but faltered. The same thought had been going through her mind. "Am I some kind of magnet who makes things happen? Or is it just this crazy business we're in?" She found herself doodling a dagger on Sharon Murphy's suspect sheet, then caught herself and erased it.

"Honestly, sweetie, I don't think all these insider trading and fraud indictments have helped."

"The public perception of brokers is awful, and lately some of the people we're dealing with make me feel so grungy I want to wash after I talk to them."

"Stop!" Smith held up her hand. "I don't want to hear any of that. We're in an insane business. Just remember, our motivation is to get the money out of their pockets and into ours." She unwrapped a refill for her gold Cross pen and replaced the old one, tossing it clattering into her brass wastebasket. "But I have to tell you that for the first time since—"

"Please don't say it." She knew that Smith was going to mention the last time Wetzon had been involved in a murder, the winter of the big blizzard.

Smith nodded solemnly. "The cards, sweetie pie. I don't know . . . I can't explain . . . it's a sense of something inevitable around you." She smiled. "Now don't get mad. I think you should consult a psychic."

Wetzon groaned. "Oh, Smith, no. I don't want to know. Can't I just let it happen? I like surprises. That's what makes life so damn much fun." She meant it, too. "Besides, Goldie Barnes wasn't murdered." She looked down at her list of people she had to talk to.

"Humpf." Smith was miffed. "Well, I'm just making a sincere suggestion. I'm afraid you're in for some—"

"Phone for you, Smith." B.B. tapped on the door frame. "Destry Bird."

Wetzon and Smith stared at each other. Smith reached for the phone. "Destry . . . yes . . . well, of course, you have our deepest condolences . . . yes . . . you know we are at your service." She was making grotesque faces at Wetzon and her eyes sparkled. "Monday? We could come at nine . . . oh, I see. Eleven-thirty would be fine." She looked at Wetzon, who nodded impatiently. "We'll see you then." She replaced the receiver.

"What is that about?"

"We've been invited down to Luwisher Brothers to talk about new hiring procedures."

"New hiring procedures? Who's taking over the firm?"

"He didn't elucidate."

"The king is dead, long live the king."

Smith eyed the phone, then Wetzon. "They couldn't meet at nine because there's going to be a police inquiry." She shivered.

"A police inquiry? Into what? Procedures? An audit? What?"

Dark clouds had slipped almost furtively over the sun without their noticing. A windstorm burst through the open doors, scooping up their papers, sending them every which way. The women jumped up and with some effort closed the French doors. A jagged bolt of lightning streaked out of the dark pewter sky and slammed into the high wooden fence that backed their neighbor's yard. Just as the fence burst into flame, the sky opened up and rain fell in heavy sheets, dousing the fire.

"It's started," Smith said.

FOUR

They took a cab to the Luwisher Tower building opposite the World Trade Center, Smith decked out in her plum suit and Wetzon in dark blue pinstripes. Smith had been late, as always, and they were now part of the snarl of cars, trucks, and cabs inching off the FDR Drive in lower Manhattan. Temperatures had risen dramatically since early morning, and it was hot.

"He says he's worried about the algebra final." Smith was reading a letter from her son, Mark, who was finishing his first term at St. Paul's and living away from home for the first time. "God, I miss him," she said suddenly, touching the corner of her eyes with a fingertip.

Wetzon patted her shoulder. "I do, too, but isn't he having a wonderful time?"

"I don't know." Smith looked out the window at the construction that had eliminated one lane of the highway, and frowned. "I can read between the lines, and I know he misses me. But Jake thinks he needs to be on his own for a while."

Wetzon hated to admit it, even to herself, but Jake Donahue was right. Mark was fifteen now, and it was time for him to ease out of the intense relationship he had with his mother.

"Well, the term is almost over. He'll be home soon." Their cab nudged the back bumper of the van ahead of them and the driver, a small

Latino, exploded from the vehicle and began screaming at their driver, a stone-faced black man, in Spanish. Their driver opened the door, yelling, "Spick mother-fuck—" when a traffic cop appeared and inspected the bumper, then waved both drivers back to their places. Horns blared through the tumult, and traffic began moving again.

"Please don't tell anyone, Wetzon, but I think Jake's jealous of Mark."

It was totally unlike Smith to sound so worried. But Smith had changed a lot recently. She had been seeing a therapist for over a year; her life appeared to have stabilized since the disaster with Leon, and she was certainly much easier to work with.

"Good grief, Smith, who would I tell? And why would he be jealous of a fifteen-year-old boy?" If indeed, the great Jake Donahue was jealous, it was because Smith had created the situation, playing her son against her lover.

"Jake's made arrangements for Mark to spend the summer in Arizona, working on a cattle ranch."

"Oh? Sounds like fun. Is Mark excited?"

"I don't know. I haven't talked to him about it. I was waiting till he got home."

"It'll be all right, I'm sure. And if it's not, *I'll* go and you and Mark can run the business for the summer."

"Wetzon," Smith said. "If I haven't told you lately, you've been a wonderful friend—and I love you." She folded the letter back into its envelope and tucked it into her briefcase.

"Why, thank you, Smith." Wetzon was amazed and just a little moved.

"Now, then." Smith wriggled to straighten her skirt, which had crawled up to mid-thigh. "Back to business. I want you to let me do the talking at this meeting."

"What—" Just then their cab came to a shuddering stop and the driver flipped his flag down. The meter read sixteen dollars and eighty-five cents.

"Give the man a twenty, Wetzon, please. I forgot to bring my wallet." Smith opened the door and slid out of the cab.

The Luwisher Tower was one of the new granite-and-glass monstrosities rising sixty-eight floors above the Financial District in lower Manhattan. Constructed on landfill, it would have boggled the minds of the small group of traders who had gathered under the buttonwood tree at 68 Wall Street on May 17, 1792, and founded what became the New York Stock Exchange.

Any other time Wetzon might have been fuming, but on this beautiful, sunny day in June, she was in a benevolent frame of mind. Smith was Smith and even with the therapy, her basic narcissistic nature was not going to change. She looked at her watch. "We're fifteen minutes early."

"See, I told you not to rush me. You always want to leave so early."

"I loathe being late."

"You're the one who should be seeing a therapist, I think." Smith beamed at her.

"Do you want to go in for coffee?" Wetzon pointed to a terminally cute croissant shop with gingham curtains on the lobby level next to a WaldenBooks outlet the size of an airplane hangar.

"No, let's go on up. We can powder our noses."

A special elevator was programmed to go directly to Luwisher Brothers, which occupied the top eight floors. The construction had been a joint venture between Luwisher Brothers and an international real estate conglomerate, which occupied ten floors of the building. The remainder of the skyscraper was divided among the New York home of a major insurance company, the headquarters of Merryweather Funds, mutual funders of some repute, and Grover, Newman, one of the largest law firms in the world.

The walls of the elevator were covered with tufted brown leather like a chesterfield, and the lighting was subdued, diffused through the mottled glass of the dropped ceiling. And the elevator talked. "Good morning," it said in a digital voice. "This elevator goes to Luwisher Brothers. Please choose your floor."

"What floor did Destry say?"

"Sixty-seven." Smith pressed the shiny brass square, and the elevator rose almost imperceptibly, like a hot-air balloon. The lights above the doors began blinking at the sixtieth floor and stopped when the doors slid softly open on the sixty-seventh.

To the right of the bank of six elevators, three on each side, was a small reception area carpeted in pale taupe. A wide corridor cut through left and right, seeming to run the width of the building. The ceiling, topped by a skylight, rose two floors, giving the space the look of a cathedral. Wetzon stifled a laugh. Some cathedral. Here everyone prayed to Mammon, god of gold. Goldie's Church, some wit had called it.

The walls were painted in a paler taupe and hung with those Georgia O'Keeffe flower paintings that always made Wetzon feel she was looking at colorful depictions of female sex organs.

A real tree, with a whitish bark and beautiful silver leaves, grew hydroponically from a huge pot of water and stones, reaching its branches up to the skylight. The windows soared from floor to ceiling.

But by far the most prominent feature in the room was the sweeping marble staircase, with an open iron railing on one side. From where she stood, looking upward, Wetzon could see a battalion of pantslegs belonging to a group of men who were milling at the top of the curved stairs.

A young woman with blunt-cut, shoulder-length hair sat behind a glass-topped desk talking on the phone and writing on a message pad. "Thank you for your thoughts," she said. "I will convey them to everyone." She hung up and smiled at them. She had perfect teeth and wore very little makeup. "How may I help you?"

"Xenia Smith and Leslie Wetzon. We have an appointment with Destry Bird."

"We know we're a bit early," Wetzon added and got a glower from Smith.

The woman picked up the phone and pressed a button. "Hi, this is Maggie. Ms. Smith and Ms. Wetzon are here." She waited. "Okay." She hung up and gave them another vision of her perfect orthodontia. "Mr. Bird is in a meeting, but he should be with you shortly."

"Where is your ladies' room?" Smith asked.

"Just past the elevators. The second door on the right."

"I'll wait here," Wetzon said. She of the slow burn was just beginning to feel abused by Smith's admonition to let her do the talking. Not on her life. Who did Smith think she was? *Don't tell me, tell her,* was what Wetzon's friend Carlos always said, but Smith was so mercurial that she seemed to sense when Wetzon had reached her boiling point and immediately became caring and attentive, deftly deflecting Wetzon's anger.

"Suit yourself," Smith said airily, "though I think you could do with a little more color in your face. You look totally washed out." She paused and, when she saw her comment had no effect, shrugged her enviable shoulders and went on past the elevators and disappeared to the right.

Two workmen in paint-streaked overalls got off the elevator, bringing with them the bitter, pungent combination of cigarettes and old sweat. The larger of the two carried a paint-spattered stepladder. The shorter one handed a piece of paper to Maggie. "You Miss Gray?"

The receptionist nodded, inspected the work order, and directed them up the staircase.

The group of pantslegs at the top of the stairs parted for the workmen, then two pairs started down the stairs and came into Wetzon's view. Surprise flushed her face pink.

The first man was tall and slightly stooped, with the pouchy-eyed look of a basset hound. The other was a stocky man with thinning dark hair; he wore a new dark gray suit. The first man was Artie Metzger, Detective Sergeant, NYPD, and the second was Silvestri, who had bought the new suit for his promotion to detective lieutenant the previous month.

What an interesting turn of events, Wetzon thought. But Destry had mentioned to Smith something about meeting with the police this morning. Wetzon walked slowly to the foot of the stairs and waited for Silvestri and Metzger to see her. But they were engrossed in conversation and probably perceived her peripherally as just another skirt.

"What are two nice guys like you doing in a place like this?"

"Les—" Silvestri stared down at her. For a brief moment, genuine astonishment stripped his face of its professional mask.

Her response was an impish grin. Silvestri always accused her of flying by the seat of her pants, interfering in police business. What would he say now? After all, she was there innocently, on business for her firm. "Hi, Artie," she said to Metzger, ignoring Silvestri's puzzled look.

She made a grand show of shaking hands, first with Metzger, and then with Silvestri, aware of the watchful eyes of Maggie Gray, and walked with them to the elevators. Metzger touched the down button and a light blinked, a door opened. The men got on and turned, facing her. "Please choose your floor," the elevator commented. "Press L to return to the lobby."

"See you later, Les," Silvestri said. He took out his little notebook and was flipping through pages as if he were looking for something. Having recovered from the shock of seeing her there, he was giving her nothing, and he knew she was dying to know what was going on.

"Wait a minute, guys." The doors started to close. "What brings you onto my turf?" She put her briefcase in the door, which opened slightly, just enough for her to hear Silvestri's intentionally melodramatic response.

"Murder," he said.

FIVE

"Murder?" she repeated, staring at the closed elevator doors.

"Murder? Is that what you just said?" Wetzon had not even heard Smith come up behind her.

"Smith!" She spun around. Running through her mind was the musical refrain, *he said murder he said, da da da dum, he said murder he said.*

"Excuse me, Ms. Smith, Ms. Wetzon. Mr. Bird would like you to go up to the conference room now." Maggie Gray, in her creamy beige silk, stood beside her desk motioning to them.

Who was murdered? Wetzon's thoughts roiled. Who had died, except . . . As they approached the staircase, the two workmen started down from the floor above. One carried the ladder, the other a large painting half covered by a dirty piece of canvas. Smith forged ahead, up the stairs, brushing between the men. The canvas was dislodged slightly, revealing an oil portrait of the late Goldie Barnes.

"The king is dead, long live the king," Wetzon said.

Smith turned and looked down at her. "Whatever is the matter with you? Come on."

The stairs led to a gallery that overlooked the floor below. On this floor were the penthouse, with the executive dining room, and the top executive offices. Only the same iron railing stood between the edge of the gallery and open space. Overhead was the skylight, through which the midday sun streamed, giving the area an inside-outside feeling. A Picasso from his Dada period—all angled, anxious edges—hung on the facing wall. Loud voices surged from the half-open door of the conference room.

Wetzon put her hand on Smith's arm, slowing her.

Johnny Hoffritz's voice, with its succulent Alabama rhythms, was unmistakable. ". . . couldn't go quietly . . . you'd know he'd try one more time to fuck us up."

"Well, you could hardly expect him to go quietly." Destry Bird's accent was strictly upper-class Virginia, fine old family. Someone guffawed, then Destry continued, "Better this way—"

"For us."

"Ladies . . ."

Smith and Wetzon, caught eavesdropping, started. They were now confronted by a royal corpulence, a grossly fat man in an immaculate gray pinstripe and crisp white shirt, the costume of an investment banker or broker.

Wetzon recognized him immediately as the man who had been sitting to Goldie Barnes's left at the banquet.

The fat man's breath came in short puffy pants, as if he'd run up the staircase, which he probably had, and under his arm he carried a flat leather portfolio. Emitting a stale minty odor, he attached himself to Wetzon's elbow, she being closer to his height than the formidable Smith, who was at least a head taller. Thus, he walked Wetzon right into the conference room, with an amused Smith bringing up the rear.

"Ah, there you are. Good. Let's get going here." Hoffritz was seated, tilting back in the big leather chair at the head of the walnut conference table, his lanky body draped territorially—in Goldie's chair. On the wall beyond his head was a big empty spot, a shade lighter than the rest of the room, where a large painting had once hung. With his small head and receding chin, there was something of the praying mantis about Johnny Hoffritz. His hazel eyes were wide apart and hooded by fine, almost transparent, lids. A cigarette lay disintegrating in the cup of black coffee, which he pushed rudely aside. "More coffee all around . . . Chris?" His hand made a lazy flick in Chris Gorham's direction.

Gorham's high-cheekboned face flushed red up to his too-short, sand-colored hair. Jaw tightening, he rose, hardly acknowledging Smith or Wetzon, and left the room. He was obviously low man on this totem pole.

"Take a seat," Destry drawled to Smith and Wetzon. He shook hands with the fat man without getting up. "Doctor—" Destry had straight brown hair neatly side-parted and round shiny cheeks, almost baby-smooth facial skin, and a small pink cupid's-bow mouth. A crooked, bumped nose barely kept him from looking effeminate.

Smith plopped herself down next to Johnny Hoffritz, of course. It was easy to see who the new *führer* was. With Goldie gone, she might be able to make some personal inroads.

The fat doctor, whoever he was, lowered his massive bulk into the chair next to Smith before Wetzon could, separating them. "I'm Dr. Ash, Carlton Ash." He said it as if Wetzon should recognize his name. She smiled politely at him and he offered her a side of ham in the shape of a hand to shake. His breathing was laborious.

"Let's get going." Hoffritz thumped the table with the flat of his hand. "Neil, will you get the fuck off the goddam phone." He pulled a cigarette from a pack and stuck it, unlit, into the corner of his mouth.

Neil Munchen, dark-haired, dark-eyed, sporting an early suntan and a bruised cheekbone, looked decidedly ethnic next to the others. He hung up the phone and sat next to Wetzon, giving her a nod. His heavy gold Rolex winked at her from under his crisp white shirt cuff.

Reaching into a vest pocket, Dr. Ash removed a small inhalator and, pressing one nostril at a time, inhaled a mint-scented spray.

Chris returned, followed by a white-haired black man in a black suit who carried a silver tray of cups and a large decanter of coffee.

Looking around the room, Wetzon saw a particularly white-bread group, except for Neil Munchen. Quite a difference from the way Goldie Barnes had run Luwisher Brothers in his heyday, she thought. Goldie believed ethnics had more hunger in their bellies.

"Get the door, Dougie." Dougie was Douglas Culver, head of financial services, a thick-waisted good ole Georgia boy, with a slow smile and a quick mind.

The particular, and most attractive, essence of Luwisher Brothers was that everyone produced; that is, everyone had clients and did the business of stockbroker-financial advisor along with his other duties. That meant partners, managers, department heads, all carried their own weight.

"I'll lay it out," Hoffritz said after all the cups were filled except

Wetzon's, who passed on caffeine. "And y'all jump in where you will. Everyone here knows Smith and Wetzon. They're supposed to be recruiting brokers for us, but we haven't seen much from them lately."

How attractive, Wetzon thought. All right. Smith wanted to talk, she'd let Smith handle this hot potato. And she had no doubt that Smith could, too. No one messed with Smith more than once.

Smith looked around the table, flashing everyone a dazzling smile. "Gentlemen, I don't have to tell you what the climate is like on the Street now. You want big producers? Pay them the upfront dollars that other firms are paying."

"We don't buy brokers. It's a *privilege* to be invited to work here." Destry was spouting the company line.

"There aren't very many big producers anymore; they've become a rare and vanishing breed since the Crash in '87, and they want to be rewarded for the fact that they're doing so well in such an uncertain climate. Brokers are nervous, insecure. They are worried about making a move and not being able to transfer accounts." She looked at Wetzon.

"That's right," Wetzon said, picking up the ball. "I interview hundreds of brokers every week, and we know the quality you want at Luwisher Brothers. We would never show you anyone who wasn't top quality." She let her eyes float around the table. "Of course if you want to see brokers with problems on their U4s, or who build production by churning—"

"That depends on the problem, doesn't it? We can look at each case individually. I suppose, sooner or later, every broker is going to have a complaint of some sort." Destry looked at Hoffritz, who nodded. It was rumored that Destry Bird had had his license suspended for two months when he was with Marcus, Jones in Richmond.

"Let's talk about this so-called climate, if we may?" Dr. Ash put his question to Wetzon. He pursed his lips, puffing as he spoke. His belly pressed against the table edge.

"The climate is the erratic nature of the market," Smith said.

"For the first time, brokers are looking for long-term security," Wetzon added. "Money, stable firms, nonpressured environments."

"Yes," Dr. Ash puffed. "Good, good." He nodded to Hoffritz.

Hoffritz smiled without parting his lips, exercising the unlit cigarette, which began to droop. "Shall we discuss the new profile of the Luwisher broker? We'd like to see as many of these people as you can show us."

"Just get them over here and we'll close them," Destry said.

Neil Munchen stared into his coffee and looked glum.

"Okay, Carl?"

Dr. Ash took a sheet of paper out of his portfolio and slid it across Smith to Hoffritz, who squinted at the page.

Smith cleared her throat daintily and looked at Wetzon, who took a legal pad and a pen from her briefcase.

"We want to see brokers who are married, with children, with responsibilities like mortgages, private schools. Good producers grossing two-fifty or three hundred."

Wetzon stopped writing. This was weird. While most brokers had heavy responsibilities, how could a firm eliminate from consideration the younger broker? It didn't make any sense.

"And we'd like to see some women—don't tell me you girls can't come up with some." He dropped the mangled cigarette into his cup.

Smith's smile froze on her face. Wetzon could almost read her mind. "Girls" was a red flag, especially to Smith. Wetzon looked up but didn't change her expression. Hoffritz didn't even know when he was being insulting.

"And incidentally," Hoffritz continued, "we're putting Tom Keegen on this, too."

"Tom Keegen!" Smith exploded, not even trying to keep her cool. Smith hated Tom Keegen, their major competitor. She had had a run-in with him years ago. "Everyone knows Keegen double-dips, and he's doing it right here at Luwisher Brothers."

"We've seen some good people through him lately," Chris said.

Wetzon put her pen down. The smarmy bastard. Chris knew Tom Keegen was a dirtbag. Everyone knew. But on Wall Street now, if Muammar Kaddafi sent them brokers, they'd work with him. The times they were no longer changing—they had changed.

"We like his work," Hoffritz said. "And we like your work, girls, so show us what you can do—"

The door to the conference was flung open with a tremendous burst of force and Ellie Kaplan stalked into the room. "What are you darling boys trying to get away with here?" She was a mess—wrinkled silk suit, her normally sleek gray hair disheveled, her face swollen and distorted—in no way like the chic woman in the glittery silver dress at the banquet. Ellie stopped in her tracks, staring at the spot on the wall beyond Hoffritz's head and yowled, "What have you done with his portrait?"

"Now, Ellie darlin'—" Dougie jumped up and put his arm around her, stroking her back, and she burst into tears and threw her arms around him. Distaste overwhelmed his face.

Wetzon, instinctively rising to help Ellie Kaplan, caught the looks exchanged by the Gang of Four, because clearly, Neil Munchen was an outsider.

"Ah, Wetzon darlin', maybe you can help poor old Ellie out to the ladies' . . ." Dougie's voice drifted off. He peeled himself away from the devastated woman and thrust her bodily at Wetzon.

"Of course Wetzon will, won't you, Wetzon?" Smith's voice was filled with meaning.

The phone on the credenza began to ring, three short ones, a pause, and another three short rings. Neil picked it up. "Yeah?" He looked at Hoffritz and pointed the receiver at him. "For you."

Hoffritz got up slowly and took the phone. "Yes. Well, you know what to say. No. Fuck it, just say we were shocked by Goldie Barnes's untimely death and are finding it hard to believe that he was murdered."

Ellie, shaking with emotion, leaned on Wetzon as they left the room. "Like hell," she said.

S I X

"Oh, they killed him all right. They sit there so smug, dividing up the booty. Well, there wouldn't be anything if it weren't for him."

Ellie Kaplan set a folding makeup mirror on her cluttered desk, looked at her image, and grimaced. She ran a tortoise-shell comb through the thick tangles of her silvery hair. In her midforties, she was what people generally referred to as a handsome woman, with startling gray hair and thick coal-black eyebrows. Today, however, the skin around her dark eyes was swollen and mottled. She pressed some keys on her Quotron and stared into the machine.

Wetzon sat in a comfortable club chair in front of Ellie's desk. "You mean Goldie really was murdered? I thought it was heart failure, from the asthma."

"We all did." Ellie brushed blusher on her face with a sable-haired brush, applied red lipstick, zipped everything back into a blue nylon pouch and dropped it and the mirror into the open drawer on her right. She lit a cigarette and inhaled deeply. "Didn't Hoffritz tell you? Does he think he can hide it? Or maybe he thinks if he ignores it, it'll go away. The police were here this morning questioning everybody. They're saying Goldie was murdered." She stabbed at the keyboard again, raising more information. "Uh-huh . . . up a quarter. . . . Excuse me, Wetzon. David!"

The door opened with such speed that Wetzon felt whoever opened it had to have been standing and listening.

"Ellie?"

"David Kim—Wetzon." Ellie didn't look up from the machine.

"Looking good, David," Wetzon said.

"So're you, Wetzon."

They grinned at each other, both amused that Ellie didn't remember how he'd gotten his job with her.

For a fraction of a second, Ellie considered them, perplexed, then she clapped her forehead with two fingers. "How could I forget you two know each other? I've really lost it."

"How could she forget I'm responsible for your being here, David?" Wetzon smiled. "A freebee, too, I might add."

"I don't know, Wetzon." David's tone was teasing.

"Go ahead, you two, have a good time. I'll just sit here and try to make money." Ellie was watching the action on the Quotron out of the corner of her eye. "Up another eighth. I think we should begin taking people out."

"Did you see the volume?" David Kim was tall, lean, and Asian— Korean in fact—about twenty-five or -six. He reached over Ellie's shoulder and tapped on the keyboard. She turned her face to him in a moment of such naked intimacy that Wetzon felt like a voyeur. Then it was gone. But it had been there.

Wetzon stood. "You're busy, so I'll get going."

"Don't go, Wetzon." Ellie did not look up. "Stay a minute." She had her thick client account book open and was studying it. "David, have Dwayne bring us coffee, okay? Get everyone out in the meantime, while I talk to Wetzon." She brushed her hair out of her eyes.

"Decaf, please, for me." Wetzon sat down again.

If David Kim resented the request, there was nothing in his face or demeanor to indicate it. He smiled at the women and closed the door behind him.

Ellie sighed. "I'm so lucky to have him. I owe you, Wetzon."

If everybody who "owed" her on Wall Street were to pay off, Wetzon thought, she could retire in luxury. When Wetzon had first met David Kim, he was one of the math geniuses in the Columbia Ph.D. program. He'd been referred to her because he was looking for a part-time job to cover his expenses and give him some pocket money, and Wall Street was the obvious place for his talents.

"Good will," Dougie Culver had called it after Wetzon introduced David to Ellie, and Ellie had promptly hired him. "Think of it as good will, Wetzon, and we'll make it up to you on a real placement."

"What's not real about David Kim, Dougie?" she'd asked. *Make it up to you* sounded a lot like *I'll take care of you, honey,* and it raised her hackles.

"You're the best, Wetzon," Dougie had said, and so it remained, in lieu of payment.

Ellie pushed the account book aside. "David has a real instinct for options. I've brought him in as a junior partner. That is, he has his own accounts and he helps me with mine. He's terrific at working out strategies and spreads. . . . I don't know, it's almost mystical."

"Do you really think one of them killed Goldie?"

"Oh, no, I didn't mean really *killed* him. Goldie had such bad asthma. He had an oxygen tank in his office, for godsakes. Look, it couldn't have been murder, but those animals—Search and Destroy—" Ellie's laugh was acerbic. "Those buzzards were forcing him out and he wasn't going to go quietly."

Hoffritz had said that in almost the same words when Smith and Wetzon had been eavesdropping.

Their coffee was delivered by Ellie's sales assistant, a slim young man with a bit of a swish. "Hi!" he said, smiling at Wetzon as if he knew her.

"Thanks, Dwayne. This is Wetzon—"

"I know."

"Anyway," Ellie didn't even wait for Dwayne to leave the room before she continued, sitting back in her chair, arms behind her neck. "I'm going to miss Goldie horribly. He was my mentor; he got me started in this business. I used to be a teacher, you know. I taught Twoey at Fieldston."

"Twoey?"

"Goldman Barnes, the second. He couldn't say his name when he was a baby so he called himself Twoey, and it stuck. Oh, what the hell. . . ." She'd started crying again.

The phone buzzed. Sniffling, Ellie picked it up. "Yes. No. Let David take care of him. No calls until Wetzon leaves."

"Who is that fat man? Dr. what's-his-face."

"Ha! Dr. Carlton Ash, that fat fuck. He's got the same degree I have—in education—and *I* don't call myself doctor." She stood up and opened the door to a small coat closet. There was a full-length mirror on the inside of the door, and she looked at herself critically. "I look like hell." She closed the door and sat down at her desk. "He's with Goodspeed Associates."

"Goodspeed? The consulting company?"

"Yes. The fat fuck's written some kind of efficiency report. Search and Destroy hired him. Goldie was really upset about it. We've always made money the old-fashioned way, he said." She laughed. "Hoffritz and Bird had other ideas." She took a sip of coffee and crushed her cigarette stub in the Steuben ashtray. "Drink up, Wetzon. We may be able to do some business together."

"Ellie, I can't take you out of Luwisher Brothers. You're with a client firm."

"You can if I ask you to. Chances are, I'm going to get out of here one way or the other." She lit another cigarette. "They're up to something. I know it. Carlton Ash has been walking his fat ass around here for the last six months with his little notepad, making notes in some kind of code."

"Code? How do you know it's a code?"

"David. He's very good at nosying around."

"So do you think one of them could have killed Goldie to get him out of the way?"

"Hell, no. Listen, they're good ole boys, real slime, but they're not stupid. They were demanding Goldie sell his stock back. They were putting on the pressure, and he was fighting back and his asthma was kicking up. Jesus, he was in the hospital twice in the last three months. So then comes what Goldie called the night of the long knives, the night before the dinner. They got that flake Janet involved, and she wanted to protect Twoey's interests, and then those Southern boys got out their honed steel." She tilted her head back and finished her coffee, set the cup on the desk and parked her cigarette on the saucer. "Funny . . . he stopped by my office the day of the dinner, said he had one last card up his sleeve."

"What is the report about?"

"I don't know." She touched some of the keys again and watched the machine. "The fat fuck kept hinting that it was going to shake out the industry. The Ash Report, he kept calling it, the pompous asshole. Pompous Ash-hole." She ran her hands through her hair. "I'm going to miss that wonderful old man."

Wetzon took a swallow of the bitter coffee. "Do you remember what Goldie said just before he collapsed? Didn't he say something about disappointing people?"

The phone buzzed.

"I honestly don't remember, Wetzon. The police asked me the same question." She frowned a furrow between her thick, dark eyebrows and picked up the phone. "Everybody? Good. And the other? Yes." She hung up. "I've got to get back to work." Her eyes focused on the machine. "Thanks, Wetzon."

Wetzon pulled her cardcase from her suit pocket. "Here's my card, Ellie. I'm putting my home number on the back. Call me." Her pen scratched a blob of ink on the number so she switched a fresh card for the one with the inkblot.

"Sure, Wetzon. We'll talk again."

They shook hands and Wetzon stepped out of the office.

She paused at the door to David Kim's office on her way back to the conference room. He was hunched over his phone and didn't see her. "It's important. Just sign it," he was saying. "I'll tell you all about it later."

Smith would say she was a fool because they hadn't gotten paid for the placement, but Wetzon was proud of what David Kim had made of himself. She walked down the wide corridor featuring the Georgia O'Keeffes and was back in the reception area.

"How is poor Ellie?" Maggie Gray asked without much interest as Wetzon passed her.

"She's okay." Wetzon climbed the curved stairs and got to the door of the conference room just as everyone was leaving.

"Ah, Wetzon," John Hoffritz said when he saw her. "I want to thank you for your suggestion. We really appreciate this." He shook Smith's hand firmly. Smith was purring benignly, looking for all the world like the Cheshire Cat. "I'm sure this will work out well for all of us." His mouth parted slightly in a constipated smile. "We'll clear the way so that you can talk to people freely."

That Smith, Wetzon thought, and was interrupted by Carlton Ash.

"A pleasure meeting you," the fat man said to Wetzon, leaning into her too closely.

She drew back. "I understand you're doing a study of the industry." He stared at her. "I'd love to read it. That is, if it's not proprietary information."

His eyes drooped. Little beads of perspiration dotted his hairline and upper lip. "What report? I don't know anything about a report."

"Whatever you say. But if you're really going to shake up the industry, I'd appreciate knowing about it." She gave him a warm and friendly smile, and judged herself to be as phony as all the rest.

"I'm here as a consulting psychologist."

"Of course."

"Do you have a business card?"

"Come on, Wetzon," Smith said. "Let's go. We have a lot of work to do."

"Just a minute." Wetzon shook off Smith's insistent fingers plucking away at her sleeve and gave Dr. Ash her card.

Smith had them on the street and into a cab heading back uptown to their office in less than ten minutes.

"How about telling me what the big rush is about, Smith?"

Smith settled back in her seat and studied her scarlet fingernails. She looked at Wetzon coyly out of the corner of her eye, but didn't respond.

"What did Hoffritz mean . . . clear the way so that we can talk to people? What suggestion was he thanking me for so profusely?"

"We're going to do some detective work for them, along with the recruiting." Smith pulled out a piece of paper from her briefcase. It was a Luwisher Brothers check made out to Smith and Wetzon for ten thousand dollars.

"Hey! They've put us on a retainer. No kidding. That's terrific, Smith."

"No, sugar. Brokers are still contingency. This is for something a *lot* more interesting."

Wetzon felt that familiar little hot coal burning her midsection. "Smith, what have you gotten us into?"

"Listen, Wetzon, with our experience—"

"*Our* experience?"

"Well, I told them it was your suggestion. You have contacts . . .

knowledge from previous murder cases. They want us to find the murderer before the police do."

"Oh, no, Smith, you—"

Smith smiled triumphantly. "They've hired us to find out who killed Goldie Barnes."

SEVEN

"I can't give him a thirty-five-hundred-dollar guarantee for three months. Not with the figures he gave me. I need his runs."

"Did you ask him for them?" Wetzon expertly kept the exasperation she felt out of her voice.

"Well, no. I thought you could do that."

"Okay, I will, but let me make a suggestion. Let's be creative. If you can't offer him thirty-five hundred, and he loves the higher payout on the back end as an incentive bonus, which he tells me he does, why not make it all incentive? What if he can keep a hundred percent of his gross for the first two months, then eighty percent for the next two months, then sixty percent for the rest of the year? It's a guarantee that he'll work his butt off."

"Say, Wetzon, that's really good. I never thought of that. I'll try it."

Wetzon hung up the phone and screamed. "What's worse than a broker who won't move?"

"A manager who can't close," B.B. and Harold chanted dutifully, this being Wetzon's big bugaboo.

Smith turned a baleful face to them. "Close the door behind you, please." She flipped her hand in a dismissing motion.

"Hold on," Wetzon said. "Just remember we're looking for the new Luwisher profile, whatever that is. Let's start putting a file together of people who fit. We'll prepare a spiel and start pitching them tomorrow."

"What's the matter with today?" Smith's tone was borderline belligerent. She stamped across the space of the office they shared, which had been the dining room of the nineteenth-century brownstone, gave Harold an extra little push across the saddle, and firmly shut the door. The front room, where once there had been a large kitchen and pantry, as well as entrance hall, was their modest reception area. It held B.B.'s desk, a small loveseat, and three narrow chairs. A cubicle of privacy had been created for Harold.

The southern wall of Smith and Wetzon's office was all windows and French doors leading to a garden, where they lunched in fair and middling weather from the first sign of spring to the first nip of autumn. The white iron furniture had been resprayed that spring and looked regal amid the reds and pinks of the tulips and the thick vines of purple wisteria that climbed the brick walls separating their garden from the houses to the right and left.

"What's the matter with starting the calls today, may I ask?" Smith said again, coming to stand beside Wetzon who was enjoying the garden.

Wetzon narrowed her eyes at her partner. "God, you're grouchy. That's what happens when you load up on caffeine and don't eat. Let's sit outside and talk." She took her straw hat with the tall daisy decoration from the shelf over her desk and opened the multi-windowed door. "I'm hungry and our sandwiches have to be getting soggy." They had stopped on their way back to the office at their favorite sandwich shop, What's Cooking, and picked up chicken salad with broccoli and dill on pita bread. "If we don't eat, I'm going to be as bad-tempered as you."

"You are absolutely right, sweetie pie." Smith's mood turned suddenly sunny. "Here, I'll take everything out and you get the plates." She gathered up the various paper bags efficiently, including her Diet Coke and Wetzon's Perrier, and was out the door before Wetzon could close her astonished mouth.

"Shit!" Wetzon said to the empty room, to the Andy Warhol drawing of the roll of dollar bills that they had bought when they first went into business together, to Smith's desk with its clutter of papers and personal items. She took two plastic plates and two plastic cups from the utility cabinet in their bathroom and joined Smith in the warm benevolence of their garden.

"Now, isn't this nice?" Smith said, as if it were all her idea. She'd pulled one of the iron chairs out into full sunlight and was using her reflector. Already her lovely olive tones were shading to a luminous bronze.

Wetzon looked at her enviously. The sun was an anathema to her own pale skin, and she used sun block creams all year round, wearing a hat as soon as the first glimmer of spring sunshine appeared. Her friend Carlos said she had a hat fetish, which she did, having at least twenty-five or thirty hats in boxes, on hooks, and piled high on the old wooden hat block in her apartment.

Smith opened the Diet Coke and the Perrier with a snap and poured with a champagne flourish. She smiled at Wetzon. "Pull your chair out and get some sun, for godsakes. You look all washed out, sugar."

Wetzon left her chair where it was, in partial shade, and sat down, feeling all at once angry and disgruntled. Somehow Smith had reversed moods with her.

"Smith, I think we should talk about this mess you've gotten us into."

"What mess? Wetzon, please. After all this time, you still don't understand this business the way I do. By investigating the murder—"

"We have no credentials to do a murder investigation, Smith." She shifted in her chair, beginning to sweat. It had gotten hot, just on the edge of downright uncomfortable.

"Look at it this way. Whatever we find out, we can turn over to your precious police. But more important, we can insinuate ourselves into Luwisher Brothers. We'll discover where all the bodies are buried and dig up so much dirt . . ." She licked her lips suggestively. "It will lock us into the company for life."

"Smith! Goddammit, that's blackmail."

"Wetzon, stop being so naive. This is business." She took another big bite out of her sandwich. "Mmmm. Delish," she mumbled, leaving considerable doubt in Wetzon's mind whether she was talking about the situation or the sandwich. "Come on, you negative old drip, this'll be fun—not to say lucrative."

"But we'll be interfering in a murder investigation."

"How? Just tell me how. By asking a few questions, fishing around a little? How?"

"Oh, I don't know." Wetzon gripped her sandwich and chicken salad oozed out of a torn space in the pita pocket.

"So, we're doing it. Okay?"

"You're too much for me. I don't want to argue." She found herself nibbling around the edges of her sandwich as if she were eating a melting Popsicle. "But I want you to promise me that if we get in the way, if the police tell us to back off, we will." Silvestri would be furious with her—and this wasn't even her fault. She had tried to stay out of it.

Smith beamed. "Well, that's easy to promise. Sweetie, I would never want us to—"

"Oh, shut up, Smith." Wetzon ate the rest of her sandwich feeling that in spite of herself, she'd been manipulated by Smith yet one more time. On the other hand, she was forced to admit, to herself only, that she found the situation they were in intriguing.

Smith put down the reflector and looked hurt. "You don't have to be so ungracious. I know you. If this had been your idea, you would be flaunting it. Besides, it sure didn't look like murder to me. It was obviously a stroke."

"Now I take it you're an expert in forensic medicine?"

"Humpf. You know I have good instincts. Besides, the cards say—"

"The cards say we should investigate a murder?"

"Well, no, not exactly." She smiled at Wetzon. "Admit it, sweetie pie, you're just a wee bit mad that I'm involved in this, and you don't have it all to yourself."

"That's not true, and you know it." Wetzon found herself sputtering. *Was Smith right? No, she couldn't be.*

"Wetzon." B.B. was at the door. "Howie Minton for you."

"Howie Minton?" Smith groaned. "Not again. How many years is this?"

"He called last week." Wetzon laughed. She stood up and brushed the crumbs off her skirt. "Tell him I'll be right there, B.B." To Smith, she said, "He wants to try again. I think I've been working with him for over five years now, right?"

"At least." Smith tucked her chin back in the reflector.

"This is it, he says."

"Humpf."

"This time may be for real. L.L. Rosenkind has stopped doing principal business. I told Howie to think it over and call me only if he was really serious."

"Give me a break."

"He's grossing over a million for his trailing twelve months."

Smith dropped the reflector with a thump. "Jeeezus!"

"Smith." B.B. appeared at the door again. "Jake."

"Oh, good." Smith followed Wetzon into their office. "Clean up out here, B.B., will you? There's a good fellow."

They separated, went to their respective corners and reached for their phones.

"Jake, precious," Smith breathed.

"Hi, Howie," Wetzon said.

B.B. came back into the room with the remains of their lunch and a stricken look on his face. "Wetzon," he whispered. "I forgot to tell you. A letter came for you by messenger. It's on your desk."

"I've thought it over, Wetzon, my friend," Howie's unctuous voice spilled out of the receiver. "I want to go forward. I'm going to take a vacation for a week and then we can get started."

Wetzon picked up the letter on her desk. It was addressed to her in violet ink. The paper was heavy rag of the Tiffany type.

"You're such a darling—" Smith was saying.

"Great, Howie," Wetzon said, turning the letter over and tearing it open with her finger. "I'm going to make up a list of firms for you and then we can talk again when you get back."

She hung up the phone in time to hear Smith say, "She's jealous that I'm stealing her thunder on this one."

Furious, she swiveled around in her chair, ready to do battle with Smith, automatically pulling the notecard from the envelope. The signature caught her eye and stopped her. It was from Janet Barnes.

The grieving widow was inviting them to lunch on Monday.

EIGHT

Wetzon came out on Fifty-seventh Street after her ballet class feeling euphoric, as she always did after class, so alive her skin tingled with antennae, decidedly an extrasensory sensation. Her long, ash-blonde hair, which she had taken down out of its usual topknot, swung back and forth in a loose ponytail, drying the damp wisps around her scalp. As she headed toward Broadway, she was thinking she might walk home. It was still light and she would be just another suit walking home in her Reeboks—the ubiquitous Manhattan professional woman's outfit.

"Yoo hoo, Birdie!" Carlos was standing on the corner of Broadway and Fifty-seventh, or rather, he was doing jetés, his slender, lithe body as limber as it was when they were both chorus dancers—gypsies—on Broadway.

"You're making a scene, you gorgeous creature." She captured him by putting her hands on his shoulders and holding him down and planting a kiss on his lips. They were exactly the same height.

"As if I cared." He tossed his dark head. The large diamond stud in his left earlobe sparkled. In fact, everything about Carlos sparkled. "I'm not the one in the business suit and the ugly shoes. Are you ashamed of your old friends?" He gave her a stern look, but he was smiling broadly, and there was that devilish glint in his jet eyes.

"What a terrible thing to say, but just what I'd expect from you."
Carlos hated her business, felt it was heartless and sleazy. It was a bone
of contention between them, so they tried not to talk about it. Or at
least, Wetzon tried and he brought it up all the time. "Where are you
heading?"

"Up to Arthur's." He slipped his arm around her and grabbed her
briefcase.

"How is Arthur?" She made a halfhearted attempt to get her case
back, then gave up.

"Up to his *pupick* in trusts and estates. How is it with the sergeant?"
They began walking up Broadway.

"He made lieutenant."

"Nice. Now he can afford a wife."

She stopped and shook her finger at him. "Look at me, monster. Do
you see me as wifey?"

He stared at her, tilted his head back and around, and closed one
dark, mischief-making eye, fluttering its eyelid. "Oh, I don't know. You
might look good in an apron."

"Don't you dare say another word." They began walking again, in
time. "I just took a class—"

"I could tell."

"How? And if this is another humorous remark at my expense you
can forget about getting the afghan back in July." They co-owned a red,
white, and blue afghan they had crocheted together in honor of the
bicentennial while they were dancing in *Chicago* for Bob Fosse in 1976.
They had agreed to share it, each taking it for a year, and this was her
year—at least until July 4th.

"No, honestly, Birdie. You've totally lost your sense of humor since
you went into business with the Barracuda."

"Don't start." Carlos and Smith loathed each other, and Wetzon
made sure to keep them apart because together there were always
dangerous fireworks.

"Darling, it makes me crazy that you don't see what a manipulating
liar that woman is." They were walking arm in arm, lefts together, rights
together.

"What's new in your life?"

"Changing the subject?"

"Trying to."

"Okay. I quit—for now. There are none so blind as those who will not see. Let's see, what's new? Oh, well, la-di-da. I'm talking to Mort Hornberg about choreographing his new musical."

Wetzon pulled them to a stop. "La-di-da? That's absolutely sensational!"

Wetzon and Carlos had known each other since Wetzon's first week in New York, where she had come to be a dancer. They'd met in a class, partnered each other in Broadway musicals, road tours, summer stock. They'd worked with Gower Champion, Bob Fosse, Michael Bennett, and Ron Field, all gone now. As chorus dancers they'd moved from show to show, opening to closing, until Wetzon had met Smith. The meeting came at a time in Wetzon's life when, having entered her thirties, she'd felt she didn't want to be an aging gypsy. She was tired of scrimping and saving, tired of unemployment insurance and living in a tiny, dark apartment five flights up.

Smith had proposed they go into business together and Wetzon had listened. That all seemed a hundred years ago. Now they were the most respected, possibly the best, of the headhunters that worked the Street. Wetzon had been able to move out of her five-flight walk-up and had bought her four and a half rooms on West Eighty-sixth Street.

Carlos, too, had seen the handwriting of time on the wall. He knew there were few parts for aging male dancers, but he'd started a business while they were still doing twinkle toes over Broadway in the chorus of *42nd Street*. Princely—for Carlos Prince—Service. Princely Service employed out-of-work gypsies and was so incredibly successful that soon enough Carlos was able to run the business from his Greenwich Village apartment, sending dancers out all over the city to clean homes, shop, get dinner started for Yuppies. Then, four years ago, Marshall Bart, who had started with them in the chorus and had become a choreographer, offered Carlos an opportunity to co-choreograph a new musical with him because Marshall was handling the director's chores as well. The rest was history. Carlos was back in the theater, now as a full-time choreographer, and he'd hired another aging gypsy to run Princely Service for him.

On Seventy-fourth Street, the Fairway market lured them with the smell of ripe strawberries for ninety-nine cents a box. Wetzon bought two boxes and found Carlos inside at the cheese department, discussing a Vermont cheesemaker with the counterman.

She put her finger in his sleek side under his ribcage. "Hand over that briefcase and keep your mouth shut."

He handed over her briefcase, deadpan, and raised his hands. "You can put your gat away now."

"The Amsterdam Festival is on Sunday. Do you want to do it?"

"Sure. After twelve. I need my beauty sleep."

"I'll call you." She kissed the back of his neck, and grinned at his elaborate shudder. He was her best friend. He made her laugh. They had shared a lot of laughter and a lot of sorrow together—sorrow particularly lately when every day someone they'd worked with came down with some form of AIDS.

"Ta ta, little one." Carlos blew her a kiss.

Bless him and keep him well, she thought. Cutting over to Amsterdam Avenue, she walked up past Baci, where Jerome Robbins sat facing the street, reading and eating a pasta dinner. No one bothered him, yet everyone must have known who he was. *The glorious West Side,* she was thinking, as Jimmy Breslin strolled toward her. She loved the Upper West Side of Manhattan. There was a casual neighborliness—a live-and-let-live attitude toward the fairly well known, even the famous. The Upper West Side did not have the ostentation of the East Side or the self-consciousness of the Village, but its own definite personality created in large part by the people in the arts—actors, dancers, musicians, and writers—who had settled in during the sixties and seventies because the rents were so reasonable. Now, almost every building was a co-op and gentrification had taken hold, with expensive condos shooting up all over Broadway. Why, even a Conran's had opened across from Zabar's. Still, the area had the same old, scuffed intellectual flavor, even if it was a lot more affluent.

Wetzon's apartment was in one of the pre-World War II buildings that were known for their high ceilings and immense closets. With its location, about halfway between the elegance of Central Park West and the equal elegance of Riverside Drive, her building did not even try to keep up. The doormen were not snappy and military, and there was something comforting in the threadbare aura the old marble lobby gave off. Its ceiling was Adam, painted in Wedgwood colors of bisque and beige. The automatic elevator was ancient and in need of replacement soon, she thought, as it lurched to a stop on her floor. That would mean an assessment. Good thing she was well able to afford it.

She unlocked her door and opened it to the wonderful aroma of tomato sauce. Facing her on the wall was the old pink-and-white drunkard's-path quilt she had found at a flea market. She dropped her briefcase and purse on the white park bench in her foyer, shrugged out of her jacket, and leaned against the arched doorway to her kitchen. The MacNeil-Lehrer report was providing background from the small black-and-white television set on the kitchen counter.

"Hi, Les." Silvestri, in jeans and the sleeveless tee shirt he referred to as his Italian wedding shirt, didn't look up. He was standing over her Creusetware stockpot stirring the magnificent sauce with a wooden spoon.

"Hi," she said, mushy as the tomatoes. She came up behind him and wrapped her arms around his chunky middle and lay her cheek on his back. Sometimes she thought she would wake up and he'd be gone, never having been.

"Something smells good," she said.

"Just the old family recipe." The Abruzzi special, he called it, for his grandparents who had come from that section of Italy. He pulled her around him and looked down at her. He had the most incredible turquoise eyes that changed to slate when he was angry or on the job. Right now they were turquoise. She and Silvestri had been together for three years and she still tingled when he touched her.

"Just the old family undershirt, too?" she asked, trying to shake off her sentiment.

"Is that a bigoted remark against Italians?"

"Me? Hell, no. I love Italians."

He held out a spoon of sauce to her for tasting. "What do you think?" He was splattered with red and there was a line of red dotting his shirt across his middle.

"I think the chef is very sexy." She touched the thick sauce with the tip of her tongue. "Wonderful. Audition is over. You're hired." She giggled. "Take off your clothes." It was a joke both of them used since they'd seen a particularly boring, much touted movie called *The Unbearable Lightness of Being*. Its hero was motivated solely by sex and "take off your clothes" was the sum total of serious conversation he had with women.

Silvestri turned down the flame under the sauce. "We're having sautéed veal chops and a salad and pasta. Okay?"

"Okay? How can I complain? I got me a macho man who can hold his own at the stove. My, my. I am just so lucky." She patted his tush and scampered out of the kitchen and down the hall to her bedroom. He was only seconds behind her.

They made love a second time in the shower and finally sat down to eat Silvestri's sumptuous meal at nine o'clock.

"Ah," Wetzon said, "this is wonderful. I'm feeling so mellow I think I'll ask you—"

Silvestri leaned back in his chair and smirked at her. "I've been waiting for this. What took you so long?" He poured the remnants from the wine bottle into his glass.

"The truth is . . . I know you hate it when I get involved in a murder investigation. . . ." She paused, hoping he would help her out, but he folded his arms and waited. The color of his eyes gave him away. They were turquoise. "You are really a prick," she said, smiling sweetly.

He laughed. "So?"

"Oh, hell! Was Goldie Barnes murdered?"

"I can't—"

"Oh, forget it." She started to get up.

Silvestri reached over and put a heavy hand on her shoulder. "Do you want to tell me what you were doing at Luwisher Brothers this morning?"

"Is this for the record, sir? Are you going to take out your little black notebook?" She kissed the back of his hand on her shoulder. "I'll tell you what. Why don't we just trade information?"

"Boy, are you single-minded. I don't have to answer any of your questions, but you have to answer mine."

"He said, after he's made mad, passionate love to her and cooked her a sumptuous feast and plied her with wine to overcome her natural reticence."

"Natural reticence. That's a good one. Talk, lady, or I'll haul your ass down to the station." He folded his arms again.

She flushed and kicked him under the table with her bare foot. "I think there's something terribly wrong with our relationship. You have all the rights."

"That's because I'm Italian," he said. "Besides, it's my job." He reached into the inside pocket of his jacket, which was hanging on the back of the chair, and actually pulled out his little black notepad. "What did you say you were doing there?"

"I didn't say, but if you must know, we do consulting work for Luwisher Brothers." She made a face at him.

"Did you know Goldie Barnes?"

"Not well. To say hello to, that's about it." She looked at him seriously. "Was he murdered?"

"What do you know about the rest of them? Hoffritz and his crew." He flipped over the pages and reading upside down, she saw he'd written down some familiar names. Hoffritz, Bird, Gorham, Munchen.

"Hey, I think I'm being used here. It's not fair. Just tell me this. Was Goldie really murdered? I won't ask any more questions. He looked as if he was choking, as if he were having an asthma attack."

"'He looked as if he was choking'?" Silvestri repeated. "What the hell are you saying, Les? Are you telling me that you were *there*, for chrissakes?"

"Well, of course I was there. I told you I was going to a business dinner with a manager. You never listen to me."

"I don't believe this." He smacked the table, rattling the empty plates. "How do you know every—?"

"It's my business to know everybody on the Street. And anyway, New York is really a small town. I never go anywhere without running into people I know or people who know people I know."

"Oh, forget it. Who were you there with—not Hoffritz, by any chance?" He was being sarcastic, and she couldn't control her giggle.

"Chris Gorham."

"Oh, for shit's sake."

"Now do you want to tell me about Goldie?"

"Nope." He started cleaning up, carrying the dishes into the kitchen.

She followed him and began stacking the dishwasher. "You already told me you were there about a murder."

"Who, me? I don't remember saying that."

"You know, when the elevator door closed."

"I was talking about the heat."

She gave him a push. "I hate when you do this."

"Do what?" He drew her to him and kissed her. He tasted sweet, of wine and tomatoes. "You can be really helpful because you know the players."

"True," she mumbled into his shirt. "What'll you give me if I cooperate, officer?"

He laughed and ran his hands slowly down her back. "God, I hate to tell you anything because you're going to make sure you get involved."

NINE

"Come on, Silvestri, face it, I am already involved, albeit peripherally." It was morning and Wetzon was standing in the open door of the bathroom watching him shave.

"Oh, hell," he said. "Goldie Barnes appears to have been poisoned."

"What does that mean—appears to have been?"

"That's it, Les."

"Don't I get to know anything else? Quid pro quo and all that?"

"Nope."

"Why are you on the case?"

"Because it happened on my watch."

"Oh." She frowned. "I just love hanging around here getting no information."

His reflection grinned at her. "I'd like you to fill me in on what *you* know. As far as we're concerned, everyone is a suspect until we eliminate him. Or her."

"But don't get involved, right?" She thought for a moment. "There must have been a hundred people at the dinner, Silvestri. That's a lot of suspects. And as far as filling you in . . ." She stopped, wondering if this was the time to tell him what Smith had done. "I've got a bit of a moral problem here."

He raised a black eyebrow at her and ran a comb through his thinning hair. "I'm listening."

She backed out of his way, following him into the neatened bedroom; she had made the bed while he showered. He groped under his side of the bed and pulled out his shoulder holster, removed the gun, and laid it gently on the quilt. After shrugging into the leather apparatus, he checked his gun and returned it to its pocket under his right arm.

Wetzon had never gotten used to watching Silvestri dress without feeling this was the same kind of personal ritual as watching a woman putting on her makeup. The gun and his relationship with it held a particular fascination for her. In some peculiar way, he handled his gun the way he handled her.

He straightened up and caught her look, and she felt naked and exposed although she was garbed in full pinstriped armor. "What moral problem?" he asked. He kissed her nose and went down the hall in search of his jacket.

She could tell his mind was on the job and he was not listening, but she followed him down the hall anyway. "What I know about Luwisher Brothers is considered proprietary information."

"There's no such thing in a murder investigation."

"You say."

"Do you want a ride?" He was impatient, standing at the door.

She shook her head. "I don't think so. I have some calls to make and I want to go through the papers." *The Wall Street Journal* and *The Times* lay on the floor near her door, demanding to be read.

He pressed the down button of the elevator and came back to stand in her doorway. "What's your afternoon like?"

"Don't know. Fridays are slow when the weather is like this. Everyone takes off early for the Hamptons. Why?"

"I might want you to come over to the precinct and talk to us about these investment bankers of yours."

"Oh, Silvestri—"

"Don't oh-Silvestri me. You've always wanted to be involved; now I'm involving you."

"I have to think about this."

"No, you don't." He closed the door on her.

She poured the last dregs of coffee from her Melitta pot and buttered the second half of her bagel, wondering where the borders of confidentiality could be crossed. What was right and what was wrong.

Was she obligated to tell her client? She smeared Sarabeth's wonderful apricot orange marmalade over the bagel and raised the mug to her lips.

What about Smith? She would have to tell her. Damn. Here she was trying to be virtuous and uninvolved, and both Silvestri and Smith kept pushing her into a homicide investigation. She set the cup down on the counter and opened *The Journal,* skimming over the articles on the front page. The headline in the center of the page read "Barnes Death Deemed Murder." The article quoted John Hoffritz's statement as she had overheard it, and no new information except that the New York Stock Exchange would observe one minute of silence at twelve noon today in memory of Goldie Barnes.

Under *What's News—Business and Finance,* Wetzon stopped to read a small item. S&S Sedlet Securities, a small Atlanta-based brokerage house, had made a buy-out offer for L. L. Rosenkind.

"Oh, no!" she said out loud. There went the Howie Minton job search. He'd probably hang in and see what kind of bonus he was going to get to stay. And he'd get a nice one, she was sure, because no firm could afford to lose a big producer. S&S Sedlet would probably follow the Street and offer a contract for two to three years with a bonus on the front end for big producers to keep them stationary and another bonus on the back end based on production at each year end for the length of the contract.

She was just thinking that Smith was right again when her phone rang. She wiped her sticky fingers and answered just before her machine clicked in.

"Wetzon!" It was Smith, breathless, as if she'd been running, which was totally out of character. Smith never exercised, didn't believe in it, and had the metabolism to reinforce this. "Wetzon?"

"Yes."

"You saw the item about Sedlet buying Rosenkind?"

"Yes. Don't say it, please."

"Say what?"

"I-told-you-so about Howie Minton. Now he's going to wait and see what he's offered to stay—"

"Well, of course he'll be offered a bonus to stay, but he wasn't going anywhere anyway. I wasn't calling you about that. I know Seth Sedlet and his brother Sean."

"You do? How?"

"Don't ask. They're *pirates.* They took over the first company I worked for and sold it off piece by piece. There was nothing left that was recognizable. They'll sell Rosenkind's assets and wipe out the company—not that it matters, except the Street is getting smaller and smaller. If they dissolve Rosenkind, we'll have one less place to pull brokers out of."

"Well, they made an offer, but they may not get Rosenkind."

"I wouldn't count on it, sugar. Rosenkind has a cash flow problem."

"Who doesn't?"

"Are you on your way down?"

"I just want to finish my coffee and skim through *The Times*." She heard a phone ring. "Where are you?"

"In the office, of course. Where else would I be? You know Jake, he likes to get up and out early."

So that's how Smith had seen the Rosenkind-Sedlet item. She should have known. It was unlike Smith to do much professional reading. She left it for Wetzon to fill her in on what was happening on the Street, while Smith let Wetzon know the social news from *W*, which Wetzon found stupid and frivolous.

"Tell me something, Smith," she said, "what does Jake really do?"

"Why are you doing this to me, Wetzon? Jake is a wonderful, caring man. He paid a harsh price for what he did. He'll have his license back in September and he's—"

"Please don't tell me that he's coming back into the business."

"Sweetie, don't be naive. He never left."

Wetzon hung up the phone, finished her bagel in big, angry bites, and put the dishes in the dishwasher. Of course Donahue never left. How *could* she be so naive? It was amazing what the Street sanctioned, even after the Crash· and the insider trading scandals.

Just three months ago, against her better judgment, she had placed Bruce Pecora, a broker with two client complaints and a pending lawsuit, at a major firm after giving the eager manager every caveat she could about the broker. Bruce had, in fact, been turned down by almost every other firm on the Street. Only two years in production and he was grossing $350,000. How could he do it? Indeed. One account of a hundred thousand dollars had generated thirty-six thousand dollars' worth of commissions in one year. He had a churn 'em and burn 'em mentality.

But the headhunting business had slowed to a crawl because brokers were nervous about moving, and production had fallen off because clients were nervous about the market. Smith was nagging at her to show Pecora, regardless. "Someone will want him, " she said, "and we'll make ourselves a neat twenty-five thou. And once he's there, he's their problem."

"God, Smith, if something goes wrong, it'll reflect on us."

"This kid is a time bomb waiting to go off," one manager told Wetzon. "We'll pass on him."

Mike Norman, who managed the Rockefeller Center branch for Loeb Dawkins, had called her, begging for brokers. "Don't you have anyone for me? Come on, send me brokers."

"I have someone, but he's trouble, Mike. Lawsuit, complaints on his U4. Hotheaded."

"What are his numbers?"

"Three-fifty, second year."

"Great. When can I see him?"

"He's trouble, Mike."

"I can handle him, Wetzon, just leave him to me."

Famous last words. The day before the Goldie Barnes banquet, Loeb Dawkins had to tell Bruce Pecora to take a leave of absence, at the suggestion of the New York Stock Exchange. It looked as if the Exchange was going to pull Pecora's license.

She'd felt terrible, responsible.

And Smith had screamed at her, "Mike's a big boy. He knew what he was doing. And we have our money."

The phone rang again just as she was outside her door locking the upper lock, the Medco. She hesitated, then unlocked the door and made a dash for the phone. Too late. The machine clicked on. Oh well, let the machine go ahead and answer it. It was probably a survey taker or some salesman.

The first sound she heard was labored breathing—exactly what she needed right now, a breather—then a voice buried in a bronchial cough. "Ms. Wetzon. I must see you as soon as possible."

She picked up the phone. "Hold on, Dr. Ash." She turned her machine off. "Are you still there?"

"I must talk to you about—"

"Let me guess," she said, impatiently. "You're going to tell me about the study."

"I'll provide you with a copy, but—"

"Oh, good." How had he gotten her home number? She wasn't

listed . . . then she remembered. She must have given him the card with the inkblot, the one she hadn't given to Ellie.

"But that's not what I want to talk about." Ash took a loud gasping breath. "Can you meet me at Luwisher Brothers tomorrow morning early—at seven-thirty?"

"Seven-thirty? Tomorrow's Saturday."

"I'm aware of that."

"Does it have to be downtown?"

"Yes. There's something I want you to see. I'll be waiting for you at the elevator bank on the sixty-seventh floor."

"Why me in particular?"

"Ms. Wetzon, why are you making this so difficult for me? I'd rather not go to the police just yet—"

"The police?"

"I want you to give me your word that you will tell no one about our meeting. No one."

"My word?" She frowned. "All right. What is all this about?"

"I believe," his voice almost disappeared into a wheeze, "I know why Goldie Barnes was murdered."

T E N

Worried L.L. Rosenkind brokers were jamming the phone lines when Wetzon got to the office. B.B. was fielding some, sending a few to Harold, fewer still to Smith—who only deigned to speak to the biggest producers—and holding for Wetzon those who had asked for her specifically.

Smith, phone clamped to her ear, mouthed, *it's about time,* and made a big X on the suspect sheet in front of her, her loathing for brokers oozing from every pore. "Yes, well, you can be assured we'll do the very best for you, but at your level you don't have much choice." She made a silent *I'm throwing up* finger-in-mouth motion. "We'll get back to you with some suggestions." She hung up the phone. "Lying scuzzball. Can you imagine? He told B.B. his production was half a mil. Sure, it was—in 1984." Her tone turned petulant. "You're never here when I need you."

"I know, I know. But I'm here now and I'll take over so you don't have to get your hands dirty."

"Wetzon, you know something? You've become impossible. You have a smart answer for everything."

"Oh, please!" Wetzon dumped her briefcase under her desk and flipped through her messages. Laura Lee had called. They were planning a tea party for a friend of Laura Lee's with whom Wetzon had become friendly as well. The friend, Anne Altman, had just gotten engaged.

In Wetzon's early days as a headhunter she had met Laura Lee Day when Laura Lee was a stockbroker with Merrill and helped her make a move to Oppenheimer. They'd become good friends, much to Smith's chagrin. Smith was, in fact, jealous of all of Wetzon's friends, forever trying to cast them in a bad light.

"Okay, forget it," Smith said. "I can see you're in a foul mood. I don't want to fight." She smiled at Wetzon as if Wetzon were an impossible creature and had to be humored. "I want to talk about Janet Barnes. I spoke with Johnny this morning and told him she'd invited us to lunch on Monday."

"Excuse me. Johnny?"

"Johnny Hoffritz. Good heavens, sweetie, who else? He says Janet had every reason to want Goldie pushing up daisies."

Wetzon, who had not been in a foul mood, felt herself losing. *Pushing up daisies? Ye gods.* She looked down at her datebook. No interviews. Just notes on whom she should talk to. She planted herself in her chair with a thump.

"Smith, if we're going to do this so-called investigation, let's do it right. We'll keep files, notes, and send a report every week on our progress. Let's not turn this into a raging river of gossip, for godsakes. Who are we supposed to report to?"

"Johnny."

"Oh sure, Johnny."

B.B. knocked on the door and opened it. "Bruce Pecora for you, Wetzon."

"Oh, great," Smith groaned. "Tell him she's not here. Don't you dare talk to him, Wetzon. That dirtbag's got compliance problems up the yin-yang. They're pulling his license."

"My, my, how quickly we change." Wetzon punched the hold button. "Hello, Bruce, how are you doing?"

"Well, I'll tell you, Wetzon." Bruce sounded like a low-life thug, but as long as he was producing big numbers, no one cared. However, now that he was in trouble—real trouble as opposed to potential problems—everyone pointed out his *déclassé* New York street accent. "I'm sitting on the beach waiting for those fuckers to reinstate me—and I don't like waiting. I'm not making any money. I want you to show me someplace else. I got business to do and it's piling up."

"Bruce, I don't know what the nature of this trouble is, but you can't go anywhere until it's cleared up. You took a hundred and fifty thou upfront from Loeb Dawkins. Even if they clear your license with the Exchange, they won't transfer it until you pay it all back."

"Fuck that, Wetzon. What do you think I was doing there for three months, jerking off? I did real business, more than most of those losers in that office. They fuckin' *owe* me. Besides, I guarantee they'll transfer my license. They have no choice."

"Dirtbag," Smith said loudly from her corner of the room.

Wetzon turned her back on Smith. "I don't understand, Bruce. Am I missing something?"

"I went to work with a wire the last week. I have everything on tape. I'll talk to the SEC if they fuck with me."

"Scuzz," Smith said.

Wetzon's head began to throb. "Bruce, look, I didn't hear that. Okay? I'm afraid I can't help you this time. They're my clients."

"Sleazebag," Smith said.

"Okay, Wetzon, no hard feelings."

"No hard feelings, Bruce." She put the phone down slowly. Again, where were her obligations? Should she tell her clients that the broker she placed there claims he has illegal dealings on tape?

"Well?" Smith demanded.

"I need a moral judgment here. Let's talk about this, Smith. Seriously."

"No hard feelings." Smith giggled. "Just a nice hard fee we get to keep because he waited three months before he self-destructed, thank-you-very-much."

"Somehow, that makes me feel grubby."

"Get real, Wetzon." She laughed. "Precisely what kind of moral judgment do you want to discuss?"

"I'm not sure you're the right person to discuss moral judgments with. I'd be better off with Oliver North."

"If you're finished being funny Wetzon, I want to tell you that Oliver North is a patriot and a hero. I'd feel privileged to be associated with Oliver North."

Wetzon laughed. Smith was so dead-on serious, she was funny. "Okay, partner mine, try this on for size. Bruce Pecora just told me he'd be reinstated and Loeb Dawkins would transfer his license because he's got them on tape doing something illegal."

"Oh, shit! Did he really?" Grudging respect crept into Smith's voice. "I didn't know the sleaze was that smart."

"Wait a goddam minute, Smith. Before you get too carried away with Bruce's brilliance, we have a problem—"

"What problem? We don't have a problem. We've gotten paid."

"Don't we have to tell Mike Norman that Bruce was wired?"

Smith jumped to her feet. "Are you crazy? We'll do no such thing. In fact, we don't know about it, never knew about it. Read my lips, Wetzon, never never never."

"Okay, okay." Wetzon threw up her hands. "He never called here."

"We can say he called and wanted us to move him—which is true, right?"

"Right."

"And we said no, right? We *did* say no, didn't we?"

"*We* did."

"You'd better leave me a copy of his suspect sheet just in case Mike calls when you're not here. Do we have Pecora's home number?"

B.B. knocked and opened the door. "Sam Herlihy for you, Smith."

"Mmm. That's nice. Stroking managers does pay off sometimes." She sat down at her desk, yawned elaborately and picked up the phone. "Well, hi there, Sam. How are you doing?"

"B.B., make a copy of Pecora's sheet for Smith."

"Okay, but who's Sam Herlihy? He got nasty on the phone. Didn't want to hold—"

Wetzon looked over at Smith. Her body language spelled fury.

"He's the manager at L.L. Rosenkind."

Smith rose out of her chair, the icy calm before the storm. "I will do nothing of the kind and don't threaten me. Oh, really? I beg your pardon, Sam, but we will talk to *anyone* from your office who calls us and we will continue to call into your office and talk to *anyone* who is referred to us. And there's nothing *you* can do about it." She paused. "I'll convey your feelings to her." She crashed the receiver down into the base. "What nerve! He demanded—would you believe—*demanded* that we stay the hell out of his office."

Wetzon smiled. "Well, of course he wants us to keep off the grass and not pick his prize flowers. Did he think he was going to intimidate two poor helpless women?"

"You bet your ass he did. So it's a good thing I talked to him first."

"You act as if I'm easily intimidated."

"And you're not?"

"Bullshit. Was that last bit a message for me?"

"Yes. Sam said after all the years we've known each other, he is not surprised by anything I do, but you are a whole different story. He is shocked, get it—*shocked,* that you would try to steal his brokers and make him look bad to new management."

Wetzon laughed. "Business is business."

Smith raised her eyes heavenward. "Thank God she's finally learning."

The calls started heating up then. Neither had a chance to talk until just before lunch.

"It's too hot for me to sit out there today," Wetzon said, having gone out to the garden and stood in the oppressive heat and humidity. "I'll stay in with the air-conditioning, blessings on Con Edison."

"Fine. I've set up six people next week. Harold or you can do the follow-ups. I hate talking to them. I'm going to leave now and try to get up to Redding early and flake out at the pool. What are your plans for the weekend?"

"Let's see. I'm meeting Silvestri—"

"Great! See what you can find out about Goldie's murder."

"Look, Silvestri wants to know about Luwisher Brothers, the inside dope, and the poop on all the top people there."

"Of course he does. Silvestri wants someone else to do his job for him. Just give him a few crumbs—you know, the throw-away stuff. You haven't told him about our deal, have you?"

"No. No. Not yet, anyway."

"Not ever, if you please. That's proprietary to *our* partnership."

"Smith, I—"

"I mean that, Wetzon. There is no discussion. Do you want to drive up and spend the day with us tomorrow? The City is going to be horrendous."

"No, I can't." She thought for a minute. "Actually, there is something I haven't told you, and I want you to promise me you won't tell anyone."

"What? Of course I won't tell. You know you can trust me, sweetie. Cross my heart and hope to die."

No, she didn't know that she could trust her. Smith had done some really appalling things in the past, but this was different. They were on an assignment. She would take a chance and tell her. Seven-thirty in the morning on Wall Street on a Saturday was a little spooky. Someone had to know where she was going, and she'd just as soon not tell Silvestri.

"Cross your heart and hope to die," Wetzon repeated. "Okay, if you tell I'll kill you."

"Will you tell me already."

"I'm meeting Dr. Ash at his request at seven-thirty tomorrow morning at Luwisher Brothers."

"On a Saturday? Whatever for?"

"He wouldn't tell me over the phone. He said he has to show me. I think it has something to do with this study he's writing. He says he knows why Goldie was murdered."

"That means he must know who did it. Maybe I should go with you."

"Saturday morning, seven-thirty, Smith. No. Besides, he specifically said I was to come alone."

"Humpf. Okay. But you have to call me and tell me everything as soon as you leave him."

"I will." Wetzon turned back to her work and reached for the phone.

"Now I'm going to tell you something that you must absolutely keep secret."

Wetzon looked at Smith. "Okay."

"Johnny wants us to outplace Ellie Kaplan and her paramour as soon as possible."

ELEVEN

The heat was blast-furnace intensity, the sun still blazing at four-thirty, with the kind of humidity that left one gasping for air. The pavement radiated under the soles of Wetzon's Ferragamos. She took off her jacket and folded it over her arm.

On Fridays in the summer, the Street emptied with the closing bell. At four o'clock, everyone was on his way to the Hamptons.

The truth was, the City became saner, more accessible on summer weekends. Restaurants weren't crowded, movie and theater tickets were easier to get, and the City burst forth with a plethora of activities—street fairs, flea markets, craft shows. And Wetzon and Carlos were the ultimate scavengers.

She was dawdling, no doubt about it. She didn't want to talk with Silvestri and his detectives. Not yet. What was it Smith had said? Give them what they'll find out anyway.

The Seventeenth Precinct was on Fifty-first Street, but Wetzon's feet took her farther up Second Avenue to Fifty-third, where she knew there was a Häagen-Dazs. She bought a scoop of chocolate chocolate chip and had them put it in a container rather than a cone so she wouldn't drip all over herself.

The precinct house looked more like a grade school than a police station. The police had become institutionalized. She wanted to see police stations in formidable concrete, black with the dirt and soot of years, with massive doors, tall stone steps, and the desk sergeant up high on a platform behind the desk so you had to crane your neck to see him.

By humanizing the police precinct house, perhaps the forbidden wrong seemed less so. In a strange way it trivialized crime, because entering a precinct house was no longer frightening and intimidating.

But Wetzon entered the Seventeenth with a feeling of foreboding. She was going to have a fight with Silvestri.

The civilian at the desk, a woman in a blue polyester pantsuit and orange hair, was new and didn't recognize her, so she was put through the formality of being announced.

The noise from the squadroom spilled out into the corridor. Inside, five or six detectives were sitting at battered gray metal desks, in various states of procedure, typing reports and on the phone. An unhappy Midwestern mom and pop and two round-eyed children in chocolate-stained overalls were reporting their Ford station wagon stolen. Typewriters clacked and two hookers were complaining about being picked up for no reason. Plastic and paper containers of food and coffee proliferated. Around the available walls were gray filing cabinets. A holding cell had one occupant, a disreputable lump who was snoring loudly. Notices were taped to every bit of wall space or were tacked to bulletin boards that hung crookedly. Dog-eared calendars were abundant, displaying everything from scenic views to cheesecake.

On the floor in a crowded corner a monstrous plant drooped, more dead than alive. A roach rested audaciously on one of its petals. *Yuk,* she thought. This place needed major sprucing up.

Silvestri had his own office now, for what it was worth, a slightly larger room among rabbit warrens, without a window, just like all the rest except for the rear wall, which was all plaster because it was an outside wall. Drab linoleum tiles covered the floor. The other walls were chipped and smudged plaster for about four feet up and then the rest was glass. Clipboards hung from nails around the perimeter of the room; on the rear wall behind Silvestri's newly painted black metal desk was a big cork bulletin board to which a map of the City was tacked and, to the side, some worksheets and yet another dog-eared calendar.

Metzger was on the phone in his office next to Silvestri's and he waved to her. She blew him a kiss and walked into Silvestri's office. A tall woman in tight pants showing off a nicely rounded ass, taut muscles flowing out of a short-sleeved white shirt, its collar stylishly up, stood talking to Silvestri. Wetzon cleared her throat.

"Detective Mo Ryan, Les Wetzon," Silvestri said, offhandedly. "Mo's working with me and Metzger."

Mo Ryan turned her cornflower-blue eyes on Wetzon and unabashedly gave her the once-over. Wetzon returned the compliment, seeing red curly hair and a peachy complexion, pink freckles and big boobs. Mo towered over Wetzon, offered her a firm hand and said, "Pleasure," without much enthusiasm.

Wetzon bristled. *Am I being ranked or what,* she thought. Mo Ryan and she were figuratively circling each other. "Nice to meet you," Wetzon lied and caught Silvestri's turquoise look. He was laughing at her and maybe even engaging in a little idle torture.

"Let's get Metzger in here, Mo, and coffee all around. Decaf for Les." He waited for Mo to leave the room and then said, "Come down off your high horse, Les." He came around his desk and stood between her and the glass and ran his finger down her side from under her arm to her waist. She could feel the heat between them through the thin silk of her blouse.

"Is she new?"

"Who, Mo?"

"No, Barbara Bush."

He grinned at her. She loved the woodsy-smoky smell of him.

"She's been around."

"I'll bet."

He made a *tsk*ing sound with his tongue. "I'm going to let that go by. Mo just made detective. It's her first case. She'll pick up some good experience."

"I hope that's all she'll pick up."

Silvestri grinned again and sat down. In spite of the air-conditioning the room was sultry. A tall fan in the corner languidly blew hot air at them.

Wetzon slipped her jacket over the back of an ugly, scarred wooden armchair and sat, catching her pantihose on a splinter. "Damn!" She looked at the gaping hole on the side of her knee and tugged her skirt down over it. "I don't even know why I'm here," she grumbled.

"You're here to help us with background on people at Luwisher Brothers who knew Goldie Barnes well enough to have a motive to put him away."

"Why do *I* have to do it? Someone else could, I'm sure. This puts me in an awkward position. They're a client. And some of these people have told me things about themselves in confidence."

"Look, Les, I'm not asking you to break a confidence"—He paused—"yet."

"Yet."

"But it will make my life that much easier because your observations are reliable."

"I think I heard a compliment." She smiled at him. "But what you don't seem to understand is what I know may be deeply personal, told to me in confidence over a drink. That I keep a confidence is the touchstone of my business. I'll damage my credibility irreparably if I break a confidence." She remembered having had a drink once with Destry Bird when he first came to New York. They had both ordered Perrier and he'd confided that he had just become a member of AA. "Too personal to reveal to anyone," she said, shaking her head.

"I'll be the judge of that—"

"No, you won't. You can't. I have a business I take very seriously, even if you don't." She felt hurt, as if he was negating what she did. "I have to be the judge of what I tell you. I just can't surrender my ethics—"

The air crackled between them, and she looked away, plucking at the hole in her hose, straightening the hem of her skirt. When she looked up, his eyes were slate and his jaw with its dark shadow was grim.

"I hope we're not interrupting anything," Mo Ryan said. She'd opened another button on her shirt and her cleavage was very much in evidence. She plunked herself down in a chair she'd pulled in from the squad room, and Metzger positioned himself against the door frame where he could get the best view of her cleavage.

Silvestri took a sip of coffee, looked pained, and set the cardboard cup down. "Jeeesus, this is hot—"

"Do you want me to get an ice cube?" Mo Ryan asked eagerly, jumping up.

Wetzon gave Silvestri a hard stare as he pointed his finger at Mo and lowered it slowly. Mo followed his finger, sinking back to the seat of her chair, somewhat deflated.

"Talk to us about Luwisher Brothers, Les." Silvestri reached behind him and pulled the worksheets from the corkboard. He took his notebook from the inside pocket of his jacket and flipped through pages until he found a blank one. "Give us a picture of the company."

"I can't tell you too much about the company itself except that it was started by the three sons of a German Jewish immigrant named Nathaniel Luwisher, who made a killing in cotton during the Civil War." She looked over her shoulder at Metzger, who seemed to have tuned out, more interested in the scenic view of Mo Ryan's bosom. "The actual operation of the company passed out of family hands, I think, after World War II. The only one of the descendants interested in running Luwisher Brothers was killed in the war. The others went into the arts, politics, and medicine. I think there's a Luwisher who is active in environmental issues, organic food or something like that."

Metzger yawned without covering his mouth.

Silvestri's phone rang. He picked it up. "Yeah?" Listened intently. "Okay." He hung up and nodded at Metzger almost imperceptibly. "Go on."

Wetzon crossed one leg over the other, feeling sweat accumulating behind her knees, and took a swallow of the cooled-down coffee. "I don't know where you want me to go with this. There may be a Luwisher descendant with the firm who doesn't have the name anymore. I wouldn't know about that. Interestingly enough, I think the first generation and the second produced nothing but sons and only one or two daughters. After that, there were scads of daughters and very few sons."

"So who owns the stock?" Metzger asked.

"I don't know. It's a private company. The employees who became partners do—certain of them. Luwisher descendants, possibly. Goldie Barnes did, of course. They don't have to make anything public, neither their stock ownership breakdown nor their financial statements. But it's easy enough, I would think, for you guys to find out who is who."

Silvestri made a note in his black notebook. "How exactly do you get to be a partner there?"

"Again, I don't know. I can give you an idea. To make partner, you'd have to be a top producer, say over a million dollars in gross production, in other words, the broker's annual total of commission charges to clients." She thought for a minute. "And the broker would have to have a squeaky-clean record, I'm sure, which means no compliance problems."

"Run that by us again, Les."

"You mean compliance?" He nodded. "Every brokerage firm has a compliance department, which works with the New York Stock Exchange to oversee market activity and to make sure trading complies with the SEC and Exchange regulations. Get it?"

"Got it." Silvestri waved his hand. "Go on."

"Partnerships get awarded to the big deal makers like John Hoffritz, who bring business into the firm through M and A, mergers and acquisitions." She caught herself wondering if Twoey inherited stock or whether the partnership had to buy Goldie's back from Twoey and Janet.

"Was Goldie Barnes related to the Luwishers?" Mo asked. She took a battered pack of Kents from her shirt pocket, rustling cellophane, and shook out a cigarette.

"Not that I know of." She watched Mo jot a note in her little book. They would check that out, but Wetzon was fairly certain they wouldn't find a connection. Goldie had come to Luwisher Brothers bare-ass naked, as he used to say, right after leaving the army. "Anything else?" The room was stifling. She got up and reached for her jacket. Mo snapped her yellow lighter and lit up, splaying cigarette fumes into the turgid air.

"Not so fast, Les. You can give us a quick thumbnail on the players here." Silvestri sorted through the worksheets and spread them out on the desk.

Sighing, she sat down. "I'd like to know how Goldie was killed, if I may?"

"I've already told you. He was poisoned."

"I know that. I meant, what kind of poison? How was it done?"

"That is confidential information."

"In other words, only you and the murderer know?"

He gave her what could only be described as a snide look. "You got it."

"Okay." She accepted that. "Fire away." She settled back in her chair. That meant it had probably happened at the banquet with everyone watching. No. She was guessing. That didn't necessarily hold up. It could have been something slow-acting, something administered at home, if he went home or—

"Hoffritz."

"He's probably going to run Luwisher Brothers. He is already. He's been a partner for a long time. Has to have accumulated a lot of stock. Very smart and very Southern—Alabama, I think." She smiled brightly at Silvestri and thought, *actually, he's a devious, lying Southern snake and would have done absolutely anything to get rid of Goldie so that he could run the company.* Out of the corner of her eye she saw Mo was writing volumes and was having trouble keeping up. Good.

"Destry Bird."

"Smooth. Probably number two now that Goldie is gone. Very upper-class Virginia. V.M.I., I think. He and Hoffritz are a formidable team. The brokers refer to them as Search and Destroy." *And don't turn your back on either one,* she thought.

"What, Les?" Had he read her thoughts?

She masked her sentiments and remembered how the two men had surrounded Goldie at the head table just before Goldie got up to speak—and to die. "Was it in his Jack Daniel's?"

Mo looked up quickly, but Silvestri was impassive. Too late. Whatever had killed Goldie had been found; it *was* in Goldie's drink.

In her mind she heard Goldie's voice—for it had been his voice, she was certain now—from the men's room, saying, "Over my dead body."

"Did you remember something, Les?" Silvestri leaned across the desk, his question an accusation, his eyes intent on hers.

She closed her eyes to keep him out and saw the head table again. "Only that everyone was crowding around Goldie. People came over to pay respects."

"Some respect," Metzger said.

She shook her head. "I really didn't see anything unusual." She saw Chris gesturing vigorously and spilling Goldie's drink. Someone had replaced it. . . . She looked up and found Silvestri reading her. She shrugged and gave him wide-eyed innocence.

"Douglas Culver," he said, reading from a worksheet.

"He's head of financial services. A really nice guy. Another Southerner. Atlanta this time, I think. The easiest guy there to talk to." She remembered Dougie's look of distaste when Ellie had collapsed on him. Either he didn't like women or he didn't like Ellie.

"Neil Munchen."

"Neil runs the telemarketing program." She uncrossed her leg and recrossed in the other direction. She felt she was sitting in a pool of perspiration.

"Telemarketing?" Mo asked, looking up from her notebook. She took a last acrid puff of her cigarette and ground the butt out on Silvestri's floor. She was wearing red pumps.

"Cold calling. They have cold callers and leads from Dun and

Bradstreet and elsewhere from all over the country. The callers place the calls, qualify the banking and background on the lead and then the broker gets back and pitches the stock of the day, usually something the firm is pushing."

"Sounds like a bucket shop operation," Mo said. "What smart, rich dude would tell an absolute stranger private financial information over the phone?"

Wetzon smiled, glad to find someone who was more naive than she was. "They do, and they buy stock like that. Heads of corporations, wealthy people, smart people. It's a very successful program—that is, the firm makes a lot of money from it and so do the brokers. Really intelligent people get conned, too."

"I just don't get it," Mo said, looking at Silvestri. "We put these creeps out of business whenever we find them."

"Don't get me wrong. This is no con. It's perfectly legal, and some investors even make money."

"What about Munchen?" Silvestri interrupted. "What do you know about him?"

"Neil was Goldie's protégé. He learned telemarketing at Lehman and Goldie brought him over to Luwisher Brothers to set up a unit to compete with Lehman's because Goldie was feuding with Sheldon Amble at Lehman."

"Sheldon Amble." Silvestri wrote the name in his book. "Was this Sheldon Amble at the dinner?"

Wetzon laughed. "In spirit only. Sheldon shuffled off this mortal coil a few years ago." *Wait a minute,* she thought, *wait a minute.* Sheldon Amble.

"Yes, Les?"

She blinked, guilty. She needed time to sort it out, try to remember. He'd read her face and knew she'd thought of something, and knew further that she wasn't going to share.

"Nothing. Honestly, Silvestri." She looked down at her hands.

"Where's this Munchen from?" Metzger asked. "Is he another redneck?"

"No, Artie, Great Neck." She laughed. "Believe it or not, none of these guys is a redneck. At least not on the surface. They're good ole boys deep down."

"So Munchen is not a Southerner?" Silvestri barely acknowledged her joke.

"Neil? No way. He's definitely Long Island." She said it the New York way with the hard *g* so that it became all one word, *longisland.* "Jewish. Too dark and ethnic for them. An outsider in this crowd. Check his suntan. A closet gold-chain wearer, if ever I saw one." She recalled the bruise on his cheekbone when he left the men's room. "Are we almost finished? I have to make a phone call."

"Really, Les?" Now he was being sarcastic.

"Oh, come on, Silvestri. I have to call Laura Lee about the tea we're planning."

"Christopher Gorham."

She made a face at him and recrossed her leg. "I was there with Chris that night because his wife—Abby—walked out on him. He was upset about that." *Was he,* she thought. He was upset about something, but she'd bet it had more to do with Goldie than Abby. "He manages the large boardroom. I've known him since he was a rookie. He is not a murderer." She couldn't imagine Chris working up passion enough to murder someone.

"Anyone could be a murderer, Les. You ought to know that by now." There was a warning in his voice. "All it takes is an irrational moment and a motive."

"Not Chris. He's from good Episcopalian stock—Connecticut, I think. Greenwich. Fine Wasp credentials. Won a bronze in swimming in the Olympics one year." And was passed over for partnership at Luwisher Brothers, she thought, holding that for herself. "Is that it?" She rose.

"One more." Silvestri frowned at her. She could see he was furious. "Dr. Carlton Ash."

She sat down. "I don't know him at all." She thought for a moment. "He's like the wild card, you know. He doesn't fit. He's a consultant with Goodspeed Associates. He was hired by Luwisher Brothers to do a secret study of some sort, and he's been hanging out there for months."

"Was he at the dinner?"

"Yes. He was sitting right next to Goldie. Can I go now?" She got up quickly, took her jacket. "Bye, guys." She opened the door. "Your air-conditioning stinks." She closed the door.

Silvestri caught up with her in the squad room. "What's the big hurry, Les?"

"I told you. I forgot to call Laura Lee."

"Why do I get the feeling you're holding out on me?"

"Me? Would I do that, Silvestri?" she said. She reached up and kissed his cheek. He was sweating; his shirt was wet, particularly around the shoulder harness.

"You're a liar," he said. "See you later." He rubbed the back of her neck and returned to his office. Metzger had taken her chair and was talking to Mo. Silvestri gestured with the worksheets.

She turned away. Around her the activity of the squad room— phones jangling, a woman screaming drunkenly, a child wailing— seemed to intensify.

Sheldon Amble, the power at Lehman, had died in the saddle, but not in his own bed. His mistress had been a young woman broker with another firm. A woman it was rumored Sheldon had taken away from Goldie Barnes.

The woman had been Ellie Kaplan.

TWELVE

New York City was her dewy-eyed best early on summer mornings. The air was clean, balmy, and faintly moist. The June sunlight came filtering through a light haze which the sun would burn off by midmorning.

In the meantime, there was something almost small townish about the empty streets, the few sleepy joggers, the dearth of traffic.

Wetzon felt overdressed in her two-piece lavender linen, even though it was lightweight and less formal than her usual business attire.

The subway platform on Eighty-sixth and Broadway was hideously hot, having not cooled off from the previous day; it probably would not cool off again until fall. But the "1" train came swiftly, and Wetzon got on a car so air-conditioned that the droplets of perspiration on her face condensed like a cold, wet slap.

The car was sparsely filled, as was to be expected at six forty-five A.M. on a Saturday. She took a seat and opened *The Times* to the business page, automatically folding it in the narrow New York subway fold so she could read without going into someone else's space when she turned a page. At the far end of the car a woman in a bright yellow sundress screamed loudly in Spanish at two children who were playing tag around one of the center poles. She was surrounded by bundles, one of which was a gigantic red food cooler. They were obviously getting an early start for the beach, maybe Coney Island.

At Seventy-ninth Street a group of athletic-looking, golden-skinned teenagers got on. They were speaking German and both girls and boys wore walking shorts and carried backpacks. Wetzon returned to her newspaper and was reading about problems at Shearson when suddenly they were bending over her, and she realized that she was sitting under the subway map. She smiled at them and slid over to another seat.

"Where do you want to go?" she asked.

"Fulton Fish Market," a very blond young man said.

"You're a little late. You won't see anything now. You really have to get there around five." She smiled at their disappointed faces. "You could try. Change to the '2' or '3' train at Chambers Street. I think Fulton is the second stop. Or, what you could do is take this train to the last stop, which is South Ferry, and take a ride on the Staten Island Ferry or walk along the waterfront to the South Street Seaport, and save the fish market for another day."

They settled down in the middle of the car to talk about it, and Wetzon went back to her newspaper.

She was on one of the newer trains, and the coolness and lack of humanity made the ride almost pleasant and certainly a lot more civilized than riding during rush hour on a weekday. But she was tired. And she resented having to get up and come down early on *her* Saturday to appease someone who wasn't even a client. On the other hand, she was really curious about Ash's secret report. What could be so topsecret it would shake the industry?

Happily, she hadn't had to answer any questions about her appointment because the night before was Silvestri's poker night, and since it was his turn to host, they'd played at his apartment in Chelsea, and he'd slept there.

The train hurtled through the five or six miles between Eighty-sixth Street and Cortlandt Street, which was the World Trade Center station, stopping every eight or nine blocks to pick up or expel passengers. Even during a busy rush hour, the trip took only about half an hour. Today, without the surges of people getting on and off, it had taken twenty minutes.

Wetzon quickly climbed the steep steps of the out-of-order escalator to the mall-like ground floor of the massive World Trade Center. Except for a few coffee shops, most of the stores in the giant complex were closed. Surprisingly, a lot of tables in the biggest coffee shop were occupied. She let her eyes flit through, thinking how much she'd like to stop for an iced decaf. But it was a quarter after seven already, and she would be late if she indulged herself.

Later in the morning, tourists would flood the area and the shops and restaurants would open. It would be a day—almost but not quite—like any other day in the Financial District, except, of course, its frenzied, high-voltage spine—the salesmen and traders—would be absent. And their absence was palpable to those who were there every day.

On Wall Street—metaphorically, not literally, because very few of the brokerage firms were actually on Wall Street—even on summer Saturdays and Sundays, the deal makers would be coming to work shortly. Sometimes a particularly ambitious stockbroker would saunter into his office in informal attire to make some calls and catch up on paperwork, but the pace was decidedly slower.

And now and again, a stockbroker (or as the firms had taken to calling them, a financial consultant) would come in on a weekend prior to his resignation and his move to another firm, to Xerox his "book," which contained valuable client account statements.

Unofficially, the firms knew brokers did this and resented it, but understood they couldn't stop a client from pulling out his account and going with the broker. The pre-resignation time was particularly treacherous, for if a broker was caught copying his book, he was usually peremptorily fired and his papers confiscated. That didn't mean that the new firm wouldn't take him, however. They still wanted him; it would just make the transition harder, longer.

Officially, the firms, particularly Merrill, fought the transfer of accounts tooth-and-nail. In some states, firms had taken to putting a restraining order on the broker when he moved, in an effort to stop him from luring his old clients to his new firm. But it never worked for any length of time. It only succeeded in upsetting the broker, which was the reason they did it. If the broker was upset and couldn't work, the account might stay with the original firm. Some firms had also taken to putting a bounty on the broker's accounts; that is, offering the remaining brokers in the office high commissions—seventy percent or more—to go after the departed broker's accounts, offering the clients huge discounts in commission charges on the first few trades. It could get vicious. One major firm actually announced over the speaker system how many accounts the firm had held on to after the broker left. It was a form of emotional abuse, terrifying brokers into staying put.

Wetzon left the World Trade Center via the Tower One entrance, crossed the street, and walked up the covered walkway to the Luwisher Tower Building.

She paused for a moment in the huge, luxurious shop-filled lobby. Where had Dr. Ash—or the fat fuck, as Ellie had called him—asked her to meet him? The elevator bank. Downstairs? No, upstairs.

The lobby was empty except for a uniformed attendant who was sipping coffee from a Styrofoam container. He looked at her and nodded sleepily. She had learned long ago that if you were pulled together and knew where you were going, or acted as if you did, no one stopped you.

She got off the elevator at sixty-seven and walked smack into Chris Gorham who was rushing to get on. They hit each other with enough force for each to stagger backward. He recovered first and charged onto the elevator, pushing Wetzon back roughly just before the doors closed. The programmed voice filled the car as Chris pressed the lobby button without releasing her.

"Hey," she said angrily, recovering. "Let go." She tried to push him away. "Do you mind? What do you think you're doing?"

"What the hell do you think *you're* doing, Wetzon?" Chris let go of her and rested against the wall of the elevator, panting. His face was flushed. He was wearing perfectly pressed khakis and a blue LaCoste shirt, deck shoes without socks, and was carrying a tennis racket in a white-and-blue-striped canvas bag.

"It's a private matter, Chris."

"A private matter," he mimicked her. "I'll bet." His eyes narrowed to slits over his high cheekbones. "Well, forget about it. It's over." He slumped, appeared to shrink like a balloon someone had let the air out of.

"Is it Abby? I'm really sorry about that, Chris." He seemed so deflated. Feeling sorry for him, Wetzon reached out and touched his tanned, muscular forearm.

"Who? Oh, yeah. Abby. Right." He looked down at her hand on his arm. "Come and get a cup of coffee with me."

She shook her head. "I can't. I'm going to be late as it is." She was sorry for him, but she didn't want to get involved in his messy private life. This was the new Leslie Wetzon, and she was making a real effort not to give too much of herself to everyone.

The doors opened on the lobby and Chris got off. He turned back. "Don't go up there, Wetzon."

"What are you talking about? I have to." She pressed sixty-seven. The elevator pronounced its good-morning wishes.

"Suit yourself." He shrugged and turned his back on her as the doors closed.

What peculiar behavior, she thought, yawning and rotating her jaw for the pop in her ears as the elevator rose. There was something about Chris that was bogus. As if he were in costume, a boy imitating an adult. She couldn't put her finger on it. As if he was blue-collar putting on white, so he wasn't entirely accepted . . . and he wasn't entirely real.

She stepped off the elevator on sixty-seven into almost total silence. No Carlton Ash. No one. She walked into the reception area past the empty desk. The sun poured through the skylight high over her head onto the tree, making dazzling patterns on the walls, carpets, and furniture. It was quite lovely.

"Hello?" she said tentatively. "Dr. Ash?" Where had he said he'd meet her? She was sure he had said by the bank of elevators. She looked at her watch. Seven-forty. The silence and emptiness were eerie, as if she were the only human being left in a world after the hydrogen bomb had been dropped.

She shuddered. What a dreary thought on such a beautiful day. She turned to the marble staircase and started up. Maybe Ash was waiting for her in the conference room.

Something glinted in the sunlight about three steps above her. She bent to get a closer look. She picked it up. It was a watch crystal, in one piece, but shattered. It was small and oddly shaped. A woman's watch. Anyone could have lost it; though there were few women brokers, the firm was full of women in subsidiary positions. She walked back down the stairs and placed the crystal on the reception desk.

She climbed the stairs again slowly, her heels clicking on the marble. Total silence, but for that. At the top, she called again, "Dr. Ash?"

No response.

She opened the door to the conference room. It was empty. Three Styrofoam cups were on the conference table. The ashtray was full of cigarette butts and ashes. She walked into the room.

Behind her, the door slammed shut with a thud. Startled, she jumped, bumping the table. Coffee spilled from one of the cups. *Get with it, Wetzon, it was only the goddam door,* she told herself. What was there to be jumpy about? A draft can close a door. She went back to the door and turned the knob to open it. It was locked.

THIRTEEN

Well, here's a fine how-do-you-do, Wetzon thought, and she laughed out loud. Then, *this isn't funny, Wetzon. You could be here all weekend, and what would you eat and where would you pee?*

That did it. She jiggled the knob and thumped on the door with her fist. "Hey! I'm locked in!" She bruised the side of her hand, looked at it, rubbed it. "Oh, shit!" she yelled and did Rumpelstiltskin with her foot. Instinct told her the room was probably soundproof. "Oh, hell, blast and corruption!" She stamped around the conference table and sneered at the spilled coffee. "And I'm not cleaning up either."

She pulled out a chair and sat down. She looked up at the large spot on the wall where Goldie's portrait had been, then let her eyes roam quickly around the room searching for an exit she had, perhaps, missed. There were twelve chairs around the conference table; three were askew. The credenza . . . *Dope,* she thought—*the phone.* She jumped up, ran around to the other side of the table and grabbed the phone from the sideboard. She got a line, punched out 411 for information—she would just call the building number and they would send someone up to let her out—got a line, tried again, got a line again. She tried her home number; the same thing happened. She pressed nine. Nothing at all. She threw down the phone. "Damn this!" She went back to the door and pounded on it with both hands, then stalked back to the table. She was dripping sweat in spite of the air-conditioning.

Only Dr. Ash and Smith knew she was here, and Smith was in Connecticut for the weekend. Smith would try to call her, but probably wouldn't worry about not reaching her until tomorrow. Silvestri would go crazy if she didn't come home. Hmmmmmm. That was a thought. He never seemed jealous—or at least if he were, he never let on.

She was composing grand scenarios about their unlocking the door on Monday morning and finding a crazy-lady, when she realized that brokers would undoubtedly come in to work this morning. She would be sensible, finish *The Times* and wait. Eventually, someone would show up. After all, it was still very early.

But Chris had been here. What had he been doing here so early? And why had he been in such a hurry to leave?

And where was Dr. Ash?

She looked at the spilled coffee forming a greasy black cloud on the table. Oh, well. If she was going to be here for any length of time, she didn't want to be sitting in a mess. She pulled a Kleenex out of her purse and dropped it on the pool, watching as the liquid turned the tissue brown. Gingerly, she pushed the Styrofoam cup away from her toward the center of the table. The cup was warm to the touch. *Chris,* she thought. She pulled the cup toward her. There was something in the cup besides coffee, but the cup was too full for her to see what it was.

Across the table was another cup and a plastic plate full of crumbs. She got up and walked around the table, picked up the almost empty cup, and poured the liquid from the first cup carefully into the second. At the bottom of the first cup was a nasal inhalator, similar to the one she had seen Carlton Ash using. *Yipes,* she thought and dropped the cup. It fell on its side and rolled away from her.

Unaccountably frightened, she got up and tried the door again, rattling the knob and banging with her sore fist. The knob turned in her hand and the door began to open. She stepped aside, astonished, as the door opened slowly and Dougie Culver, in jeans and a blue-and-white-striped shirt, stood there holding another Styrofoam cup, shock on his face.

"Good heavens, Wetzon, you scared the livin' daylights out of me. What are y'doin' down here at this ungodly hour?"

She looked at her watch. Only twenty minutes had passed in the locked—or was it?—conference room. She felt a little foolish. She looked at Dougie, who was waiting. "I was supposed to meet someone here at seven-thirty, but he's not around. I thought he might have meant the conference room, but as soon as I came in, someone slammed the door behind me and locked me in."

Dougie listened, amusement all over his face. "Aren't we gettin' a little theatrical here, Wetzon?" He fiddled with the latch. "I guess it could have slipped," he said dubiously. "Or maybe you pressed the button accidentally and locked yourself in."

"I am not an hysterical woman, Dougie Culver, so get that patronizing tone out of your voice."

He chuckled. "That's what I like about you, Wetzon. You let it all hang out." He patted her arm. "Come on, be kind and split my Danish with me." He patted his plumpness spilling over the waist of his jeans. "And you can tell me who y'all were meetin'." Without waiting for her response, he walked off down the corridor toward his office.

"Dougie—" Oh, hell. Her stomach growled. Just the thought of being locked up for two days without food had made her hungry. *What a baby you are, Wetzon*, she thought. She followed Dougie Culver.

"Have you seen my office, Wetzon?" He walked through the open door and waved her in after him. The focal point of the office was not the *de rigueur* massive mahogany desk, the computer, the Quotron, the Telerate machine, and the collection of four separate telephones, or even the incredible view of New York Harbor and the Statue of Liberty rising out of the morning mist, but rather, a floor-to-ceiling glass-enclosed vitrine with all kinds, shapes, and colors of seashells displayed on its shelves.

"Wow!" Wetzon said, drawn to the shelves. A huge chunk of rosy coral beckoned her on eye level.

"My grand collection." He closed the door.

"You scuba?"

"Every chance I get."

"It's stunning."

"Come on and sit down," he said. He cut the cinnamon Danish on the plastic plate into wedges. "Help yourself."

She tore herself away from the display case with difficulty and took a wedge of Danish, plunking herself down in one of the two upholstered chairs in front of his desk. The fabric was the same shade of red as the coral in the case.

"I see you matched the decor—" She pointed her wedge of Danish at the display case.

"Pure coincidence, Wetzon." He smiled his slow smile at her.

"I'll bet." She took a bite out of the Danish. It was surprisingly fresh and buttery.

He looked at her expectantly. When she did not pick up his cue, he drawled, "Don't tell me y'all have taken to interviewin' brokers here at dawn on a Saturday."

"No, Dougie. Not a broker, although I've been known to meet people in odd places at odd times. You know how paranoid you brokers are."

He smiled at her, his bald dome shiny in the bright natural light.

"I'm not going to tell you anything, Dougie, so don't try to wheedle it out of me." She helped herself to another slice of Danish. "This is good. Not your usual greasy-spoon variety."

"Wetzon!" He mocked horror. "Y'all know I wouldn't let that kind of junk past these lips. No, no. One of our employees has a connection for gourmet baked goodies. We get supplied six days a week. Sundays you're on your own." He picked up the last piece of Danish and ate it. "So, Wetzon, my word of honor as a Southern gentleman that I won't reveal—"

"No. I keep confidences."

"I know that. You're a real pro. Everyone on the Street respects you. You have a top-notch company, and we rely on you to keep sendin' us the good-quality people you have been."

"Why, Dougie, that's a really nice commercial. Just put in a good word for us with Hoffritz."

Dougie smiled, slowly eased his feet in their Cole Haan moccasins onto his desk, and leaned back in his leather chair. "Now, Wetzon, y'all know you're never goin' to get the recognition you deserve from Johnny Hoffritz because you sit down to pee."

She stared at him for a moment, not sure she'd heard right. "I'm not sure I got what you said." She was having a hard time keeping a straight face.

"You heard me." He was deadly serious.

She laughed. She couldn't help herself. "That's what I like about you, Dougie, you let it all hang out."

A muffled scream, a woman's decibels.

Their eyes locked. Wetzon got to the door first and threw it open.

The scream came again and again, agonizing, from the floor below, piercing, then filling the silence.

FOURTEEN

Ellie Kaplan's face was contorted by the soul-wrenching sound that poured from her.

"Ellie, for godsakes," Dougie said, coming to the edge of the balcony.

The screaming subsided. Ellie stared up at Dougie with pure hate and loathing, her hands to her face, then backed away out of sight toward the elevator banks. Dougie said something under his breath that sounded like, "Women."

"What's goin' on here?" John Hoffritz appeared in the hallway in tennis whites. The perpetual unlit cigarette dipped from the side of his mouth.

"Oh, my God," Dougie said, stumbling backward, crushing Wetzon's toes under the heel of his moccasin. He was looking down toward the foot of the staircase.

"Dammit, Dougie," Wetzon murmured. She turned and limped away from him, rubbing her foot. There was now a dark smudge on her white pantyhose.

"Wetzon?" Destry Bird was standing in front of her. *Where had he come from?* He looked down, behind her, toward the staircase. "What the fuck—"

She straightened up and spun around. What was everybody so engrossed with?

"Do something, do something!" Ellie screamed.

Wetzon went to the edge of the balcony and looked down. Something lay on the marble staircase below. She saw the shoes first, the soles, new shoes, black shoes . . . and knew who it was before she saw the man's face, which was hidden by his immense bulk. Carlton Ash was lying on his back like a beached whale, upended, his lower torso on the steps, his head twisted awkwardly on the carpeted floor. A dark aureole of blood had formed around his head. His face was blue.

The Danish began a trip back up to Wetzon's throat and she swallowed again and again, hand to her mouth.

"Stand back, Wetzon," Hoffritz said, trying to shoulder her out of the way. "What the hell are you doing here anyway?"

She didn't move; her feet felt cemented to the floor, her eyes cemented to the thing on the stairs. Neil Munchen was downstairs now. He bent and lifted Carlton Ash's limp wrist, taking his pulse. He looked up at the faces looking down and shook his head. "We'd better call the police."

"Not yet," Hoffritz said. "Call 911 and tell them there's been an accident. I want to buy us some time. Get Jed Backer up here so we can get a statement out quick. And move his head. That's a quarter-million-dollar Persian."

"You can't move him, John." Wetzon spoke quietly, when all the time she wanted to shout at him, *Are you crazy?* "He's dead. You have to leave him that way for the police to see."

"Stay out of this, Wetzon. It's not your affair," Destry snapped.

"Wetzon is right," Dougie said smoothly, letting his hand travel lightly over her back.

"Oh, fuck it," Hoffritz said. "But put somethin' under his head so he doesn't ruin the goddam carpet. I'm calling Jed Backer." He went off down the hall.

"Trust Johnny to make the appropriate comment every time," Dougie said. "Class will out."

"Good thing it didn't happen yesterday; otherwise, we'd never get any work out of anybody." Destry made a sweeping gesture and followed Hoffritz.

Neil looked up at Wetzon. "Would you call please, Wetzon?"

"No, I'll do it," Dougie said. "Neil, you get somethin' to put over the poor clumsy slob. Can't have him lookin' at us that way."

Wetzon looked down at Dr. Ash. His right hand was clenched, his index finger pointed up at them—an accusation. She turned to Dougie, who shrugged.

"Gallows humor." His hand rested on her waist. "Wetzon, go deal with Ellie, would you?" He gave her a little pat on the back and went into the conference room. Wetzon started down the stairs and remembered the inhalator in the coffee cup. Carlton Ash's inhalator. What was it doing in the cup of coffee—and more important now, what had happened between the time it was left in the cup and Ash's death?

She followed Dougie, stopping at the door. Dougie made the call to 911 as she listened. The phone seemed to be working fine.

When he hung up, she asked, "Did Dr. Ash have an office here?"

"He was usin' Angelo's office down on the floor."

"Who is Angelo?"

"Was, not is. Angelo La Rocca. He was our man on compliance. Took a flyin' leap in front of the 'F' train about six months ago. Forty-five years old. Damn shame. We haven't found a replacement yet, so I've been coverin' compliance. We put Ash in Angelo's old office, near Ellie."

As if in response, Ellie's voice could be heard below, rising to a high pitch, shrieking for Neil to call an ambulance, cover him, get him off the stairs.

"Please, Wetzon." Dougie's eyes beseeched her.

"Okay, okay." She left the conference room, again thought of the inhalator, and started back. Dougie was talking on the phone again.

"Fortune shines on 'us," he said. "They're in check and don't know it." He paused. "Later." And hung up.

Wetzon dashed away from the door and was halfway down the stairs, eyes averted, when she felt Dougie's presence above her. She did not look back, afraid of her footing on the slippery marble.

"Watch it, Wetzon." Neil was coming down behind her. He was carrying a linen tablecloth, which he flapped open and dropped on Dr. Carlton Ash, obliterating him.

They're not even bothered he's dead, Wetzon thought. "Where's Ellie?"

"In her office probably." Neil's tan was tinged with gray. He was wearing a gold chain around his neck under his sportshirt.

"Neil, what about that study he was doing?"

"What about it?"

"Well, you know. It was supposed to be top secret."

"It is, Wetzon. He'd just finished it." Neil looked miserable. He seemed the only one to be emotionally affected by Carlton Ash's death, except for Ellie perhaps.

"Where is it then, Neil? Have you seen it?"

He shook his head. "He—"

Three brokers came bounding down the hall, steaming with curiosity. "Hi, Wetzon," one greeted her. Juggy Greenfield. Wetzon had placed him at Luwisher Brothers last year. "What's up? Ellie just told us someone took a header on the stairs."

"Someone did. Best to stay out of the way until the medics get here."

"Oh, okay." Juggy said, but he and his cohorts kept going toward the reception area. Wetzon shrugged and made her way to the boardroom and the surrounding offices.

The boardroom was empty, just a sea of L-shaped desks, the Quotron machines eerily silent. She passed the closed door of David Kim's office, hearing the faint murmur of voices. It made sense that if Ellie were working, David would also be. She passed the closed door of Ellie's office, heard talking. Ellie could wait.

The door to the last office on the floor was shut tight. No sound came from within. This had to be the office Carlton Ash was using. Wetzon opened the door boldly and stepped in—then, shocked, took an involuntary step backward.

Carlton Ash's office had been trashed.

FIFTEEN

She moved slowly into the small office thinking someone might be hiding behind the door. No. The office was deserted. Drawers hung open, papers lay in snarled masses, books had been pulled from bookshelves. The desk had been made a catchall for the wastebasket which lay upended on its surface. There was no sound, except for the computer. A tornado had swept through the room, and it didn't much matter anyway because its previous occupant was dead and that's all there was. *This is the way the world ends, this is the way the world ends,* T.S. Eliot's words floated up from her memory. *Not with a bang but a whimper.*

A whimper. She could hear it. It was coming from the computer. Someone had left it on. The someone who had trashed the room—or Dr. Ash? She came around the desk and stared at the screen. It was blank. It was making a wheezing sound not unlike the breathing noises Dr. Ash had made. When she touched W for Wetzon, it gave her a lunatic hodgepodge of letters and numbers, as if it had had a nervous breakdown.

On the desk chair lay Carlton Ash's soft leather portfolio, brutalized, its binding ripped open. She lifted the torn leather flap with her fingernail. Nothing. Whatever had been there—the mysterious report he'd been working on, no doubt—was gone.

She stared out the window. The haze had lifted and the view, the statue, the boats, seemed as sharp and gleaming as if painted on glass.

What could be in that report that would make someone kill for it? But wait. Not so fast. Had Ash been murdered? And if so, was it because he knew something about Goldie's death?

She fished into her purse for her pen and, crouching, used it to sift through the papers on the floor. Nothing that even looked remotely like pages from a report. Standing, she checked the gaping drawers. Nothing except the usual desk paraphernalia. A stapler, tape dispenser, a tin of paperclips, pencils. One drawer was set up for hanging files, folders ready but empty. She skimmed through, just to be sure, using the closed tip of her pen. Whoever had done this had been thorough. She sighed and put her pen back in her purse.

A row of tall bookshelves covered the short wall next to the door, but the books were on the floor, tossed like rag dolls. Some spines had been broken. She picked her way through the wreckage. She recognized the red Standard & Poor's *Securities Dealers of North America*, pages rent, the green *Securities Industry Yearbook*, binding in shreds, and several other reference books, all on the subject of compliance in the securities markets. A dictionary, in tatters. A book on trading, two books on options, a half dozen or more books on securities law. She shuddered. Destroyed books were like dead bodies. This was a bad luck room. Its *two* previous occupants were dead.

Silvestri, she thought. *He should be in on this, even though it's not his precinct.* She would be breaking no client confidence by calling him because he would get to know soon enough anyway.

She strolled out of Dr. Ash's office, past the closed doors of the other offices into the boardroom, and waved casually to Juggy Greenfield and his friends a dozen desks away. They were guffawing, as if someone had just told a joke. The worst possible situations were breeding grounds for Wall Street's black humor.

Picking the closest desk with a phone, she sat down and called Silvestri. No trouble getting a call out. Silvestri and Metzger were both unavailable and she was bumped to Mo Ryan.

"Please tell him I'm at Luwisher Brothers," Wetzon told the detective. "There's been an accident here. Dr. Carlton Ash is dead." She gave Mo Ryan the address and hung up in the middle of Mo's response. Her hands were shaking.

She walked back to Ellie's office. Inside, she could hear Ellie talking to someone. Wetzon knocked and opened the door. The room reeked of booze.

Ellie was alone, talking on the telephone. She beckoned to Wetzon and said into the phone, "Gotta go," and hung up. She was wearing gray linen trousers and a white wrap-around silk blouse, cut in a low V. A gold ball charm dangled from a long mesh chain around her neck. "Horrible, isn't it?" She pointed to the open bottle of Jack Daniel's on her desk. "Want a swig?"

"No, thanks," Wetzon declined. "Too early for me." But it was tempting. The office was freezer-cold. She could feel goosebumps on her arms under the sleeves of her jacket. She sat down in front of Ellie's desk, sitting on her cold hands to keep them still.

Ellie poured a generous amount of whiskey into a taupe coffee mug, inscribed with the legend WOMEN MAKE THE BEST BUSINESS-MEN, and drank most of it. "I told them to carpet those goddam stairs, I told them to put up another railing, but no, they never listen to me. They always know better." She drained the contents of her cup and poured again. "If the fat fuck had a wife and kiddies, they'll sue our brains out."

"Accident? You think it was an accident?"

"Well, of course, Wetzon. What else would it be? I was just telling David—" She pointed to the telephone.

"David called you?"

"Yes. Why?"

"From his office?"

Ellie frowned and pushed her hair back behind her ears. "No, he's not here. I just spoke to him on the phone. He helps his parents out on Saturdays. He was . . ." She stared at the phone, her face haggard.

"I heard someone in his office. I thought it was David."

Ellie shook her head violently, her hair rippled forward like a gray satin curtain. "No. You couldn't have." Rising suddenly, she picked up her mug and left the room. "Come on, Wetzon."

Wetzon followed her into David Kim's office. Ellie turned to face Wetzon and gestured with the mug. "See, he's not here," she said.

The office was neatly arranged, functional and attractive. An open black attaché case was standing under the desk. "His briefcase is."

"Oh, he often leaves it here. Trust me, Wetzon, you were mistaken." Ellie patted the back of David's chair in a vague, almost distracted manner. Still, there was something unmistakably proprietary about the gesture.

Wetzon nodded. "I must have made a mistake." Someone could have been using David's office, or for some reason either Ellie didn't know David had been there, or she was covering up for him. It was multiple choice, pick one.

They drifted back to Ellie's office. Ellie closed the door behind them. "I think you'd better get me out of this place, Wetzon."

"Where do you want to go?"

Ellie rolled the gold ball charm between her thumb and forefinger. "Oh, I don't know. I always thought I'd be here for life, but with Goldie gone . . ." She sank into her chair, her eyes half closed, mouth sagging. "I'm so tired of all the infighting. Doug is the only decent one in the group, and who knows for sure about him. He's got such a coating of Southern honey that it could be covering something equally disgusting. Find me a nice quiet, quality regional firm, like Tucker maybe."

"You and David, too?"

"Yes. And my assistant, Dwayne." She looked up at Wetzon. "Our trailing twelve months come to two million."

"Not bad."

"Yeah. Not bad for an ex-schoolteacher." She drained her mug and poured a last dollop from the bottle, emptying it. Then she screwed the cap back on and dropped the bottle in the wastebasket next to her desk, with a crash. "So much for that." She raised her mug. "To the late, great Dr. Carlton Ash. His demise gives the lie to the adage that only the good die young." Her mouth twisted. "Are you sure you don't want to join me, Wetzon?" There's enough here for you to have a taste."

"Those are pretty hard sentiments, Ellie."

"You didn't know the fat fuck."

"Is this all about the study he was doing for the firm?"

"What do you mean *this*? What are you doing here today anyway, Wetzon?" Ellie stared at her with clear hostility.

If one more person asked her that, Wetzon was going to start screaming. But now probably there was no harm in telling. "He asked me to meet him here."

"He? Who?" She took a swallow of bourbon and closed her eyes.

"The late, great Carlton Ash."

Ellie set the mug down hard. "He did?"

"He was going to give me a copy of the study."

"Hot off the press, no doubt." With unsteady hands she drew a cigarette from a crumpled pack and lit it.

"No doubt." Wetzon paused. "He also said he knew who killed Goldie."

Ellie smiled. "I don't think anyone killed Goldie except Goldie. The fat fuck was just trying to make himself look important. Wetzon, you've been had." She laughed and swung around in her chair to study the view. "He'll make a nice headline in the *Daily News*."

"God, Ellie—"

"Don't judge me, Wetzon. You don't know."

The door opened and one of the young brokers Wetzon had seen earlier poked his head in. "The cops want to see everyone out in the boardroom, ASAP."

Ellie sighed. Turning, she took out her blue nylon bag and the makeup mirror and ran a comb through her hair, carefully reapplying powder and lipstick.

Wetzon rose. "Is there a ladies' room on this floor?"

"Of course. Just past the fat fuck's office. Men's on the left, ladies' on the right."

"I'll be back."

The corridor narrowed as Wetzon came to the far end of the floor, where it formed a T. She went left, walked about ten paces down a hall, and when she saw MEN in bold black letters on the door, realized she'd made the wrong turn. She backtracked. Stopped. She opened the door to the men's room tentatively. No one there. *Good thing, too, Wetzon. Fancy catching someone in the middle* . . . a giggle welled up in her chest.

The narrow hall went beyond the men's room. Curious, she followed it to where it ended. The sign on the door said, EXIT STAIRCASE 2.

SIXTEEN

Police procedure, she thought, yawning, was never the same from precinct to precinct, murder to murder, but the nitty-gritty of it was always boring, especially when it meant waiting around, and there was always a lot of that. Like rehearsals. The chorus people were always waiting around for the director or the choreographer to get his act together.

The detective in charge was a lieutenant named Weiss, a swarthy man with a great shock of black hair. He was wearing a very well-tailored, summer-weight gray suit, blue button-down shirt, and crisply tied light-blue-on-dark-blue dotted silk tie, soft black Bally shoes. Very fashionable for a Saturday morning.

Wetzon, sitting in the boardroom—*bored* in the boardroom—waiting her turn, felt her mind wander restlessly. Hoffritz, Bird, Dougie were not here. Presumably they'd been questioned separately, treated with some deference. After all, they were managing directors. The three other brokers were also gone, having been dealt with—and out—quickly, probably each vouching for the others.

She picked up the phone, pressed 9, and called Smith in Connect-icut. Smith answered in a voice smothered in sleep. "Sorry I woke you," Wetzon whispered.

"Speak up. Where are you?"

"I can't talk any louder. Carlton Ash was just murdered." She overrode Smith's gasp. "I'm still at Luwisher Brothers. I'll talk to you later." She hung up on Smith's squeal.

She got up and stretched; she would have liked to put one leg on the desk and fold herself over it, but her skirt was far too slim and she wasn't alone. She looked at her watch. Ten o'clock. It seemed as if she'd been here all day. She walked over and sat down next to Ellie, who was wearing red-framed half glasses and was thumbing restlessly through *Barron's*.

"So?" Ellie said. Her eyes met Wetzon's over the top of her glasses.

"They're taking a long time with Neil."

"This is ridiculous." Ellie slapped the magazine down and looked at her watch. "Damn, I've lost the crystal again."

"Do you often work on Saturdays?"

"It's very hard to keep up if your eyes are glued to your Quotron all day—the sweet sad song of the options broker."

"Does that mean yes or no?"

Ellie smiled ironically. "What is this, Wetzon? The third degree?"

"Sorry." Wetzon looked at her hands. She'd broken a nail.

Two uniformed policemen stood in the entrance to the boardroom, talking. Both were young men with bushy mustaches and long hair curling over their collars.

Ellie sighed. She took off the glasses and folded them into a blue nylon case and tucked the case into her quilted Chanel handbag. "No, *I'm* sorry, Wetzon. I miss Goldie, I hate what this place has become, and God save me, I didn't wish that poor slob dead, but I'm not sorry he's gone. Ash was a troublemaker."

"What kind of trouble?"

"Oh, I don't know. He was a snoop. He had us all at each other's throats. Oh, dear." She giggled. "I didn't mean it like that."

"You against Goldie?"

"Oh no, never. Goldie, Neil, and I on one side and Search and Destroy on the other."

"And Dougie?"

"Who knows? He's his own best friend." Ellie shrugged. "How long have you known Dougie? Years, I'll bet. Me, too. He's a sphinx. I mean, do you get any sexual vibes from him?"

Wetzon considered that. "No," she admitted. "Although he is touchy-feely."

"Yes, isn't he though. But my guess is it doesn't mean anything. He's probably lined up with Search and Destroy, but only if he thinks they're going to win."

"Win what?"

"Everything. This firm. Luwisher Brothers is a pot of gold. That's all they really care about."

"I don't get any sexual vibes from any of them. Oh, maybe Neil."

"Well, Neil has real blood running through his veins."

"And Goldie?"

"Goldie was sexual. Oh, my, yes." She looked at Wetzon, exposed, daring her to comment.

"Ms. Kaplan?"

Startled, both women stood up. An overweight detective in tan slacks and a brown sports jacket looked from Wetzon to Ellie.

"I'm Ellie Kaplan."

"Come with me then, if you don't mind. Lieutenant Weiss is ready for you." The detective turned and walked past the uniforms, toward the reception area.

"But am I ready for Lieutenant Weiss?" Ellie murmured. "And of course I mind. I could put this time to better use."

So could I, Wetzon thought, watching Ellie go off down the hall. Still standing, she called out to the uniforms, "May I be excused for a minute?" She pointed to the rear of the floor.

The men looked at each other and nodded. Tweedledum and Tweedledee. Good thing one wasn't a woman because then she'd have company she didn't want.

She went back past David's office, staying close to the wall, and ducked through Ellie's open door, closing it quietly behind her. Her back against the door, she surveyed the room. What on earth was she doing here? What was she looking for?

Ellie's desk was an organized chaos of papers. The machines were shut down. Wetzon sat down at the desk and opened one drawer after another. Stationery, envelopes, notepads. Nail polish—a nice pink Estée Lauder—and a top coat. Nail-polish remover. A bottle of oyster-shell calcium pills. A prescription container of Valium. Ten milligrams. Heavy stuff. She closed that drawer.

The bottom drawer contained the blue makeup bag and the standing mirror. She unzipped the bag. Three lipsticks, a compact, shadow, mascara, an eye pencil. Brushes. She turned one of the lipsticks over to see the color label on the bottom, and a little square of white paper fluttered off and to the floor. She picked it up; there was some writing on it. It looked like the fragment of a letter. Wetzon dug into the bottom of the makeup bag, and found other little squares of paper, most with writing on them.

She was taking too long, she knew. She had to get back or they would be suspicious. Gathering up all the scraps, including the one from the floor, she dropped them into her change purse with her tokens and loose coins.

Probably nothing. Certainly none of her business. God, she was getting like Smith. Betray a friend. No conscience whatever. No. Wrong. Wasn't she working for Luwisher Brothers? Whatever, she'd talked herself into a good case of the guilts. Ellie was a nice woman. *So put the scraps back where you found them, Wetzon,* she said to herself. Fat chance.

She made sure the drawers were closed and slipped out of the room.

"Wetzon?" Neil Munchen was walking toward her from the direction of the men's room. "How's Ellie doing?"

Oops, she thought, *caught in the act.* She smiled at him. "I think she's okay. She's being debriefed. I just rinsed out her mug for her."

He seemed to accept her dopey explanation, as if his mind were elsewhere, and her exit from Ellie's office was not a surprise. "Are you last?"

"I guess so. How did it go?"

"They just want to know who saw what and when. Alibis et cetera. All this bureaucratic crap about an accident."

Wetzon walked back into the boardroom with him. "What was the report about, Neil—the one Ash was writing for the firm?"

"I can't tell you that." He was going from one desk to another, checking that everything was locked up and put away.

"Do you know?" She followed him.

"He hadn't completed it. He was going to present it on Monday at the managing directors' meeting. It was being finalized this weekend."

"This weekend?"

"Yeah."

"Was he working with anybody? A secretary?"

"I don't know." He turned on her. "Get outta my face, will you, Wetzon?"

"No, Neil, I won't. You have to have an idea of what that report was about. You're a director here."

His dark eyes flicked over her wearily. "All right, I do. We hired Ash to do a feasibility study, but we don't know what his conclusions were."

"A feasibility study of what?"

"It wasn't my idea, and Goldie was against it."

"What? *Dammit,* Neil."

"I can't tell you, Wetzon."

"Okay, don't tell me, but you'll have to tell the police. Jesus, Neil, Goldie is dead. Now Ash is dead. What if it's connected? What if it's murder?"

He brushed his hands over his eyes.

"It *was* murder, smart old Wetzon." Neither had noticed Ellie until she spoke. They spun around. Her face was ghastly in the fluorescent light. "The medical examiner just told Weiss that the fat fuck was dead before he cracked his head open on the marble stairs."

SEVENTEEN

Weiss was holed up in the conference room, which was so dense with floating smoke and acrid fumes from his cigarettes that Wetzon's eyes began to burn and tears seeped down her cheeks. She dabbed them away with a tissue, coughing, while Weiss conferred with an athletic-looking light-skinned black man who was chewing vigorously on a reeking cigar.

"Oh, shit, cigar," she said faintly. That and the increasingly evident death odors from the body of Carlton Ash, which had yet to be removed from the staircase, were playing havoc with Wetzon's digestion. The tablecloth Neil had thrown over Ash's remains was gone, and they were chalking the site when she squeezed past. While a cop in uniform took lengthy notes, two technicians were making precise measurements with compasses and rulers as if they were architects. A photographer snapped away. All were seemingly oblivious to the person who lay exposed, vulnerable, and dead.

She pressed the tissue over her mouth. She was going to be sick. They had sat her in the end chair, nearest the door, but she'd never make it to the bathroom.

Weiss looked up. "Get some water for the lady, Drake. And see if you can find a paper bag."

Drake had one of those carved-out-of-oak faces, with a heavy sprinkling of freckles across his prominent nose, cheekbones, and forehead. He rolled the cigar stub in his mouth and chewed some, staring at her skeptically.

"And dump the cigar," Weiss said, putting some papers aside and sitting down opposite Wetzon.

Wetzon put her head on the conference table, miserable, past caring that she felt foolish, and gasped for air.

Drake opened the door and left the room without closing the door behind him. Some of the smoke drifted out with him.

"Take deep, slow breaths." Weiss looked down at his notes and frowned. ". . . Ms. Wetzon . . . Through the mouth. Why do I know your name?"

Somewhere Drake found a paper bag, and they had her hold it to her mouth and breathe into it. Her nausea subsided. Drake, sans cigar, closed the door to the conference room and sat down beside Weiss. He exuded the rankness of the cigar. Wetzon's throat tightened.

"Do you want to wash up, Ms. Wetzon?" Weiss shuffled through pages of his notepad and didn't look up.

Do I look that bad? she thought. But she shook her head.

"Well?" he asked, impatiently, putting his notepad aside and fixing his eyes on her.

"No." She was annoyed. Some detective. He might notice more if he looked at the person he was talking to.

"You are—"

"Leslie Wetzon. My company is Smith and Wetzon. We're recruiters and management consultants to Wall Street firms. Luwisher Brothers is a client."

Weiss picked up a fresh pack of Camels, tore the cellophane and slipped a cigarette out. He was about to light it from the butt of his old one.

"Please don't do that," Wetzon said.

"Do what?" He raised a hairy black brow at her and lit the cigarette. The fingers of his right hand were stained yellow-brown.

"That. The cigarette." She felt he knew what she meant and had lit the cigarette anyway. "It'll make me sick." She didn't bother keeping the anger out of her voice.

Weiss heaved an exaggerated sigh. He put the cigarette out in the overflowing ashtray to his right, spilling ashes and stubs onto the already ash-dusted conference table.

"Ashtray!" she said out loud.

"What do you *think* I'm doing, Ms. Wetzon?" His tone was faintly contemptuous.

"No, not that. I just remembered that the ashtrays were full when I got here this morning, which meant there had probably been an early meeting, since I'm sure everything was cleaned last night. Did you smoke all over what was already in those ashtrays?"

"Ms. Wetzon, what do you take us for?" He spoke sonorously, with a patronizing edge.

She didn't answer. Where were all the Styrofoam coffee containers? "What about the coffee cups?"

"What coffee cups?" Weiss looked at Drake, who shrugged.

"There were at least two on the table. And an empty plastic plate with crumbs. The coffee was still warm."

"Okay, that's enough," Weiss said, smacking the table with the palms of his hands. "Start from the beginning."

Drake took a notebook from the inside pocket of his tan jacket, opened it on the table and made a note with a ballpoint pen.

"Dr. Ash asked me to meet him here at seven-thirty this morning. He was going to give me a copy of the study he did. He more or less told me that there was something in it that led to Goldie Barnes's death. He said he knew why Goldie was murdered."

"Tell me, Ms. . . . Wetzon"—Weiss seemed to have trouble with her name—"if Luwisher Brothers is your client—and we haven't established that for certain yet—why would you have to sneak around to get a copy of this study?"

Wetzon did a slow burn. Maybe he had a point, which made her even angrier. She sat poker-straight, summoning up as much dignity as she could. "Clients keep secrets from consultants; consultants keep secrets from clients. This is a business of secrets and it runs on confidentiality. I felt—and Ash led me to believe—that there was something in his study that would shake up the whole industry. I had to know what it was."

"Tell me what you know about this Goldie Barnes's death." Weiss shifted his eyes to Drake without moving his head. "See what you can get from the computer on that. And check Arditti on the forensics. I want every scrap of material bagged." Drake got up and left the room. His gun bulged through his jacket from the back waistband of his pants.

Normally, she would have smiled and tried to charm Weiss,

considering him a challenge, but she didn't like his attitude. He probably hated women, particularly successful businesswomen.

"Well?" he said. His snide tone confirmed her assessment.

"It was at a dinner in Goldie's honor, Wednesday night. He was sort of retiring."

"Sort of?"

"Supposedly he didn't want to. They were pushing him out."

"He told you this?"

"No, Jesus, everyone knew—"

"Who's *they*?"

"They? Oh, Hoffritz, Bird, maybe Culver, maybe others."

"That was Silvestri's homicide," Weiss mumbled, more to himself than to her.

"Yes," she said, wondering if she should tell him she'd called Silvestri.

"What were you doing here so early on a Saturday morning?"

"I told you. Dr. Ash called me. He asked me to come here."

"Why you?"

"I have no idea. Were there coffee cups here on the table when you got here?"

Drake returned with a sheet of paper. Weiss took a cursory look at it and handed it back to Drake. "Were there coffee cups here when we got here?" Weiss asked Drake. "I want to be sure they went over this room with a fine-toothed comb."

"I'll check." Drake left the room again.

Weiss moved to light another cigarette, stopped, and put it away. Wetzon's heart sank. Without his nicotine fix, he would get meaner and meaner. "Go on," he said.

How did she get herself into these messes? "I was supposed to come up here—I mean, meet him at the elevator bank on the sixty-seventh floor at seven-thirty, but he wasn't there. No one was. So I came up here thinking maybe he'd meant the conference room. Someone slammed the door and locked me in." *How was Chris involved?* she thought suddenly. Had he come back, locked her in, and murdered Carlton Ash? No. Chris was long gone. She'd seen him leave. But what had he been doing here, and why had he made such a point of telling her not to go up?

"That's when you saw the coffee cups?"

"I thought I was locked in for the weekend." She smiled in spite of herself. "Without anything to eat. Some of the cups still had coffee in them. And the coffee was still warm. That's when I found the inhalator." She dropped that on him, trying to keep the glee out of her voice.

"Wait a minute. Stop." Weiss held up his hand. Now she had his full attention. For the first time, he was looking directly at her. "What inhalator?"

Drake returned and sat down.

"Well?" Weiss said, keeping his eyes on Wetzon.

"No coffee cups, no cups or plates or anything," Drake said.

"Swell." He stared at Wetzon without speaking, then said finally, "You want to tell us about the inhalator?"

"I think it was Dr. Ash's."

"Why would you think that?"

"He had a breathing problem, maybe because of his weight—or asthma, I don't know. But I saw him using one at the dinner and also at the meeting we had here yesterday."

"Where was it?"

"The dinner or the inhalator?"

"You know damn well I meant the inhalator." He glared at her.

"It was at the bottom of one of the coffee cups."

"You drank the coffee?"

"No." God, what if she had? "Do you think there might have been poison in the coffee?"

He shrugged. "Without the cups, it's all conjecture, and we don't work on conjecture."

"I poured off some of the coffee to the other cup, which was empty, and the inhalator was on the bottom."

"What did you do with it?"

"Nothing. I didn't touch it. Someone came and let me out and I was so relieved I forgot about it."

"Who let you out?"

"Doug Culver."

"Let's get back to this report. No one mentioned a report until now."

They were covering up, she thought. "I don't know anything about it except that Dr. Ash claimed it would change the face of the retail brokerage industry."

"Get a seal on his office," Weiss mumbled to Drake.

"It's too late," Wetzon said.

"What do you mean? Goodspeed is at Rockefeller Center. How would you know—"

"I'm sorry. I don't know about that office. He had an office here."

"No one told me."

"Maybe they forgot."

"Conveniently. How do you know it's too late?"

"Because"—she felt her face flushing—"because I went down to look for the report."

"And tampered with evidence. Give me a break, lady!"

Wetzon hard-eyed him right back. "I'd like you to know I don't tamper with evidence. The drawers were already open. I used a pen to sift through the papers."

"What the f—what difference does that make?" Weiss stood up, disgust in his every movement. "Where is the office?"

"I'm trying to tell you something important," Wetzon said, matching his disgust with her own. "His office is downstairs in the boardroom, on the other side of Ellie Kaplan's. It's a mess, it's been trashed." What was keeping Silvestri?

Weiss grunted and moved toward the door. He gestured to Drake to precede him, but spoke to Wetzon, slowly and deliberately. "Where do you fit in all of this, Ms. Wetzon? Why would Ash call *you*?"

Obviously, neither Hoffritz nor Bird had mentioned the investigation job. "Because I work for the firm. Maybe he thought I was detached enough—gosh, I don't know. His call came as a big surprise to me. I'd been introduced to him only yesterday. He knew I was curious about the report. I can't believe no one else said anything about the report."

"You have the distinction of being the first."

"I just can't believe it. What did they say he was doing here?"

"They said he was working for Goldie Barnes."

"Working for Goldie?" Now she was at a loss. "I had the feeling that Goldie didn't like him."

Weiss put a cigarette in his mouth and this time, he lit it. He inhaled deeply and smoke came from his nostrils in a thick, white stream. "They said Ash was terminated yesterday."

E I G H T E E N

Ash had been terminated, which was why he'd called her. When Wall Street terminated, keys were demanded, desks and offices were padlocked. How had he gotten into the building? Chris. Chris could have let him in.

These guys—Search and Destroy, Dougie, Chris, Neil—were all killers, but only in terms of making money. Any one of them would sell his own crippled grandmother for a profit. Would one of them also commit murder to ensure his place in the sun? What could possibly be in this report that would make someone kill two people?

Wetzon looked at Weiss, who was smoking with unconcealed gusto, getting his nicotine fix. "I guess he didn't stay terminated," she said.

"Now he is," Weiss said, the cigarette parked in the corner of his mouth. "Give Drake your address and work and home phone numbers, please." He coughed, a hollow catarrhal cough.

Still hacking, he walked her out the door. "That finishes us here," he said to Drake.

Silvestri, sunglasses hiding his eyes, was standing at the top of the stairs with Metzger. They were talking to a squat man carrying a medical bag, whose side-combed hair covered a center bald spot so that it looked like a bad hairpiece. They were joined by a lumpy-faced woman in a cotton shirtwaist dress. Wetzon recognized her from newspaper and television coverage as the Assistant D.A. who had just successfully prosecuted the murderer of a young coed at City U. Two attendants had wrapped Dr. Ash's remains in a white sheet but were having difficulty packing him into a blue body bag, the same color as Ellie's makeup bag.

"What brings you here, Silvestri?" Weiss spoke with just a hint of territoriality.

"I had a call," Silvestri said.

Wetzon knew he was looking at her but it was disconcerting not to see his eyes. "I called him," she said. "I thought he ought to know about it since—"

"I'm working on the Goldie Barnes case." Silvestri cut her off. "I'd like to have a look at the First Officer Report."

Wetzon stuck her chin out and said stiffly, "Silvestri, Dr. Ash told me he knew why Goldie was murdered."

"Hey, Artie." Drake clapped Metzger on the back. "Haven't seen you in a dog's age."

Metzger's basset hound face brightened. He and Drake shook hands.

"If you guys don't need me anymore, I have an appointment." She suddenly felt redundant, as if she had gone too far, been too much of what Silvestri always said she was, a wiseass.

They ignored her.

"Come on, Silvestri," Weiss said. "I'll fill you in." He started back to the conference room.

"Silvestri—"

"Get lost, Les." He didn't take off his glasses. She knew he was angry with her, and she'd hear a lot more about it later.

Why hadn't she told him what Carlton Ash had said on the telephone? *You were playing poker, Silvestri. Shit, Les.*

Going down in the talking elevator, she thought about it. It wasn't only because Ash had sworn her to secrecy. She had not felt herself in any danger, not even when she'd been locked in the conference room.

She'd come to get a copy of the study, that's all.

You're rationalizing, she told herself, getting off the elevator in the lobby. Silvestri would let her have it. Ah, yuk. Why did this always happen to her? *Because you think you're so fucking smart,* she heard Silvestri say.

She looked at her watch. Eleven-thirty. She was supposed to meet Laura Lee at the Burger Heaven around the corner from Saks at twelve-thirty. There was just one thing she wanted to do before she headed uptown.

Circumnavigating the lobby, she found a bank of telephones. It wouldn't have been easy for someone to kill Carlton Ash, trash his office, then race down the stairs, all sixty-seven floors. But it could have happened. For that matter, even David Kim could have called Ellie from the lobby. Ellie wouldn't have questioned where he was calling from.

She'd better update Smith or there'd be hell to pay. "Collect, please," she told the operator after dialing a long progression of numbers.

"Are you all right? What did he say?" Smith's voice was distorted.

"Are you eating breakfast?" Wetzon was envious. She was starving, and it wasn't even noon.

"Yesh. Tell me what happened."

"Dr. Ash was dead . . . to begin with."

"What are you talking about, Wetzon? You're making no sense."

"It was a joke, Smith. You know, 'Marley was dead to begin with.'"

"Who the hell is Marley, Wetzon? What does he have to do with this?"

"Forget it. I'm being silly." She was silly to even try a literary joke on Smith. It served her right. "I mean, when I got here, no one was around. I got locked in the conference room by someone and when I was let out, Dr. Ash was lying dead on the staircase."

"Good heavens!"

"But I'm fine, Smith, thanks for asking."

"Don't make jokes, please. I think maybe I should come in and be with you. You sound hysterical." Smith made mumbling noises, obviously talking to Jake with her hand over the telephone.

"I'm not hysterical. Please don't share this with Jake."

"Wetzon, sweetie, you know you can trust me. I still think maybe I should come in and strategize with you."

"Whatever. I'm hanging up now because I'm late for an appointment. I just wanted to let you know before you heard it on the news."

She replaced the receiver, cutting off Smith's protests and, bypassing the escalator, trotted down the covered staircase to the street, wondering if Carlton Ash had had a secretary at Goodspeed.

The heat on Vesey Street was fiery. The midday sun careened off the concrete like a drunken, suffocating blanket, leaving everyone gasping for air. Summer in New York, but it was not yet even officially summer.

Wetzon hesitated at the entrance to the World Trade Center. The thought of standing on the unair-conditioned subway platform below, where the temperature was likely to be well over one hundred, made her feel faint.

A cab pulled up directly in front of her, disgorging a man, a woman, and two teenagers, all wearing shorts, all carrying cameras from shoulder straps. They were jabbering in French, craning their necks, pointing upward to the top of the towers.

Wetzon held the cab door open. "Are you looking for a fare?"

"Get in, lady, and close the door. You're letting all the hot air in." The driver had dark hair in kinky curls and spoke with a Russian accent.

She got in and settled back. "Forty-ninth and Madison." The cab was air-conditioned but you could hardly tell.

"Very hot today," the driver said. "Over ninety, I think."

"Um," she said, not really wanting to talk. *Just sit here, close your eyes and think cool,* she thought. Her pantyhose clung damply to the back of her knees and thighs. She plucked at her sleeves, then turned them up to the elbow, opened a button on her shirt, then another. She could open all the way, for all the cleavage she had—or didn't have.

She looked up and caught the driver watching her in his rearview mirror. "Just drive," she mumbled. His I.D. said Ari Savarti.

"So what brings you downtown on such a hot day?" Ari Savarti asked, making a smooth turn onto the FDR Drive.

The East River was dotted with sailboats, giving it the illusionary look of Marblehead. The sun streamed down a brilliant yellow, deceiving someone on the air-conditioned inside into thinking it was cool and dry and breathable on the outside.

"You okay back there?"

Wetzon sighed. Her luck that she had to get a talky driver. "You want to know what brought me down there? Business."

"Oh, yeah? What kind of business?"

"I'm a headhunter."

"No fooling? Do you do computer people? I'm a very good programmer. I do word processing, too."

"No. Stockbrokers only."

"Stockbrokers? No fooling. I have a friend, is a stockbroker."

"Oh?" She perked up and sat forward. "What firm is he with?"

"Dean Witter. Long Island. Garden City. You know it?"

"Yes. What's his name?"

"Rueben Silver. You should call him. Maybe he's not so happy. You can mention my name. Ari Savarti."

When she got out of the cab at Forty-ninth and Madison, it was ten after twelve, she had an unexpected lead, and she was feeling definitely more chipper. It was too early to meet Laura Lee, which was good. She wanted to make a phone call.

The sun blazed down; the tar of the street gave under Wetzon's little heels like dough. She slipped into Saks by the side entrance on Forty-ninth Street and made her way across the store for the phone area on the Fiftieth Street side.

The store was jammed with shoppers, locals who were doing their final shopping for the summer before heading to the Hamptons or Connecticut, and tourists, mostly Japanese, all carrying shopping bags and cameras and wads of American money.

She passed a saleswoman with a spray bottle, who offered her a splash of Elizabeth Taylor's Passion, which she rejected, having quite enough of her own. Two other saleswomen were huckstering Estée Lauder's latest giveaway.

An extremely tattered phone book, open on the counter, locked in a metal plate, showed Goodspeed Associates was at Forty-five Rockefeller Plaza. She jotted the phone number down on a page from her Filofax and waited her turn for a phone. Maybe she could talk with Carlton Ash's secretary and find out what the study said. Once the police got to her, that would be it.

A gray-haired man with a Slavic face and a small paunch was just finishing a call. He was being tugged at by a small boy, barely a toddler, who took his hand and pulled him to a woman waiting with the empty stroller. "Daddy, Daddy," the child said. The woman smiled at the boy and sat him back in the stroller. She wasn't far from fifty herself.

So many women were waiting into their thirties and forties to have babies, which wasn't so bad either, because children became a choice and were born because they were wanted. What a wonderful world it would be if the only children born were the ones who were wanted.

Here she was, thirty-eight years old and not particularly maternal. Did she want children? No. Certainly not now. Did she want the option to have them later? You bet.

Wetzon dialed the number for Goodspeed Associates. It was Saturday. Who knew if anyone would be there. Six rings . . . seven . . . eight . . .

"Goodspeed Associates." A young man's voice, slightly high-pitched.

"Hi, I wonder if you can tell me the name of Dr. Carlton Ash's secretary."

"Dr. Ash?"

"Yes, Carlton Ash. He's one of your consultants."

"Oh, Dr. Ash hasn't worked here in a while, six months at least."

"Are you sure? Is this the answering service?"

"Hold on a minute." There was a whispered conversation. "Who is this?"

Wetzon very quietly hung up the phone.

NINETEEN

"And then the check came, and mind you, there were fourteen of us, so I just divided fourteen into four hundred dollars and said everyone owed twenty-eight dollars." Laura Lee took a vicious bite out of her Roquefort burger. "And would you believe this weenie started carryin' on about how she hadn't eaten any rice so she shouldn't have to pay for it."

Wetzon cut her Roquefort burger into four pieces, setting the top of her bun aside.

"You can well afford to eat the whole thing, you know," Laura Lee said. "And then I said to her, do y'all think we're just goin' to sit here and wait till everyone figures out what he owes without an addin' machine at eleven o'clock at night?" She took another bite out of her burger. "Annie was wild. Here we were, it was Vittorio's birthday party. He'd invited all these people, everyone came knowin' full well it was pay for yourself. Annie and I chipped in for the cake—damn." Her burger was oozing out of the bun, dripping juices and melted cheese. Laura Lee dropped the burger on her plate, licked the melt off her fingers, picked it up, and finished it off.

Wetzon grinned at her. "You do have an adventurous social life." She reached into her purse, found a Wash 'n Dry, and handed it to Laura Lee.

"And then Annie was sayin' in such a loud voice all the way down in the elevator, 'What a bunch of stiffs.' I had to keep shushin' her." Laura Lee's eyes gleamed. She'd let the blond tips in her chestnut hair grow out and now wore it in full waves on top of her head and very sleek and short on the sides and back. It was incredibly becoming, making her look like a sophisticated pixie.

"I do love your hair."

"Why don't you think about doin' it yourself?" Laura Lee rubbed her fingers and hands with the Wash 'n Dry.

"Doing what?"

"Changin' your do."

"Me? God, no. I'd never have the nerve." Wetzon patted her topknot, which she'd worn since her early days as a dancer. "God, it would be like an amputation."

Laura Lee laughed. "You're such a stodge. One day I'll get you in a weak moment."

They finished off the Diet Cokes, paid the bill, and crossed the mushy street to Saks. If anything, the air was more humid, the sun hotter.

"Jesus," Wetzon said. "It's like being in hell."

"What would you know about that, darlin'? Of course, you are dressed to the gills." Laura Lee looked cool in a short silk skirt, black with white polka dots, and a silk tee-shirt, white with black polka dots. She had a full half dozen beaded Indian bracelets on her wrist, and her bare feet were in black patent sandals.

"I had to be at Luwisher Brothers for a meeting this morning."

"On a Saturday? Isn't that carryin' things too far?"

"One does what one must."

They took the escalator to the second floor.

"The Max Maras are on sale," Laura Lee said.

"I like Armani better."

"Yes, but who can afford Armani, even on sale?" She stopped at the Calvin Klein area and rummaged through the rack of sales items. "I hate those guys."

"What guys?" Wetzon looked at the price tag on a linen jacket. "Yipes."

"You know. Hoffritz and Bird. Search and Destroy."

"How do you know them?" She gave Laura Lee her undivided attention.

"Come on, Wetzon, everybody knows *everybody* on the Street. Now Goldie, he was somethin' else. Look at this, Wetzon." She had pulled a navy skirt from the rack. "Your size."

"Laura Lee, the police say Goldie was murdered."

"I know. I heard it on the news."

Two women with too much curly hair and chunky gold jewelry on the other side of the rack stopped and listened.

Wetzon pulled Laura Lee to a less populated corner of the sportswear section. "This is just between you and me, not including the two ladies from Great Neck. While I was there this morning, a consultant for the company was murdered."

"Ooooh?" Laura Lee's mouth formed an O. "Well, it's no wonder you're off your feed. How could I be so dumb, goin' on and on about last night? Why didn't you stop me? Was it awful? Who was it?"

"Well, it wasn't pretty. He was from Goodspeed Associates. Dr. Carlton Ash. Or at least, I thought he was from Goodspeed. He was doing some kind of secret study for Luwisher Brothers."

"Secret study, eh? Come on now, Wetzon, nothin' is truly secret either on the Street. That's why they'll never be able to really stop insider tradin'."

"Well, I think this was so secret that someone killed him to keep him from telling me."

Laura Lee clucked her tongue against her teeth. "Mmmm. I'll see what I can dig up about this so-called secret, Wetzon. Now let's hit these racks."

It took them two hours to work over both the second and third floors. Wetzon bought two suits and some DKNY sportswear, and a black linen dress. "I'll never wear it," she moaned.

"Of course you will. Where will you ever again see a six-hundred-dollar Valentino dress reduced to two hundred dollars that fits you as if it were designed for you? Now, let's see." Laura Lee leaned against the counter and peered at the leather belts. "Two dresses, a Max Mara jacket, Calvin trousers and blazer, two Vittadini sweaters, and two Gloria Sachs suits."

"Let's get out of here," Wetzon said. "I'm bleary-eyed. And we have to talk about the tea for Annie. Do you realize we have ten women coming to my apartment a week from tomorrow?"

"We'll plan it all out this afternoon." Laura Lee picked up her shopping bags. "I know exactly what we have to do. But first let's see if the Ferragamos are on sale."

Wetzon groaned. The Ferragamos *were* on sale, and it was after four when Wetzon and Laura Lee staggered out to Fifth Avenue.

"Let's get a cab and go to my place," Wetzon said. "That way we can decide what serving plates to put what on."

"I just want to go across the street to Dunhill's for one li'l ole minute."

"What for?"

"I want to see if they have pajamas."

"Is there a new man in your life, Laura Lee? One you haven't told me about?"

"They're for *me*."

"Pajamas?"

"Wonderful, fine cotton. Feels like silk. What do you sleep in, smarty?"

"Oversized tee shirts. Fine cotton. Feels like cotton. Or just skin. I hate anything confining, like pajamas."

"Why, Wetzon darlin', you never cease to amaze me."

Dunhill, thank God, was out of pajamas so they hailed a cab and loaded their packages on the front seat next to the driver, then collapsed into the backseat, exhausted.

"I'm starving," Wetzon said. "Not to mention hot and sweaty."

"So am I. Do you have somethin' to munch at home?"

"Nada, nothing. Bagels, maybe."

"No. I want a tequila sunrise and somethin' really spicy to eat."

"Why don't we drop our stuff with my doorman and go over to Panarella's? We can have a big salad and talk the party through there."

Fifteen minutes later, that's exactly what they were doing, sitting at a small table on the narrow upstairs balcony overlooking the bar. Wetzon had shocked Laura Lee one more time by surreptitiously rolling down her pantyhose, tucking the clammy nylon hose into her purse. She wriggled her toes. "Oh, my, that feels wonderful." She had a cold Amstel in front of her, and they'd ordered Italian salads.

"Okay," Laura Lee said. "What do you think? Scones, muffins, a couple of tea breads, and some open-faced sandwiches."

"And a chocolate torte."

"Of course."

"Who makes what? I have a good scone recipe."

"You do the scones, then, and I'll do the muffins. We'll each make a tea bread." Laura Lee took a long sip of her tequila sunrise and sighed. "I can do the chocolate torte. We'll need *pain de mie* for the sandwiches. We'll have to order it from somewhere."

"I'll do it. We can make the sandwiches up in the morning and store them under a damp towel."

"Good, now that that's settled." She reached for her drink and knocked her fork to the floor. Bending to pick it up, she exclaimed, "Oh, my, look who's there." Laura Lee, twisted like a pretzel, was looking down at the small bar below them.

Wetzon couldn't see the bar from where she sat. "Who?"

"Chris Gorham. The one in the tennis whites and the thinning hair." She laughed. "Boy, that must bother him a lot."

"Chris?"

"Oh, I forgot. I heard he's at Luwisher Brothers now. You must know him." She came out of the pretzel.

"I do. I guess I shouldn't ask how you know him."

"Don't."

Wetzon frowned. Chris Gorham's appearance had clearly thrown a damper on Laura Lee's mood. "Are you sure it's Chris?"

Laura Lee gave her a scornful look and became a pretzel again. "Oh, oh, he's got company."

"This I have to see." Wetzon twisted herself around and squinted down over the railing. Below, a dark-haired man in gray pants and black tee shirt was shaking Chris Gorham's hand. Chris seemed to be ordering drinks. The second man turned and leaned against the bar. "Jeeezus," Wetzon said. She untwisted herself and sat back in her chair.

The delivery of their salads diverted them for a few minutes.

"What was that about, Wetzon?" Laura Lee asked when the waitress had left.

She didn't answer Laura Lee. Her eyes were drawn below even though she knew she couldn't see anything from this position. The man with Chris Gorham was David Kim.

TWENTY

In a quilted blue satin vest, his small head perched between his hunched shoulders, John Hoffritz grinned demoniacally. "Ante up, everybody." He punctuated his words by blowing smoke rings as big as inner tubes, which hung over the conference table.

"How about freshenin' our drinks here, girlie?" Destry Bird snapped his fingers in Wetzon's face.

"Deal me in, deal me in," someone pleaded from the shadows.

"What?" Wetzon shook herself. Where was she?

"Drinks!" Destry shouted at her.

"Women," Hoffritz said.

"They don't belong in the game," Dougie said. His fingers lingered on her bare arm.

Wetzon found herself dressed in an off-the-shoulder, almost off-the-bosom, gold moiré dress, trimmed in black lace. God, how tacky. She tugged at the bodice of the dress with her free left hand as she balanced the metal tray with a bottle of bourbon and six glasses in the palm of her right. Gee, she thought, just like one of those waitress jobs she'd had when she first came to New York to be a dancer.

She was wearing black fishnet stockings and high-heeled shoes with ankle straps. Gwen Verdon in *Sweet Charity*. *This is not reality,* she thought. Was it a rehearsal?

The men around the smoke-draped conference table were waiting for her to do something, so she did a Bunny tilt, set the tray on the table, and unloaded it.

"Deal me in, deal me in," came again from the shadows at the back of the room.

The players looked up and exchanged sly smiles.

"There's a king," Hoffritz said, "and a trey. No help here."

They were playing with huge cards with strange markings. Wetzon pressed in to get a closer look. A hand crept confidently up her leg, getting to her thigh before she swung around, halting the incursion. Chris Gorham, in a black SS uniform, a Heidelberg saber scar on his cheek, leered up at her and threw his chips into the game.

"Kings, pair of kings, over here."

Wetzon looked around the table. Hoffritz was dealing. Bird, wearing a black patch over his eye, sat next to Hoffritz. Neil, Dougie, Chris—they were all playing. She peered through the smoke. She had brought six glasses to the table. The sixth man was David Kim. He was building a house with another deck of cards.

"High man on the board, he's got the power."

"Over here, Miss Ellie," David Kim called suddenly. "Blow on my cards for luck." He had built an enormous house of cards, with terraces and turrets.

"No," Wetzon cried. "Don't do that. You'll blow the house down."

Ellie Kaplan, voluptuous in a green velvet dress made like a merry widow corselet, materialized out of the smoke and blew sexily into David Kim's ear. The house of cards tottered but didn't fall.

"Eights, see it, pair of eights."

"Deal me in, deal me in."

"Deuce of diamonds, nothing. Ace of spades. Ace bets."

"Aces and eights," Neil cried, jumping to his feet. "Dead man's hand. Count me out."

"Sit down, Neil, I'm dealing," Hoffritz snarled. "Bring on the entertainment." He clapped his hands, and a veiled dancing girl in a red taffeta harem costume, with a red bow on her ample breast, flitted into the room carrying a huge tray with a covered dish.

"Deal me in, deal me in." The voice had become more threatening.

"Aces and eights high. Okay. Pot right."

"I raise," Dougie said quietly.

The woman in red taffeta wove around clod-footed in a semi-dance to some creepy New Age music and then, when the music stopped, dumped the tray peremptorily into the middle of the game. She snatched the cover off the dish. There, resting on a plate of arugula was the head of Goldie Barnes. His eyes were open and staring, his white blond hair shocking against the blue of his face.

"What are my options?" Ellie screamed.

"Get me out of here," Wetzon cried.

Goldie's head winked at her. "Over my dead body," he said.

"I'll take the pot because deuces are wild," Dougie said, reaching for Goldie's head.

Wetzon screamed. Hands clutched her. Arms pressed her down. "No, no, no!"

"Les—"

She struggled against the pressure.

"Les, let it go."

She stopped struggling. Silvestri had his arms around her, holding her against the crinkly hair of his chest.

"Oh, God." She opened her eyes and groaned, snuggling in his arms. The rough bristles of his chin scratched her cheek. He stroked her back, playing his fingers down the bumps of her spine. "Oh, God," she said again, listening to her heart thump helter-skelter against his slow, even beat.

The air conditioner droned, the blinds were drawn against the unrelenting sun.

He came up on one elbow and stroked her face. "Do you want to tell me about it?"

"Not yet." She pulled him down beside her.

Sunday. Day of rest. Day to recoup.

"Love in the morning. Lieutenant take warning," she sang in his ear. Her stomach made an anguished growl. "I'm starving," she said, sitting up.

"Can't you just lie here for a minute calmly," Silvestri said, pulling her down again beside him. Her head found the crook of his arm and rested there. He smelled of sweat and smoke and spicy aftershave. "Now tell me what scared you."

She rubbed her eyes. "Well, there was this poker game, like *Maverick*—"

His beeper went off.

"Shit," she said.

Silvestri kissed her, sat up, and called in.

He's gone, she thought. *That's it.* She got up and into the shower. He joined her a minute later.

"Gotta go downtown," he said, soaping her back.

"Too bad. We could have spent the day together making love."

"Liar. Knowing you, you've already made plans. I did want to talk to you about yesterday."

She rubbed shampoo into her hair. "Uh-oh, I was wondering when that would come up."

"Les, you're a mule. I don't want you to get hurt."

"You can't protect me from life, Silvestri."

"I'd like to."

"I'm turning on the cold water," she said.

"Thanks, I needed that," he said, ducking, but not soon enough. The icy water shot out of the shower over both of them.

"Yeow!" she screamed.

He laughed and stepped out of the shower.

"I'm glad you're not yelling at me," she said.

"Would it do any good?"

"I really didn't think I was interfering. I just wanted to know what was in the study so Smith and I could have a head start." She rolled her long hair into a towel.

"Is that like having inside information?"

"Oh. God, Silvestri. No. This is different."

"How is it different?"

"I wasn't offering to buy it and I wasn't going to use it to trade the stock market with."

"Not the stock market, but what about the placement market?" He grinned at her.

"That's enough. You have a really mean streak in you, Silvestri, you know that? Stop torturing me. I have to think about that."

"Fine, Les. I think it bears thinking about." He was suddenly deadly serious.

Wrapped in a towel, she followed him around the apartment as he dressed. He put on a suit. "Why a suit today?"

"It's not just any meeting."

"Oh? Is it something to do with Carlton Ash and Goldie Barnes?"

She stood behind him. In the mirror, his turquoise eyes flicked over her. He combed his dark hair back, past his receding hairline. "You have a nice scalp," she said.

He turned and grabbed her before she could escape. "You have no respect for anybody," he said, holding her face in his hands.

"I do, Silvestri. You just don't understand women."

He laughed and kissed her. "I. don't understand *this* woman. I'll never understand her. Being around her is a complication." He picked up his jacket.

A sharp flash of lightning and then a tremendous clap of thunder drowned out the hum of the air conditioner. She opened the blinds. "It's really dark out there."

"I'm not afraid," Silvestri said. He strode down the hall to the door.

"No coffee, no breakfast?"

"I'll grab something on the way." He patted his slight paunch and opened the door. *The New York Times* lay on her doormat. He picked it up and handed it to her. "What are your plans?"

"Don't you think it's time you let me in on what the poison is?" She stood in the doorway as he waited for the elevator.

"No."

"Don't you trust me? I'll never tell." God, she sounded like Smith.

"I bet."

Her downstairs bell buzzed. She dropped *The Times* on the floor and let the door slip shut while she went to respond. "Yes?"

"Ms. Smith coming up."

Shit! What the hell was Smith doing here? She went back to the door. Silvestri was still waiting for the elevator, now with impatience, jiggling from foot to foot, pacing. "Smith is on her way up."

He stopped and eyed her. "You were going to spend the day with her?"

"No, I was not going to spend the day with her," she mimicked. "We, you and I, were supposed to meet Carlos and Arthur at Sarabeth's for brunch and then we were going to do the Amsterdam Avenue fair, which may or may not be rained out."

The elevator door opened and Smith stepped out and Silvestri stepped in, managing with some finesse to avoid Smith's quickly proffered cheek. The door closed.

Smith wrinkled her nose. "Humpf."

"You might have called me and let me know you were coming," Wetzon said.

Smith pushed her door open and stepped around her into the apartment. "You'd better get some clothes on."

Wetzon shut the door. "Oh? Why?"

"Jake is parking the car and is on his way up."

TWENTY-
ONE

"Oh, for pitysakes," Smith said. "I don't know why you're being so pigheaded about Jake. He's as much involved in this as we are." She was wearing washed silk bluejeans and a black silk camisole with spaghetti straps. Her arms were tanned a walnutty brown. "I'll just give him a kiss and be right back." She closed Wetzon's door.

Wetzon opened her door, still in her towel. "Furthermore, I wish you'd kiss the bastard off for keeps."

Smith pressed the elevator button and looked wounded. "I don't tell you who you should or should not see."

"You don't? Since when? Who's kidding who?" Wetzon slammed the door, stamped down the hall, and thundered at the thunder. Damn Smith. What did Smith mean, *he's as much involved in this as we are?* She'd probably told Jake everything.

Wetzon threw on a pair of shorts and her red Murder Ink tee shirt that sly old Carlos had found at a bookstore by the same name in the neighborhood. "Murder," he'd said, "is your middle name."

When her doorbell rang, she was pouring water through coffee in her Melitta pot and grinding her teeth. "Cool your heels," she growled.

"Sweetie pie, where are you?"

Wetzon let her in. "I'll bet you've told him everything, the agreement with Luwisher Brothers, Janet Barnes's invitation to lunch—"

Smith's eyes opened wide and innocent. "You know I wouldn't break a confidence." She frowned. "Why are you in such a foul mood? Did you and Silvestri have a fight?" She sounded so hopeful, Wetzon almost laughed.

"If you didn't tell him, why would Jake want to come up? And how is he as involved in this as we are?" She poured coffee into mugs and put Sweet 'n Low in one for Smith.

"Jake wants to be friends."

"Sure. You be friends with him, not me. I hope you haven't forgotten what he did. People like him give the industry a bad name. I don't like the games he plays." She offered the mug to Smith. "I'm wondering what kind of game he's playing right now."

"Oh, I give up. You're awfully hostile, Wetzon. You know, I try really hard to please you." Tears welled up in Smith's eyes and spilled over. She went into the living room and sat down on the sofa. Taking a tissue from her pocket, she dabbed carefully at her makeup.

"Oh, shit. I'm sorry. Come on." Wetzon sat beside her and gave her a hug. "I'm a jerk. First Carlton Ash expires mysteriously just before we're supposed to meet and then I had this horrible dream."

Smith stopped snuffling and pulled away from Wetzon's embrace. "That's really why we—I came back to the City early. Did he tell you who killed Goldie?"

"No, my dear partner, he didn't have the grace to do that before he died. I never even saw him." Wetzon thought for a minute, staring off in space. "Damn. You want to hear something really fascinating? All the players were there yesterday. Any one of them could have killed him. Just like in my dream." She got up, bemused, and went back to the kitchen to get the mugs of coffee.

"Come on, tell me. I'll interpret."

Rain rapped at the windows, clattering like pebbles on her air conditioner.

Wetzon sipped her coffee and closed her eyes. She saw the table, the smoke, the faces, and the cards. "They were playing poker—all of them—with these big cards."

"Tarot cards, you mean. I knew it when I did my reading this morning. You've had a psychic dream, sugar. What cards did they play? Who played what?"

Wetzon searched her memory. "I don't know enough about them to remember specifics."

"Maybe we should have you hypnotized."

"Forget it. One of them tried to feel me up."

"Ooooh, goodie. Who?"

"I don't know. It was a spooky Technicolor dream. But the worst was the dancing woman with Goldie's head on a plate." She shuddered. "It was disgusting."

"Lovely!" Smith jumped up, almost spilling the coffee from her mug. "Think back, did any of them talk?"

"They were all talking, including Goldie's head." She giggled.

"That's not funny, sugar. You were getting a message of some sort."

"Oh no, Smith. You know I'm not into that."

"Tell me, what did Goldie's head say? Don't laugh, Wetzon."

Wetzon laughed. Smith's mouth twitched.

"It said," Wetzon intoned, "*Over my dead body.*" They stared at each other and then shrieked with laughter.

"I've got to go," Smith said regretfully. "He said he'd be back in an hour."

Wetzon sighed. "Please don't tell him anything."

"I promise."

She walked Smith to the door. "I guess we're just not going to be able to find out what was in that report Ash was working on."

"Unless Janet Barnes knows and we can get it out of her."

"Why would she know?"

The phone rang.

"I'll let myself out," Smith said. She seemed suddenly in a hurry to leave.

"Hello," Wetzon said into the phone.

"La-di-da, Birdie." Carlos's voice was ebullient. "The heavens have opened up, but the Festival will probably go on. Are we still on for brunch?"

"I am. Silvestri had to go to work."

She hung up the phone and did some pliés and stretches at the barre, which ran along one wall of her dining room, backed by mirrors from floor to ceiling. She was in good shape again; her body felt long and limber. *My, but you're such a tiny thing,* people always said to her, and she didn't understand why. She thought tall, therefore she was. She laughed out loud and looked at herself in the mirror. She'd looked pretty sexy in her dream with fishnet hose.

She soft-shoed her way down the hall to her bedroom and put on a loose yellow Laura Ashley sundress, the coolest thing she had. There was little hope that the rain would bring a respite from the heat.

As if in response, the sky began to lighten, and by the time she left her apartment and sauntered down Amsterdam, the sun was back to summer-heat-wave normal, and the humidity was tropical rain forest. On both sides of the street the displays of clothing and antiques were being set up. Sausages were frying, and the Belgian waffle makers were cooking. Streams of balloons decorated the Avenue, strung from lamppost to lamppost. A salsa band was warming up.

The Avenue itself was blocked off for traffic and was already beginning to fill with people. Security guards in short-sleeved shirts mumbled into walkie-talkies and eyed the crowd.

Wetzon arrived at Sarabeth's Kitchen before Carlos and Arthur. "Three," she said, giving her name to the young woman in the entrance to the dining room.

"It'll be about a ten-minute wait," the woman said. "Nice to see you again."

The front left side of the restaurant was a bakeshop, with wonderful scones, muffins, cookies and cakes, jams and jellies on sale. She ogled the showcase and decided she might be forced to have a sticky bun for breakfast.

"Ms. Wetzon, your table is ready."

She was seated at a table to the rear of the restaurant when Carlos arrived with Arthur in tow—serious Arthur, with his solemn face and gray beard, and wildly exuberant Carlos. They'd been together two years, and she'd never known Carlos happier. He blew her a kiss and then stopped at every single table where it seemed he knew someone.

"He's unbelievable," Wetzon said, holding her hand out to Arthur.

"He's exhausting." Arthur watched Carlos with delight. He squeezed her hand, then lifted it to his lips. Across the room, Carlos beamed at them.

"Will you get over here already," Wetzon called, "I'm starving."

"Coffee?" the waitress asked, dropping three menus on the table.

"Decaf for me. Orange juice and a sticky bun, please."

"Black coffee with all of her caffeine," Arthur said, smiling. "Orange juice, scrambled eggs, and a bran muffin."

"What's Mr. Wonderful having?" Wetzon said, as Carlos closed in on them.

"Oatmeal and black coffee," Carlos said, pelting her with kisses. "So, Birdie, what's going on in the jungle these days?"

"Very funny."

"There's a bit of activity at Luwisher Brothers," Arthur said.

"Quite a bit. They're a client."

"She attracts murder like a lightning rod," Carlos said. "I think we have to have you exorcised."

"You're starting to sound like Smith."

"Heaven forfend," Carlos said dramatically, rolling his eyes.

They had just been served when the maîtress d' came over to their table. "Ms. Wetzon?"

She took a sip of coffee. "Yes." Her fingers touched the sticky bun.

"There's a police officer in the entrance asking for you."

"Oh me, oh my." Carlos stood up, side of hand cupping his brow to cut the glare, and stared toward the front of the restaurant.

"Sit down, Carlos." Her heart was thumping. Had something happened to Silvestri? "I'll be right back." She got slowly to her feet, licking the honey from the bun off her trembling fingers, and followed the young woman to the front of the restaurant.

A burly uniformed cop was standing outside in front of the restaurant. He had pale pink skin, and carrot-colored hair crept from under his hat. He was watching the people and the activity of the street fair. Wetzon opened the door and stepped out.

"I'm Leslie Wetzon. Is it Silvestri?"

He looked puzzled. "Silvestri?" He took off his hat and wiped the sweat off his brow. "The deputy chief wants to see you downtown."

"The deputy chief?"

"Yes, ma'am. Deputy Chief of Detectives Ian McMann."

TWENTY-
TWO

"Where are we going?" Wetzon squinted at his nameplate. SIEGEL. The street beneath her feet was radiator-hot. Groaning, overloaded window air conditioners spewed hotter air down on them.

"One Police Plaza." Officer Siegel wiped sweat away from his forehead with a handkerchief and held the back door of the blue-and-white open for her. Perspiration stained his light blue summer uniform shirt. She climbed in as two young men walking a Doberman stopped to stare. Across the street, a mother and two small children, bound for the fair, paused.

"*Mira, mira,*" the little boy cried, pointing.

A *New York Post* headline—*Headhunter Moonlights Selling Sex*—flashed across her mind. She'd done nothing wrong. Why did she feel guilty?

It got worse when Siegel, who had left his patrol car double-parked with the rest near the Twentieth Precinct on Eighty-second Street, pulled out onto Columbus and turned on his siren. Unaccountably humiliated, Wetzon sank deeper into her seat. She straightened the skirt of her dress and realized that her present costume of sandals, sleeveless yellow cotton dress, and the yellow print scarf she'd tied jauntily around her ponytail was not the proper dress to meet with the deputy chief of detectives.

Once she knew that nothing had happened to Silvestri, she began to hatch scenarios as to why she had been sent for. Siegel took a corner like a race car driver, barely swerving out of the path of a *New York Times* delivery truck. Wetzon slid back and forth across the lumpy leather seat like a rag doll. She hit the opposite door with a thump.

"What's the hurry, Officer Siegel?" She sat up and grasped the back of the seat, checking her upper arm, sure she'd show black and blue there later.

"The D.P. said posthaste, Ms. Wetzon, and the D.P. gets whatever he wants." Red hair, dripping droplets of sweat, curled on the back of his neck.

"Just like Lola," Wetzon said.

"I'm sorry, Miss?"

Am I that old, she wondered, *that no one gets my references anymore?*

They tore off the FDR Drive, plunging into lower Manhattan which, except for the occasional tourist bus headed for Chinatown or Little Italy, was devoid of traffic on this hot summer Sunday.

Sweat ran like salty rain from her forehead onto her lips and chin. The open windows of the car let in steamy drafts of air pollution in the form of oil, grease, gasoline, and exhaust fumes, leaving her gasping. Her sunglasses did a wet slide down her nose. She pushed them up; they slid down again.

This had to have something to do with the murders. Silvestri had left this morning dressed to the nines. Was he meeting with the Deputy Chief of Detectives?

One Police Plaza, where the Commissioner had his office, and from which all important NYPD decisions were made in the City of New York, was one of the truly ill-conceived buildings in Manhattan, hanging like a huge crate over Madison Street near the foot of the Brooklyn Bridge. It rose fourteen stories and appeared to have been dropped down behind the Municipal Building, intentionally ugly, as if to let the people of New York know that looks were not important. What was important was how the job was done.

Siegel hustled her through the nearly empty garage to the elevator and pressed the button for thirteen.

Great! Here she was being escorted like a suspect to an office in one of the few buildings in New York that dared to have a thirteenth floor.

Siegel led her through an open door into a large room, not unlike a squad room, holding beat-up desks, some with computer terminals, others with typewriters. On the wall facing her, Wetzon saw in large blue letters: DETECTIVE BUREAU. Framed photographs, of past chiefs no doubt, decorated walls which may have been white originally but were now leaning toward gray. Siegel went to the desk and pressed the intercom. The line opened, crackling static. She didn't hear a voice.

"Ms. Wetzon is here," Siegel said.

"Send her in." The voice was harsh with the residue of years of beer and cigars.

She was shown into a meat-locker-cold office, acutely aware of her informal dress and of the man in the smart gray business suit, white shirt, and dark red silk tie, who overpowered the massive mahogany desk he sat behind.

Out of the corner of her eye she saw Silvestri and Weiss at a small conference table, papers, notebooks, and photographs spread out between them. Weiss coughed and cleared his throat. Smoke hung over his head like a dark cloud.

Chief McMann stood up. He was a hulking man probably close to sixty, with slumping shoulders and keen dark eyes. His face was deeply seamed from nose to chin and the skin under his eyes sagged. He had a full head of gray hair and enormous ears that hung down his short thick neck almost to the collar of his shirt. "Ms. Wetzon," he said. His voice rumbled like a diesel engine. He offered a curiously small, blunt-fingered hand, which she shook, and a small smile, which she returned. "I'm sorry to bring you down here on such short notice. Please, have a seat. I understand you may be able to help us, and your cooperation is appreciated."

Wetzon shot daggers at Silvestri, who deflected them impassively. She felt cornered. Silvestri slid over one chair, leaving the one closest to the Chief vacant for her.

The room was unbearably cold, and she shivered violently. Without a word, Silvestri took off his jacket and put it around her shoulders, tucking her in, straightening the lapels. It was either an act of tenderness or he was staking his claim to her as "my woman." She gave him a suspicious once-over, but couldn't figure which, and he was avoiding eye contact.

"I understand you two are acquainted," McMann said with a faint quiver of a smile.

"I've met Lieutenant Weiss also." Wetzon nodded at Weiss, who sat smoking, reading from a clipboard, not looking up.

They sat, the three of them, facing the Chief like students with a professor, waiting for him to begin a lecture. Behind him, on the walls, everywhere there was space, were plaques and framed citations. On his desk were two telephones, a huge Rolodex, a box with buttons and lights—NYPD's version of a Quotron. A gray computer sat to the side, seemingly unused. On one wall hung a large electronic map of the City with blinking colored lights.

McMann's eyes fastened on hers. "We have two connected murders here. Both victims worked for the same firm, both were killed with the same substance—"

"Substance?" she repeated and got a rough nudge from Silvestri's foot under the table. She resisted the urge to kick him back.

"You are working as a consultant for Luwisher Brothers."

"My partner Xenia Smith and I are."

"Yes. This must remain strictly confidential, Ms. Wetzon. That means no discussion, whatever you decide, with your partner."

"Sir, excuse me. What is this all about?"

"We'd like you to work with us. You know these people. The evidence points to someone on the inside, someone at Luwisher Brothers, but we have not found a clear motive for either murder. The department uses outside consultants from time to time, and we're prepared to put you on the payroll."

"Put me on the payroll?" In spite of her efforts to stay calm and Silvestri's knee pressing against hers, she heard her voice rise an octave.

"We want information that will lead us to a murderer. Someone who has already killed twice. We believe there are people at Luwisher Brothers who know why these two men were killed and maybe even who did it. We think you can help us."

"Sir—I'm sorry. I'm really sorry. You want me to be a mole. I can't do that."

She watched McMann's hands reach for a giant black stapler, which he slowly took apart, emptied, and refilled with the same staples. Neither Weiss nor Silvestri spoke.

Nervous, Wetzon stumbled verbally into the silence. "I just can't. Please don't ask me."

Still no one spoke. McMann snapped the stapler shut, set it aside, and fastened his eyes on her again.

"This is serious, Ms. Wetzon. I understand you have a natural inquiring instinct. If you uncover anything, your life will be in danger."

She dusted imaginary lint from the lapels of Silvestri's jacket, chastened. "Look," she said, gesturing unconsciously with her hands, watching McMann's eyes travel to her hands and then back to her face. She felt her cheeks flush. "I feel I'm breaking a confidence by telling you this."

Silvestri glowered darkly at her. What was his problem? For once, she had Weiss's complete attention.

"They . . . . please don't give me away on this. . . ."

Silvestri made a noise in his throat.

The Deputy Chief waited.

"This was before Carlton Ash was murdered. They hired my partner and me to investigate the murder—that is, Goldie's murder."

"Jesus H. Christ, Les!" Silvestri jet-propelled out of his seat.

"Sit down, Silvestri. I want to hear this. You said *they?*"

"Hoffritz, Bird, Culver, Munchen. All of them. But Hoffritz, really."

"Now we're talking!" McMann thumped his desk with his fist, and the intercom spat static. He turned it off without glancing at the box, as if this happened frequently. "I want your cooperation on this, Ms. Wetzon. I'm leaving it as a request. I want to remind you that you and your partner have already exposed yourselves to some danger by agreeing to do an internal investigation. I might add, this was a very foolish thing to do, Ms. Wetzon."

"Hoffritz wanted us to find who did it before you did," Wetzon blurted, suddenly realizing how dangerous that was.

"These people are all prime suspects. And, I repeat, they all know you're investigating the homicide. Think about it."

Damnation, Wetzon thought. *He's right.* No outsider committed these murders and Hoffritz knew it. What had Smith gotten them into?

"I'll do what I can," Wetzon said, softly.

"Silvestri and Weiss are going to handle it between them from Midtown North," the D.P. said. "I'm going to leave you here now to work out the details. Ms. Wetzon, don't pursue any lead without clearing it with Silvestri or Weiss. Or me. I'd like your word on that."

"Good luck," Silvestri muttered without moving his lips, so only Wetzon and Weiss heard him.

A frisson of excitement ran up her spine. "Of course," she said, after taking a moment to wonder if she ought to cross her fingers. *This is not fun and games, Wetzon,* she chided herself. She smiled at the Chief, who looked at his watch and rose.

Wetzon stood, too. "May I ask—" Silvestri clamped a hand on her shoulder, and she shook it off. She came around the conference table and held her hand out to McMann, who took it. "May I ask what the murder weapon was?"

"Don't you know?" He gave her hand a reassuring squeeze. "I'm late for lunch with the Mayor. Tell her, Silvestri. Good to have you on board, Ms. Wetzon."

TWENTY-THREE

"Those are very nice numbers, Bert," Smith said. "You must be doing something right over there." She laughed seductively. "Mmmm, I'll bet." She made some notes on the suspect sheet in front of her. "I'll put the bill in the mail. I hope this time we don't have to wait till Christmas to get paid." She turned and winked at Wetzon, who was talking to Sharon Murphy on the other phone.

"Sharon, I set up two appointments for you this week after the close. One tomorrow with Marty Rosen at Loeb Dawkins and the other on Thursday, with Carl Fisher at Dayne Becker. Both are good managers. Marty is a little more unstructured. Both firms have a decent muni bond inventory for these days."

"And they're both in midtown, right? I don't want to go downtown."

"I know. Both are midtown."

"I'm really nervous about this, Wetzon. If they find out here I'm interviewing, they'll fire me."

"They'll never find out if you don't tell anyone, Sharon. And besides, if they fire you, it's their loss. Your trailing twelve come to over three hundred and fifty thou. Any firm would be thrilled to have you.

Just make sure you have copies of all your statements." Wetzon hung up the phone.

"You spend altogether too much time propping up these sleazebags' egos," Smith scolded.

"I like Sharon, and I meant what I said to her. I wish you wouldn't be so cynical, Smith. You'd have a lot more fun."

"But would I make more money, sweetie pie? That's what counts." She pulled the calculator to her and put in some numbers. "You know what I always say, Wetzon, the secret of success is—"

"Getting the money out of their pockets into ours," Wetzon finished for her.

"Humpf."

"Were those Jordan Shapiro's year-end figures you were getting from Bert?"

"They were." Smith had a beatific smile on her face. "Would you care to hear?"

"Tell."

"Four hundred thou."

"Wowee! That means sixteen lovely little thou for us on the back end, plus the twelve we got last year on the front end. We did all right. I knew he'd do it. All he needed was the right environment." Wetzon was thrilled for Jordan. On the fifty percent payout he got as part of his deal, he'd made himself two hundred thousand dollars.

Harold knocked on their door and came right in without waiting. "Hi." His eyes blinked nervously behind his glasses.

"Insufferable," Smith said, eyes to the ceiling. They had asked him again and again to wait for a response before opening their door.

"Don't make a big deal," Wetzon said, out of the corner of her mouth.

Smith brought her eyes back to Harold's rolled-up shirtsleeves and pants riding low on his hips, dragging over the heels of his shoes. "What is it, baby pie?" Her tone was saccharine.

Harold looked uncertainly from Smith to Wetzon.

"Go on, please, Harold," Wetzon said.

"We have five candidates for Luwisher Brothers ready to be set up." He held a stack of suspect sheets.

"Excellent. Give them to me and I'll introduce them," Smith said, holding out her hand.

"Er . . . ah, I thought I could do it." He did not turn over the suspect sheets.

Smith snapped her fingers at him. "Think again."

Harold's face fell as he gave her the sheets. "We're still talking to people."

"Fine. Close the door behind you." She turned her back on him. The door closed. "Is he gone?"

"Smith, you are being dreadful to him."

"I don't trust him. Don't you notice how he doesn't look you in the eye? How do we know he isn't going to go out and join a competitor or open his own company? You said yourself he thinks he knows everything."

"Oh, come on. He wouldn't do that. He's kind of attached to you, don't you think?"

"Humpf." Smith opened the bathroom door and looked at herself in the full-length mirror. "I think we ought to go over the questions we're going to ask Janet Barnes today over lunch."

"Okay."

Smith patted her slim hips and turned and looked over her shoulder at her rear view. "I think I'm putting on weight." She was wearing a snug white linen dress that only the tallest, thinnest woman in the world could get away with.

"You're not. But if you think you are, why don't you try some exercise?"

"Exercise?"

"You know—dancing, aerobics, jogging."

"Sex?"

"I won't touch that." Wetzon grinned. "Do you want me to call Chris with our candidates?"

"Oh, would you, sweetie? I thought I might run over to Vicki's and get my polish changed. It's only ten o'clock; lunch isn't till twelve-thirty." She dumped the suspect sheets on Wetzon's desk.

"Go ahead." Wetzon flipped through the sheets. "These are pretty good people. If they don't work for Luwisher Brothers, we can remarket them to the Bear." Smith didn't respond. Wetzon was talking to an empty room. Sighing, she picked up the phone and punched out Chris's direct number.

"Hi, what've you got?" His tone was always so intimate, almost as if he was coming on to her over the phone. This was the style of the brokers trained in a cold-calling boutique. Chris talked to everyone that way.

She talked bullets to him, running quickly down the candidates and setting up appointments. She was about to hang up when he said, "How're things?" He hadn't said a word yet about Carlton Ash.

"You missed a little excitement on Saturday."

"So I heard."

"I don't suppose you ran into Dr. Ash up there before I saw you?"

"Don't suppose, Wetzon. It might be bad for your health."

"Hey! What kind of thing is that to say?"

"No, I didn't see Ash. I was there to pick up some papers I had to read over the weekend. The place was empty." He laughed harshly. "Trying to earn your fee as a detective, I see."

"Oh, come on, Chris. I thought we were friends. What is this about?"

"You're so serious about everything, Wetzon." He laughed again. "Can you meet me for an early dinner on Thursday? I'll pick you up at the office."

"Oh? Care to give me a clue what this is about?"

"Didn't you just say to me you thought we were friends?"

"Yes."

"Well, I have some business to discuss with my friend. What else?"

She found the whispered intimacy in his voice suddenly disquieting, but her schedule was clear for Thursday dinner. "Thursday is fine," she said.

"Don't sound so enthusiastic, Wetzon," Chris said.

She hung up. He wanted to move out of Luwisher Brothers. Or were they pushing him out, as they were Ellie? She grimaced. This was such a puzzle. And she was a mole. She wondered if she should tell Silvestri she was having dinner with Chris on Thursday. She had to admit to herself, she liked being on the inside of an investigation. It was exciting, and the tiny element of danger was a turn-on.

Pacing, she opened the door to the outer office and left it open. She wanted to hear noise, people talking. She moved the blinds aside and stared out the French doors to the garden, unseeing. She saw Goldie's blue head on the platter of arugula.

She thought again about how she had confronted Silvestri after the D.P. left. "So now, Silvestri, you've got what you wanted. Give me my quid pro quo." She'd been angry that he'd trapped her into agreeing to work with them. Now there was no doubt she would be betraying a client.

Weiss's face wore an amused smile. He'd lit a cigarette, tilted his head back, and blown perfect smoke rings.

"Come on, Silvestri," she'd said. "Give. What was it? Arsenic? Strychnine? Cyanide? Lye? Rat poison?" Her feet had punctuated each poison with a tap step.

"Cut it out, Les." Silvestri's eyes were slate cold. "They were both killed with a massive dose of sulfite powder."

That had stopped her dead. "Sulfite powder?"

"Yeah," he'd grunted. "Now are you any smarter than you were before?"

Silvestri was right—knowing what the poison was didn't make any difference one way or the other, except to satisfy her curiosity.

The phone rang.

"Smith and Wetzon," B.B. said. "Hold on." He looked up. "Len Bernhardt for you."

"Good. That'll be about Tony Weinstein, if you want to listen, B.B. Come on in." B.B. had cold-called Tony Weinstein and turned him over to Wetzon as a very viable candidate. Tony was a million-dollar producer who was unhappy with the merger of Hutton and Shearson. "Hi, Len."

"He didn't show up again, Wetzon. I've had it. You call him and tell him if he doesn't get his statements over here and give me a start date, it's finished. Over." She held the phone away from her ear. Len was so angry, B.B. could hear every word.

"Oh, dear, I'm sorry. I'll see what happened." She hung up.

B.B. was upset. His bonus was based on the candidates he'd cold-called who were placed. "That's terrible. Where else can we send him?"

"Tony does well over a million in production, B.B. Len will forgive him. Everyone will lie a little, and Tony will eventually go there because it's the best deal on the Street."

By the time Smith got back, Wetzon had made most of her calls and had smoothed things over between Weinstein and Bernhardt.

"It's ghastly out there," Smith said. She fanned herself with *The Journal*. "What did I miss?" She held her long fingers out for Wetzon to admire the white-tipped French manicure.

"Very nice."

"Goes great with my tan. Anything I should know about? Have you talked with Ellie Kaplan?" She frowned. "Fix your hair, it's slipping."

"No, I haven't talked with Ellie yet, but I will. We've had the usual cancellations, reschedules, and Tony Weinstein stood Len Bernhardt up again." She'd forgotten about Ellie. Or maybe she was avoiding dealing with her.

"A day like any other day." She flipped through her pink message slips. "I have a couple of possible new clients to talk to."

"Good ones, I hope. No more small firms with cash flow problems, please," Wetzon said, checking her makeup in the bathroom mirror and repinning her hair, although there was nothing wrong with it.

"Why, Wetzon, sweetie pie. You're beginning to sound like me."

Lie down with dogs, get up with fleas, Wetzon thought, as they sat in the cab on their way to Janet Barnes's apartment on Park Avenue. God, that was awful, she admonished herself. How could she think such a thing? She was definitely losing it.

Wrightman House, an apartment building with the look of an armory, stretched the whole block between Ninetieth and Ninety-first Streets. It had been built in the twenties and had a huge drive-in courtyard, similar to only about five or six other buildings in Manhattan, including the Apthorp on Broadway and Seventy-ninth Street and the Dakota on Central Park West.

A doorman dressed like an English bobby took their names, writing them on a card. The card was then delivered into the hands of another bobby, who took it into a sideroom and phoned upstairs.

Smith and Wetzon were invited to wait in a plush reception room just like the lobby of a grand hotel, complete with oil paintings of medieval scenes and a Max Ernst sculpture.

"Jesus," Wetzon said. "Is this the palace?"

Smith giggled. "Don't be gauche, Wetzon."

"Ms. Smith and Ms. Wetzon?" The phone bobby came to the entrance. "You may go up now. Mrs. Barnes is in apartment nine. That's the elevator to your left."

Smith rolled her eyes at Wetzon and stood up.

"Don't be gauche, Smith."

They walked in the direction the bobby had pointed. "What floor did he say?" Smith asked.

"I don't remember. You distracted me. Did he say nine?"

"I don't know. Be a sweetie and run back and ask him." Smith pressed the up button on the elevator.

Oh, well, what the hell, Wetzon thought, walking across the thickly carpeted floor to the phone room, from which the sound of buzzing could be heard.

"Yes, Mrs. Barnes."

Wetzon stopped outside the door.

"I will, Mrs. Barnes. Yes." Then, "Patrick, have a cab ready for Mr. Culver. He's coming down in the service elevator."

TWENTY-FOUR

"Miss Smith and Miss Wetzon, madam," the butler announced in a formal English accent.

Janet Barnes looked remarkably well for a woman who had just lost her husband of forty years. Her hair was the same glinty auburn it had been when she was the spokeswoman for a washing machine company decades earlier. She broke off her conversation with the two men in the room and rose to meet them. "Thank you so much for coming." She was gushy, and dishonest, and seemed to be performing for the men, who didn't take their eyes off her.

Like the entrance gallery, the room they stood in had a high ceiling. Sheer white organdy covered the tall windows along one wall, and the furniture was slipcovered in a green-and-white lily pattern. An elaborately inlaid parquet floor peeked out from under Turkish rugs that lay one on the other in an ostensibly careless configuration.

"Do you know Alton?" Janet Barnes waved her hand casually at Alton Pinkus, whom Wetzon recognized from the disastrous dinner for Goldie. Pinkus had stood when they came into the room, and now he shook hands with first Smith and then Wetzon. Although an effort had been made to comb his iron-gray hair straight back, it hadn't worked, and in fact, gave him a shaggy appearance. Humor and intelligence radiated from his warm brown eyes. He was wearing a navy blazer and navy pants, but with a white LaCoste tee shirt and scuffed loafers with white socks.

"And this is Twoey," Janet said.

The other man, who had also risen, came forward. His auburn hair was a natural version of his mother's. "Ms. Wetzon," he said, speaking with a slight and not unattractive lisp. Goldie's son had hazel eyes with dark brown flecks that looked out from behind gold-rimmed glasses, and a multitude of freckles covered his cheeks, chin, and forehead. He looked to be in his late thirties and was a big man, with his late father's build.

"Mr. Barnes," Wetzon said. Twoey had a firm, slightly damp handshake and freckles under the orange hair on the back of his hand.

"Ms. Smith." Twoey turned to Smith and was gone. Wetzon, watching, couldn't believe it.

"Mr. Barnes," Smith said, in her little-girl voice, out-gushing Janet. She put her hand in his as if she were offering herself to him.

"Please call me Twoey. Everybody does." He was still holding her hand, almost leaning into her.

Smith smiled, enveloping everyone in her aura. "If that's what you want . . . actually, Goldman is a very nice name."

"It is now, Ms. Smith," Twoey said. He kept trying to tear his eyes from Smith, but it wasn't working.

"Oh, dear, please call me Xenia. And everyone just calls Wetzon, Wetzon." Smith smiled into Twoey's eyes.

He's a total goner, Wetzon thought, revolted by Smith's performance. *What a wuss.* And then she remembered how Smith had done much the same thing to Silvestri when she'd first met him, and he'd recovered. Wetzon mentally forgave Twoey. Smith was the most seductive person Wetzon had ever known, and she should be used to Smith's effect on men by this time. The mark of a real man, for Wetzon, was how long the spell lasted.

"Luncheon is served, madam," the butler said. He looked like a comic-opera butler, a gangly, cadaverous man with a face so narrow it looked as if it had been squeezed in a vise and set that way. When he bowed, Wetzon saw that his hair barely covered his pink scalp.

"Oh, thank you, Sheldon. Come this way, everyone." Janet was wearing flowing green silk pants and a matching blouse with, unlike

Barbara Bush, a triple strand of the real thing around her neck. She carried a bowl of white roses with her into the dining room and set it down in the center of the graciously set table.

Her walk and slightly disjointed motions triggered a memory for Wetzon, but it wasn't until they were seated that she recognized the dancing girl in her dream who carried Goldie's head on a platter—only the girl was really a woman, and the woman was Janet Barnes.

"You sit here, dear, and Ms. Smith—"

"*Xenia*, please."

"Xenia, then, you sit next to Twoey. Ms. Wetzon—er, Wetzon—my, you're such a petite little thing—on my right next to Alton."

Petite little thing, Wetzon repeated to herself. She loathed people who said that. It was grounds for murder. The woman was practically chirping. There was not one sign that she was in mourning.

The table was set with white linen placemats and cut-crystal glasses and silver place settings. They were served a thick, piquant gazpacho and then sliced chicken and bacon sandwiches in wedges of warm pita bread. A pitcher of iced tea was on the sideboard, along with a chilled bottle of a California chardonnay.

Wetzon passed on the wine, but Smith and the others were drinking. The conversation hovered innocuously around the problems of being a mayor of the City of New York, and a gas explosion that had taken place on Roosevelt Island.

Macerated berries and fragile sugar cookies arrived for dessert, and Janet said, "That will be all, Sheldon."

Sheldon pulled the sliding mahogany-paneled doors to the dining room toward him from either side, backed out, and closed them.

At last, Wetzon thought. *Now we're going to get to the nitty-gritty.*

"Shall I speak for all of us, Mother?"

"Oh, yes, please, Twoey. I'll stop you if I want to add anything." She smiled at Smith and Wetzon. "Alton is here as a close personal friend as well as a member of the Board of Directors of Luwisher Brothers."

"Before we proceed," Twoey said, still looking at Smith, "we'd like you to give us your word that everything you hear today is confidential."

Again? This time Wetzon crossed her fingers under the table. Everybody seemed to demand her word that she wouldn't tell. This time she knew she wasn't going to keep it.

"Of course," Smith said, a little too rapidly. Wetzon looked at her. Smith wasn't going to keep her word either.

"Luwisher Brothers is part of our family history," Twoey began. He looked at Wetzon, who nodded, she hoped encouragingly, and then at Smith, who gave him one of her most dazzling smiles. "Er . . ." He looked dazed.

Wetzon choked back a giggle with a light cough, covering her mouth with her hand, and was caught in the act by Alton Pinkus, whose eyes crinkled, acknowledging he was reading her mind.

"What Twoey is saying—" Janet said impatiently.

"I'm doing all right, Mother." Twoey's freckled skin colored. "We now own, between Mother and me, forty-five percent of the stock in Luwisher Brothers."

"I thought the retirement or death of any partner meant that stock had to be sold back to the company," Wetzon said. She put her dessert spoon down on the white placemat and immediately some of the remnants of the deep red macerade spread into the white fabric . . . like wet blood.

"It's been tradition since Nathan and Jeremiah Luwisher started the firm at the turn of the century, but there is nothing to say we have to do it. My father put his life into that firm."

My father, Wetzon thought. At last, Goldie had entered the equation.

"We believe," Janet said emphatically, "that we will get enough shares on our side to put Twoey into the Chairman's seat."

"Hoffritz is not going to like that," Wetzon said.

"John Hoffritz is a nonentity." Twoey's temper flared.

Smith smiled, a slow, lazy smile like a cat stretching in the sun.

"Alton has the board lined up and ready to call for a vote of the shareholders as soon as we give the go-ahead."

Alton nodded. He was a bulky man, not as tall as Twoey, built like an athlete who'd let himself go a little. His hand holding the tall slim wine glass was tanned copper, the nails impeccably manicured. He looked at Wetzon, and she felt a faint palpitation of intrigue in her breast. *Oh, no you don't,* she thought, and pushed it away.

"I don't understand," Wetzon said carefully, "where we fit in."

"I'm getting to that," Twoey said. "We know you do good work for the firm and we want to continue the relationship. In other words, we want you on our side in this."

"But—" Wetzon began, pushing back her chair.

"We're on your side," Smith assured him.

"Wait a minute, Smith," Wetzon countered swiftly.

"There's going to be a fight for control and it may get ugly," Twoey said, looking at Smith.

"That's all right," Smith said, "we're prepared to hang tough."

"Wait just a minute." Wetzon stood. Had Smith already known what was going to be said and had Smith set her up again? "Hold it right here." Now she had everybody's attention. "We can't work for everybody. What do you really want, Twoey? And why is nobody mentioning the fact that Goldie and Dr. Ash were murdered and that the report Dr. Ash was writing is missing?"

"That's just it, Wetzon," Twoey said. "We're dealing with murderers."

"And what about the fact that Dr. Ash was supposed to be working directly for Goldie on this report?"

"Dr. Ash? Goldie?" Janet looked confused. "Dr. Ash wasn't working for Goldie. Goldie was against hiring him at all."

"Forget Dr. Ash," her son interrupted. "We'd like to know you're on our side when the firm is in play."

"I don't think—" Wetzon said.

Smith stood, too. "Of course, we'll want some kind of financial arrangement up front."

"*Smith!*"

"Agreed," Twoey said.

"I'll have my lawyer call your lawyer," Smith said.

TWENTY-FIVE

"Let's go to Bloomie's," Smith said, linking arms with Wetzon in the lobby. "I have the urge—"

Wetzon yanked her arm away. "Smith, how could you? We're working for Luwisher Brothers, and that means Hoffritz and Bird. Now you've agreed to work for their enemy." *And,* she thought, *I'm working for the NYPD.* It made her head spin.

"I don't see any harm in giving to both political parties. People do it all the time."

"Cab?" the doorman bobby asked.

"Yes," Wetzon said to Smith, ignoring him, "but we're not just giving, we're taking. It's an entirely different thing."

"Wetzon, in the words of my old housemother, 'if they give, you take, and if they take, you scream.' Let me handle this. I know what I'm doing. I just have a feeling that the winning team is"—she pointed upward—"up there. Besides"—her expression turned beatific—"I'm in *love.*"

The tulips on the divider between uptown and downtown traffic on Park Avenue shuddered in the hot breeze. They drooped, dry, withered, and burnt. Overhead the sky was blue and cloudless, while on the street the exhaust of a million cars and trucks burned Wetzon's nasal cavities and coated her throat. She looked up at Smith. "What did you just say?"

"You heard me, sweetie pie. He's adorable, isn't he?"

"Spare me. What about Jake?"

"Jake who?"

"Oh, my." Wetzon couldn't help laughing.

"Well, isn't that what you wanted?"

"Yes, gee, thanks a heap. I really appreciate it."

Smith tilted her head toward the doorman. "Cab, please."

The doorman whistled down a cab and held the door for them. They crawled in and sat recuperating in the air-conditioning. Salsa music blasted from the radio.

"Bloomingdale's," Smith ordered. "And would you kindly lower that noise, please."

An agonized Jesus on a gigantic cross hung from the rearview mirror and swayed spastically to the motion of the cab. Their driver was a middle-aged Hispanic. "Where is?" he asked.

"What?" Smith leaned forward.

"Where is you're going?"

"Bloomingdale's, for pitysakes. I can't believe you are living here and taking our money and you don't know your job."

"Fifty-ninth and Lexington," Wetzon said, elbowing Smith.

"Thank you, nice lady."

"Now let's get to what you just got us into, Smith."

"Leave everything to me, baby cakes. I've got the best instincts. You know that. Believe me, we just left the winning team."

"I think we are honor-bound to tell John Hoffritz that we can't take any money from him," Wetzon said, thinking that Smith did have good instincts, but half the time they were warped.

"Honor-bound? What century is this? Don't you see, sugar, we're only taking money from them to find the murderer. The rest of the work we do on contingency."

"But there's an implied contract." Wetzon's head began to throb. "Oh, I give up." Smith had created such a maze of everything it was impossible to negotiate a way out.

"Stop over here, driver," Smith said.

"This Sixtieth Street, lady."

"This is Bloomingdale's," Smith snapped. "It runs an entire block between Fifty-ninth and Sixtieth Streets." She took some bills from her pocket, put them in the metal drawer attached to the glass partition, and slammed it closed.

They stood in front of Bloomingdale's trying to talk above the yowling of a beggar in tatters, who thrust a plastic cup at them. "I want to go back to the office, Smith. I have work to do." Wetzon felt in her purse for some change and dropped it into the plastic cup, which looked as if someone had chewed on the rim. "I have to call Ellie. I have things to do." Her voice sounded querulous.

"Just come in for a minute with me, sweetie. I want you to help me pick out a tie for Mark."

"Oh, well. Only for a few minutes." She let Smith lead her through the revolving door into the store. "What did you decide to do about this summer?"

A small troubled cloud drifted over Smith's face. "I'm sending him to the ranch, but only for June and July. He and I are going to spend August together in Connecticut."

"That's lovely, Smith. What about Jake?"

Smith brightened. "Well, of course, you never know, do you?"

"Twoey's mother-led, so be careful."

"You underestimate me, Wetzon. I can handle Janet." Smith laughed. "She can be eliminated just like Goldie."

"That's a horrible thing to say."

"I was only kidding. Wetzon, why are you so serious about everything? It's a real pain. What happened to the good-time-get-up-and-go girl—pardon the word—I used to know?"

"She got up and went. She couldn't take the turmoil you always create around her."

"*I* create turmoil? Really, sweetie. I want to remind you which one of us always finds herself hip-deep in murder."

They picked out a rep tie for Mark, and Wetzon left Smith going through the sale rack of designer clothes on the fourth floor.

She felt an odd sense of unease when she left Bloomingdale's, almost as if there was something she'd forgotten. Everything had gotten so convoluted. She started down Third Avenue, but the intense heat was torture; surrendering, she hailed a cab and took it back to the office.

B.B. was alone, dealing with calls incoming and outgoing. "Where's Harold?"

"He took a late lunch. Silvestri called twice. He left a number." B.B. handed her a pile of pink message slips.

"Okay. I'll get to him . . . it's hellishly hot out there."

Riffling through the messages, she trailed into her office and closed the outside door. At once she began to peel off her top layer—jacket, blouse, shoes. Soaking a towel in cold water, she washed her face, neck, and underarms, holding her wrists to the cold water. She patted herself dry and replaced the blouse. Her feet were swollen; she sat down at her desk and lifted them up.

"Aaah." She closed her eyes. Smith was crazy, but she was sharp and intuitive. And hard to take. Sighing, Wetzon dug out Ellie's suspect sheet and called her direct number.

"Ms. Kaplan's office. Dwayne speaking."

"Ms. Kaplan, please."

"Who's calling?"

"Leslie Wetzon."

"Oh hi, I'll get Ellie for you." Again Wetzon heard that extra familiarity in his voice, as if he and she knew each other.

"Wetzon?" The voice was hoarse and cracked; it didn't sound like Ellie.

"Ellie? Is that you?"

"I don't feel like talking, Wetzon." Her voice faltered. "Call me in a month."

"Ellie, wait a minute. What's the matter?"

"Don't ask me, please. Nothing is going right."

"Ellie, meet me for a drink tonight."

"No, Wetzon. I'm not feeling sociable. Besides, I have an appointment."

"Then tomorrow. Please. Just us girls. Come on, how about the Four Seasons? I guarantee you'll feel better."

"Oh, I don't know." Ellie wavered. "Actually, the Oak Bar at the Plaza would be more convenient—"

"Okay, the Oak Bar it is. At five o'clock."

Wetzon hung up and dialed Silvestri. She did not recognize the number he'd left. When he answered, "Silvestri," she said, "where are you?"

"Midtown North. I'm with Weiss."

"Will you be home later?"

"Yup."

"Smith and I had lunch with Janet Barnes today."

"Oh? Want to fill me in?"

"Not here, not now. I'm going to try to find a broker to have a drink with this afternoon."

"Busy, aren't we?"

"Jealous?" Alton Pinkus's face materialized in front of her and she waved it away.

"Sure. It's in my blood."

"Do you want to bring a pizza home?"

"I'll think about it."

She was about to hang up when she heard him say, "Les—"

"Yes?"

"Be careful. Please. Don't go off anywhere half-cocked."

"*Moi?*"

He hung up on her.

Well, she guessed she deserved it. She laughed. This investigation would be safe for her. It was really just a question of using her brain. Like right now. She pulled out her Filofax and looked up the phone number for the New York Public Library information line and called it. "Sulfites or sulfite powder," she said to the male voice who answered. "Can you tell me what it is?"

"Hold on, please." She pulled a blank piece of paper from the Filofax and doodled with her pen while she waited. He was back on the phone only seconds later.

She listened, then hung up, going over in her mind the gist of what he'd said. A salt or compound . . . used as a preservative until it was banned from fresh fruits and vegetables by the FDA in 1986 because it can cause severe allergic reactions in susceptible people. . . .

The lights on the phone lit up all at once and it rang, over and over. Where was Harold? She padded to the door and opened it. B.B. was trying to deal with all the calls. Harold was still not back and it was three o'clock.

"Jeeeeezuz!" Wetzon picked up one line. "Smith and Wetzon," she said.

"Wetzon? Is that you?" The voice was familiar, but she couldn't immediately place it. "This is David, David Kim. Something's happened and I need to talk to you right away." He was stumbling over his words.

"David, calm down. Whatever it is, we can deal with it." She looked at her watch. "I can meet you at five-thirty at the Berkshire, on Fifty-second Street between Fifth and Madison. How's that?"

"Okay. Just hang in there if I'm a little late."

"Is this anything to do with what's been happening at Luwisher Brothers, David?"

"You're not going to tell anyone I called you?" Panic.

"I wouldn't do that, David."

"Good, because I don't want to be history like Goldie and the fat fuck."

TWENTY-SIX

She had three candidates meeting this afternoon with Keith Burns, Northeastern Regional Sales manager for Marley, Strauss; there were two openings for managers, one in New Haven and one in Wellfleet on the Cape. Only one of the three was already licensed for management. Carolyn Johnson.

Wetzon had sandwiched the appointments, putting Jeff Lewin first at two o'clock, then Carolyn at two forty-five, and finally, Gary Walsh at three-thirty. She'd had to do some further juggling because both Carolyn and Jeff worked in the same Dean Witter office, and it would be death if they ran into each other. So it was arranged that Carolyn would wait on the twentieth floor and Keith, who was interviewing on the twenty-first, would let reception know when Jeff had left.

All very cloak-and-dagger but necessary to ensure confidentiality. In her early days as a headhunter, Wetzon had discovered what a small street Wall Street really was. Everyone knew everyone, and secrets were hard to keep. Brokers moved around so much that it was nigh to impossible that a broker going on an interview wouldn't run into, or be recognized by, someone he'd once worked with, or a friend of someone he'd once worked with. If his present manager were to find out he was doing something disloyal, like considering a move to another firm, his books could be confiscated before he had a chance to copy them and he could be fired outright. Or, if he were a big enough producer, his manager might bribe him to stay with perks like paying for a cold caller, picking up certain expenses, throwing him house accounts.

Confidentiality was often breached because brokers forever talked among themselves, semi-trusting each other. News, rumors, gossip swept the Street like a raging brushfire. Once, Wetzon had been working with a broker whose gross production ranged between four hundred and four hundred fifty thousand dollars. He didn't like his manager and made the mistake of telling another broker in the office, a friend, he thought, that he was seriously considering joining another firm. The friend let the manager know, the manager confronted the broker, confiscated his books, and ordered him out. The friend was rewarded with some of the broker's accounts. Moving was never easy, and moving before one was prepared to move could be a disaster. This particular broker's manager picked up the phone and called every client, offering the client free trades and implying that the broker had been fired for doing something disreputable and that he had not handled the client's account professionally.

Wetzon checked the time. It was almost four o'clock. She could probably reach both Jeff and Carolyn. Gary would head for the Port Authority and his bus to New Jersey. She'd catch up with him tomorrow.

Her hand was on the phone when she heard the outer door slam and a sudden bustle of activity, then a knock. "Yes?"

Harold opened the door tentatively. He was dripping wet, as if he'd been swimming. Harold was a sweater. When he realized Smith wasn't there, he breathed relief and straightened himself, becoming less apologetic and more full of himself as she watched.

"Late lunch, Harold?"

"Gosh, I'm really sorry it took me so long, Wetzon."

"Where the hell were you?"

"I was at the eye doctor and I had to wait forever."

Anyone other than Harold, and she would have thought he was doing a matinee—hot sex on a hot afternoon—but *Harold*? She looked at him objectively. Nah.

"Okay, Harold. I'm sure you have a deskful of work. I know I do—" She turned back to the suspect sheets on her desk.

"Will Smith be back?"

"I don't know. Don't think so." She waited until he closed the door and then picked up the phone and called Jeff Lewin.

"Jeffrey Lewin."

"Hi, Jeff. Wetzon here. How did it go?"

"Well, I think. He offered me the job."

"What? He offered you the New Haven office?"

"Yes. I said I would really have to think about it."

"My word. You don't even have your licenses. You'll need the Series 8 and the R.O.P., the Registered Options Principal. . . ." This was really crazy.

"I asked him when he would need an answer, and he said last week. Does that mean there's no manager there now? I'd like to know what happened to the other manager."

"I don't know." She'd have to do some dancing. "They're probably moving him up in the system. Did you talk money?"

"Yes. He said about thirty-five as a base, plus my own production. An upfront package and a higher payout. But listen, Wetzon, I'd really like to know what happened to the other manager. I have to talk with Amy. We just moved into the new apartment . . ."

"Okay, Jeff, you talk to Amy, and I'll talk to Keith and find out about the old manager."

She hung up the phone. Was Keith out of his fucking mind? Jeff was top quality, no question; Wetzon had known him for seven years. How could Keith spend a half hour with him on a first meeting and make an offer for him to run an office? No wonder the industry was in trouble. It was being run by lightweights.

She tried Carolyn, who had all the licenses and could sit down quickly and smoothly.

"Keith was very nice, but he said he didn't have any management openings right now."

"Oh? Did you limit him on area?"

"No. I said Connecticut, Massachusetts, or even New York would be fine."

"Okay. Consider this a get-acquainted meeting. Now he knows you, and you can bet he'll think of you next time there's an opening." *What a liar you are, Wetzon*, she thought, hanging up. This was just another case of we-don't-want-a-woman-in-our-private-club. Imagine the professionalism of offering an important job to someone after half an hour, good as he might look, and Jeff looked terrific. He was one of the best-dressed brokers she'd ever known. He could model for GQ. Still, Carolyn was an attractive candidate on paper and more so in person. And she was licensed. It wouldn't take months to get her through the exams.

"Ah, fuck," she said out loud, throwing down her pen. She punched up Keith's number.

"Gary just left," Keith said. He talked so fast, his tongue got caught up in his breathing and made his words come out in spurts. "He's a good, solid baloney-sandwich, meat-and-potatoes kind of guy. Our kind of guy, Wetzon. We want him for the Wellfleet office."

"What about Jeff Lewin?"

"Want him, too. Offered him New Haven."

"You have a manager in place now?"

"Yeah, but he's not staying."

"You're replacing him?"

"Yeah, but he doesn't know it yet. I shoulda told Lewin not to say anything . . . you do it, Wetzon. It's strictly confidential. It could be very embarrassing if it got out."

"I would think so. What about Carolyn? She has all the licenses."

"Yeah, Carolyn. She's okay. I liked her. Good lady I just don't have anything for her right now. Tell Jeff and Gary I'll talk to them next week. We want to get moving on this."

"Sure, Keith." So much for equal opportunity on Wall Street. She hissed. We're just not one of the boys.

She sorted out the papers on her desk and made a list of the calls she had to make the next day. The air conditioner was chugging with some difficulty, and the office was not as cool as it had been; perhaps Con Ed was cutting back on power.

Outside, their garden looked limp and seared, baking day after day in the sun. Still, there was little sun now, only the sulfuric haze of an air inversion. She stepped back from the window and sat down. What she wouldn't give now to be pulling on white socks and her pink Reeboks, instead of pantyhose and pumps for her appointment with David Kim.

Sharon Murphy was meeting with Loeb Dawkins tomorrow. Wetzon hoped that went well. Sharon was high-strung and a little crazy, but she had a good business and her numbers were really super.

Wetzon opened the door to the front office. B.B. was on the phone. The other light was on and not blinking, so Harold was probably on that one. The phone rang. "I'll get it," she said, then thought maybe she shouldn't. If it was a problem, she'd be late . . . oh hell, "Smith and Wetzon."

"Will Ms. Wetzon accept a collect call from a Ms. Smith?"

"Oh, for godsakes." Smith was always doing this. If she had half a mind, she wouldn't accept. But instead she said, "This is Ms. Wetzon. I'll accept the charges."

"Wetzon—"

"Smith, you're impossible. Only you would call collect when you're less than fifteen blocks away."

"Be still and listen," Smith said. There was street noise in the background and she sounded agitated.

"Where are you?"

"On Third Avenue, near Bloomie's. Is anyone else on the line?"

"Who would be?" Wetzon looked down at the phone. Three lines were lit and not blinking. "Just you and me, sweetheart," she said, doing Bogart.

"I don't have time for your jokes, Wetzon. I've been running around trying to find a phone in this goddam city that works. You won't believe what I saw. *I* don't believe what I saw."

"What did you see? Tell me please and put me out of my misery."

"Everything is a joke to you, Wetzon, but you're not going to find this funny, any more than I did."

"Oh, God, Smith—*what?*"

"I was so upset I had to sit down in Yellow Finger and have a lemonade to calm myself."

"Smith, I'm going to kill you personally if you don't get on with it."

"Who is the scumbag slimeball—our biggest competitor?"

"Tom Keegen."

"Well, Wetzon, not one half hour ago guess who I saw *tête-à-tête* with that dirtbag?"

"I give up. Who?"

"Your precious Harold."

TWENTY-SEVEN

The front lobby of the Berkshire was formal without being ostentatious. In the rear and a couple of steps down was an upholstered open, nicely carpeted area set with comfortable chairs and sofas and marble-topped coffee tables arranged in small conversation groups. Here, someone could order tea and tea cakes, coffee, or drinks. It was a gracious refuge from the persistent rush and frenzy of the City.

She saw David Kim immediately because he was pacing back and forth, wild-eyed, seemingly unaware that he looked a trifle mad to the arriving and departing guests of the hotel who gave him a wide berth. He did not fit the stereotype of the imperturbable Asian. A slim, somewhat prissy concierge in a medium-brown suit was just bearing down on him when David caught sight of Wetzon, stopped pacing and waited for her to come to him.

"David." She touched his arm and led him to the rear of the lobby, where he flung himself on the loveseat and Wetzon took the Louis XVI chair next to the harp.

He was wearing a gray pinstripe, white shirt, and considering the heat, showed hardly a wrinkle, Wetzon thought, looking down at herself. His hair was a smidgen too long for the Street and fell across his forehead to his dark eyebrows. With an impatient, boyish gesture, he brushed it back. He looked a little like Rob Lowe, if Rob Lowe were Korean. All in all, a charmer, particularly when he smiled, which he did just then.

Wetzon found him engaging, as she had almost two years ago when he'd followed up his resume with a phone call and persuaded her to see him, although she had assured him she could do nothing for him because he didn't have a track record. He was in the Ph.D. program in mathematics at Columbia.

"I want to be the first Asian-American to run a brokerage firm," he'd said.

"You're too late, Gerald Tsi got there ahead of you."

"He's Chinese, and besides, he didn't do so well with Smith Barney and ended up selling to Sandy Weill. I want to be Sandy Weill." His black eyes were serious, but he was sharp as a tack and full of beans, and Wetzon had liked him immediately.

He was looking for a summer job, something he could build into a career once he'd finished his Ph.D., and Wetzon had reiterated that not only did Smith and Wetzon not do entry-level positions, but they certainly never touched summer employment. But David was beguiling and wrested a promise from her that she would keep him in mind if she heard of anything with one of her clients.

And she had. It was only two weeks later that she'd heard from Doug Culver that Luwisher Brothers was looking for a temporary sales assistant for Ellie Kaplan, and Wetzon had suggested David Kim. The temporary job had turned into a permanent job, and everyone had benefited from the introduction except Smith and Wetzon because no fee was paid.

Wetzon preferred to chalk it up to bread on the waters—good will and all that. It would eventually pay off with referrals, useful contacts. But Smith had been very displeased. "We can't pay the rent on freebees," she'd bitched.

Wetzon ordered iced decaf and David a bourbon on the rocks. He had, she saw, adopted the drink of choice at Luwisher Brothers.

"Okay, David, spill it. What's the matter?"

"I don't even know how to tell you . . ." He stopped and stared at her. "I don't know if I'm doing the right thing." He shook his head and his hair fell into his eyes. "Everything I've ever dreamed about can be wiped out. I—" He shrugged and held up his hands.

Their drinks were served on gold-embossed cocktail napkins. A woman with long blond hair sat down at the harp and began to play. Every conversation area in the room was now occupied, and just beyond them Wetzon could see two women talking animatedly, one taking notes all the while. An interview of some sort. She turned back to David.

"What's going on down there, David?"

"Something bad, I think. A mess. It'll get out and I'll never be able to get another job."

"But how does it involve you?"

He looked miserable, suddenly, and took a big swallow of the bourbon. "Ellie . . ." He let it hang like that and Wetzon's mouth dropped.

"Ellie? Ellie is involved in something illegal?"

At first, he didn't respond, then with some reluctance, said, "I think so. I haven't had a chance to make sure. They could be setting her up, too."

"I can't believe it. Make sure. Maybe talk to her."

He shook his head. "I just can't. I—we—" He looked down at his drink.

"Who else?"

"Chris Gorham would have to know . . . and the others, too."

"What about Goldie?"

"I don't know."

"Do you want to tell me what you think it is?"

He shook his head and took another swallow. "Not till I'm sure. A lot of money is involved."

"Why are we talking, David?"

He smiled at her nervously. "Because I trust you, Wetzon. Because you're my friend. Because you helped me get here. Because I know you're not going to tell anyone what I've told you. Right?"

Wetzon sighed. "Right."

Warily, he said, "If I'm right, I would have to notify the SEC of a violation if there was one—wouldn't I?"

Was he asking her permission to become a whistle-blower? She couldn't figure out what he wanted of her. "Are you telling me that Hoffritz, Bird, and Culver are all in on this scam, or whatever it is?"

"That's just it, Wetzon, I don't know. And if I tell the wrong person, I could be dead." His hand shook when he raised his glass to take another drink. "It's getting so I'm scared to go in every day."

"Why not take a week off, then? Maybe it'll all be out in the open sooner than you think."

"It might be. The auditors are coming in this week. Chris told me."

"What do you want me to tell you, David?"

"What would *you* do, Wetzon? I think you would do the right thing."

"I would go to the police because my life was in danger, and what good is money and position or anything, if you're dead? But David, I'm not you and this has to be your call." She remembered the poker game in her dream and the house of cards David had been building in it.

"Will you help me get out?"

He was asking her to move him. That's what this was all about. "You know I'll do everything I can. Do you have your own business, separate from Ellie's?"

"Yes, some. And some of her clients may prefer to stay with me."

"But suppose Ellie's not involved?"

"They may still want to stay with me. They trust me. Ellie—well, she took this thing with Goldie very hard." He rose and leaned over to shake her hand. "Thanks, Wetzon. I'll keep you informed."

"Xerox your books," she said automatically, putting ten dollars in the leatherette folder where the bill lay. *Poor Ellie,* she thought. David had become a broker.

TWENTY-EIGHT

Wetzon walked past the Plaza Hotel, the long line of limousines parked and double-parked in front, crossed Central Park South, with its horses and carriages ready and waiting, and went into Central Park. The hush was almost instantaneous. She walked slowly; the air quality was terrible. A horse and carriage clopped by, carrying a family of tourists, the driver pointing out the Wohlman Rink, which New York's own Donald Trump had repaired with a flourish three years ahead of schedule. Summers it was used for roller skating, winters for ice skating.

From the hill where Wetzon walked, she could see through the dry, sparse leaves of the massive oaks the miniature golf course, another Trump triumph, near the Rink. The carousel, which had been renovated, was working again. She loved the carousel. She loved to climb on one of the elevating horses and go around and around.

She moved on, replaying her conversation with David, trying to figure out what it all meant. There was no more horse manure to dodge since the City ordered that carriage horses must wear plastic bags. Silly looking, but not as silly as the Canadian diapers.

Two teams of young men were playing volleyball with a modicum of energy. A Good Humor salesman leaned on his cart nearby and watched the game. Wetzon sat down on a bench shaded by an old chestnut tree and put on her pink Reeboks.

So "my precious" Harold was meeting secretly with Tom Keegen. Smith had been right not to trust him. Then again, Smith had been treating Harold so shabbily that maybe Smith had driven him to Keegen. Wetzon had wanted to confront Harold immediately, but Smith was firm. She wanted to be there.

"See that he doesn't take anything out of the office with him."

"If you don't want me to send up a red flag, that's not going to be easy. Why don't you come back and we can do it now?"

"I just can't cope with Harold now, Wetzon, it's too hot. I'm going home."

Wetzon had hung up and thought for a minute, then she went into the outer office. "Yo, I have an announcement to make. It's too hot to work. Go home, guys. I'm closing down the office for the day."

She leaned on the doorframe to Harold's cubicle. Harold was gathering up suspect sheets and stuffing them into his attaché case. "No, Harold. I mean it. No work tonight. The heat will make us all sick if we overdo. I want you and B.B. to go home, get cool, have a good night's sleep. No calls tonight. No work. We'll all be better for it tomorrow."

"But—" His eyes looked at her innocently from behind his glasses. Maybe Smith was wrong.

"No, really. Come on. Leave everything. You don't need your case, Harold." She waited in the doorway until he returned the sheets to his desk.

Under the guise of concern, she'd amiably escorted B.B. and Harold out the door, and once they were gone, she'd locked up. Good thing Harold didn't have a key. Or did he? She couldn't remember. Without a qualm, she inspected his attaché case. Yesterday's *Journal* and *Time*. Among the suspect sheets on his desk she found a list of the Merrill brokers in New York. That little creep. She confiscated the list.

There could be a logical explanation for Harold's meeting with Keegen. *Sure, Wetzon, if you buy that, I have a bridge to sell you that runs between Brooklyn and Manhattan.*

"Watch the *ball*, lady!" The soccer ball hit the bench with a slam, just missing her.

"Sorry." A wiry little guy in gym shorts and an iridescent blue sleeveless tee shirt grabbed the ball on the bounce. He grinned at her from under a pimpy mustache.

"S'okay," Wetzon said. She got up and started walking again, north and west.

The fenced-off area, Sheep's Meadow, where New York farmers had grazed their sheep into the twentieth century, was empty except for a few diehards braving the smog and heat, lying in the grass. Its great expanse was usually lush with grass and people, reading, talking quietly, meditating, or just plain sleeping. Designated a quiet zone by the Parks Commission, no radios, shouting, or ball playing were allowed. She had never thought of Central Park as anything but an oasis, and as much as she disliked the country, whenever she walked through the magic door into the Park, she felt a sense of awe, pleasure, and yes—peace.

Wetzon's Reeboks crunched on a short length of gravel path; her jacket, lying over her arm, was drenched with perspiration. She decided to leave the Park at Seventy-second Street and Central Park West, taking the steep, uphill walkway past Strawberry Fields, the John Lennon memorial. A few elderly people were sitting on the benches near Seventy-second Street looking dazed by the heat. Two teenaged boys on bicycles whizzed out of the Park onto Central Park West without looking and narrowly escaped being run down by a black stretch limo making a left turn to the Dakota. The Dakota, a residential fortress with turrets, was the oldest apartment house on the West Side, and had a list of inhabitants from the arts, politics, and business that was unimaginable. It had been John Lennon's home—he'd been murdered in front of the building—and Yoko still lived there.

By the time she got to Seventy-seventh Street and the Museum of Natural History, Wetzon was having trouble breathing. On Columbus, she went into a supermarket and bought a six-pack of Amstel Light right from the cooler.

Javier, her doorman, was sitting in the lobby under the huge standing fan, which was blowing hot air around. He made a move to get up and help her, but she waved him back. Parking the grocery bag near the elevator, she pressed the button and went around to the mailboxes for her mail, too tired to look through it.

The elevator had a pizza smell that made her smile. Silvestri had beaten her home, which meant the air conditioner would be on and the apartment reasonably cool. She was right.

After dinner they sat in the living room drinking the remainder of the six-pack. Silvestri had his feet in his white cotton socks up on the coffee table. Wetzon had just finished telling him about her lunch with Janet Barnes.

"Your partner's a piece of work." He took a handful of jelly beans and popped them in his mouth.

"Beer and jelly beans?"

"Smith and Wetzon? You two fit together like beer and jelly beans."

"Have you and Carlos been comparing notes? Let's talk about something else—say, the way you set me up yesterday? I should be mad as hell at you, but I'm too nice a person."

He chucked her under the chin. "I set you up because we need you. We're at an impasse. And by the way, how come the Chief got you to do something I couldn't?"

"Wholesale flattery and ego-building."

"Sure. You just want official permission to snoop." He put his arm around her and kissed her nose. "Love that nose."

"So, what do you want to talk about, besides my nose?"

"Let's see, we have MOM to look at for each suspect." He got up and left the room, coming back in moments with his notebook.

"Mom?"

"Motive, opportunity, method. We know the method; let's look for a motive."

"Listen, I forgot." She sat up. "I had a strange conversation with David Kim this afternoon." Hand on her mouth, she mumbled, "My God, what am I doing? I can't tell you."

"What's this about? Why can't you tell me?"

"Because he spoke to me in confidence, as a headhunter, and I can't reveal what he said, except—Silvestri, don't be mad at me—I can tell you he's scared to death."

"Okay, I'll haul his ass in and find out what he's scared about."

"Oh God, Silvestri, do you have to? He'll know I gave him away."

"We're talking to everybody. He'll never know you had anything to do with it."

She rubbed the side of her head to ease the sudden twinge of pain, a band of tension circling her brow. "I've just broken all the rules," she said, abashed.

"Les, goddammit. This is not a game. We're talking about two murders. Just because there was no blood shed, don't think for one minute it's not as deadly."

"I'm not allergic to sulfites, Silvestri."

"He could change his modus operandi at any time. We're dealing with a sociopath."

"He?"

"Okay, let's look at our group. Ladies first. Janet Barnes. She had opportunity and, possibly, a motive."

"What motive?"

"Maybe Goldie Barnes and his son didn't get along. Son of powerful father and all that. With Goldie out of the way, Twoey Barnes could join Luwisher Brothers at the top."

"But why would Janet kill Dr. Ash?"

"Say his report discredited Goldie in some way, which would then reflect badly on Twoey. What about Ellie Kaplan? She also had opportunity."

"She hated Dr. Ash—but enough to kill him? I don't know. She's supposed to have been Goldie's mistress, though."

"Well! That's news. When were you going to tell me that?"

"I just did. I didn't think it was pertinent before."

"Why did Ellie hate Ash?"

"She said he was going around asking too many questions. I think she was worried about that report."

"Hardly a motive for a normal person. Was Goldie breaking off their relationship?"

"I don't think so. I like Ellie, Silvestri. She's a nice person. She's wonderful at what she does. Somewhere I read she's very active with AIDS help organizations. But I think she has something going with David Kim."

Silvestri raised a dark eyebrow at her and took another swig of beer. "Let's consider David Kim."

"Was he at Goldie's banquet? I didn't see him, but then, I wasn't looking for him. I suppose he could have done either murder. But why?"

" 'Who will free me from this turbulent priest?' " Silvestri looked pleased with himself.

"Why, Silvestri. I had no idea you knew *Murder in the Cathedral.*" She leaned over and kissed the dark-whiskered shadows of his cheek. "Would David have done it for Ellie? Maybe. What about Twoey? Patricide?"

"Motive maybe, but no opportunity. He wasn't at the dinner or at Luwisher Brothers, was he?"

"Now that you mention it, no. Odd, though, that he'd miss a banquet in his father's honor. Alton Pinkus?"

Silvestri shook his head. "No opportunity or motive that we know of for Dr. Ash."

"Okay." She reached over and picked out two licorice jelly beans from the glass compote and rolled them around in her palm. "That leaves Hoffritz, Bird, Dougie Culver, and Neil Munchen. They all probably had opportunity, but what was the motive? I just know it had something to do with the report. Why haven't you guys been able to find it?"

"There is a report floating around somewhere. We think Hoffritz has the original, and we haven't been able to pry it out of him without a subpoena. He says he'll disclose its contents in a public press conference later this week."

"What the hell?" Wetzon popped the jelly beans in her mouth and let the licorice melt on her tongue.

"He claims it has absolutely nothing to do with either murder."

"He had motive and opportunity. So did Bird."

"Hoffritz put himself through college doing stand-up comedy."

"You must be kidding. He's about as funny as a crutch."

"Destry Bird's degree is in biology."

"Do you think he was heading for med school? God, medicine's gain, Wall Street's loss. But really, Destry's not a people person—has no bedside manner, so to speak. He would probably have ended up in a lab." She glanced at Silvestri. "So he might know his way around poisonous substances."

Silvestri shrugged. "What about Culver?"

"He plays his own game. I don't know about Dougie. I don't see him as a murderer. He's more like a vulture who hovers over the murder scene and then moves in to pick the flesh off the bones of the dead."

"Jeezus, Les." He was looking at her hard.

She shrugged. "You asked me and I'm telling you. Neil Munchen, graduate of MIT. He was Goldie's protégé. He probably didn't like Ash. I don't know about Neil. He's like Ellie, I think. He would never have killed Goldie. Just before Goldie keeled over, I heard either Neil or Goldie through the wall that separates the men's room from the ladies' room say to the others what sounded like 'over my dead body.'"

He looked at her quizzically, raising an eyebrow. "One of these days, lady, someone is going to catch you listening at keyholes."

"Oh, come on, Silvestri, it was an accident. Serendipity."

"Sure." Silvestri frowned, thinking. He drummed the table with his pen. "Neil's folks own a kosher deli on Second Avenue."

"No wonder they all look down on him. He's far from a blue blood. But what does that have to do with Neil and the murders?" Her head was pulsing. "Oh-h."

"Right. Who's to say there wasn't a stray can of sulfite powder lying around in the deli's storeroom after it was banned?"

TWENTY-NINE

"Tom Keegen." Smith's lip curled as she drew the syllables out slowly. She was resting one hip on the edge of her desk, half sitting, swinging an elegant leg.

"Tom Keegen?" Harold's left eyelid twitched violently behind his horn-rimmed glasses. His head swayed from Smith to Wetzon, back to Smith.

"Yes, Harold. You've heard of him?" Wetzon said.

"Well . . . ah, yes. . . ." He stood in front of them squirming.

"Who is he, dear?" Smith purred. There was so much venom in her voice that even Wetzon was startled.

"I . . . ah . . . he . . . I mean . . ."

"Speak up, Harold."

"He . . . ah, he's a headhunter." Harold jiggled on his feet and looked to Wetzon for help, but she'd rotated in her chair, turning her back on him.

"That's quite right, dear. And what is his area of specialty?"

"Um . . . ah, you mean . . . brokers?"

"That's wonderful, dear. Isn't that wonderful, Wetzon?"

Wetzon rotated again. "Oh, yes, truly. What were you doing with Tom Keegen yesterday, Harold?"

"I . . . uh . . . oh . . ." Harold looked down at his scuffed brown shoes and up again. "You saw me?"

"Not I. Smith saw you. I was in the office working, wondering why you were taking so long at the doctor."

"Oh."

"Do you like working here, dear?" Smith asked sweetly.

"I do . . . ah . . . I do." He began to sputter.

"I don't think he does, do you, Smith?" Wetzon said.

"No, I don't think he does."

"Please . . . Smith, Wetzon. We have the same eye doctor. Honest. He had the appointment before mine. He said he recognized my name because the brokers say such nice things about me."

"Oh Harold, how could you? After all we've done for you?" Smith's voice was steely.

"No . . . I . . . oh, please, Smith. I didn't do anything. He . . . uh, invited me for a drink. I didn't want to go."

"But you did?"

"Well . . ." Harold brightened. "I thought to myself, what would you do, Smith, and I knew right away I should accept and string him along to hear what he was going to say."

Ha! That little weasel, Wetzon thought. He was right, though. And not just about Smith; Wetzon would have heard Keegen out, too.

"Humpf." Smith's eyes were dark slits. "And just what did he have to say?"

"I was going to tell you—honestly," Harold said. "But you weren't here when I got back."

"You could have told me," Wetzon said. "I was here, wasn't I?"

"Yes, but I wanted to tell you *together*." He'd stopped stammering and was gaining confidence. "He offered me a job."

"Did he indeed?" Smith said, with an exaggerated yawn.

"Did you talk numbers?" Wetzon asked. Now she felt he was telling the truth.

"Well, yes. He said I would make a lot more money with him."

"Give me a break," Smith said. "Haven't you heard that line before? Haven't you used it yourself?"

"But, Smith, I wouldn't think of leaving you. You taught me everything I know and I feel good here—"

"I'd like to remind you, Harold," Smith said, "that you have a contract with us. You signed it when you started and it is understood unless there is a three-month notice on either part, it is renewed every year."

Wetzon had forgotten the contract. Now she remembered that Leon, their original attorney, had drawn it up at Smith's insistence, with the comment that it probably wouldn't hold up in court.

"Oh. Right . . . the contract." Wetzon could tell that Harold had forgotten it, too. "But I would never do anything with Tom Keegen. You don't have to worry."

"Loyalty is all that we want, Harold."

"Did Keegen ask you anything about how we do business?" Wetzon said.

"He asked, but of course, I wouldn't tell him."

"We'd like your word on this, Harold," Smith said.

"Honestly. I swear. You don't have to worry about me." He held up his hand as if he were taking an oath.

Smith stood up. "All right, then, Harold. You may leave us."

Harold, with unnatural dignity, turned and left, closing the door softly behind him.

"Do you *believe* him?" Smith demanded, hands on her hips. "I'd like to *kill* him."

"Kill Harold? He's not worth it."

"Harold? No, that dirtbag Keegen."

"Forget it. About Harold, I don't know. Let's not make anything more of it for now, but I think we should keep our eye on him."

Smith sighed and sat down. "It depresses me that we can't even trust him. But he was right, about meeting with Keegen. Either one of us would have done it to hear what the slime had to say." She smacked the top of her desk with the palm of her hand. "The *nerve* of him. *Who* does he think he is? I have half a mind to call him and let him know what to do with himself."

"A waste of energy. Doing well is always the best revenge," Wetzon said thoughtfully. "Maybe we should raise Harold's percentage up to thirty-five."

"I hate to reward the creep when he's been disloyal."

"We don't know that. It's all circumstantial evidence, isn't it?" Wetzon smiled. "Think about it." She looked down at the papers on her desk. "I have a ton of work to do. . . ."

"Do you want to have dinner tonight and talk this through?"

"Can't tonight. I'm meeting *la belle* Ellie for a drink. Where's Jake?"

"In Atlanta checking out a company that wants to go public."

"How about tomorrow?"

"You're on."

"We could go have pasta at Baci."

"But that's on the West Side."

"So? What's wrong with the West Side? Too ethnic for you?"

"Oh, for pitysakes."

Wetzon grinned at her, picked up the phone, and called Sharon Murphy. "I'm confirming your appointment today with Marty Rosen at Loeb Dawkins, four-thirty."

"Oh, Wetzon, I'm glad you called. I'm really nervous about going there. Someone might recognize me. I just can't do it. Please see if he can meet me outside."

"All right. I'll call you back." Wetzon looked at Smith, who was making notes on a yellow legal pad.

"Now what?" Smith asked, not raising her head.

"She wants to meet outside the office."

"You indulge their paranoia."

"Sharon has a point, Smith. Everyone knows everyone on the Street. Someone in Marty's office could recognize her and let someone in her office know, and that someone could tell her manager. . . ." Wetzon tapped out Marty Rosen's number.

"Sure," Rosen said. "Tell her I'll meet her at the Pierre at five o'clock. And tell her what I look like, Wetzon."

"What *do* you look like, Marty?"

"Like a broker, Wetzon. Dark blue suit, glasses, six feet, one eighty, dark hair. Who am I looking for?"

"I'd spot you anywhere. Sharon looks a bit like Tina Turner, if Tina were Irish."

"Is that white Irish or black Irish?"

"You figure it out."

Rosen chuckled. "Well, that'll be interesting."

"I'll talk to you tomorrow, Marty. Remember, Sharon's looking for an aggressive office, wants her own cold-caller, and she's really nervous about making a move."

"Trust me, Wetzon."

Wetzon hung up. She was not reassured. The phrase *trust me* always triggered the memory of what a broker told her in her first year in the business—"*Trust me* is code for *fuck you*."

"Marty Rosen just said 'trust me,'" she said.

Smith sighed and threw down her pen. "I can't concentrate on this now."

"What are you doing?"

"The report for Hoffritz. I'm still furious about Tom Keegen. We just can't let him get away with it. I have half a mind to—"

"We have no choice unless you put your devious mind to work and come up with a way of fixing Keegen without hurting us. Come on, let's work on the report. We don't have that much to say, I'm afraid."

"I'll fudge it."

"What are you going to say about yesterday's lunch with Janet *et al*?"

"Just that we talked with Janet and Twoey, and we've eliminated Twoey as a suspect."

"That's a real work of genius. Jeezus, Smith, Twoey is the only one who couldn't possibly have done either murder. And Janet wasn't around for Dr. Ash's, so we should probably tell them that we've eliminated her as a suspect."

"Okay." Smith began writing again. Wetzon stood up and came to look at Smith's scrawls over her shoulder.

"By the way, both Goldie and Dr. Ash were killed with sulfites."

"Sulfites? What's that?"

"It's a colorless, tasteless powder that some people are horribly allergic to."

"You mean both Goldie and Dr. Ash?"

"Yes . . . Good God, how could the murderer possibly know they were *both* allergic to sulfites? Isn't that a little bizarre?"

"How about a little coincidental?" Smith added. Her eyes glinted. "I wonder if Tom Keegen is allergic to sulfites."

"Oh, Smith, be serious. Cool it on Keegen. You're letting him get to you. What are you writing?"

"That they were both killed by sulphur."

"Sulfites."

"Whatever. It'll look good on the report. Was it in their food?"

"Yes. Goldie via his drink. Dr. Ash, probably in coffee." The nub of a thought darted through her mind and was gone. She frowned. It was too coincidental. Smith was right. And one death followed hard on the other. She remembered that Ash had been seated next to Goldie at the dinner.

"Ouch, Wetzon, what's the matter with you?" Smith pulled her shoulder away from Wetzon's squeezing hand and stared at her.

"God, I'm sorry. I just had an incredible thought. The killer couldn't be sure the sulfites would kill his victim, so he had to be really desperate and have no other options. And he might have gotten away with it if there hadn't been a double fluke of another allergic person sitting at the same table. A person who picked up Ash's drink by mistake."

"What are you babbling about, Wetzon?" Smith made an exasperated face at her.

"Try this on for size. What if Goldie was not the intended victim?"

THIRTY

Ellie Kaplan was late. So what else was new. It gave Wetzon time to think about her theory. If Carlton Ash was the intended victim all along, Goldie had been killed by mistake. Then either Neil or Ellie could have done it. It all led back to the study Ash was doing.

The Oak Bar of the Plaza was crowded with end-of-the-day people having their little drinkies. Tourists mostly. It was not a place she normally met brokers, although it wasn't a bad place to meet someone who didn't wish to be seen by anyone else in the industry. There was something a little tacky and run-down about it. The waiters were older, jaded, their black tuxedo uniforms seedy; the service was terrible, the contents of the snack bowls often stale. It was nothing like Wetzon's beloved Four Seasons, which she preferred over any other environment for an after-the-close drink.

But the Oak Bar had been Ellie's choice.

Actually, Ellie's choice had been not to meet at all, when Wetzon had called her to confirm their appointment.

"I'd like to put it off," Ellie'd said, her voice thick and foggy. "I just can't deal with anything in my life right now, especially moving."

"We don't have to talk about that at all. Come on. We'll do girl talk."

"Girl talk," Ellie had repeated. "God. All right, Wetzon, but remember, I warned you."

"Duly warned," Wetzon now murmured to herself, plucking a cheese-flavored fish cracker from the bowl in front of her and sipping the Perrier. She looked out at Central Park South at the clustered cabs and limousines. Rush-hour traffic clogged the broad, spacious street that fronted the lower portion of Central Park. The street temperature still hovered in the high nineties, and people walked slowly, looking wilted and frazzled. The horses and carriages, usually in evidence, were banished to their shelters according to law when the heat was excessive.

"Oooooh, Dar!" The scream came from a middle-aged woman at the table next to her with thick, curly ash-blonde hair and thick curly bangs that covered her eyebrows. She waved wildly to another woman who had paused in the entrance to look around. Dar had the same hairdo in brown. Another woman with the same hairdo joined the two, and now there were so many shopping bags—Saks, Bergdorf's, Bloomie's, Bendel's—that they needed two extra chairs. It was some kind of reunion, and Wetzon, eavesdropping as always, learned that Dar had flown in from Boston. They were soon joined by a tall woman with a cap of reddish hair and another, about Wetzon's height, with bobbed white hair. They seemed so glad to see each other that Wetzon, watching them, smiled.

She never learned the occasion for their reunion. Ellie Kaplan appeared, and Wetzon raised her hand high to get her attention.

Ellie, at quick glance, could have been a bag lady. Her yellow linen dress was wrinkled, her silver hair hung dank in her eyes. With its smear of makeup and swollen raccoon eyes, her face looked ravaged.

Brushing her hair back with a nervous gesture, Ellie sat down heavily. "I'll have a Booth martini, straight up and very dry," she told the waiter. She took a gold cigarette case from her handbag, opened it, and offered a cigarette to Wetzon, who shook her head.

"Nice case."

Ellie removed a cigarette, closed the case with a snap, tapped the cigarette smartly on the closed case, and lit it with a gold lighter. She gave Wetzon an intense, appraising look. "Let's not talk about where we get our hair done."

"Okay."

Instead, they talked about the early heat spell, transportation in the City, politics, and had just polished off an assessment of the nation's budget deficit when the waiter, an aged man in a threadbare tuxedo, brought the martini and set it in front of her. An olive pierced by a toothpick lay at the bottom of the glass. Ellie spoke to him. "Why don't you just bring me another one now so I don't have to look for you later? Is that okay, Wetzon?" She took a short, sharp drag on her cigarette, inhaling the smoke and exhaling through her nostrils.

"Of course." Ellie had been drinking, Wetzon saw, and was well on her way to being drunk.

"I know you want to talk business, Wetzon. You're in business; I'm in business." Ellie laughed. "And I don't want to talk about business. What else do you have to offer?" She drained half the martini, took hold of the toothpick with thick fingers, and popped the olive into her mouth, then broke the toothpick into little pieces.

"I *love* it!" one of the women at the next table shrieked.

"How about friendship?" Wetzon said.

"How about it?" Ellie finished the martini and stared into the empty glass. "Do you know what it's like for women in this business if you don't play along with Them?" She stared at Wetzon. "What's the matter with me? Of course you know. I'm sorry, Wetzon. You know, life never turns out the way you want it. You make plans, you think you have it right, and then it just melts away, and the detritus is worse than what was before."

Wetzon shooshed the ice around in her glass. Was Ellie talking about David?

"You're not saying anything, Wetzon. Come on, you have to keep up your end of the conversation."

"Where are you from, Ellie?"

"Originally?" She took a big swallow of the martini.

Wetzon nodded. Ellie was sitting with her back to the window, and Wetzon, facing her, saw only her silhouette framed in the late-day sunlight.

"Grew up in Forest Hills. My father taught history at Queens College. I went to Vassar on a scholarship, and ended up teaching at Fieldston, where Goldie Henry-Higginsed me." Her words began to slur badly. "Should never have . . . should have let me be. . . ." She took another sip of the martini, holding the liquid in her mouth before swallowing. "Too many fucking responsibilities . . . I could use a friend. . . ." She stared at Wetzon, then let her chin sink wearily to her breast. ". . . Someone who won't judge me. Will you be my friend, Wetzon?"

Wetzon felt a rush of sympathy; she reached out and touched Ellie's hand. "Ellie, talk to me about what you do. The options market is so specialized, I'd love to learn more about it."

Ellie pulled her hand away. "Is this from course number two-oh-two, humor the broker? Get her to talk about herself."

"There aren't very many people on the Street who do with options what you do, and certainly not very many women. I'd really like to understand it."

"Thinking of switching careers?"

"No way. I like what I do. Now you humor me. Pretend you are teaching a retarded person about options."

Ellie's laugh was sour. "Do you have a man in your life, Wetzon? Are you married?"

"Yes to the first, no to the second."

"I hope he's not on the Street."

"Not in the sense you mean." *More like these mean streets,* she thought.

"Is he nice?"

"Yes. He's my friend."

"Ah, Wetzon, it's never that simple. *Options* are simpler than the adversarial relationships between men and women. Options are cleaner." Ellie sighed and reached for her second martini. "Okay, and this is really for the simple-minded; present company excepted. Options are wagers. There are two kinds, puts and calls. Calls are wagers to buy a security at a fixed price within a fixed time, and puts are wagers to sell. A call bets the stock is going to go up and a put, down. Options trade in three-month cycles. They expire on the third Friday of every month at the end of the day."

"The triple witching hour?"

"That only happens four times a year. The final hour of trading just before the contracts expire for equity and index futures contracts." Ellie played with the toothpick and the olive marinating in the gin in her glass. "So much trading goes on because the arbs and traders want to unload their positions. The stock prices can swing incredibly."

"What if I want to say that I think General Electric is going to go up in three months?"

"First you'd have to sign an agreement with the brokerage firm that you understand the risks of options and are able to pay in cash the next day if you guess wrong. Then you'd buy one contract for each hundred shares that you want to control. Because you're using leverage, if you guess right, you could make a lot of money, and if you guess wrong you'd lose your original equity. It's a good bet, if you know what you're doing."

"But it's a bet."

"What do you think, Wetzon? Better odds at a craps table? Only if you're not in good hands. It's treacherous, if you don't know your way, and most brokers lose their shirts in options."

"What about you, Ellie?"

Ellie smiled a slow, satisfied smile. "I do very well. It's instinct, experience, and confidence. It works for me. I wish I could handle the rest of my life as well." She polished off the martini and stabbed out her cigarette. "Got me to talk about myself, didn't you?"

Wetzon smiled and said nothing.

"Don't ever do options, Wetzon. God, I must be a mess. I've got to go." She stood. "Thanks."

"For what?"

"You know. Why don't you set me up with Tucker next week?" Ellie patted her hand and moved away, turned suddenly and came back. "Oh, by the way," she said, "I found out what the fat fuck's study was about."

Wetzon's pulse quickened. "You did?"

"It was a feasibility study about eliminating commissions and putting brokers on straight salary."

"Oh, come on."

"Really."

"It could never happen."

"Don't kid yourself, Wetzon. It's *going* to happen."

THIRTY-ONE

While she waited for the bill, Wetzon took out her Filofax and flipped to the blank note pages. If their clients were to put stockbrokers on salary, where did that leave the headhunter?

She wrote *Personnel Placement,* and under it, *one percent per thousand dollars,* which was the way salaried jobs like secretarial and clerical were paid. God, Smith would have a real fit. She'd always said that kind of work was déclassé. Besides, you had to be licensed by the state to do low-level placement. On the other hand, just about anyone could open an office and declare himself or herself an executive recruiter. The difference was that placement firms for executives, whose salaries were well over twenty-five thousand, were not regulated and thrived or died on good will, good work, and good business development.

The noise level in the room was at its peak, helped along by the women at the next table who, she decided, were college buddies because they were recounting tales punctuated by howling laughter and "do you remember when Dean Kushinsky . . ."

Wetzon looked out the window onto Central Park South. Underneath *Personnel Placement,* she wrote *Dinosaur.* The headhunter would be eliminated. If draw vs. commission were to be eliminated, it would please some critics of the industry because it would take away the incentive of payment on gross commissions. It would please some of the low-end brokers who needed the stability of a regular salary, but what big producer would want to work on salary? Even with bonuses when he reached certain designated levels, the broker would never earn what he could on commission. She wrote KILL INCENTIVE!.

She paid the bill with her credit card and wrote *Less Motivation to Move*. At least that's the way it would be at the wire houses. Why move from one to another for the same thing? It was even possible the houses would collude and fix base salaries and commissions. After years of intense rivalry, price-fixing. Of course, the we're-all-in-this-together mentality. The broker would get royally screwed.

She shook her head, dismayed, and wrote *Boutiques and Regionals*. Never. It would be ludicrous for them to go along and put brokers on salary if the wire houses did. They couldn't compete. Very entrepreneurial big-firm brokers would begin to consider the smaller houses as real alternatives. Some might even go into business for themselves and clear through the Bear, or Pershing, or one of the other houses that offered back office services to small firms for a price. And that price was low enough for the broker to keep a lot more for himself than he could working for a listed firm. A big producer at a major firm got roughly a sixty-forty split, sixty for the firm, forty for the producer. At a much smaller firm, one that didn't carry the heavy overhead of marketing and research and information and other designer support systems staffing, the split could be fifty-fifty or even higher, in favor of the broker.

The firms would say to the general public, See, we are safeguarding you from the few bandits that get through our rigid screening by eliminating the possibility of churning—buying and selling of securities by the broker for the purpose of raising his gross commissions.

She wrote *Order Taker*. The stockbroker would be reduced to the uncreative position of order taker. He would sell the firm's products instead of shopping for the best product on the Street. The clients would cleave to the firm, not the broker.

Stockbrokers would have to organize, she thought suddenly, to protect themselves. Brokers, who considered they were running their own businesses, would find themselves so manipulated by management, they would have to look for representation. She wrote *Teamsters?* Then she wrote ALTON PINKUS!.

Maybe Smith and Wetzon could switch gears and become labor organizers. The thought was so insane, she laughed out loud, and she was still laughing as she trudged over to Sixth Avenue in sauna heat and caught the "7" bus. It was only moderately air-conditioned, but better than the street; she found a seat in the back next to a small, white-haired woman who was sorting newspaper clippings into a gigantic accordion file. Her feet, encased in Nike running shoes, dangled well off the floor of the bus.

Wetzon pulled *The Oldest Living Confederate Widow* from her briefcase and opened it to her bookmark.

"Do you own a dog?" the woman asked.

"What?" Wetzon looked up, startled, into pale blue eyes, set into a cascade of wrinkles.

"Don't get me wrong. I love dogs. My grandchildren have dogs. What can I do about it? Nothing. It's not the dogs, it's the people who own them. Dog crap everywhere—in the park where children play. I can't tell you what I've seen. Horrible eye diseases, infections, parasites. Of course, everyone acts as if I'm crazy." She touched Wetzon's arm gently. "Goldie Hawn wanted to do my life, but I wouldn't compromise. I have a good heart, what can I tell you? But we are surrounded by dirty dogs and disease and careless owners."

The woman gathered up her material and got off the bus at Seventy-ninth Street. On the street Wetzon saw her stop another woman with three German shepherds on a leash. Probably telling her that she didn't need three dogs.

When she opened the door to her apartment, it was as hot as the street, and she ran from room to room turning on the air conditioners. She'd have a monumental Con Ed bill this month, but who cared? Comfort was everything.

She stripped off her moist clothing and took an icy shower, then put on short bicycle tights and one of Silvestri's sleeveless tees. The apartment had cooled off some. She sat cross-legged on the bed and called Sharon Murphy.

"Sharon? Wetzon."

"Hi, I just got in," Sharon said. "Hold on while I get something to drink." Her voice was huskier than usual.

Wetzon waited patiently and was rewarded in a couple of minutes by the click of ice against glass. "Okay," Sharon said.

"What did you think?"

"I liked Marty. We talked for over an hour. They have a decent bond inventory. He showed me what they have on a given day."

"What else did you talk about?"

"Oh, I don't know. Direct investments. Marty's going to set me up with the guy who runs that department."

"Good. How did you leave it?"

"We're going to talk again. He also gave me the number of a friend of his in Boston who just switched from Slutton to Loeb Dawkins so he could explain the differences."

"Did you say Slutton?"

"That's what we're all calling it. Apt, don't you think?"

Wetzon laughed. Shearson Lehman Hutton. Slutton. "If you say so." The industry was a breeding ground for witty, cynical jokes, which traveled like viruses, usually from the trading floors. "That's a good beginning, don't you think?"

"Wetzon, to tell you the truth, I don't think I'm very interested in Loeb Dawkins. You see, I've been interviewing pretty seriously with Luwisher Brothers, and I really like what they're about."

Wetzon almost dropped the phone. "Wait a minute, Sharon. Luwisher Brothers? They're downtown. I thought you wouldn't, under any circumstances, go downtown?"

"Oh, I know I said that, but there are express buses from my neighborhood. It won't be easy, but I can do it. It would be worth a little discomfort for what I could get down there."

"Well, Luwisher Brothers is a client firm, and it's a wonderful place to work. I did mention it to you last week and would have had you look at it as an alternative if you hadn't been so adamant about not going downtown. Who are you talking to there?"

"Chris Gorham. He's really nice. We had dinner together last week, and we really hit it off. I'm sorry about this, Wetzon, but I'm close to a deal. I would love to work with you, but after all, you didn't show me Luwisher Brothers and someone else did."

"Oh, then you're working with another headhunter?"

"Yes, I am, and I'd rather not say who. I met everybody up at Luwisher Brothers yesterday. John Hoffritz, Destry Bird. They wouldn't let me leave without giving them a commitment."

"Okay, Sharon. Chris is a super guy. They're all terrific, but I really think you should take your time about this. Working downtown will change the quality of your life."

"I know that," Sharon said regretfully. "My shrink is uptown."

"Well, look, as I said before, I love Luwisher Brothers. They are an aggressive equities house. Are you going to switch your business to equities? Don't you do over fifty percent bonds?"

"Why would I have to switch?"

"Because Luwisher Brothers is very weak on bonds. I'm not saying you shouldn't go there because there's no better place to work. If I were a broker I would want to work there, but ask the right questions before you commit yourself. Check out their bond setup."

"Okay, I will, Wetzon. And thank you."

"What do you want me to tell Marty?"

"Tell him I'm thinking about it."

Wetzon hung up the phone feeling really shot down. Not only was she going to lose the fee on Sharon, but Sharon was making a terrible mistake. On the other hand, Wetzon couldn't tell her that because she could not put herself in the position of bad-mouthing a client, even if it meant the broker was making the wrong career decision. And it would also look as if she was trying to poison the well. Besides, Wetzon had always liked the atmosphere at Luwisher Brothers—until the events of the last few days.

She reached for the phone to call Smith and break the news to her, when it rang. "Hello!"

"Well, don't bite my head off, darlin'."

"Oh, Laura Lee. I'm sorry. It's been a torturous day, so it's really good to talk to you. What nice news do you bring me?"

"I don't truly know that you'll think it's such nice news."

"Uh-oh. Don't tell me the wedding is off?"

"No, not at all. Remember I told you I'd check out the subject of that mysterious study?"

"Yes, and if you're going to tell me it was a study about how to put brokers on salary, I already know, and it doesn't seem likely."

"Well, Wetzon darlin', I'm glad to hear you know what's goin' on, but what I have to tell you is barf-in-a-bag news. Prepare yourself."

Wetzon groaned and lay back against the cool pillows. "Tell me."

"Search and Destroy are goin' to announce the new program at a news conference at Luwisher Brothers on Thursday."

Wetzon punched her pillow with her fist. "*What* new program? They're my clients, why aren't they telling *me*?"

"Well, darlin', let me be the first then to tell you the news. On July first, your esteemed clients are puttin' all their brokers on salary."

THIRTY-TWO

Wetzon wandered around her apartment in a state of *agita*. Smith was the only living human being left in the world who wouldn't use an answering machine, so there was no way to leave a message for her. Well, fuck it then, Smith would have to wait to hear the news tomorrow.

She did a hundred warm-up brushes, then twenty minutes of pliés and relevés, giving herself a fair workout, grumbling almost continuously under her breath, before collapsing on the sofa in the living room. A copy of the latest issue of *Forbes* lay on the coffee table. She flipped through it without reading anything and dropped it on the floor.

Obviously Silvestri wasn't coming home. Too bad. She wanted to try her theory about Goldie's death being accidental out on him. Feeling frustrated and abandoned and hungry, she drifted into the kitchen, found a bagel, cut it in three slices and stuck the two outside slices in the toaster oven. She made iced coffee with espresso beans and foraged through the refrigerator for something to eat with it.

Aha! She pulled out a container of cured olives in olive oil and half a beefsteak tomato wrapped in plastic. Her favorite sandwich was a bagel lathered in fruity olive oil and topped with thin slices of tomato, peppered and drizzled with more olive oil. Oh, boy! She dropped a few olives on the dinner plate for nibbling.

At ten o'clock she gave up on Smith and Silvestri and went to bed with the oldest living Confederate widow, but it was hard to concentrate on the page because her mind kept returning to Luwisher Brothers's scheme to put brokers on salary. She felt betrayed. If it worked at Luwisher Brothers, you could bet that Merrill Lynch, Shearson, and Dean Witter would jump at the chance.

The words wobbled on the page.

She looked up and saw she was sitting on a bench in Central Park, near the volleyball games. Chris Gorham sat next to her in gym shorts and a shirt that said LUWISHER BROTHERS. He was bent over his hairy, muscular legs, tying the laces on his Avias.

The game was Luwisher Brothers against the Teamsters, or so the other team's sweatshirts said. Alton Pinkus, chubby and a little winded, was playing for the Teamsters. Hoffritz and Bird, Neil, even Ellie were dolled up in matching gym shorts and tees. David Kim zapped the ball smartly back at the Teamsters. Now and then Dougie Culver would make a play while Ellie stumbled around drunkenly. The ball came back, and Hoffritz gave Ellie a hard push, knocking her down. "Get out of here," he said. "You're slowing us down."

Ellie lay crumpled on the tarmac, not moving. The players stepped around her.

Wetzon jumped to her feet. "Stop!" she cried. "Someone help Ellie." Ellie lay on her back like a corpse, hands crossed over her breast.

"Get out of here, Wetzon," Hoffritz snarled. "It's too late to help Ellie. She did herself in."

"Duck, Wetzon!" Alton Pinkus shouted. "This isn't your fight."

The ball was coming toward her with tremendous speed. She flung it away, using both hands; the follow-through almost slammed her to the ground.

Wetzon soft-shoed herself over to Ellie, but Ellie was gone. In her place was an antique leather-and-wood pirate's treasure chest, decorated with brass fittings. She knelt and opened the chest; it was filled with money, paper and coins. Oh, she saw it all now—they were fighting for the chest.

Silvestri put a whistle in his mouth and blew it.

"What are you doing here, Silvestri?" she demanded.

"Pay attention to the game," he said.

"You call this a *game*?"

"Take off your clothes." He smiled and faded away.

She stood up. The game was getting violent; the ball became a round trajectory covered with nails like a mace. Everyone was getting hurt, bleeding. Hoffritz had a bloody rag tied around his head. Neil had a bad cut on his cheek, Destry's thigh was gashed, Chris bled profusely from a cut just over his eye, and blood ran from David Kim's nose. Only Dougie remained untouched. Wetzon, standing on tiptoe, saw that the other team was similarly battered and bloody.

"Stop this, Dougie. They're killing each other." And for what? "Here!" she shrieked. She plunged her hands into the chest and flung bills and coins at both sides. "Take it, take the money, just stop this."

Dougie took her arms and pulled her away from the trunk. With a benign smile, he said, "This is a perfect example of why women don't belong on the Street, Wetzon."

"Are you crazy, Dougie? Let go of me."

"What you don't understand is, this is only a *game*, Wetzon."

A fierce clap of thunder tore the atmosphere, lightning following hard on. Then the sky opened up and dense snow began to fall, just like the old-fashioned paperweights you shook and turned upside down. The snow hit her face, stinging eyes and lips—but it wasn't snow. It was a white powder of some sort. *Danger, danger,* sounded a siren in her brain. It was snowing sulfites.

All the players looked like ghosts now, covered with the white powder. The game had ended. When the next clap of thunder came, she convulsed, knocking the book to the floor, waking herself up.

Be still, my heart, she thought, pressing her hands to her thumping chest. She'd fallen asleep with the lights on and had one of her tops-in-pops dreams. Silvestri had come home; she could hear him moving around in the foyer, rattling his keys. He'd probably slammed the door and woken her up. She looked at the clock. Twelve-thirty. She got off the bed and picked up the book.

"Hi," he said, thumping down the hall. Before he even came into the room, she knew he was in a temper. He hung up his jacket in the closet and shrugged out of his shoulder holster, hooking it on the door-knob. Sweat stained his blue oxford-cloth shirt liberally. When he finally looked at her, she saw his eyes were red with exhaustion. His face was dark with beard bristles.

"You're in a foul mood," she said.

"I've been up for twenty straight fucking hours. I have the Chief on my back and that fucking prima donna Weiss to deal with. And the fucking Mayor making demands. You bet your ass, I'm in a foul mood." He sat down on the edge of the bed and pulled off his shoes. "Shove over."

She rolled over to his side of the bed, and he lay down and offered her his hand. He smelled of cigarettes and coffee and sweat. "I can tell you've been with Weiss. You smell like an ashtray."

"I'm fucking wasted, and we're not getting anywhere."

"Have you had dinner?"

"Grabbed a few slices with Weiss." He closed his eyes. He had thick silky lashes, like a girl. He opened the eye closest to her. "Nice outfit," he mumbled and closed it again. "Sexy."

"Anything new on the case?"

"Nada. A few odds and ends. Nothing real."

"I have a theory. Wanna hear?"

He opened the same eye and gave her a fish-eyed turquoise look. "Do I have a choice?"

She tickled him along his ribs. "I could tell the Chief directly. He and I are like *that*." She brought two fingers close together.

He rolled over on her without warning and pinned her down. "Oh, yeah? Talk, lady."

"Okay. Think about this," she said, kissing his chin whiskers. "Beast." She rubbed her fingernail on the bristles.

"I'm waiting."

"Okay. What if Goldie was not the target? He was sitting next to Ash at the dinner. They both had asthma or emphysema or whatever. There was so much activity at that table. Everyone was around Goldie. I think I remember a drink getting spilled. Goldie could have picked up the wrong glass . . ."

Silvestri rolled off her. "Sit up, Les. I want to go back over this. You're saying that Ash was the target and Goldie Barnes was—"

"A mistake—an unfortunate accident."

"Tell me again what you saw."

"Everyone was around the table talking to Goldie just before he got up to speak. Destry, Hoffritz, Dougie, Neil, Ellie, Chris. Dr. Ash was sitting next to Goldie. They each had drinks." She closed her eyes. "Chris knocked over Goldie's drink, and Dr. Ash jumped up to get out of the way. Some of it got on him anyway. Someone brought another drink."

"Someone?"

"I don't remember who."

"A waiter?"

She racked her brain. "I don't know. The drinks might have gotten mixed up. Can you find out if Goldie and Ash were drinking the same stuff?"

"Yup."

"Yup, you can find out, or yup, they drank the same drink?"

"Yup, they drank the same—Jack Daniel's on sulfites."

"You know something, Silvestri, you have a ghoulish sense of humor."

"Interesting theory, Les. It would mean that someone wanted to get rid of Ash badly enough to try a second time and with the same method."

"Methodical and uncreative."

"Panicked." He got up and began stripping out of his clothes. "I need a shower." He stopped in the doorway. "Oh, by the way, I dropped in on Goldman Barnes II tonight."

"Oh? He's not a suspect, is he?"

"We're not ruling anyone out yet."

"Did you get anything new out of him?" She rolled back to her side of the bed and crawled under the covers. Her eyes were heavy. She'd be asleep before he came out of the shower.

"There was a woman with him—"

"Oh?" She felt herself begin to drift off. "Anybody I know?"

"Yeah, Xenia Smith."

THIRTY-
THREE

Wednesday seeped in with a greasy phlegmatic haze; the local news reported that night temperatures had never dipped below eighty-five. The City vibrated heat, and New Yorkers were beginning to take on the bleary-eyed look of people living through a natural catastrophe.

Wetzon, wearing a lime short-sleeved silk shirt under her cream silk suit, the jacket folded neatly over her arm, found an air-conditioned cab on Central Park West and arrived at her office a little later than her customary time. She wasn't moving very fast, but in this unremitting heat, nobody was.

The Times gave the Mayor front page coverage when he announced a ban on cars holding one person only from entering the City and threatened to ban all cars entirely if the inversion continued. Days ago both *The Times* and *The Journal* had banished major coverage of the Wall Street murders to the back pages, leaving it to the hysterical headlines of the *News* and the *Post*. But now the extreme heat had pushed everything to the side, including politics.

She paid the driver with the five-dollar bill she took from the zippered compartment of her purse and made a dash to the door of her office, holding her breath, trying not to breathe the polluted air.

"She's heee-yer," Harold sang out. He was sitting on the edge of B.B.'s desk, reading a suspect sheet, a slightly smug expression, quickly there and gone, on his face. B.B. looked at her, then away, nervously.

"Good morning . . . I think," Wetzon said, picking up on something in the air.

"Wetzon!" Smith cried. "Get in here right away."

"What's going on?"

"Come in and close the door. No interruptions, B.B. Just take messages." Smith looked frantic; her hair ragged, as if she'd been pulling at the ends. She was waving her arms and pacing the room like a caged animal, a leopard in a white-with-black polka-dot dress. "You've really done it now. How *could* you? You know how careful we have to be."

"Wait one minute here. What am I supposed to have done?" Wetzon threw her handbag and briefcase on her chair and put on the jacket of her suit. Then she faced Smith, properly armored.

"John Hoffritz just called and told me you bad-mouthed Luwisher Brothers to Sharon Murphy. He says we will never work for them again. I don't think you realize how hard I worked on that relationship, how difficult Hoffritz is to deal with. All *you* have to handle are the brokers." She stopped pacing and stood in front of Wetzon, hands on her hips. "How *could* you?" Her voice rose in an hysterical wail. "And they owe us so much money."

"For your information, I did *not* bad-mouth Luwisher Brothers. Who says I did?" Wetzon demanded hotly.

"You didn't?" Smith sank into her chair, deflated. "You must have said something. They wouldn't just make it up."

"What I said, after telling her I thought Luwisher Brothers was about the best place on the Street to work, was to check out their debt side. She does more than fifty percent of her business in bonds, and Luwisher can't compete with the majors on inventory."

"This is true, of course, but did you have to *tell* her?" Smith complained.

"Smith, it's something I would have told *our* candidates. What's the point of sending a broker to a firm where he or she can't do business? What happened, did she tell the other headhunter what I said?"

"What other headhunter? Didn't we show her to Luwisher Brothers?" Smith looked confused.

"No, we didn't. She insisted she wouldn't go downtown. And she also does too much bond business."

"The other headhunter, then . . ." Smith said slowly, the light dawning.

"Yes. I'm calling Hoffritz right now." Wetzon set her bag and briefcase on the floor under her desk, sat down and punched out Hoffritz's direct number, hoping she wouldn't be deflected by a secretary.

"Hoffritz." Good, he'd picked up his own phone.

"John, this is Wetzon."

"Wetzon, I've been reading your report on the murder. Congratulations. I want to show it to Destry and then sit down and talk with you both to strategize."

Not a word about her bad-mouthing the firm. "John, I did not bad-mouth Luwisher Brothers, and anyone who says I did is a liar."

"Wetzon—"

"John, I told Sharon you're a terrific firm, that I'd want to work for Luwisher Brothers if I were a broker, and that she should check out your bond department because so much of her business is in munis. Do you want to hire a broker who does a huge bond business and then not be able to feed her?"

"We have hired on a couple of bond traders now, Wetzon, and we're making a real effort to build up the department."

"Fine, show her what you can do for her. Don't wait and let it be a surprise after she's on board. I've known Sharon for years. She calls me for advice all the time. She's high-strung and has trouble making a decision, but she's a good producer."

"Wetzon, if you'll help us close her, we'll make it up to you."

Wetzon knew that was bullshit. Where money and loyalty were concerned, the men at the top had short memories. "Thanks, John, but I really resent your jumping to conclusions about what I said and I resent the threat—"

"Ahem!" Smith was waving her hand back and forth, trying to get her to stop talking.

"Oh, I was just letting off a little steam, Wetzon. You know I didn't mean it."

"Sure, John. Do you want to tell me who the other headhunter is?"

"I have no problem with that. He's a good man. Tom Keegen. Talk to you later, Wetzon."

Wetzon put the receiver down in a fury.

"Who was it?" a subdued Smith asked.

"Need you ask?"

"I'm going to kill him," Smith said through gritted teeth. "In a slow, painful way."

"Not if I get to him first. I'd like to nail Tom Keegen's thumbs to the outside sill of the penthouse in Luwisher Tower." Her mouth was dry and she headed for the door to get a cup of coffee.

Smith rose and stood in her way. "I'm really sorry I attacked you, sweetie pie."

"You should be. Why do you always think the worst of me? We've been together almost eight years. I'm not the girl from the chorus anymore who's learning the business. I've learned it. Don't you think it's time you accepted that? And what makes you think that dealing with brokers is any easier than dealing with clients?"

"You're absolutely right, I know." Smith put her arms around Wetzon and gave her a quick hug. "It's just that you're so tiny I think you're a little girl. I forget. Please forgive me, sweetie. You know I love you. You're my best friend."

"Okay, okay, you may stop groveling."

"Are you kidding? It's part of our job, what we do best."

Wetzon laughed. Smith was so right. She held Smith at arm's length and decided Smith was definitely mellowing. "We have some more important things to talk about right now."

"Oh?" Smith flushed and looked down, as if contemplating some important object on the floor. "I suppose that nosy boyfriend of yours told you—"

"Told me what?" She was not about to give Silvestri away. "I tried to call you all last evening, but you weren't home, and without an answering machine, how was I to leave an important message?"

"Oh, good," Smith said coyly, ignoring what Wetzon had just said. "Well, if you must know, I was with Twoey last night . . ."

"Really?" Wetzon said.

"He's wonderful."

"And rich."

"*Very* rich."

"I'm thrilled your love life has taken this magical turn, Smith, but we really do have a problem. Are we still on for dinner tonight, or are you ditching me for the new love in your life?"

"Harold seems to have settled down, I think, but why would you think I'd ditch you for Twoey? We had a date. Dinner is fine. Baci's at seven."

Wetzon laughed. Smith would have no compunction about cancelling if something more interesting came up. "This is not about Harold. I heard last night that Luwisher Brothers is going to put their brokers on salary."

"I'm sorry?" Smith stared at her, wrinkling her brow.

"Wait a minute." Wetzon took her Filofax out of her briefcase and tore her notes from the book. "We're going to be out of business if this goes through. I'd better spruce up my buck and wing." She handed the pages to Smith, who barely glanced at them, then threw them on her desk.

"What are you talking about, Wetzon? I can never make sense of you. You *heard* they're putting brokers on salary? You have to be wrong. They can't do that; it would *kill* incentive."

"It would *kill* the headhunter."

"Damn it all, Wetzon, you must be wrong. How would you hear about it, anyway? I have the inside track with management." When she saw Wetzon's face, she held up her palms and shrugged. "Sorry."

"Ellie told me that's what Dr. Ash's missing study was about, and then Laura Lee called me and told me they are going to announce it tomorrow at a news conference."

"They can't do that without telling me—us."

"Oh, yeah? Do you think they told Keegen?"

"We're going to have to confront them."

"I don't trust them, Smith." Wetzon opened the door. "Give us our messages now, B.B." She took the two pink stacks and handed Smith's to her.

"We must have a policy, a response ready, because we'll be asked how it affects us."

"Yes. I can just see the front page of *The Journal*—'Headhunters accuse Luwisher Brothers of castration.'" She laughed.

"This is no time for your weird humor, Wetzon." Smith scowled and thumbed through her messages. "This is serious. It's our livelihood. We're going to have to fight it, but not before they pay us what they owe us."

"We can work out some strategy over dinner." Strategy. That

reminded her of Hoffritz's comment about the report Smith had given him.

"God, just when everything was going so well." Smith lowered her heavy eyelids and gave Wetzon a sultry smile.

"You're just dying to tell me about it."

"Mmmm. Sex in hot weather is so low-down and dirty. I love it."

"I can't wait to see how you're going to handle Jake." *This might be fun to watch,* Wetzon thought. The worm would finally get his.

"We'll work out that strategy tonight, too. I can use your input."

Strategy again. "Haven't the phones been eerily quiet? It's as if the industry is on the brink, waiting."

"It's not that, it's this godawful weather. Everyone is too hot to think about anything—"

"Except sex."

"Oh, shush. Did Ellie agree to see some firms?"

"Yes. I'm going to set her up next week with Tucker." Wetzon sat down at her desk and took her notes out of her briefcase. "By the way, what did you say in that report you sent to Hoffritz? He congratulated me and said he wants to sit down and strategize." When there was no response from Smith, Wetzon looked up. "Smith?"

Smith ran her fingers through her hair dramatically. She sauntered over to her desk and made a show of looking through her papers, all in slow motion.

"Smith!" Wetzon shrieked.

"Don't get so excited, sweetie pie, and lower your voice, please."

"What did you say?"

"I just told them that we know who the murderer is."

THIRTY-FOUR

It had been a long, dull day. At five o'clock Wetzon called it quits and declared she was going home. She'd meet Smith at seven at Baci.

The heat glanced off concrete, glass, stone, and steel. It had to be one hundred and ten in the shade, and there was not one cab in sight. Eyes burning, Wetzon walked over to First Avenue and took a bus uptown, transferring for the crosstown at Eighty-sixth Street, where, wonder of wonders, she got a seat. It was then she noticed that the air-conditioning had broken down, and the open windows let in more hot, unbreathable air. As more and more people crowded on, weary and rank with sweat, the bus took on the aspect of a cattle car. An elderly woman fainted somewhere up front, and people were so jammed together that no one noticed until the Central Park West stop, when everyone began to push out.

The driver radio'd for an EMS truck, and two men picked up the poor woman and laid her across the front seats, fanning her with hot air as they waited for the paramedics. An athletic young woman in Reeboks took a bottle of Evian water from her backpack, poured a little into the cap and pressed it to the woman's lips.

Wetzon got off the back exit of the bus and walked the block and a half to her apartment, finding it more and more difficult just to pick up one foot and then the other, counting in her head, *left then right then left then right.*

She took a cold shower and lay on her bed letting the air conditioner revive her body, get her brain functioning again.

Smith had done a colossally stupid thing. *If we know who the murderer is, and the murderer is among us, then Smith has put us both in imminent danger.* Wetzon plucked her phone from the painted washstand next to her bed, balanced it on her stomach, and picked out Silvestri's office number.

A strange voice answered his phone. "Brafman."

"Hi, this is Leslie Wetzon." She vaguely remembered him. Short, blondish, thin.

"Oh, yeah." He seemed to know who she was. "He's not here. Try Midtown North."

"Is Metzger around?"

"They're all at Midtown North. Silvestri, Metzger, and Mo."

Silvestri, Metzger & Mo. It sounded like a law firm. "Do you have the number there?"

"Hold on." Brafman came back on the line and gave it to her.

"Thanks." She hung up and called Midtown North, asked for Silvestri, then Metzger, and finally Weiss, got passed around for ten minutes, gave up and left her number. She probably should have asked for Mo, but she couldn't bring herself to do it. She put the phone back in its place. He'd taken Mo with him. *Get a grip on yourself, dummy,* she commanded. *The heat is definitely affecting your brain.*

In the dining room, which alternated as a workout studio, she rolled a mat out on the floor and did some slow yoga stretches, the bridge, then rolled into a shoulder stand. The blood rushed to her brain as she did deep, measured breathing.

The cast of characters with the opportunity in both murders could be narrowed down to Hoffritz, Bird, Dougie Culver, Neil Munchen, Chris Gorham, Ellie Kaplan, and possibly David Kim, if he had attended the dinner. Still in the shoulder stand, she swung her legs apart and then behind her. Earlier, she had mentally eliminated both Ellie and Neil because of their obvious affection for Goldie, but if Goldie's death had been an accident, they had to go back on the list. All told, seven. The not-so-magnificent seven.

She stretched her legs up in the air, holding hands on hips, and continued deep breathing. She felt a pink glow, a brilliance surge through her. *Oh, dear God,* she thought. What if all this business about Carlton Ash's report had nothing at all to do with the murders? The study was a distraction, a wrong turn, all unfortunately her own creation.

Slowly, she came out of the shoulder stand into a backbend and lowered herself, vertebra by vertebra, into the sponge position and lay there. Better than a massage because the brain was not left out.

Carlton Ash had stumbled on something when he was nosing around Luwisher Brothers working on his study. Something that had made him quit his job. As a consultant with Goodspeed, Ash had to have had an income of upwards of six figures. So unless he had a trust fund, he couldn't afford to just quit a job like that.

If he'd had an independent income, he probably wouldn't have been breaking his ass working at Goodspeed, because they were notorious for working their people into burn-out. He had to have felt that whatever he'd discovered was going to fix him for life. Except it had fixed him for death.

Damn Smith. Damn every last one of the magnificent seven. It had to be one of them. She was fairly certain that neither Ellie nor David would be privy to Smith's report for Luwisher Brothers. Ergo, if someone tried to kill Smith and Wetzon, they could narrow the suspects down to five. *Very funny, Wetzon,* she thought.

Regretfully, she rolled herself up into a standing position and did a few pliés. Her skin tingled. Where was Silvestri? She didn't want to go out without talking to him, telling him how Smith had set them up as decoys.

"Well, quack, quack, sweetie pie," she said, mimicking Smith, and danced into the bedroom. She dressed in a long white Bis skirt and short-sleeved, V-neck cotton shirt, slipped sandals on her bare feet. Tying her hair back in a ponytail, she covered the band with a violet-and-white cotton scarf.

How brave you are, Wetzon, she thought, mocking herself. She was not frightened, just a bit hyper. Was she being stupid? Her watch said quarter to seven. She went into the kitchen and pulled a Post-it off the pack next to the phone, and stuck it to the outside of her door under the peephole. Then she wrote on it: *S—Meeting Smith at Baci's at 7. Urgent news. Please come. L.*

It all seemed melodramatic, and he would probably return her call and not get this message until he came home, which he might not even do. *Merde*. She went back inside, grabbed her handbag, went out, closed the door, double-locked it.

A phone rang. She put her ear to the door. Her phone. Damnation. She fumbled with the lock, got it open, lunged for the phone before the fifth ring when the answering machine would activate. "Hello," she gasped.

"Wetzon?"

"This is Wetzon. I can hardly hear you. Please speak louder. Who is this?"

"Wetzon," the voice whispered. "You said you'd be my friend. I need a friend right now."

"Ellie? Is that you? What's wrong?"

"Wetzon . . . help me . . . please. Everything went wrong somehow . . . I . . ." A clattering noise, as if Ellie had dropped the phone.

"Ellie, speak clearly. I can't follow you."

There was no response.

"Ellie? Ellie!"

She heard a soft cry like the mew of a cat and then the line went dead.

THIRTY-FIVE

Wetzon cradled the receiver. Ellie was drinking. Ellie had passed out and dropped the phone. Ellie was in some kind of trouble. Should she call 911? Nah, that would be overreacting.

"Okay, let's think this through carefully," she said aloud. Where did Ellie live? Wetzon searched her memory. Somewhere on the West Side . . . Lincoln Towers?

The NYNEX white pages listed thirty E. Kaplans, seven of whom were West Siders, and one Ellie, in the wrong part of town. What to do? She didn't remember taking Ellie's home address for the-suspect sheet—always a bad move, as she'd frequently admonished Harold and B.B.—but her home phone number was probably neatly written in, and it was on her desk in the office.

She sat down on the floor, legs crossed yoga style, and closed her eyes. Think. Maybe it would come to her. The phone rang and she grabbed it, relieved. Silvestri would know what to do. "God, I'm glad you called," she said, without saying hello or waiting.

"Well, la-di-da, Birdie," Carlos said. "I'm glad it's me, too."

"Oh, Carlos, I can't talk now," she wailed. "I've got this broker who called me and she's in some kind of trouble, and I don't know where she lives and there are thirty E. Kaplans in the phone book and Smith is probably waiting for me at Baci and I'm late. . . ."

"Tsk, tsk, that last problem is the least problem. Let the Barracuda wait. She's kept you waiting often enough."

"Goodbye, Carlos."

"I'm fine, dear heart, thank you for asking."

"Carlos, this is important. I have to hang up right now. I'm sure Silvestri's trying to reach me and I've got to tell him about Ellie."

"*Ellie* Kaplan? Do you mean the Wall Street Ellie Kaplan?"

"Yes, yes. This is no time for jokes, Carlos."

"Not to worry. Stay right where you are. I'll call you back."

"Carlos!"

He'd hung up.

It was almost seven o'clock. Wetzon got up and ranged anxiously around the apartment. It was hot as a tomb because she'd turned off the air conditioners before she left. Surely a mistake. She turned all the air conditioners on low. She'd leave them on. Smith was always late, she thought. She looked up Baci's phone number and left a message that she was delayed.

As soon as she'd hung up, the phone rang.

"If you weren't such a hard head and had call waiting, darling, I wouldn't have gotten a busy signal these last few crucial minutes—"

"I loathe call waiting. It's rude and nasty. What did you find out?"

"Four-eight-o West Seventy-first Street. It's a dead end street, the last house. The lower duplex." He reeled off the phone number, which she quickly jotted down.

"Carlos, you're wonderful, a genius. Good-bye."

"Hold on there! You will pick me up in a cab in front of Arthur's. I'll be downstairs."

"Oh, no I won't."

"Don't argue, Birdie. Somebody has to look out for you." He hung up.

"Men!" Wetzon muttered under her breath. She called Ellie's number on the off chance that someone would respond. Ten rings. No answer.

She hung up, and again, the phone rang immediately.

"Wetzon," Smith said, "I'm glad I caught you. I'm running late. Why don't I pick you up in my cab?"

"I'm running late myself. Ellie Kaplan called and sounded really strange, then she disconnected or passed out. I'm just going to stop by and see that she's okay."

Smith groaned. "She's a lush. I've heard stories about her. I don't know why you have this Goody Two-shoes thing about helping people—"

"Good-bye, Smith. I'll see you about eight—or do you want to cancel?"

"No, I don't want to cancel. You have to get your priorities straight. You yourself said we have important business to discuss. More important than Ellie Kaplan's drinking problem. Don't make me wait—"

Wetzon hung up on her without saying good-bye, certain again that the milk of human kindness curdled in Smith's veins.

She stood at the door ready to go and stared one more time at the phone, commanding it to ring again, and when it didn't, she quickly locked up and left. While she waited for the slowest elevator on the Upper West Side, she crossed out 7 on the Post-it note she'd stuck to the door and wrote 8.

It was twenty minutes past seven when she hit the street and less than half an hour since Ellie's call. The heat was smothering, and the polluted air brought tears to her eyes. Daylight was a sickly yellow. A cab dropped off someone in front of her building, and Wetzon got in and directed the driver to West End Avenue and Ninetieth Street where Carlos and Arthur lived.

Carlos, looking fresh and crisp in khaki shorts and a blue-and-white-striped shirt, hopped in beside her, brimming over with energy.

"Seventy-first and West End, please," Wetzon snarled.

"Oh, I see we're going to be grumpy gus," he said, leaning over and kissing her cheek.

"I'm not a baby," she said stiffly. "I'm only going to look in on Ellie. I don't need a keeper." She curled her lip at him.

He rolled his eyes. "Quaint, darling, really quaint."

The cab lurched, seeming to hit every pothole head-on, and she fell against him. "Learn how to drive," she mumbled under her breath, trying to right herself, but Carlos held on to her.

"My, aren't we churlish." He looked at her somberly, eyes brimming with mischief, and said, "Now why don't you break down and say, 'Dear, wonderful Carlos. I am so grateful to you for telling me where Ellie lives. . . .'"

Wetzon felt foolish and contrite. Putting her arm around him, she said, "Dear, wonderful Carlos, I *am* grateful. Tell me how you knew."

He smiled. "Now that's more like the Birdie I know and love. I called Dwayne. He was in that jazz class I taught at the Y three years ago."

"Trust you to be everywhere and know everyone."

"You know I always say there are only thirty people in the world, darling." He paused and got serious. "Listen, Birdie, Dwayne says Ellie's in bad shape—very depressed, drinking. We don't know what we're going to find. He's going to meet us there."

"Do you mean she's suicidal, Carlos?"

"Let's hope Dwayne is wrong."

"God, Carlos." She hugged him. "I owe you."

"Listen, I know this is a stupid question to ask you of all people, Birdie, but are you sure you want to get involved?"

"She asked me to help her, Carlos."

"I knew it was a stupid question."

The fare came to four dollars even. "Let me," Wetzon said, "it's my deductible." When she picked at the coins in her change purse to find two quarters for the tip, she saw the torn scraps of paper she'd found in Ellie's makeup bag. *What kind of detective are you, Wetzon,* she thought, disgusted with herself. She had a mind like a sieve. She got out of the cab behind Carlos, willing herself to remember the scraps and put them together later.

A tall jogger in shiny gray shorts, wearing a white breathing cone over his nose and mouth, a cap backwards on his head, turned onto West End Avenue from Seventy-first Street, oblivious to traffic, then continued running in a measured pace south toward Lincoln Center. He wasn't the only one out on the street running either; these joggers were fanatical about never missing a day, no matter rain, sleet, snow, hail, or poisonous air.

Ellie lived in a Georgian-style redbrick townhouse on one of the prettiest streets on the West Side. The houses on both sides of the street were beautifully maintained with window boxes, dense with flowers in spite of the heat, brass doorknockers, and solid oak doors and leaded glass windows. Some were freshly whitewashed with window sashes painted in blue. The street was quiet except for the soft drone of the air conditioners that hung from many of the windows.

Dwayne wasn't standing in front of the building waiting for them. "Now what?" Wetzon looked at Carlos, who wriggled his shoulders.

Two identical front doors at street level in a small brick courtyard, each with a grillwork outer door, indicated that Ellie's building held two occupants. The door on the right stood slightly ajar.

"The one on the left," Carlos said behind her. And sure enough, when she opened the door she saw *E. Kaplan* written on the mailbox next to the bell. A bamboo umbrella stand with two furled umbrellas stood in a corner of the tiny space.

"I guess we have to wait for Dwayne."

"He should have been here by now. He lives only twenty-eight blocks due south, in Manhattan Plaza." Carlos frowned. "Let's see if she answers." He pressed the buzzer, but they heard no responding buzz from within the apartment. He waited, pressed the buzzer again. Nothing. No sign of life. Wetzon jiggled nervously.

They looked at each other, reading each other's thoughts.

"I'm worried, Carlos. Damnation! Where the hell is Dwayne?" Wetzon rapped on the inner door. "Ellie!" She knocked again, harder.

"Wait a minute." Carlos turned the brass doorknob. The door opened. Just like when she'd been locked in at Luwisher Brothers. It hadn't been locked.

Now she was really worried. Maybe someone had broken in and hurt Ellie.

"Jesus," Carlos said, peering in. The apartment smelled musty; it was dark as pitch. He held out his hand to Wetzon, and they stepped inside. Somewhere an air conditioner whirred, ineffectively.

"Do you know what you're doing?" she whispered.

"I'm improvising. Why are we whispering?" He moved forward, pulling her behind him. The outside door slid shut. "*Merde.* Now we've lost our light."

"I'll get it." She went back and opened the door. Daylight brought a dusty haze into the small foyer.

Someone groaned.

"Ellie!" Wetzon cried.

Carlos found the round dimmer button, and pressed it. Nothing. "Uh-oh," he said.

A faint tremor of fear crept up her spine.

"The fuses must have blown." Carlos's voice had lost its usual buoyant lilt.

Not uncommon, Wetzon told herself sternly, *when every window has an air conditioner and the wiring dates back to pre-World War II.* They edged forward along the wall.

They came to an opening, perhaps an archway. From here the darkness seemed fathomless. A floorboard beneath Carlos's feet squeaked loudly. He called, "Ellie?" and Wetzon heard the uncertainty in his voice.

Another groan came out of the darkness. The muscles in his back tightened under her hand. The floorboard squeaked again. Why were they hesitating? There were two of them. Thank God, he hadn't let her come alone. But Ellie sounded awful. "Let's go to her, Carlos," she urged in a whisper.

He turned. "Birdie . . ." She could feel his anxiety. "We may not be alone. Caution would be smart. You stay here and I'll go on. If something happens to me, you run for it."

"No way! We'll go together."

She felt him shrug. He moved forward, but she'd lost his shoulder. Determined, she felt her way along, her fingers touching picture frames, leaving them askew, no doubt. They seemed to be in a hallway leading to a larger room. Carlos stopped abruptly, and she bumped into him with an "Ooof."

"Wait here," he said, firmly. "Not one step farther. I'm going back to the foyer to see if I can find the fuse box."

She looked over his shoulder. It was pitch black. "Okay," she said. He passed her and she could hear him moving toward the foyer. If she only had a match. . . . Wait. She had picked up a matchbox at the Oak Bar—or had she? She groped inside her bag and found a matchbox. Clumsily, she tried to light a match by feeling. She'd probably torch herself. She scraped a match on the side of the box and a little flame burst forth. Very pleased, she held it out in front of her and almost dropped it. In the arched entranceway to what seemed to be a huge living room, a body lay spread-eagle on the carpeted floor.

"Ellie!" Wetzon dropped her bag and jumped forward. The match went out. Something crunched under her sandals. It was too dark to see what. She could hear Carlos in the other room, mucking with the switches, but no light.

Ellie groaned again. Wetzon lit another match. "Ellie, I'm here. It's okay."

She dropped to her knees beside Ellie and felt a sharp pain in her knee as something cut through her skirt and into flesh. Holding the match higher, she saw the floor was covered with sharp shards of glass. The cut stung. The match went out. She could feel blood burning from her wounded knee. Bending, she touched Ellie's shoulder, brushing her fingers on clammy stems and flowers, felt the damp clothing, and a surprising amount of sinew. She put her hand out and stroked Ellie's hair, stopped, rubbed her fingers together and recognized the unmistakably sticky wetness of blood.

"Are you okay?" Carlos called.

"Yes," she lied. "Ellie, can you sit up? No, wait." Wetzon rose. Brushing the soles of her sandals along the floor, she tried to sweep the largest slivers of glass away from Ellie's body. "Okay now, try, Ellie. I'll help you."

She lit another match. In the flickering light, she could see Ellie's pale skin and slim muscular legs. What the hell was she wearing? Shorts. Somehow she'd never pictured Ellie in shorts. Ellie groaned again and rolled over onto her side. Wetzon leaned over to help her.

Porcelain lamps awoke suddenly, spreading soft light around the room.

Wetzon looked down at Ellie, but the figure on the floor wasn't Ellie. It was Dwayne.

THIRTY-
SIX

A scream rose into her throat and she choked on it. "Good God,
Dwayne!" Wetzon squatted beside him, flinching from the cut
on her knee. "Are you all right? I'm sorry, what a dumb
question. What happened?"

"Birdie?" Carlos called.

"Carlos, it's Dwayne."

Dwayne groaned and put his hands on his head. He groaned again
and opened his eyes. "The mother crocked me with Ellie's Baccarat
vase." The floor was alive with pink roses and petals and broken glass.

Wetzon stifled an hysterical giggle as Carlos came racing into the
room. He dropped down beside Dwayne, opposite Wetzon.

Dwayne struggled up on his elbows; a limp rose fell from his back.
"The fucker didn't even take the flowers out." He touched his cheekbones gingerly. "Did he hurt my face?"

"No," Carlos said. "Good thing your head is so hard. Come on, let
me help you up."

"Should we get an ambulance?" Wetzon looked around the room.
No Ellie.

Carlos helped Dwayne to his feet. "Dwayne," Wetzon said, "where's Ellie?"

Dwayne tilted like a leaning tower. "Don't know." He swayed. "Sofa," he said, pointing to the overstuffed floral chintz affair drowning in pillows.

"What happened to the lights?" Carlos had his arm around Dwayne and was half carrying him. "Lean on me."

"The dirtbag must have thrown the main switch," Dwayne mumbled.

"He did just that."

"It was dark when I got here. Ellie must have gone out and left the door unlocked." Dwayne collapsed on the sofa.

"I can't believe she'd do that." Wetzon heard the sharpness in her voice. In the back of her mind she heard herself saying the same thing to David Kim.

"Oh, yeah?" Dwayne rubbed his head. "Well, that lady does a lot of things you wouldn't believe."

"Forget it, you two." Carlos spotted the phone on the floor near a side chair. He picked it up, listened, and shook his head. He stared at Wetzon. "Birdie, there's blood on your knee."

"It's Dwayne's. I think we'd better get him to a hospital." She was not about to have him start fussing with her. She also had no intention of accompanying them to the hospital.

Dwayne groaned. "Are you sure my face is all right?"

"What I can see is fine," Wetzon assured him. "I'm worried about Ellie."

"There's a phone and the answering machine in the kitchen," Dwayne said. He started to stand, turned an alarming shade of gray-green, and keeled over.

Wetzon touched his forehead. It was clammy. "Carlos—"

Carlos was on his way to the kitchen. He was back less than a minute later with a clean kitchen towel. "The phone is dead." He wrapped the towel around Dwayne's head like a turban. "There, now you look gorgeous. I'm going to go out on the street and call 911 and get an ambulance."

"No!" Dwayne came to howling. "I don't want an ambulance."

"Carlos, I'll stay with Dwayne and you get a cab. You can take him to Lenox Hill Hospital. They have a good emergency room."

"Okay, Birdie. I'll be right back. Lock the door after me."

She followed him down the hall, disguising her limp magnificently. *I should never have left the theater,* she thought.

After locking up, she went back to the living room, past the squeaky floorboard, and sat down next to Dwayne. She hiked up her skirt and inspected her knee. A nice big tear and plenty of blood. And it smarted when she moved. Where could Ellie be?

"What a mess," Dwayne said, trying to get to his feet.

Wetzon put her hand on his arm and held him down. "Cool it, Dwayne." Light came filtering through the wall of curtains along the rear wall and from three large Chinese porcelain lamps.

Dried blood streaked Dwayne's shirt, which said, SOME OF MY BEST FRIENDS ARE. "What a mess," he said again. He looked at her. "You're bleeding."

"I know."

"Every sliver of glass is a hundred dollars."

"What?"

"The Baccarat vase."

"Oh." Wetzon's eyes skimmed the house-and-garden room, full of chintzes and fat upholstered pieces, set off by a whitebrick fireplace. On the floor near the arched entrance to the room were the remains of the heavy glass vase that had dented Dwayne's head. Except for the water, some bloodstains, and the shards of glass and scattered flowers, nothing looked . . . A chair was overturned near the staircase, and a rust-and-gold geometric oriental rug was lumped up as if someone had tripped over it. A built-in corner china cabinet's drawers were half open, their contents bulging haphazardly.

"Dwayne—" She turned back to him and saw he'd passed out, his bloody head staining the chintz sofa cushions. Damn. She checked her watch. It was eight o'clock. Smith would be having a fit. Too damn bad. Dwayne moaned. Why wasn't Carlos back? She got up and went into the kitchen, which was long and narrow with gray granite countertops and white glass-doored cabinets. There was a full pot of coffee in the coffeemaker, and two cups were set out on the counter.

On an open shelf she saw a white telephone sitting on an answering machine. A little light blinked, indicating someone had left a message. She tried the phone, hoping optimistically that it had healed itself. Not even a dial tone. It was dead. Her eyes followed the white wire of the phone to a jagged end. The phone line had been cut.

She returned to the living room with a cool, wet paper towel and took a close look at Dwayne. Color was back in his face. She'd have to go out on the street and look for Carlos.

The doorbell rang twice, and she dropped the paper towel on the sofa and raced down the hall.

"How did you know who it was, Birdie? You just opened the door without checking," Carlos scolded, spinning her down the hall in front of him. "I have a cab waiting on the street."

Together, they got Dwayne out and into the cab.

"Come on, Birdie," Carlos said, pulling Dwayne closer to him to make room for her.

"I'm not coming. You don't need me. I'm going to leave a note for Ellie and then go meet Smith."

He looked at her doubtfully, and Dwayne groaned.

Wetzon waved them off and went back into Ellie's apartment. She wanted to take a quick look around to make sure Ellie wasn't passed out somewhere, and then she really was going to Baci and have dinner with Smith.

The upstairs space was divided into a front bedroom overlooking the street, with tall windows curtained in sheer white gauze. The walls were papered in a pale gray stripe, the floor covered in pale gray wall-to-wall carpeting. A low queen-sized bed and all the other furniture in the room were in black lacquer, very spare, very sophisticated. The bed was made up formally with a gray-and-white quilted spread. A large armoire stood on the left of the doorway wall, its doors wide open, its contents tossed. Damn.

To her right another door led to a large dressing room, all black and white marble, and further, a huge bathroom sporting a Jacuzzi. *Very nice,* she thought enviously, opening a door on the far wall of the bathroom and walking into another, smaller bathroom.

The back of the house held another bedroom, a guest room with a four-poster bed and lots of frilly linen, also fully made up with an antique quilt, and a big old teddy bear with one eye and a surprised look on its face. But no Ellie.

Wetzon had just started back down the staircase when she froze. Had Carlos come back? No, too soon. From where she stood she could just barely see the arched entrance to the living room. Hand on the banister, she waited, listening, heart thumping.

Now, clearer, the sound came again, and this time she placed it. It was the creak of the loose floorboard.

THIRTY-SEVEN

Wetzon stepped back up the stairs and flattened herself against the side wall. Her hands shook; she could hear her heart. A tall shadow loomed along the wall below. It couldn't be Ellie; Ellie would not be creeping stealthily into her own . . . the tall shadow merged into a real person.

"*Smith!*" Wetzon charged from her hiding place and stood at the top of the staircase.

"Oh!" Smith let out a small shriek and toppled into one of the overstuffed club chairs, holding her hand to her breast. "Wetzon, for pitysakes, you almost gave me a heart attack."

Wetzon limped down the stairs. "Let's not talk about who almost gave who a heart attack," she said, giddy with relief. "What the hell are you doing here?"

"I couldn't wait at that stupid restaurant forever, you know. I hate being stood up."

"I wasn't—"

"So I got into a cab and came on over. I figured you might have run into a problem with Ellie." Her eyes roamed the room.

"But how did you know where to come?"

"The Browns live next door."

"I'm sorry." Wetzon sat down on the sofa and flexed her foot gently. "The Browns?"

"You know the Browns, sugar, that nice young couple. They catered my last party." Smith got up and examined a chalkware dog on the mantelpiece, picking it up and turning it upside down to read the markings.

"I'm still not following you."

"The *Browns,* sweetie pie," Smith said, talking to her gently as if she were retarded. She replaced the chalkware dog. "Jen and Tom Brown live in the duplex above Ellie. I knew she lived here because they asked me if I knew her. Wall Street to Wall Street. We all know each other."

All that trouble trying to find where Ellie lived, and Smith knew all the time. "Why didn't you tell me you knew where she lived?"

"You didn't ask me." Smith was working her way around the room, taking inventory. "Is Ellie lying down? This is a very nice piece." She stroked the fleur-de-lis-inlaid end table. "What's this?" She crouched. "My, how careless. Baccarat," she said, looking up at Wetzon, who was standing now, hands on hips, growing more and more angry.

"Smith, do you see anything you *just* can't live without?" Wetzon asked, dripping sarcasm.

Smith straightened and brushed her hands off on her short cranberry skirt. She gave Wetzon a hurt look. "Smart remarks do not become you, sweetie. What a mess this place is. Did you get Ellie to bed?"

"I didn't find Ellie. I found her assistant lying on the floor with a Baccarat bump on his head."

"Really? So she's one of those violent drunks."

"No, it wasn't Ellie. She wouldn't have done it. The door was open and someone had been here, looking for something—maybe."

"You know, you could have called me." Smith turned back the edge of the oriental rug with the toe of her white slip-on Keds.

"The phone is dead."

"Where's the assistant?" She wandered into the kitchen and came out again.

"Carlos took him to the hospital."

"Carlos? Really, now? You took Carlos when you could have taken me." Her tone was accusatory.

"I didn't know you knew where she lived and her assistant turned out to be one of Carlos's dance students." There she was, on the defensive again.

Smith sat down on the sofa. "You never let me in on anything anymore, sweetie. Aren't we supposed to be partners? We used to have so much fun."

Wetzon sat beside Smith. "Come on, Smith. Things haven't changed." But Wetzon knew they had. Their friendship had always been a rocky affair, close only when Smith was in charge. Smith was definitely an eccentric; always in an adversarial posture, she saw the world differently from Wetzon. In the beginning Wetzon had let Smith's more dominant personality run their business and their friendship, but in the last couple of years a more confident Wetzon had replaced the pliant one, the one Smith missed. "I'm the same person, Smith. I've just grown up. Don't you think it's about time?" She gave Smith's clasped hands a squeeze. "Come on, think about it. I'm still here."

Smith gasped, looking downward. "Your skirt, your knee—"

Wetzon's eyes followed hers. The gash looked pretty ugly. "It'll be okay. I cut it on the glass when I found Dwayne."

"I knew it. The tarot never lies. We'd better get that cleaned up before you get an infection."

"Oh, Smith."

"Listen to me. I'm a mother. I know." She stood up, capturing Wetzon's arm. "Is there a bathroom down here?"

"I didn't see one, but the kitchen—" She paused abruptly. "Wait a minute. Did you lock the outside door?"

"I don't remember." Smith frowned. "I'll check." She went so obligingly down the hall, past the creaking floorboard, that Wetzon smiled. The new Xenia Smith. Wetzon heard the door open, slam shut, the click of locks turned. Then silence.

"Smith?"

Her return was announced with a lilting, "Coming!" And a pronouncement: "That's a lovely piece of tapestry in the foyer."

"Smith!"

"Now then, baby cakes," Smith said, ignoring her, "where were we?"

"*Claire's Knee.*"

"Claire? Oh, I see, another one of your jokes, Wetzon. Spare me."

"It was a French movie."

"Yes, the kitchen." Smith marched into the kitchen, turned on all the water taps and opened all the closets.

"What are you doing, may I ask?" Wetzon said, trailing after her.

"Do you want to take off your skirt?"

"No, I don't. I'll hike it up."

Smith rummaged through a drawer and held up kitchen shears. "Here we are."

"Oh, no."

"Stand still. Don't be a baby. This skirt is ruined anyway." Smith cut the skirt above the tear. "You wear your skirts far too long."

The bottom of the skirt dropped to the floor around Wetzon's ankles and she sighed. "I always loved this skirt."

"Sit down, here. Let me look at your knee." Smith pulled a clean linen towel from another drawer and soaked it, wrung it out, and gently wiped the crusted blood from Wetzon's knee.

The tepid water stung and Wetzon flinched. "Ow!" she said. "That hurts."

"Sweetie, this is deep." Smith's head was bent over Wetzon's knee, her voice was worried. "I'm just going to clean it a little. I think you'll need stitches."

Wetzon's eyes popped open. "Oh, no, I don't want stitches." She looked down at her knee. It was bleeding again. "Shit," she said.

"Oh, yes. I've seen enough of these, believe me, I know."

"Can't we stop the blood?"

"Just stay put," Smith ordered. "There must be bacitracin and Band-Aids in the bathroom upstairs. Don't move."

Smith left Wetzon sitting with her foot up on the second chair. Wetzon closed her eyes. She felt dizzy and nauseated. She opened her eyes. The kitchen clock said nine-fifteen. Food. She looked around the kitchen. She knew she had to eat something—a cracker, something.

The light was still blinking on the answering machine. She could hear Smith's footsteps overhead. This was an old house; it made settling noises. The light on the answering machine blinked on, an invitation. *Not your business,* she told herself.

Then, gingerly, she took her leg off the chair. Blood seeped from the gash and ran in rivulets down her leg. She stared at the wound. Smith was right. It was ugly. The light on the answering machine called out to her, a siren's call. "Fuck it," she said. She limped over and studied it. It was a Panasonic, like her own. Play me, it blinked. She pressed the playback button.

Click, click, clatter, clatter, beep, it said, then a man's voice, "Eight o'clock tonight, Ellie, my place. We have to stick together on this."

Beep.

"Ellie?" Another masculine voice, this one angry. "Ellie! Pick up, damn you, I know you're there. I got your message. Ellie? Do you hear me? Don't do anything stupid. I'm warning you—" Then a hang-up, a few beeps, and the machine clicked off.

"Oh, my God," Smith said. She was standing in the doorway, holding a first-aid kit; her mouth hung open.

"You recognized the voices?"

"Didn't you?" Smith set the first-aid kit down on the granite counter and motioned Wetzon back to the chair.

"Yes." Wetzon sat down and put her leg up on the other chair. "The first voice was Neil and the last was John Hoffritz."

THIRTY-EIGHT

Wetzon watched as Smith squeezed the bacitracin ointment from a tube onto the gauze bandage.

"Hold this," Smith said, handing her the bandage. "I'm going to wash the blood off again. If you'd sat still, it wouldn't be bleeding like this."

"If I'd sat still, we wouldn't have heard Neil tell Ellie about what could be a policy meeting on the salaries, and we wouldn't have heard Hoffritz threaten her—*ouch*. That hurt."

"Give me that." Smith wrapped the wound loosely with the bandage.

"It's going to slip off."

"I'm not going to make it too tight because it'll stop your circulation. Just sit still." She rolled adhesive tape expertly on the top and bottom of the bandage and dumped everything back willy-nilly into the first-aid kit.

"Here, I'll do that," Wetzon said, taking the kit and putting the cap back on the tube, rolling up the gauze.

Smith washed her hands in the sink and dried them on another clean towel. "I'm starving," she announced.

"So am I." Wetzon did a waist bend and picked up the blood-stained remnant of her skirt from the floor. Regretfully, she dropped it into a plastic-lined garbage pail under the sink.

"Well, let's get out of here then. Ellie's obviously gone out to that meeting." Smith chuckled. "Or maybe she went out with dear Johnny Hoffritz."

"Laugh," Wetzon said, "but dear Johnny Hoffritz—all of them, in fact, have sold us out. I wonder what Ellie has on him. Do you suppose he killed Goldie and Ash?"

"Oh, Lord," Smith sighed. "If they wanted to put brokers on salary, and Goldie was against it, it was very convenient for him to die. How's your wound?"

"Actually . . ." Wetzon flexed her leg. "It's okay. You did a good job—Mom." She flexed again and winced. Pink stained the bandage.

"Why do you sound surprised?" Smith was pouring coffee into the two waiting cups. "Don't yap about caffeine, please. A little stimulation will do you good, sweetie, perk you up."

They drank the hot coffee slowly, both lost in their own thoughts.

"There goes my theory about Goldie being killed by accident," Wetzon said.

"Oh, Hoffritz wouldn't be such a fool."

"You're sure of that?"

"Hmmmm, well, they were pushing Goldie out—"

"What if he threatened to go public with their plans before they could get everything in place?"

"I don't know, sweetie. It's very confusing."

"I was certain that Carlton Ash was getting money for keeping something quiet. Now I don't know."

"How do you want to handle it?" Smith put her empty cup on the saucer.

"What?"

"The announcement, of course—if that's what it is—about salaries."

"I think we should not send them any more brokers, collect what they owe us and start raiding *them* with a vengeance. The really entrepreneurial brokers will want to leave." Wetzon took the cups and saucers to the sink, rinsed them, and stacked them in the dishwasher.

"I'm inclined to agree with you. What do you think the meeting at Neil's is about?"

Wetzon shook her head. "Don't know. Maybe the brokers are strategizing, too."

"How about organizing?" Smith walked into the living room, leaving all the kitchen drawers and cabinets yawning. "I have to pee."

Wetzon picked up the first-aid kit, closed the drawers and cabinets and followed her. "Where did you find this?" She held up the kit.

"In the sink cabinet in the second bathroom. I'm going to use Ellie's." Smith ran up the stairs and disappeared.

Wetzon followed her slowly, one step at a time. Her wound had stiffened and felt numb. From the top of the stairs she looked back down at the living room. There was something empty and forlorn about it. She shuddered, dreary thoughts.

She found the light switch on the right-hand wall in the guest bedroom and turned on the light. Two lamps on either side of the bed came on.

The first-aid kit went back under the sink in the bathroom, then she washed her hands and face, dried herself with a guest towel. In the medicine cabinet, she found a bottle of moisturizer and rubbed it into her face and hands. *We are certainly making ourselves at home in Ellie's house,* she thought with a spasm of guilt, as she wandered into the guest bedroom. It was a pretty place. Girlish, almost. The one-eyed teddy bear stared knowingly at her.

"Smith?" Smith didn't respond, but Wetzon heard the toilet flush and the water running.

The window had white ruffled curtains with tie-backs, over closed pink slat blinds. Several books rested on the bedside table, next to a photograph in a silver frame. Guest room or not, this had a personality. You could almost feel it. David Kim? No, certainly not. This was a feminine presence.

She went into Ellie's austere bedroom and knocked on the closed dressing room door. "Smith! Come on!"

"I'll be right out."

She ambled back into the pretty bedroom. The windows must look out over the garden. New Yorkers would kill for a garden. She wondered how Ellie had fixed it up. Every garden in Manhattan was a tiny, unique pocket of a place. It was probably too dark now to see it.

Wetzon opened the pink blinds and looked down. Moonlight drizzled through the dark fuzz of the hot June night. Glazed light came from surrounding apartment windows. She could make out a high fence, a tree, a glimmer of water—perhaps a Lilliputian fish pond—bushes, yard furniture. A striped umbrella attached to a white metal table was open, shading moonbeams.

Positioned near the tree was a cushioned chaise, its back to the windows. Someone had left a towel or piece of clothing on it. She stared down, thinking, choked, backed up into Smith, whom she hadn't heard come into the room.

"Excuse *me*," Smith said.

"Smith—" Wetzon pulled the side cord of the blinds and opened them up and away from the windows.

"What are you doing?"

"Smith, look down there. What do you see?"

Smith glanced down at the garden. "A garden. A big one. This building must be worth a fortune."

"Smith," Wetzon nudged her. "Look at that chaise. What do you see?"

"What do you mean . . . oh, dear God!" She grabbed Wetzon.

Wetzon broke away from her, forgetting about her knee, and made for the stairs.

THIRTY-NINE

"Wait!" Smith's cry flew over Wetzon's head as she plunged down the stairs.

All she could think was, *Ellie* . . . Ellie had been lying out there on the chaise for at least the last two hours, or longer—sick, hurt, perhaps. Wetzon fumbled with the cords, all thumbs, trying to find the right one for the floor-to-ceiling draperies that covered the rear wall of the living room. She finally pulled the proper cord, and the draperies slid open to the left, revealing a door and a large double window. The garden seemed etched in the cold light of the full moon. From here, she couldn't see the figure on the chaise.

Smith's icy fingers touched Wetzon's bare arm. "I don't think we should go out there. She's probably just sleeping off her drunk."

"You don't have to come with me." Wetzon threw open the door leading to the garden and stepped out onto a flagstone deck, narrowly missing a high-heeled sandal, which lay on its side.

Aloft somewhere a plane rumbled sluggishly in its descent toward Kennedy. The air was bloated, hot and moist, hung over with the sweet smell of roses coming from large rambling bushes growing along the western fence. And something else. Whiskey and urine. City street odors, not the odors from a private garden.

The path separated, one route leading to the umbrella'd table she'd seen from upstairs; she followed the other to the small fishpond, the tree, and the chaise.

Marbleized by the moonlight, Ellie's left hand seemed poised over an uncapped bottle of Jack Daniel's that lay on the ground.

"Just look at her," Smith said, coming up beside Wetzon. "What did I tell you?"

Ellie was sprawled on her back in a partially buttoned pink terry robe, head tilted forward over her breast, hair covering her face. Her right hand rested on her waist, not quite holding a rose. The bottom of the robe was askew, barely shielding lacy panties and her legs. One foot was bare; the other wore the mate of the high-heeled sandal.

"Ellie?" Wetzon leaned over her. Clammy sweat formed on her brow and upper lip, ran down her underarms.

"She's wet herself," Smith said. "This is disgusting. I'm going back inside. I suggest you leave her to sleep it off and come with me for dinner." She turned away, starting back.

Wetzon placed her hand on Ellie's forehead and raised her head to the back of the cushion. Ellie's head sagged to the side oddly, as if her neck had no vertebrae. Gently, Wetzon brushed the tangled mass of hair away from Ellie's face. "Oh, God!" Wetzon jumped back, arms flailing, smacked into the trunk of the tree, and held on.

The moonlight shimmered down like a follow spot, highlighting Ellie's face. Her eyes were open, bulging and staring. Wetzon's knees buckled; the earth swayed. "Smith!" The stench of urine was overpowering.

Smith, who had just reached the door to the living room, came running back. "What is it?"

Wetzon pointed at the chaise. Ellie's jaw was slack, hanging open, tongue out, her face distorted and bloated. Pinpoint hemorrhages were dark cobwebs across her eyes, tongue, and cheeks. On her neck and throat were dark bruise marks.

"Is she dead?" Smith's face was ashen in the cold light.

"I think so." Wetzon felt the bitter taste of coffee in her throat. She rubbed her neck as if she were the one with the bruise marks.

"I'm going to be sick," Smith said in a faint voice. She pressed her hand to her mouth, but she didn't move away.

"We've got to call 911. I think she's been strangled," Wetzon said. Her head was spinning, but she, too, couldn't move.

"You're turning green," Smith said. "The Browns will let us in—come on."

"No." Wetzon shook her head. "You go. I'll stay here . . . just in case." *Just in case what?* she asked herself. She tore herself away from the tree. "I'll lock up after you."

"Who could have done it?" Smith whispered, fumbling with the door. They stepped inside. "Close it, close it." She motioned to Wetzon. Wetzon closed the door but didn't draw the draperies, then followed Smith to the front door. "I'll be right back," Smith said. "Just don't go out there."

"Tell 911 to get a message to Silvestri at Midtown North."

"Midtown North." Smith nodded woodenly. Her eyes were glazed.

Wetzon locked up after Smith left. Then she slung the strap of her bag over her shoulder, took a deep breath, and went out to the garden again. The moonlight cast elongated shadows from the surrounding brownstones and the highrises to the south at Lincoln Towers, a cinematographic effect, as if Fritz Lang were directing.

Somewhere nearby a car alarm went off, its relentless whine cutting through the quiet. People were inside hiding in air-conditioned rooms, barricaded against the heat of the streets and their fellow man. No one inside could possibly hear the alarm over the drone of air conditioners. It seemed so fruitless. Tears ran down Wetzon's cheeks. Poor Ellie. She hardly seemed the kind of person who would let a stranger into her home, but she'd been drinking and possibly forgot to lock up, which was something one didn't dare to do in New York anymore.

Or it could have been someone she knew. Wetzon stopped at the fishpond. An empty tin floated on the surface, along with—she counted—seven dead goldfish of varying sizes and colors. Had someone attacked Ellie while she was feeding the fish, making her drop the whole container of food into the pond?

She knew better than to touch anything at a murder scene. On a blank page, which she pulled from her Filofax, she wrote *fishpond—fish food,* then, *answering machine messages.* She would mention those to Silvestri.

Steeling herself, she looked more closely at Ellie. It was horrible. And worse, there was something surreal about the scene, almost as if it had been artfully created. Ellie lay there like a composition, with a rose in one hand. But on closer scrutiny, although her hand was indeed clenched, she wasn't really holding the rose. Someone had placed it there; someone had posed her on the chaise, having strangled her elsewhere. The fish pond, perhaps. *Come on, Wetzon,* she thought. *You have nothing to base that one on except gut instinct.*

Wetzon touched the terry cloth robe at Ellie's shoulder. It was damp, damper than it should have been for a hot summer night. She shuddered and pressed her lips together tightly, ran back to the living room, slammed the door shut and leaned against it, panting. She would never get used to death as long as she lived . . . Hysterical laughter burbled up from her diaphragm. She sank to the floor.

The doorbell rang. Twice. Three times. Emphatically. Pounding.

Wetzon scrambled to her feet and let Smith in.

"They weren't home," Smith complained. "I had to call from the street." Smith looked a bit ragged. "I can't believe I'm involved in something like this." A trickle of pleasure colored this last comment. "I'm happy to see you stayed inside."

"What did you tell them?"

"I said someone's been murdered and to get a message to the Italian prince."

"You didn't!" Wetzon stared at Smith, outraged, then she laughed. "You're terrible."

"You're not the only one with a sense of humor, you know." Smith took Wetzon's shoulders in her hands and gave her a little shake. "I didn't say it, but I wanted to." She considered Wetzon. "You look ghastly. We can both use another cup of coffee."

Wetzon's head throbbed. Her face felt stiff where the salt of her tears had dried, and a gnawing pain, half nausea, half hunger, clawed at her stomach.

Smith pulled a bag of pretzels from the pantry, tore the bag open and held it out to Wetzon. "Ellie's beyond minding," she said, reaching into a cabinet and taking down two coffee mugs.

They sat at the kitchen table like zombies, spent.

"How long do you think they'll be?" Wetzon asked, catching the drip of the coffee down the side of the mug with her finger before it hit the table. She licked her finger.

"You know this City as well as I do."

They both heard the sound at the same moment, their heads

snapping up, eyes meeting, widening. Wetzon set her mug down gently, put her finger to her lips, and rose. The sound came again.

"What was that?" Smith rasped.

"Shshsh." Wetzon shook her head vigorously.

There it was again. A rattling sound, as if someone were trying the front door.

She turned to Smith, who had come up behind her and was clutching her arm with clammy fingers. The sound stopped. They both took a breath and fell into each other's arms, giggling. "We're stupid," Wetzon whispered.

But there it came again—only different.

Someone was unlocking—*unlocking*—the front door. Wetzon tiptoed out to the living room, Smith at her heels, barely breathing.

Who was it with a key? Certainly not the EMS or the police. Someone like David Kim? The murderer returning to the scene of the crime? Who?

Smith's cold hand clasped hers. They stood just beyond the doorway to the kitchen, listening.

The outside door opened. A dull thud as of something heavy that was dropped. Then a yell. "Hi, Mom, I'm home."

FORTY

Smith released Wetzon's hand, and Wetzon's first thought was, *What is Mark doing here?* But this wasn't Mark. She shook her head trying to clear her thoughts. *Ellie had a daughter.*

"Mom?" Rapid footsteps came closer. The floorboard creaked.

Tell her, tell her. Wetzon propelled herself into the doorway. "Please don't be frightened," she said. The figure in front of her stopped. "We're friends of your mother—" She motioned to Smith.

A girl of about eleven or twelve came into the room, puzzlement distorting her features, her long red hair in the intentionally wild, unkempt fashion of the day. "Where's my mother?" she asked, looking around.

Wetzon exchanged concerned glances with Smith, who said, "I'm Xenia and this is Leslie."

"I'm Melissa."

"Well, Melissa—" Wetzon stopped short. She felt a lump in her throat yea big.

"Come sit down, Melissa," Smith chimed in. "You're a bit of a surprise."

"I know." Melissa brushed her hair from her face in a gesture reminiscent of Ellie. "I said I'd be home tomorrow, but I got a ride." She was wearing shiny blue short tights that ended about midthigh, red ankle-high Reeboks and a trimmed cotton shirt that rode off one skinny shoulder. Lolita.

The doorbell rang.

"Oh, dear," Smith said. She looked at Wetzon.

"Melissa . . . oh, God." Wetzon swallowed. Smith put her arm around Melissa and nodded for Wetzon to continue. They stood awkwardly near the archway entrance to the living room. Melissa's eyes traveled beyond them to the open draperies.

The doorbell rang again.

"Melissa," Wetzon said, thinking she'd seen Melissa before somewhere, or a picture of her. "Your mother's been in an accident."

The girl's face blanched. "Where is she? Is she okay?"

"Hold on to me, sugarplum," Smith said with unusual gentleness. She steered Melissa to the sofa and sat down with her.

Pounding came from the door. "Police. Open up."

Wetzon raced down the hall, almost tripping over the huge canvas duffel bag and leather knapsack near the door. "Just a minute, I'm coming," she called, and yanked the door open.

A uniformed policeman—short, thick-waisted, and sweating—stood in the vestibule, two EMS attendants behind him. Beyond them on the street, competing, were the whirling lights of the squadcar and the blinking lights from the EMS van. His eyes took in her snarled hair, puffy eyes, bandaged knee. "You are Ms. Smith?" His mustache covered his upper lip; his nametag read KALISH.

"I'm Leslie Wetzon. Ms. Smith is inside with Ellie Kaplan's daughter." Wetzon stood aside to let them in, kicking the baggage out of the way.

A plaintive howl came from the living room, and when Wetzon followed the traffic down the hall, she saw Melissa struggling to get to the garden, Smith trying to pull her back to the sofa.

"Please, miss, stand aside," Kalish said, firmly. "You don't want to be out there. It's best to let the EMS guys handle it. They know what to do."

Melissa crumpled, and Smith helped her back to the sofa.

A lanky policewoman, her dark skin shining with sweat, appeared. She took off her hat and wiped her face with a big white handkerchief, and looked around, puzzled.

"They're outside," Wetzon said, standing near the windows. "In the garden."

The policewoman replaced her hat and went out to the garden.

Dazed, Melissa was sitting bolt upright, her hands twisted together in her lap. Smith looked sick.

Wetzon knew the place would soon be swarming with detectives, technicians, and medical specialists, not to mention someone from the D.A.'s office. This was no place for a child. It was no place for anybody.

Abruptly, the EMS attendants trooped back through the living room and left the apartment. There was nothing anyone could do for Ellie anymore.

The policewoman stepped into the living room and closed the door to the garden. "Where's the phone?" The tag on her breast said ANDREWS.

"It's in the kitchen, but the wire's been cut," Wetzon said.

Andrews shrugged and thumped down the hall and out.

Melissa had all but disintegrated in Smith's arms, and Smith didn't look too copacetic herself. *So much for the pleasure she had felt about being involved,* Wetzon thought. Agitated, she walked down the hall and stood in the front doorway. The siren blast from the EMS van filled the air for a minute as the van pulled away from the curb, then silence, broken from time to time by radio static from the squadcar. A small, curious crowd had gathered. Another squadcar pulled up where the EMS van had been, and a cop methodically began to put up a barricade in front of the entrance and string yellow tape around. He hummed off-key as he worked.

Sweating and shivering simultaneously, Wetzon pressed her forehead against the cool doorjamb. Ellie's daughter. Why had she never mentioned—?

An unmarked car arrived and two detectives got out. They stopped to speak to Andrews, who sat in her cruiser talking on the radio. She pointed to Wetzon. A second car disgorged technicians and equipment. A third car pulled up with a screech of tires and Silvestri and Weiss got out of the front, Metzger from the back.

Wetzon watched all the gold shields flash at each other and choked back a giggle. Then she stepped aside and let them all troop by, Silvestri hanging back last. "Why are you always at the murder scene, lady?" he said over his shoulder.

She followed him. "That's a rhetorical question, isn't it?"

"What's that bandage for?" This time he didn't bother to turn around, just kept walking.

She caught up with him. "It's nothing—a scratch. Silvestri, it was awful." She felt as if her face were melting, eyes drooping, cheeks slipping into her jaw.

He turned and slipped his arm around her shoulders.

"Out here," Weiss said, poking his head in from the garden.

Wetzon looked around the living room. Smith and Melissa were gone. Had they taken the girl out to see her mother? God. No. No one would be that cruel. "Where—"

"I told the woman and the kid to wait upstairs out of the way." Weiss dematerialized.

Silvestri took in the staircase, then surveyed the rest of the room. He noted the broken glass, the open drawers. "What time did you get here?"

"About seven-thirty, quarter to eight."

She told him about Ellie's call and about coming in with Carlos and finding Dwayne. He listened, nodding. "Go on upstairs," he said. "Try not to touch anything."

"Couldn't I just hang around here for a while? I'll stay out of the way." She sat on the sofa. "See."

He shrugged and put his head in the kitchen. "Why should I think this time you'll listen to me?" It was another rhetorical question.

"Smith and I had coffee after she cleaned up my cut." She caught his frown. "We didn't know there was anything wrong. I mean, we knew there was something wrong, we just didn't know Ellie was dead. We thought she was at the meeting—"

"What meeting?"

"The one Neil mentions on the answering machine. Oh, God, I'm sorry. There are two messages on the answering machine in the kitchen."

"Jesus H. Christ, Les, everything is always so complicated when you're involved." He went out and yelled for one of the uniforms. "I want someone in here to inventory the kitchen," he said when an older, stout giant appeared.

Wetzon let her head loll on the back of the sofa; she was exhausted. Her eyes followed Silvestri into the entrance to the garden, already strung with CRIME SCENE tape. The small spot was crowded with cops and officials. No one paid any attention to her. She got up and climbed the stairs. No one was in Ellie's room. She found Smith and Melissa curled up together, both asleep on Melissa's frilly bed.

Sighing, she went back downstairs. She was very tired. She kicked her sandals off and settled into the womb of the overstuffed sofa. If one didn't know better, the activity in the garden looked as if there were a party going on.

Wetzon leaned back and closed her eyes. What, she wondered, would become of Melissa? Did Ellie have an ex-husband around somewhere? She conjured up the child's face. She looked like Ellie . . . no, she didn't . . . yet she looked familiar.

She was becoming drowsy; her eyelids felt weighted; the sofa was so soft. Who . . . Wetzon felt herself sinking into sleep, but she knew.

Melissa looked like Twoey.

FORTY-ONE

It was snowing a confetti of little bits of paper, but this time she knew she was dreaming because no way would it snow during a New York June heat wave. She awoke all tangled in the top sheet and quilt, tense and sweaty. That was it for fitful and disturbed sleep. She didn't need it.

The white box of her Sony clock beamed five-thirty at her. She turned off the alarm, which was set for six-thirty, and put her feet on the floor. A burning pain shot up her leg. Blast! She'd forgotten about her cut, which a doctor at Roosevelt Hospital had cleaned, stitched up, and lightly bandaged in the wee hours. It had been about two-thirty when she'd finally crawled into bed. And then she'd lain there trying to wipe the chilling image of Ellie Kaplan out of her mind.

Silvestri hadn't come home at all. He seemed to make do very well with much less sleep than she needed, she thought resentfully.

She did a messy bath in the sink because she was not supposed to get her stitches wet and ended up with a swamp, water everywhere. Her mirror reflected back at her a haggard witch of a woman. *You're not going to be young and cute forever, at this rate,* she told herself. She filled her glass with water and threw it at the reflection. *Take that, you old bag.* Her reflection dissolved into rivulets and she laughed. *You've lost it, Wetzon.*

In the kitchen, hobbling, she did her coffee routine with her ancient Melitta, then checked her answering machine, which was blinking.

"Dwayne is okay, but is giving Lenox Hill his bod for the night," Carlos said. "Birdie? Are you there? Where are you at this hour? You're obviously not there. Well, I'm where I'm supposed to be. So ta-ta and all that."

The other, infinitely more intriguing message, came after the next beep. It was from Doug Culver. Just his name and phone number in that soft drawl of his.

She dawdled over orange juice and her line-up of vitamins, then took her mug of coffee into the dining room, eyeing the barre, which she didn't dare use lest she open the stitches. Something in particular was prodding her, something that had troubled her sleep. Confetti. Scraps of paper.

She found the scraps of paper she'd filched from Ellie's blue makeup bag in her coin purse and spread them out on her dining room table, turning them this way and that, to position the pieces with writing face up. Some of the pieces were blank on both sides. She stared at what she had and shifted the pieces again, and again. Some pieces had to be missing because . . . it was like working with a complicated jigsaw puzzle. Uh-oh . . . wait one fine minute here.

Across the top she pieced together a heading: *Memora   ton Ash.* What followed looked like a list of names and addresses, with numbers after the names on the right-hand side of the paper. Social Security numbers? No, not enough digits. She frowned. This was a photocopy, not an original. And Ash may or may not have written it on his stationery.

She found a piece of her own gray stationery. Rolling a bit of transparent tape around her finger, she mounted each scrap the way one preserved a stamp collection. Once the mock-up of the note was complete, she made a tube of it and slipped it in a baggie, then put the baggie in her briefcase. Silvestri would take it the next step, if a next step were warranted.

At seven she called Smith. "Did I wake you? How's Melissa?" Melissa Kaplan had spent the night with Smith, at Smith's insistence, in Mark's room.

"No, you didn't wake me. Gail Munchen woke me. And Melissa's in shock."

"Neil's wife? How did she know where Melissa was?"

"I don't know and I don't care. Why don't you ask how *I* feel?"

"How *do* you feel, Smith?"

"Beat up, thank you very much. She's coming for Melissa in about an hour, after her tennis class."

"Gail?"

"What's the matter with you, Wetzon? I'm being perfectly clear," Smith snapped.

"Gee, I'm sorry. I didn't have the same experience you had last night, did I?"

"Oh, for pitysakes! Why are you being so sensitive? I can't worry about you and your feelings right now." The whistle of a teakettle shrilled. "Gail said Ellie would have wanted her to take Melissa. I'm making tea."

"I'll come over and have breakfast with you."

"Bring some muffins and some milk—and coffee, if you want decaf. I'm out."

When Wetzon arrived with a bag of groceries from Zabar's, Melissa was sitting at Smith's dining table staring at a tulip champagne glass of orange juice. She looked wan and heartbreakingly younger than her twelve years. The doctor had given her a sedative the previous night. Now smudges bled from under her eyes into her pale cheeks. Her jaunty outfit from the day before managed to look droopy and inappropriate for the morning after her mother's violent death.

Gail Munchen turned up only minutes later, young, very blond, and moderately pregnant. She wore a loose red cotton top over pink cotton leggings and Tretorn sneakers and carried a tennis racket in a canvas cover with G.L.M. in gold letters.

"How far are you along, dear?" Smith asked. "Will you have tea or coffee?" Smith's face was still sodden with sleep, or the lack of it, and Gail's fresh, youthful appearance was a marked contrast that even Smith could not miss.

"Five and a half months. Orange juice." Gail gave Melissa a hug and kissed the top of her head, stroking her wild hair.

Smith glowered at Gail and stepped into the kitchen. Wetzon smiled. Smith was behaving as if she'd had the tragedy in her life and everyone was being selfish and uncaring.

"I'll get my things," Melissa murmured. Head down, she left the room, her orange juice untouched.

"This is a terrible thing," Gail said to Wetzon.

"I would have been happy to keep Melissa. She's a lovely child," Smith said, handing Gail a tulip glass of orange juice. "But my work, you know . . ."

"Ellie was a good friend to us. She would want us to take Melissa."

"Why don't you sit down for a moment?" Smith said, picking at the ink stains on her fingers, the remnant of last night's fingerprinting. Wetzon's were already on file with the department, and Ellie's apartment had been thoroughly dusted. "Of course, you'll have to get in touch with her father."

Wetzon started, remembering her feeling that Melissa and Twoey looked enough alike to be related. Brother and sister? Goldie's progeny. Goldie's *heirs*. And Goldie was dead.

Gail did not respond to Smith's ploy for information, but lowered herself into a chair.

"Weren't you concerned when Ellie didn't show up for the meeting last night?" Wetzon asked, cutting a bran muffin into quarters. She felt, rather than saw, Smith's attention.

"Oh, you know about it, then?" Gail looked at Smith, then at Wetzon.

"Well, of course we do," Smith said. "We're with Neil all the way."

"Actually, I think Alton was even more upset than Neil. They thought she'd copped out on them, but I told them Ellie isn't that kind. She's true to her word."

Alton, Wetzon thought, chewing on a piece of the bran muffin. *Alton Pinkus.* She said, "Alton is a visionary if he thinks brokers can be organized." She wiped her greasy fingers on a small paper napkin she pulled from a package Smith had dumped rather ungraciously on the table.

"I would see it more as a threat to management, wouldn't you, Gail dear?" Smith asked coyly.

"Only if Luwisher backs down and the other firms don't go along. If it should become Street policy, the brokers will go union," Gail said.

"They'll have to," Wetzon added, "to survive."

Smith's scowl at Wetzon was lost because at that moment Melissa dragged her duffel into the foyer, and Smith muttered, "She's scratching my floor."

"Here, let me help you." Gail got to her feet.

After Gail and Melissa left, Smith piled the dishes in the sink and Wetzon packed away the muffins.

They cabbed it to the office and got there in time to hear the market was dropping like a stone. It had opened down ten on bad news about the trade deficit. Then word seeped out that the junk bonds for the LBO of Southeast Delta weren't selling. The halcyon days of leveraged buyouts were over. Down twenty-five. By ten-thirty the program-trading sell orders kicked in and the market really began to plummet.

Over the wire came Luwisher Brothers's announcement that brokers would be offered a salaried base up to $250,000 of gross commissions earned. Anyone grossing more than that would earn incremental bonuses. The announcement officially marked the death knell for commission sales, at least at Luwisher Brothers. Whether the other firms would follow remained to be seen.

Laura Lee had called with the news, saying, "Don't freak out."

"Thanks a heap, Laura Lee, bearer of glad tidings." Wetzon hung up. "Well, they did it." She looked over at Smith, who had a pensive expression on her face. "'Every day a little death,'" Wetzon sighed. "So now we know what the meeting was about."

"I thought that was very clever of me." Smith came out of her fugue.

"Yes, very clever. You did it all yourself." Smith was at her narcissistic best and was beginning to irritate her.

"I didn't see anything in *The Times* about Ellie."

"*The Times* doesn't follow murders, usually."

Smith opened the door to the reception room. "B.B., run out and get the *News* and the *Post*, there's a dear. Harold can cover the phones."

"We've had some calls from Luwisher brokers who want to jump ship. What do we do?" Harold stood in the doorway behind B.B. atypically well-dressed in a new light-gray pinstripe and yellow power tie.

"That was fast. Just say I'll get back to them, not to do anything in haste," Wetzon said.

"We shouldn't say we work for the firm and can't take them out?" B.B. asked.

"Not yet," Smith said. "This is only Thursday—by Monday we may no longer be working for them. Be circumspect. They owe us money. We can't look as if we're taking brokers out, even if we are. On your way, B.B." She closed the door.

"I'm supposed to have dinner with Chris Gorham tonight." Wetzon rubbed her tired eyes and smeared her mascara. "Damn!"

"Eat with brokers, get up with fleas."

Wetzon laughed. "I think the expression is, sleep with dogs, get up with fleas."

"I know that, for pitysakes." Smith sat down at her desk and pawed through her papers. "I'll probably have to tell Hoffritz and Bird who we think murdered Goldie. They called." She held up her messages. "So leave Monday clear."

"Enlighten me, oh sagacious one," Wetzon intoned. "Who did it? We've lost one of our suspects, so now we're down to"—she ticked them off on her fingers—"Hoffritz, Bird, Culver, Gorham, Munchen, that's five, and David Kim is six."

"If I had to choose now, I couldn't, and I've never even met this David Kim person," Smith admitted. "But I'm going to do a deep meditation tonight before I consult the tarot, and I'm sure it will all come to me."

The phone rang, stopped, rang again, stopped. A light blinked. "There's a call on hold. Harold must be on the first line."

Come to think of it, Harold was pretty unobtrusive today, Wetzon thought, considering the condition of the market and the explosive announcement from Luwisher Brothers. *Subdued* was a better word. But subdued in an expensive new suit and tie. Maybe he was thinking he might be forced to go to graduate school after all, as he'd originally planned when he'd been their summer intern.

Wetzon picked up the third line when the phone rang again. "Smith and Wetzon."

"I'll come by for you at six." It was Chris Gorham and he sounded harassed.

"How did the announcement go over?"

"Great. At least no one has gotten up and left. I hear Merrill and Shearson are creaming."

"It's awful about Ellie, isn't it?"

"Yeah, well, you can't always keep your clients happy."

She wasn't even shocked. Long ago, she'd learned the denizens of the Street had particularly ghoulish senses of humor and spewed out vulgarities with a relish that defied good taste. "It could have been a break-in, or perhaps it's related to Goldie and Dr. Ash."

"Sure," Chris said offhandedly. "She killed them and then killed herself because she couldn't live with it."

"Chris, that makes no sense. Ellie was strangled."

"Whatever you say, Wetzon. The auditors are here and I'm up to my ass." He hung up.

Baffled, Wetzon cradled the phone. Was she crazy or were everyone's reactions decidedly odd today, starting with Smith and ending with Chris Gorham?

B.B. had returned with the papers, and Smith was holding up the *Post*, shaking it at Wetzon. The headline read: STOCKBROKER STRANGLED. A picture of Ellie in a bathing suit, looking twenty years younger, decorated the bottom left of the front page.

"Tasteful," Wetzon said. "I hope Melissa doesn't see that."

The phone rang.

The *News* headline, like the *Post*'s in heavy 100-point type, screamed, MILLION $ MURDER, and hinted at dark secrets involving sex and money with Ellie's business at Luwisher Brothers, citing unnamed sources.

B.B. knocked at their open door. "Destry Bird for you, Smith."

"Okay. Close the door, please." Smith dropped the papers on the floor and reached for the phone. "This is it. We've got to know by Monday." Her look at Wetzon was accusing, as if it were Wetzon's fault they didn't know who did it. "Destry, congratulations," she oozed seductively into the phone. "Well done." She listened intently. "Monday. No, we'll come to you. After the close is fine." She replaced the receiver.

"Goddammit, you should never have told them we knew. You've made us an open target." All the pent-up fury Wetzon had been holding back came spewing out.

"Nonsense." Smith sucked on her stained fingertips.

"In all the mess about Ellie, I never got the chance to tell Silvestri what you did, but I will. And he'll be furious."

"Oh, my, I'm just shivering with fear," Smith drawled.

"It was a particularly stupid thing to do, Smith. You've put our lives in danger—"

"Puh-leeese, Wetzon, you constantly overdramatize everything. All those years in the theater . . ." Smith let her words hang there.

"Oh, shut up, Smith." Wetzon jerked out her chair, then plunked herself down. Smith made her feel like a pouting child, yet Wetzon knew she was right. "Doug Culver called me last night."

"Oh? What did he want?"

"I wasn't home, remember? I'm going to call him back now. Do you think he knows you told Hoffritz who the—"

"Don't say anything, sweetie pie, just in case."

"'Don't say anything, sweetie pie,'" Wetzon muttered. She punched out Dougie's direct number.

"Doug Culver."

The outside doorbell rang.

"Doug, this is Wetzon. You called me last night? I was at Ellie's—"

"Oh? Tragic."

"Yes." She let a vacuum develop, waiting for him to say something to fill it, which he finally did.

"Do you have plans for dinner?"

"Yes, I do. What's on your mind, Dougie?"

"I hear you gals know who murdered Goldie."

"How on earth did you hear that?"

"Everyone here knows. You can't keep something like that a secret for very long. Is it true?"

B.B. knocked at their door.

"Come," Smith called. "What do you have there?"

"A package for Wetzon and Mr. Barnes on the phone for you, Smith."

"No, it's not true, Doug."

"Well, fine, then. I'd like to try an idea out on you, Wetzon," Dougie was saying.

"Me? I'm flattered." Wetzon played with the clasp of the package, which was candy-box sized, in a fat manila envelope sealed with thick tape. "How about if I call you when I get home? Where do you live?"

"Gramercy Park." He gave her his phone number.

Wetzon hung up the phone and looked over at Smith, who was making love to the telephone. Sighing, she turned her attention to the package. No return address. She picked it up and turned it over, squeezing it gently. It wasn't a book. She reached for the letter opener. Stopped. The label said "Wetzon, Smith and Wetzon," in dot matrix printing. *Private and Confidential* was written directly under their names.

She stood up slowly. What was it? She held the envelope in front of her. Was she being stupid or overreacting or—

Smith hung up the phone. "Where are you going?" she demanded.

Wetzon didn't answer her. Her only thought was, *Get it out of here.* She opened the door to the garden and ran out into a wall of heat and humidity. *Move it, move it,* she told herself. She set the envelope down carefully on the bricks in the middle of the garden and ran back to the office. "Smith," she cried, "get away from the window!" She pulled Smith after her into the reception room and closed the door. "Everybody, down. Now! B.B., call 911," she commanded.

Smith, still standing hands on hips, began, "What is the matter with you, Wetzon? I—"

A loud boom, like a giant backfire, came from their garden, followed almost immediately by the sound of shattering glass.

FORTY-TWO

A deadly stillness.

Wetzon raised her head and looked around. She was kneeling in front of B.B.'s desk. Smith was prostrate, mouth agape, on one of the chairs. Harold stood in the doorway of his cubicle, looking dazed. Her bad knee began throbbing.

B.B. was clutching the receiver in midair, speechless, while a metallic voice repeated, with increasing irritation, "911 operator, hel*lo*."

From their inner office, Wetzon heard a delicate tinkling sound and hoped it wasn't the glass on their Andy Warhol drawing. She stood up and took the phone from B.B.'s rigid fist, giving the emergency operator her name and their address. "I think," she said, very calmly, "a bomb just went off in our garden."

"A bomb?" B.B.'s eyes were blue pennies.

"Jesus." Harold took his glasses off and rubbed his face.

"I don't believe this! I don't believe any of this," Smith muttered.

The phone rang. "At least our phones are still working." Wetzon opened the door to the inner office with trepidation.

"Smith and Wetzon," B.B. said in a squeaky voice behind her.

Shards of glass lay everywhere, smithereens. And dirt—garden dirt, shreds of plants and flowers. It must have been blown through the windows, all of which were broken. The air conditioner groaned mightily, surging, not comprehending why it had become impossible to cool the large room. The blinds hung awry, twisted and torn by the blast. They would have to be replaced. The smell of sulphur, as if a thousand matches had been lit all at once, filled the room.

Suspect sheets and papers and loose pages of newspapers were scattered helter-skelter on the floor, but that seemed to be all the damage. Andy Warhol was whole.

A siren came closer and then stopped in front of their office. Wetzon came back through the reception area and opened the door to the street. The heat and humidity fell on her, weighing her down. She rubbed her tearing eyes. A blue-and-white van that looked like a combination tank and cement mixer was parked in front of the house. And in front of the van was a red fire car with a blinking red light on its roof.

"Please, sugar, I'm all right," she heard Smith say irritably. "Of course I miss you, but I can't talk now because the police are here."

Leave it to Jake to phone at the proper time, Wetzon thought.

Another siren shrieked over and over, and a fire engine turned down the street from First Avenue. Three hulking spacemen in blue padded suits and blue caps came toward her carrying metal suitcases. She could hear them bitching about the firemen and hoped this wasn't going to become a competition between the police and fire departments, as it often was in New York.

"It's already gone off," Wetzon said. "In the garden." She followed them as they tramped through the mess on the floor and out the back door, which had been blown off its hinges.

Two sweating firemen in rubber coats trudged through, carrying axes. "Stand back, Miss," one of the men said. Another lifted the door and leaned it against the side wall. They went out slowly, checking the area, and collided with the two men from the NYPD bomb squad.

"Hey, this is our job, get the fuck outta here. You're destroying evidence," a burly fireman said.

"Can it," one of the spacemen from the bomb squad replied. "There's no fire here. You boys can take your little red engine and go back to your little red house."

"Listen, you muth—"

"Hey, you guys," Wetzon, pissed off, called from the dirt-laden brick deck. "A bomb exploded here. Can we please concentrate on that?"

The garden was a mess. Chunks of bricks lay everywhere; plants were uprooted. She could see a charred hole where she had set the envelope. People were standing at windows, calling down questions. Some of the windows looked blown, though most of the explosion seemed to have been contained in the garden.

"This is what happens when you get us involved in one of your murders," Smith hissed, just behind her.

"When I? When who? Goddammit, Smith." Wetzon found herself quivering. "This is *your* doing. We're lucky we're not in little slivers all over this room."

Smith burst into tears. *Dammit,* Wetzon thought. And not one clean spot to sit or stand.

"Oh, shit, stop that. Go home. I'm sorry. I'll take care of everything." Wetzon put her arm around Smith. Why did she always end up apologizing to Smith for something Smith had done? "Harold!"

Harold was standing in the doorway gawking at the chaos. The phones rang incessantly. "B.B., get the goddam phones. Harold, go out and get a cab. Smith is going home."

"I can't go home," Smith sniffled. "Our papers, our work." She pulled a tissue from a box on her desk, shook off the dirt, and dried her eyes.

"We'll take care of it. You go home and get into bed. I'll call you later."

"Cab's outside," Harold crooned. "Do you want me to see you home, Smith?"

"No," Wetzon said, walking Smith to the cab. "My, isn't he sweet and solicitous."

"Who?"

"Harold." She smiled. "Gee, Smith, we must have made Tom Keegen really mad."

"Tom Keegen?" Smith had opened the cab door. "You think this was his doing?"

"No! Don't get so excited. I was kidding. No, what I'm really saying is, this is what I warned you about. Telling Hoffritz we know who the murderer is has put our lives in danger."

"You're wrong. It was Tom Keegen. I know." Smith got into the cab and closed the door. The cab pulled away, then screeched to a stop and backed up. Smith rolled down the window. "The Tarot never lies. Call me later."

Spare me, Wetzon thought. Trust Smith to try to cast off culpability. She said, "I'm having dinner with Chris."

"Good. Work him over, but be careful. He may be the one."

"I doubt it, but thanks."

Smith rolled up the window and the cab took off.

"Silvestri," Wetzon murmured. It was all getting too confusing.

Three more technicians, probably fire department because they came in a red station wagon, arrived and began combing through the debris in the garden, packing things up in plastic bags. Wetzon gathered up the storm of papers and sorted them, which were hers, which were Smith's.

"B.B., see if you can get Mr. Diamantidou over here," she said. "I want a glazier to fix these windows today. Without air-conditioning, we won't be able to work."

After a technician sifted through the mess in the office, Wetzon swept the dirt and glass from the desktops to the floor and then gathered the floor mess into one pile in case the bomb detectives wanted to go through it once more. *Silvestri,* she thought again. She couldn't put off calling him. The office was uncomfortably warm although she'd left the air conditioner on . . . but of course, there were no windows . . . Her knees began to shake violently. She tipped her chair to empty it of glass and dirt and sat down, putting her head on the desk. A hand touched her arm and she jumped.

"Sorry, Miss. Didn't mean to startle you. I'm Sergeant Gans. I'd like to go over what happened." Gans was well over six feet tall, and broad, broader still because of the padding. Sweat stood out in glistening beads on his face, dripped from under his cap, and ran through his hair, which was long even for a present-day cop.

"A bulky package came—"

"In the mail?"

"I don't know. I don't remember postage on it. B.B?"

"Yes?" B.B. came to the door. There was a long smear of dirt on his face.

"Did that package come in the mail?"

"No. A messenger delivered it."

"Did you sign for it?" Gans asked.

"No . . . yes. Yes, I think so." B.B. rubbed his cheek, smearing more dirt on his face. "Wait. Yes." He went back to his desk and began searching through papers. "I know it's here."

"Take your time," Gans said.

"Sergeant." Wetzon returned to her desk and sat down. She was beat. Her neck and shoulders were stiff. Her knee was killing her. At this rate it would never heal. "Close the door and pull up a chair," she said.

Gans closed the door and pulled Smith's chair over, shaking off a gnarled bit of rosebush, and sat down near Wetzon.

"I'm working with the P.D. as a consultant on a case," Wetzon said. "There've been three murders of Wall Street people." She stopped. Gans was listening politely, but he was registering doubt.

"Let me get this straight. You got this package, but didn't open it." He took off his cap and mopped his head, which was mostly bare scalp, with a handkerchief. Wetzon wondered whether he combed the long side hair over the bald spot when he was off duty. Gans put the cap back on and took out a notepad. "What made you take it outside? And good thing you did," he added.

"I don't know. No return address . . . Intuition . . . Something. Look, I know you're having trouble believing me, and I'm having trouble finding words for all this." She swept her hand around the room. "Call Midtown North. Ask for either Lieutenant Silvestri, or Weiss . . . or Sergeant Metzger. Here." She shoved the phone at him. "Wait." She found her Filofax undamaged in her briefcase under her desk, looked up the direct number and gave it to him.

Gans punched out the number and waited. "Silvestri," he said. "Gans, bomb squad."

"Excuse me," Wetzon said. "I'd rather not be involved in another explosion." Gans threw her a this-lady-is-off-the-wall as she went into the bathroom and closed the door, turning on the cold-water tap full force. She washed her face and neck, patted the moisture off with a paper towel, and stared at her drawn face in the mirror. Strings of hair flew every which way. *You do look insane,* she thought. No wonder Gans hadn't believed her. She undid her topknot and combed her hair with her fingers, rolling it up again into a neat knot. *Okay, Wetzon old girl,* she thought. *Gird your loins.* She opened the door.

"Yeah. We have a piece of the envelope," Gans said. "The kid is looking for the messenger slip. Yeah. One big firecracker can do a shitload of damage. Yeah." He looked at Wetzon. "Here she is." He held out the phone.

She took the receiver and lilted cheerily, "Hi, there."

"Les." Silvestri cleared his throat. "Gans says you're okay."

"I am. I'm fine. I'm scared, though. I should have mentioned it yesterday, but with everything . . . Smith told the guys at Luwisher Brothers that we know who the murderer is and we'll tell them on Monday."

"Of all the fucking, harebrained—"

"Stop!"

"That's it. I want you off the case."

"It's too late for that." She could hear him fuming over the wires. "I'm having dinner with Chris Gorham tonight and Doug Culver called me. I'm supposed to call him back later tonight."

Gans got up and looked outside. The head of the fire department crew came over and they talked quietly, turning once and looking at Wetzon.

"Fuck that shit, Les." Exasperation colored his every carefully spaced word.

"Silvestri, please—just give me some protection. And Smith, too, I guess."

"I'd feel a damn sight better if you were out of this, but I know you'd find a way back in. Okay, okay. I'll cover you. How long will you be there?"

"I'm going to call Chris and see if I can meet him at the restaurant."

A triumphant shout came from B.B.

"Les, be careful. 'No chances, do you hear me?"

"Yes, honest, Silvestri. I'll be good. You can depend on that."

"That's what I'm afraid of." He hung up.

The door popped open with a bang-slam. "I found it." B.B. was waving a yellow slip of paper. "It was in my pocket all the time."

Wetzon reached for it.

"Here, I'll take that." Gans was across the room in three steps. He took the paper and held it out in front of him and they both looked at it.

It was a narrow slip of paper, about three inches by six inches.

Across the top it said: LUWISHER BROTHERS.

FORTY-THREE

So there it was. The bomb had come from someone at Luwisher Brothers. Why should she be surprised? She had known all along the murderer was not an outsider.

She dusted the dirt off her calendar. Sharon Murphy was supposed to meet with Carl Fisher at Dayne Becker after the close today. It needed confirming. The show must go on.

When Sharon came on the line, Wetzon heard reluctance in her voice. "I don't know, Wetzon," she evaded. "I don't think I want to go there."

"Have you decided on Luwisher Brothers, then?" Wetzon asked, disappointed.

"No. Chris Gorham keeps pressuring me, but after that announcement this morning, I wouldn't consider a firm that would limit what I can make."

"Good thinking, Sharon."

"So I think I'm going to stick around here for the time being. Look at the market today. We're down a hundred and forty-eight points already. Besides, Wally said he'd give me some of the accounts of people who've left."

"Okay, Sharon. I'm not going to pressure you. Just know that Marty Rosen wants you and will do what has to be done to bring you on board."

"But not give me thirty percent upfront."

"He can't. It's firm policy. At your level he can only give you twenty-five. Your trailing twelve months would have to come to five hundred thou for him to get approval on thirty percent."

"Call me in three months, Wetzon. I feel just too pressured now to do anything."

She's *too pressured,* Wetzon thought as she disconnected and called Carl Fisher at Dayne Becker to cancel Sharon. "She has a meeting with an important client," she lied, promising him she'd reschedule. He sounded depressed; as the Street contracted and firms merged, managers were finding it more and more difficult to hire brokers. And now with another major dip south, brokers would be more gun-shy than ever.

When she got Marty Rosen on the phone at Loeb Dawkins, he informed her, "We had dinner with Sharon last night."

"We?"

"Yeah. Bob Kankowitz, the head of our direct investments, and I. I think we got her."

"I just spoke with her, Marty, and I think you will get her, but she said she wants to back-burner it for a couple of months. She's landed a couple of huge accounts and wants to cement relationships before she drops it on them that she's switching firms, especially in this climate."

"Listen, Wetzon." Marty sounded crushed. "We all know that if you don't catch 'em before the first bounce, you probably won't get 'em. They'll pop out somewhere, but not to you. The momentum is gone."

"I know, but I promise I'll keep after her, Marty. I do know she's decided against Luwisher Brothers."

Marty chortled. "No broker worth his salt would be crazy enough to go there. I heard they took a hickey today in United Can. How about pulling out some of the good ones for me, Wetzon?"

Wetzon sighed. "I can't do that, Marty. They're a client firm."

Marty's parting shot was a cynical, "You can't work for everyone, Wetzon."

"I know, I know," Wetzon said, after he'd hung up.

With all the mergers, the Street was getting so small, she and Smith would end up pulling brokers out of any one of the three majors and placing them at the other two. That's all that would be left. She wondered if what Marty had said about Luwisher Brothers taking a major loss in United Can was true. Their traders were known for smart arbitrage, but was it worth the risk? They would load up on a stock they were guessing would be a buy-out candidate. If the buy-out came through and the stock surged, they'd make a million, but if the buy-out failed, the loss could be devastating. You had to risk millions to make millions.

The room was stifling. The air conditioner kept groaning, surging and rattling. She got up and turned it off. It was doing no good and was already on overload.

"Mr. Diamantidou is here," B.B. announced.

Wetzon opened the door and got doused with a refreshing gust of cold air from the reception room.

Peter Diamantidou was the block superintendent. He saw to all the brownstones and townhouses. It was a time-consuming job, but not as difficult as being the super in a high-rise co-op or condo and having to deal with a hundred or more diverse families. A short, dark man of about fifty, he spoke with a transitional Greek-American accent.

"Oh boy, oh boy," he was saying as he surveyed the mess, hands waving, his gray workpants hanging baggy on his hips. Swaybacked, belly protruding, he was not at all fat. "Whatta job I got here." He gave off the rank odor of many layers of dried sweat. "I dunno what Mr. H. is going to say." He had his worry beads out and was rolling them in his fingers.

"I think we're insured, so we'll be responsible," Wetzon said, hoping she was right and trying not to breathe in through her nose. The stagnant air in the room was rapidly taking on his ripe smell.

"Okay, okay, don't you worry, miss. I gonna get a glass man in." He inspected the door, turning it. "No damage, just needs a touch-up and maybe new hinges. I check the bolt." He stared at the bomb squad technicians, who were finishing up their work in the garden, and backed away from the opening as they barred the door to the garden with yellow police line tape.

After the technicians trooped out, Wetzon said, "I'm going to leave all this in your capable hands, Mr. Diamantidou. We just have to be able to work here tomorrow with the air conditioner operating."

"Okay, okay, miss. I do my best." His calloused hands were stained dark with the marks of his job. He wouldn't even notice ink stains if he were fingerprinted . . .

Damn. Her mind was wandering. *Concentrate,* she told herself. She had only one more call that needed to be made, then she would go out for a quick late lunch at Il Nido Cafe. She had a sudden craving for a stuffed artichoke and an icy espresso. But first she'd call Chris and switch their meeting place.

"He's on the other line, Wetzon, do you want to hold?" Chris's assistant Ruth asked.

"Tell him we're having some work done in the office so it's better if I meet him at the restaurant." Specks of glass winked and twinkled at her from various places on her desk.

"Okay, hold on. I'll see if I can get his attention."

"How's the market behaving, B.B.?" she called. Their phones had become eerily still.

B.B. opened the door. He'd finally washed his face, although his suit was a mess. "It's recovering. The buy programs kicked in after it dropped a hundred and sixty points and now it's only off twenty-nine."

Wetzon shook her head. This was the second precipitous drop in as many months, each time triggered by something wrong with a junk bond or commercial paper, a company's being over-leveraged, or worry about the strong dollar, the weak dollar, inflation, recession, inventories, or the balance of trade. And each time there was a drop, the brokers had margin calls up the wazoo. Which explained why Smith and Wetzon's phones had stopped ringing. *Hi, there, Mr. Wazoo. You've got a margin call. You'll either have to sell some stock, or you'll have to quickly send me a check for a mil to cover.*

"Wetzon?"

"Yes, Ruth." The heat was getting to her brain. She took a hard look at the Andy Warhol; it was hanging rakishly cockeyed. She got up to straighten it.

"Chris says to meet him at six at the Bloomsbury Court. It's on the corner of Madison and Twenty-ninth."

"The Bloomsbury Court? I don't know that restaurant. Is it new?" When Ruth didn't answer, Wetzon thought they'd been cut off. "Ruth?"

"That's not a restaurant, Wetzon. That's where he lives."

FORTY-FOUR

An acrid haze hovered over the City like the remnants of a smoky brushfire. The cut on her knee twinged under her pantyhose. It began to itch.

A Tuscan restaurant on the expensive side, Il Nido had, as did several other restaurants, a less costly cafe. This one was wedged into the atrium of 875 Third Avenue, between Fifty-second and Fifty-third Streets. The string quartet on the balcony, the cathedral-like sweep of ceiling, four rows of faux marble cafe tables one next to the other, linen napkins, gave the spot, which was open to the public, a cafe-in-a-garden atmosphere.

Along the far wall was the showcase of foods for taking out or eating in, everything from veggie lasagna to sweet pepper salad, hot and cold. After looking at the tempting offerings, Wetzon ordered a stuffed artichoke and a decaf espresso freddo from the waiter and sat down at one of the tables. It was two o'clock. The lunch crowd was back at their desks, tourists were minimal. A gray-haired man with horn-rimmed glasses, torn jeans, and a short-sleeved workshirt was sitting at a table drinking an espresso and writing in a notebook.

Wetzon's stomach growled. It was cool as an oasis here, with none of that New York feeling of obsessive energy. She dug into the artichoke and listened to the music. She could feel herself loosening up, letting the tension go.

"More coffee for the *signorina*?"

She shook her head at the waiter.

An elderly couple, both bent, looking so alike they could have been twins, came and sat down near her, holding hands across the top of the table.

Somehow she couldn't picture herself and Silvestri that way.

With her front teeth she continued to scrape the flesh of the artichoke leaves until she got to the tender heart. She and Silvestri would be the old couple who yakked at each other. She laughed. Where were her thoughts leading her? Dangerous territory. Was she thinking about spending the rest of her life with Silvestri? She felt a sudden sense of panic. *Afraid of commitment, Les?* she asked herself. Maybe. She actually felt more panic at the thought of marriage than she'd felt about the bomb.

She picked at the heart of the artichoke. Think about something else. The list of names, for example. She patted her briefcase. It must have something to do with the three murders. Why would Ellie have torn up a Xeroxed memo from Carlton Ash but not thrown it away? Perhaps she had torn it up in anger, then realized it was important. Who would know, then, what it meant? Someone who worked with Ash?

Replenished, Wetzon left money on the table for the check and tip and caught a cab on Third Avenue, letting her thoughts spin and roil unfettered. But, alas, no new ideas, no inspired possibilities came to her.

At home, once all the air conditioners were humming, Wetzon unrolled the paper and studied the list of names. Two had the same post office box numbers. She took a Diet Pepsi from the fridge and filled a glass with ice, pouring the soda over it, watching as the bubbles subsided, thinking.

David Kim might know what this meant. She chewed on her lip. She ought to call him anyway—offer condolences about Ellie. What would he do now? she wondered. He would have all of Ellie's business. His line rang and rang. No one answered. The Luwisher Brothers operator didn't even pick up. She hung up.

Dwayne. She called Carlos and left word on his answering machine that she had to talk to Dwayne about something important and to please leave his phone number on her machine. Then she peeled off her damp, wilted clothing, took another icy sink bath and stretched out on her bed in her terry robe.

It was a real puzzle. Everything was connected, but unconnected.

The phone woke her. She grabbed it and mumbled, "Hello."

"Well, Ms. Birdie Marple, I was wondering when you'd get around to calling your best friend." Then, more seriously, Carlos said, "I read about Ellie. I'm really sorry. She was a nice lady."

"Carlos—"

"And why are you not haunting the caverns of Wall Street today looking for warm bodies?"

"Well, you see, our office exploded."

"La-di-da. Just another day in the life of Leslie Wetzon, head-hunter."

"Carlos, I'm not kidding."

"Birdie—" His tone changed.

"I wasn't hurt. No one was hurt," she added, answering the question he wasn't going to ask.

"Dare I inquire whether it was one of Con Ed's fine asbestos-lined gas mains?"

"More like a package bomb. Smith let it be known that we know who the murderer is."

"Wouldn't you just know the Wicked Witch of the North would do that to make herself look good."

"It almost made us look dead."

"*Do* you know who the murderer is?"

"Not a clue."

"And I'll bet you're not going to let a few minor things like explosions and murders scare you off, hardhead."

"You win."

"Birdie, I hate this. You need a keeper, you do, and I'm getting too old to keep up with you. Dwayne's at home. Why do you want to talk to him?"

"A hunch."

"Good God, when this lady has a hunch, the sky falls in."

"Never you mind. Just give me Dwayne's phone number."

He gave her the number. "Now be careful."

"It's okay. Silvestri knows about everything and he said he'd cover me."

"Oh, great," Carlos groaned. "You'll get caught in a shoot-out."

She hung up and called Dwayne. His answering machine picked up and played "What I did for Love" from *A Chorus Line. Give me a break,* she thought. After his message and the beep, she left word for him to call her after nine.

She put on her black silk suit with the green lining and the matching green-with-black-polka-dots shell and low patent leather pumps and took a cab to Twenty-ninth Street and Madison Avenue. She felt naked without her briefcase.

The cab let her off in front of a grand newish condominium. This was a strange neighborhood. Until recently the streets here had been seething with derelicts and the homeless because they were being housed in the Armory nearby. The area had the piquant, pervasive odor of curry issuing from the many Indian restaurants and foodshops that proliferated in this section of New York, and which would probably soon be driven out by gentrification. And on Twenty-ninth Street, near Fifth Avenue, was the landmark Church of the Transfiguration, known as the Little Church Around the Corner, dating back to before the Civil War. It became known as the actors' church in 1870, because unlike most other churches it didn't refuse to admit actors. Edwin Booth had worshipped there, as had Sarah Bernhardt. It was a beautiful, accessible church.

She looked around at parked cars, at pedestrians. If she was being watched, she couldn't find the detective. A boy practicing jumps on a skateboard narrowly missed her as she stood under the wine-colored awning in front of the building. Glass and brass was the motif of the facade and continued into the lobby.

A doorman in a gray uniform approached her. "Yes, Miss?" His accent was Hispanic, but not Puerto Rican.

"I'm here to see Mr. Gorham."

"Your name, please."

"Ms. Wetzon. W-E-T-Z-O-N."

"Please wait. I don't think he's come home yet."

"Miss Wetzon for Mr. Gorham in 24L," the doorman told a second, younger man who was carrying a package into what was probably the mailroom.

The second man returned after a minute. "No answer. He's not home yet, and the wife is out of town." He looked Wetzon over appraisingly.

"Do you want to wait?" the first man asked. "Is he expecting you?"

"Yes," she said with a finality that finished off the conversation. She sat down on a black leather chair next to a potted tree to wait for Chris, and watched a continuous stream of men and women in business suits coming home from work. It was after six; Chris would be late; they would have dinner late; she would get home late. . . . Dammit all.

She'd about worked herself into a snit when she heard the doorman say, "Here he is now," as if he were saying, *H-ee-ere's Johnny*.

Chris came down the four steps to the dropped lobby, where she sat vegetating with the vegetation. "Oh, Wetzon, good, you're here." He looked harried. His shirt collar was limp and slightly yellowed around the neck. His dark suit was wrinkled. He took her proffered hand, and instead of shaking it, tucked it into the dank gabardine crook of his arm, carrying her along to the bank of three elevators.

"Where are we going?" she asked. He seemed to have taken possession of her.

"I thought maybe Park Bistro."

"I think we're going in the wrong direction then."

"It's been a really tough day. I don't have to tell you," he said, pressing 24. The button lit up. The elevator was small and sleek, glass and brass again. "And I've got the goddam auditors."

"I thought we were having dinner," she said, trying to take her hand back. She felt the muscles tighten in his arm. He had done this to her before, the day Ash was murdered. She felt a tremor of uncertainty.

"We are. I just want to shower and change my clothes. I wouldn't want to offend."

"You wouldn't." She laughed nervously. "You don't."

"Oh, yeah? Well, why do you think my wife left me?" When he saw she wasn't laughing, he said, "All you have to do is have a drink and wait for me in cool comfort. How's that?"

"Sounds okay to me," she said, but she thought, *this is a little odd*. She didn't want to seem unsophisticated, it was just not the kind of thing she did. In fact, she didn't remember ever going to a broker's home—except for Laura Lee's, of course.

"Here we are," he said, setting his attaché case on the houndstooth carpet and unlocking the door. The corridor had been cool, but nothing like the blast of cold air that shot out of Chris's apartment. "Ah," Chris said. He held the door for her to walk in before him.

One wall of the apartment, which had a huge L-shaped living room, was window with a door leading to the terrace. She walked as if pulled by a magnet to the wall of windows. "What an incredible view." Straight ahead she could see all of downtown New York, past the pointed gazebo spire of the Met Life Building to the twin towers of the World Trade Center. To her left she saw the East River and to her right, the Hudson and the cliffs of New Jersey. The whole scene looked like a set piece, painted on, unreal. She turned to say so to Chris.

He had taken his jacket off. He was wearing red paisley suspenders. He'd rolled up the sleeves of his white shirt, flexing muscular forearms. "What are you drinking?"

"Perrier . . . Pellegrino . . . club soda."

"How dull, Wetzon. Loosen up. I'm going to have a beer."

She would have loved to tell him to fuck off, but she smiled and said, "I heard you guys took a big loss in United Can."

He removed two glasses from a cabinet and closed the door, his back to her. His shirt was custom-made and fit his athlete's body like a leotard. "Yeah, we took a hickey, but we're all right. We didn't get hurt badly—only our clients did. Neil's boys in the boardroom sucked some wind."

"Oh, gee, that's good. Only the clients. So it's okay."

He shot cold bolts at her. "Get outta my face, Wetzon."

"What do you want to talk about, Chris?" She felt impatient and she resented his making her feel like Goody Two-shoes. What was she doing here, anyway? *Let's get this show on the road,* she thought. Her nose tickled and she sneezed twice. "Excuse me." She found a tissue in her purse in time to sneeze again. Was she catching cold?

He opened the refrigerator and took out a beer and a can of club soda. The kitchen, which had no door on either end, was a small compact affair, a galley, really. He poured the club soda into a glass, added a slice of lime, and opened a Becks for himself, drinking from the bottle. A child's pull toy, a long orange caterpillar on wheels, lay on the floor.

"I'll be ready in a jif. Then we can grab some dinner," he said, catching her looking at the caterpillar. He shrugged. "Make yourself at home." He turned on the stereo and disappeared into what must have been the bedroom. "Warren?" she heard him say, then the door closed.

Carly Simon filled the room while Wetzon inspected the premises, like a good detective. Warren? Who was Warren? When she heard the shower come on, she gave herself permission to prowl. Sofa, club chairs, coffee table. She set her drink down on the latter. More evidence that children lived here, toys, photographs. A bookcase filled with books. She sneezed again. Two gleaming yellow eyes blinked at her from the top shelf of the bookcase. Her heart lurched. Good grief, a cat. A huge black cat. No wonder she was sneezing.

"Hello, cat." The cat stared at her and jumped down, then up again on the coffee table and watched her tour the room. A desk. A stack of newspapers, *The Journal* and *The Times*. A *desk,* she thought. Drawers. She opened them quietly, listening to the shower, riffled through papers, closed them.

On top of the desk several letters sat under a Steuben apple paperweight. They were personal, handwritten. She moved the paperweight and fingered the letters. She couldn't. She wouldn't. She did. One was from his mother. It was postmarked Kennebunkport, Maine. She skimmed through it hastily. Mom was berating him about the separation, about his career. Nice, Mom. Back in your cage. A letter from Abby, his wife. She bypassed that. At the bottom of the pile was a blank envelope with just his name printed on it.

She drew the single sheet of paper out and unfolded it. It was a Xerox copy of the list of names, intact, just like the scraps of Ellie's she'd pieced together.

FORTY-FIVE

Wetzon froze, caught by a change in the room. The shower. The sound had stopped.

She slipped the sheet of paper back in the envelope, hesitated for only a minisecond, then folded the envelope into her purse. She could feel eyes boring into her, but Chris was not in the room. It was Warren, the cat.

"Stop that." She shook her finger at it.

It continued its unblinking stare.

Brazenly, she reached around its bulk for her drink, and a black paw with a white mitten caught her hand and whacked it playfully, as if she were a mouse. Wetzon's hand shook and tipped the glass over. Warren leaped to the sofa and commenced staring at her again.

The glass lay on the coffee table upended, its contents spilling onto the table and the carpet. "Damnation," she said to the cat. Thank goodness it was only club soda. She rushed into the kitchen, tore paper towels from a roll on the wall and began blotting up the mess.

"I see you've met Warren," Chris said softly, coming up behind her. His hair was damp from the shower.

Startled—she hadn't heard him come in—she jabbered, "I've made a mess, I'm sorry."

"Forget it. Warren has a habit of jumping out at people. He likes to see them squirm. Here, I'll take that." Chris took the soggy paper and the empty glass back into the kitchen. The fridge door opened and closed. The icemaker growled.

Wetzon looked down at Warren. She felt stupid. Made a fool by a cat. "You," she said. Warren continued to stare at her insolently as he licked his right paw with a pink tongue.

"Here, let's start all over." Chris was holding another beer and handed her a fresh glass of club soda. He sat down on the sofa and crossed his legs. He seemed in no hurry to get to dinner.

"So what's the story downtown?" she asked. Why was she feeling so discombobulated, so off-kilter?

"Sit down, Wetzon, you're all wound up about something. I can see that." Chris patted the cushion next to him. "Clear off, Warren." He gave the cat a slap and the cat hissed and jumped to the coffee table.

"Warren. What kind of name is that for a cat?" Wetzon asked lightly. Maybe she should just excuse herself and leave. Now there were four eyes staring at her. Illogically, she wondered if Chris knew she'd taken the envelope. Had Warren told him?

"Warren Buffett," Chris said.

"Warren Buffett?" She was confused. Had she missed something? Warren Buffett was a first-rate entrepreneur–financial wizard, whose company, Burlington Hathaway, held interests in many companies. Buffett himself had bought a piece of the investment banking firm of Salomon Brothers because Solly had gotten into financial trouble and was being stalked by takeover artist Ron Perelman of Revlon. It was said that Buffett was invited in to forestall Perelman, and it had worked. What was Chris talking about?

"Warren is named for Warren Buffett."

"Oh." She smiled at him. "Well, why not. Maybe he's a good stock picker."

"Yeah, he uses the blindfolded monkey method. Come on and sit down. I want to finish my beer before we head out. Tell old Uncle Chris why you're so jumpy." He treated her to a boyish, toothy grin.

She took a sip of the club soda. It had a tangy taste. "Did you put something in this?" She set it down on the coffee table.

"Just lime." Chris got up and went into the kitchen. Again, the fridge door opened and closed. He returned with another beer.

She walked over to the window wall and looked out. Lights were beginning to pop on all over the City. The gazebo affair on the top of the Met Life Building was glowing green in the streaky yellow sunset.

The music stopped. Chris rose and changed the CD. Neil Diamond. "So, you want to tell me what you're upset about?"

"I'm not upset. I'd like to get some dinner."

"I can read you like a book. How many years have we known each other now?"

She hesitated, back to the window, thinking how she hated when someone said that to her—that he could read her like a book. It was so smug and condescending and, in this case, anti-female. She looked back at the panorama of New York rooftops. "Someone sent us a package bomb." Turning away from the window, she continued, "It exploded in our garden. No one was hurt."

Chris looked surprised. "Why would anyone do that?"

"Because someone thinks we know who the murderer is. Haven't you heard? Didn't Destry and Hoffritz fill you in?"

"No, but I was putting out fires all day in the boardroom." He paused and studied her, his face a handsome mask. "Do you?"

Could he be the one after all? she thought suddenly. Was she being stupid? Where was her protection? "Was Dr. Ash blackmailing Ellie?"

Something quick flashed across his eyes, then disappeared. "I don't know. Why?"

"Was he blackmailing you?"

"Me? Hell, no."

He'd answered too quickly. "Did you and Ellie have a meeting with him early last Saturday, when I met you getting on the elevator?"

"Wetzon, you have some imagination, you know that?" Chris said unctuously. He got up and came over to the windows, standing near her.

"Chris, be honest. If he was, fess up because you might be the next one."

"Next one what? Don't be so melodramatic."

"Next one murdered. If you know something, don't keep it to yourself. Is that what you wanted to talk to me about?"

He laughed then, showing all his teeth, throwing back his head, but real mirth was absent. He took a long swallow of beer. "I've had an offer from L.L. Rosenkind," he said. "Good package, and a piece of the action, which I'm certainly not getting at Luwisher Brothers. Come on, sit down for a minute."

"Oh." She let him lead her to the sofa. "They have new owners."

"Yeah. Canadians. I don't know if I want to work for them."

"Canadians? Didn't I read they were from Atlanta?"

"They are. For chrissake, Wetzon, where've you been? When we say someone's Canadian, we mean a Jew. Everyone knows that, even the Canadians." He took another long swig from the bottle.

Yes, she thought, *where've you been, Wetzon?* Bigotry on Wall Street just made it part of the real world, albeit an exclusive part. She sneezed, then again. It was ugly, yet everyone wore it like an old school tie. "Stop staring at me, Warren," she told the cat.

Chris laughed. Warren reached a paw out to him, and Chris flicked it away with his finger. Warren purred loudly. "You're a funny girl, Wetzon," Chris said.

"Are you going to take the offer?" she asked, trying to bring business back into the equation. She stared at Warren and took another swallow of the club soda. No. She set it down. He'd put vodka in it. Or sulfites? Her fingers were wet from the sweating glass.

"Should I?" he said, giving the words a peculiar intimacy.

"Should you what?"

"Take the offer . . ." He put his arm around her. He smelled of cologne and soap and beer.

"I don't think this is smart, Chris," she said sharply, trying to move away.

He had his hands on her shoulders then, forcing her down on her back. "You want it," he breathed in her face, "You know it. You want it."

"Stop!" she cried, but he was kissing her, holding her down, right arm across her shoulders, his left hand groping at her jacket. She struggled, terrified, turning her head away. "No! Let me go." He was the murderer. He was going to murder her. She threw her legs around, trying to knee him.

"Come on, baby, come on," he said, "you know you want it, and I'm going to give it to you better than you've ever had it."

He rolled the shoulders of her jacket back, pinning her arms to her sides as she fought him, legs flailing, but he was lying on top of her like dead weight. Panicked, she knew she was fighting for her life. His hands were under her blouse, on her breasts.

"Chris, stop this, stop!"

His fist came up before she saw it and smashed into her face. Pain rolled over her, numbing her, pulling her down in the undertow. Her left eye was on fire. Warm liquid flowed from her nose. *Oh God, oh God,* she thought. *Don't pass out.* He was pushing up her skirt, tearing at her hose. *I'm going to be raped and murdered. Raped and murdered.* She tried to kick, but his legs were pressed against hers and he was the swimmer, all muscle and sinew. Don't struggle, they said. Or did they? You had to struggle. It was crazy not to, but she was starting to let go. She could feel herself tuning out.

"Good girl, just lie back and enjoy it," Chris whispered. She heard her blouse tear, felt her bra give way.

"No, Chris, please." Her lips were numb, useless. She knew it was over. *Poor Silvestri,* she thought, beginning to feel she was leaving her body. He would blame himself.

A high unearthly shriek—then another, and another. She came back. She was shrieking. No. Chris had shrieked. He'd let go of her. She opened her eyes. He seemed to be clawing at his back, shrieking. Or was it Warren shrieking? Warren stood like a vulture, his claws dug into the back of Chris's neck. *Move, move,* she told herself. *Move.*

She moved, blocking out pain, shrugged her jacket up her shoulders. *Run.* Grabbed her purse from the coffee table. *Run. Go, go, go.* She ran, awkwardly, struggled with the door, and all the time the terrible shrieking of cat and man. Opened the door. *Run.* Ran into the hall, screaming for help, banging on the doors of the other apartments, ringing doorbells. In vain. *Keep running.* Down the hall. No one helping. But they were there, hiding behind their doors. *Run.* She stopped short. The hall ended on a fire door. Noise behind her. She plunged through the door.

FORTY-
SIX

A whitewashed concrete-and-metal staircase stretched upward and downward. Wetzon took a sobbing breath and tore down the stairs, thankful she was wearing low heels, astonished that she'd been able to keep her shoes on her feet. *Well, you dummy, he wasn't exactly interested in your feet.*

Twenty-two . . . twenty-one . . . twenty . . .

She turned swift corners on each landing. The fire stairs were not air-conditioned, but her sweat was cold and rested on her body like a glaze. The left side of her face, jaw, cheekbone, eye, throbbed in different rhythms. Her stitched knee complained. Her nose dripped. Holding onto the stair rail, she paused and dabbed at her nose with a Kleenex from her purse. It didn't feel right. What if it were broken? She looked down at the tissue. It was bloody. Oh, God. He'd broken her nose. Tears burned her eyes. Her fingers probed her puffy, swelling cheek. *Keep going. Don't stop. Get out. Get away. Get help.*

Nineteen . . . eighteen . . . seventeen . . . sixteen . . .

He would have killed her. *You're not safe yet. Keep going. Run. Run.*

Fifteen . . . fourteen . . . thirteen . . .

If it were not for Warren, she would have been raped for sure. Beaten. Dead. *Concentrate on the stairs.*

Twelve . . . eleven . . . ten . . .

Almost there. *Go. Go. Go.* Had she done something to lead him on? No. No. He was crazy. But what if he thought she'd come up to his apartment with him because she wanted it? No. No. She hadn't led him on. What was she thinking?

Nine . . . eight . . . seven . . . six . . .

She slowed down, gasping, and listened, looking back up the stairs. No one was following her. How could that be? Oh, God, what if he had taken the elevator down? What if he was waiting for her at the bottom of the stairs? She was trembling so violently that she staggered like a drunk, gripping the rail, forcing herself on.

Five , , , four

She lost her footing and half fell, half slid on her butt to the third-floor landing and lay there moaning, fighting to catch her breath. If Chris were the murderer, he would have to find her and kill her now because she knew. She knew. Dragging herself up, she tottered down the remaining two flights to a red door that said EXIT—USE ONLY IN CASE OF FIRE.

She pushed on the door, aching with the effort. It didn't give. No sound came from upstairs. The staircase went further down, and she followed it to LEVEL I. Peering down, she saw what must be LEVEL II and heard the rumbling sigh of the building's innards, like those of a giant passenger liner. The boiler was down there, and God knew what else. She crawled back up to street level. She would have to make one last try on the fire door. What else could she do? Go out onto a floor and beg for help? Who in New York would open a door to a stranger? But maybe she could get someone to call the police.

She gathered up all her strength, leaned on the bar handle, and pushed. The door swung open and she lost her grip on it, tumbling into the street, landing on her knee—the torn one. Spasms of pain shot up her leg and she collapsed on the sidewalk. *Don't quit now. Get up. Get up.* Where was she? She rolled over on her side and sat up. Twilight. An overcast sky. The unbreathable air. She was near a vacant lot on the quiet side of Twenty-ninth Street because she could see the Little Church Around the Corner across the way in the middle of the block. Everyone was indoors cooling off except a bag lady across the street, sitting in the gutter, dozing against her overloaded shopping cart.

Holding on to the open metal door, she got up and slammed the door shut. She needed a doctor. She had her purse. She'd hail a cab. She leaned against the smooth marble side of the building. She'd never make it to the street. Looking down at herself for the first time, she saw that her blouse and bra hung in tatters. She buttoned her jacket, brushed her hair out of her face with quivering fingers. It was hanging around her shoulders, her back. It was so hot. It was so cold. She seemed unable to keep her balance. A car made a left from Madison and came slowly west on Twenty-ninth Street, pulled over to a fire hydrant and stopped. It shouldn't park there. It would get a ticket. A horn blared.

She couldn't see. Was it a cab? She willed herself to leave the side of the building, but her feet wouldn't move.

"Ms. Wetzon?" Someone was calling to her from the car. "Leslie?"

A figure was getting out of the car, coming toward her. She cringed. Who was it? She covered her face with her trembling hands. Chris had found her. He was coming for her. No. It was a woman. It wasn't Chris. Someone who knew her, who would help her.

"Leslie? What happened?"

She squinted her good eye, trying to see who it was. Mo. It was Mo. And she was beautiful. Wetzon pitched forward into soft but total darkness.

Her mouth was so dry. She moved her head and opened her eyes—but only one of them responded. The other was stuck. Her face felt as if it had been horseback riding and the horse had stepped on it. It was dark. A faint light came through the windowed door. She saw the bed, the white linen, the buttons, the switches. The antiseptic smell. She tried to sit up, but the blanket was too heavy. People were talking in low voices, but the room was swimming and swirling around her. In the distance she heard someone say, "She'll sleep now." And she did.

When she awoke again, sunlight spattered the room with yellow rectangles. Silvestri was smiling down at her. Smiling at her, she thought. He stroked her hair. "Where am I?" she said, but in a stranger's voice. Her nose felt funny, heavy. There was packing in it.

"Bellevue. Mo brought you in last night. You were a mess."

"Water," she croaked.

He held the straw for her and she sipped the cool liquid. It had no taste.

"Chris did it," she said. She held her hand out to Silvestri. "Did you get him? He was going to rape me, then murder me." Her lips quivered. *Stop that,* she ordered herself.

"Les, you agreed to press charges last night."

"I did?"

"Yeah. Gorham's cooling his heels waiting for bail."

"Bail? He's getting *bail*?"

"He's getting bail."

"He can't. He almost killed me."

"He claims you led him on."

Anger careened through her, running amok, burning her veins, her fingers, her gut. "He almost killed me. Do you believe him?"

"No."

"Then why is he getting out?"

"It's the law if he makes bail."

"But who set the bail low enough—oh, shit. He's a murderer and he's going to walk."

"He's not a murderer . . . at least he didn't kill Ellie Kaplan."

"How do you know for certain?" She was angry . . . hurt . . . burbling, crying, shaking. . . .

He sat on the bed and took her in his arms. "We know for certain."

"He did it, Silvestri. He did it. I know. He has to be the one." She pounded weakly on Silvestri's arms.

"He has an airtight alibi."

"What kind of airtight alibi?"

"He was in custody that night . . . arrested on another charge."

"No! It can't be. What other charge?"

"Assaulting his wife."

FORTY-SEVEN

"It's the helplessness more than the pain," Wetzon said, combing her hair gently because everything hurt, even her scalp. "Shit." She was going to cry again. She couldn't seem to get her emotional balance back. The mirror over the sink in the small bathroom revealed a frightening image. The left side of her face was grotesque— eye black and blue, swollen shut, cheek red and raw, black and blue, swollen, nose swollen and full of packing. "How am I going to go out looking like this?" she wailed.

"You look beautiful to me." Silvestri took the comb from her hand. "You're alive. Right now that's all that matters." He put his arm around her and led her back to the bed. The hospital gown and robe flapped around her knees. "When I got the call from Mo—"

Tears watered her good eye. She felt edgy, even whiny. "I was so scared. He could have done anything he wanted to me. If it weren't for Warren—"

"Who?"

"The cat. Warren. What happened to him?"

"I don't know, but Gorham looked as though he'd battled a tiger." He smiled. "I thought you did it."

Wetzon didn't smile. "I wish he'd killed him," she said fervently. "I hate him." Her hand moved restlessly back and forth; she fiddled with the clasp of her purse. "For making me feel weak and unable to control what happens to me. I keep thinking, what did I do that made him think—"

"Listen to me, Les, the man has problems. You just happened to be there. You came up to his apartment—"

"Silvestri, it was a business dinner. He invited me up. I couldn't very well insist I'd wait in the lobby or meet him at the restaurant. It would have been insulting. I would have felt like a bumpkin, like an unsophisticated fool—" She stopped. "I guess that's what he wanted me to feel."

"You had a drink."

"Club soda."

"Whatever. These guys who beat up on women have a cracked perception of the world, Les. It gives them power they don't normally have in their work or on the street. It turns them on. Gorham took your presence there as a deliberate come-on."

She felt her heart thumping against her rib cage as if it would explode. "Silvestri, I swear I didn't do anything." She was crying again. Why couldn't she stop? Enough already.

"I know that, Les, but do you?" His beeper went off.

"I'm trying," she said, giving him a small flicker of a smile. "When did Carlos say he'd be here?"

"Ten, ten-thirty." He returned her comb and picked up the phone on the table next to the bed, punched out some numbers, waited, then said, "Silvestri." He adjusted his shoulder holster while he listened, grunting.

Wetzon slipped the comb back in her purse and saw the folded envelope containing the Xeroxed list. "Hey!" Silvestri looked a question over at her. She plucked the envelope out, feeling a welcome surge of adrenaline, and waved it at him.

"Yeah," he said into the phone. "I hear you. About fifteen minutes." He hung up. "What's this?" He looked at the envelope, then slipped the sheet of paper out and unfolded it.

"I found it in Chris's apartment."

"So?"

"It's exactly like the one I found torn in small pieces in Ellie's make-up bag at Luwisher Brothers—the day Dr. Ash was killed."

"Oh, yeah? Well, when were you going to tell me about it?" He sounded pissed.

She felt wounded. "I forgot. It didn't seem all that important, I guess. I couldn't tell it was written on Ash's memo paper. Please don't be mad. Please, Silvestri. I pasted it together yesterday and would have shown it to you last night—"

"Jesus Christ, Les."

"Don't yell. I'll cry." She couldn't help herself then. She did, pressing her palms to her eyes.

He held her, and she cried on his clean white oxford-cloth button-down, feeling the gun in its case and for once, found its presence reassuring. *It's a good thing I don't own a gun,* she thought. *I would have blown Chris Gorham away.*

"I love you," Silvestri said. He kissed her swollen cheek gently and took a tissue from the box next to the bed and blotted up her tears. "You fly solo all the time, by the seat of your pants. I'm the detective here, you know, and if we're working together, you've got to share."

"You're right," she said. "But about the list—with everything that happened, I'd forgotten about the scraps of paper until yesterday."

"Who would this mean anything to?"

"You might ask Chris, since you have him in custody."

"That's what the call was about. He's out. His wife arranged bail."

"What about what he did to me? Wait, I don't understand. Abby got him out? I thought—"

"She dropped the charges."

"Oh, shit, what a stupid thing to do. He'll do it again if he doesn't get help. Do you think she moved back in with him?"

Silvestri shrugged and folded the paper back in the envelope. "How about you?" He put the envelope into the inside pocket of his tan jacket.

"How about me what?"

"The charges."

"I'm not dropping them."

"Good girl."

"You don't know me very well if you think I'd do that." She was hurt.

"I don't know you at all. You're a mystery to me." He smiled at her, his eyes doing their deep turquoise number, the skin crinkling up at the outside corners.

"I love you, too, Silvestri. Thanks for the chocolate."

He kissed her forehead and left.

The gigantic dark chocolate Lindt bar lay on the table next to the telephone. She'd save it till she got home. All she wanted right now was to get out of there. She looked at her watch, but it wasn't on her wrist. Where was it? Had she lost it? She emptied her purse on the bed and found her earrings and her watch, putting them on. Very considerate of someone. Mo maybe. Somewhat chagrined, Wetzon thought, *I owe her. If she hadn't* . . . She balled her hands into fists, then thought, Silvestri had said he loved her. Just like that.

"Are you decent?" Carlos poked his head in the door. He looked like vanilla ice cream—slacks, jacket, a straw Borsalino on his head, carrying an Armani shopping bag.

"You look like an ethnic Tom Wolfe."

"And you look like the elephant woman."

"Thanks a heap. Silvestri told you, I suppose."

"Here are your duds." Carlos handed her the shopping bag. "Yes, he told me. Scared the shit out of me, he did." He leaned over her. "Let's have a look at you."

"What do you think?" she asked anxiously.

His mischievous eyes studied her face. "Ooooogly."

"Oh, shut up, you monster." She held her bruised cheek and laughed. "I could use one of those things Arab fundamentalists make women wear."

"A burqa? Forget it. Not glamorous enough. I brought you just the thing." He handed her a pair of dark glasses with enormous round lenses.

She put them on gingerly. "How do I look?"

He clasped his hands over his chest. "My word, Miss Garbo, may I please have your autograph?" He grinned at her. "Do you need help getting dressed?"

"Really, Carlos. Just step out and pull the drapes, my man." She got to her feet slowly and emptied the shopping bag on the bed as he drew the curtain around her bed, closing her in. "Where did you find this? I haven't worn it in ages." She pulled out a yellow cotton, short-pants jump suit. He'd brought her DKNY white cotton bodysuit, bra, panties, and Keds. "I'll be ready in a minute, but you'll have to help me into these," she said.

"Into what?" He had a mocking lascivious expression on his face as he parted the curtains.

"My Keds."

"Shucks."

She sat on the edge of the bed and he fitted her feet into the sneakers and laced them. "What's it like outside?"

"I passed a camel caravan on the way over."

"Great. What do you think I should do with my hair?"

He cocked his head, put a finger to his chin. "Here, let me." He expertly braided her hair into one long braid, felt in his pocket, produced a rubber band, and banded the end. "How's that?"

"It feels good. How does it look?"

He cocked his head again. "I rather like it. Are you ready to face the world?"

"I have to check out, I think."

"Okay, let me trot on down the hall to the nurses' station and see what you need. Do you have a Blue Cross card on you?"

"Are you kidding? They tore it out of my hands last night."

"I'll be right back. Just sit there and don't get into any more trouble, Birdie, there's a good girl."

She stuck her tongue out at him. When had everyone started referring to her as "good girl?"

Sitting on the edge of the bed, feet dangling, she suddenly thought, *oh m'God, Smith!* She picked up the phone and called the office. How was she going to tell Smith? Smith would be—"Oh, hi, B.B. May I speak with Smith, please?"

Several seconds passed. "Who is this?" B.B. sounded cautious.

"B.B. it's me—it's I, Wetzon." Was her voice that distorted?

"Oh gosh, Wetzon, I'm sorry. Hold on. She's been trying to find you."

"Wetzon!" Smith shrieked. "Where in hell have you been? I've been trying you—I heard what happened."

"You heard? Who told you?"

"Destry. Where are you? We must talk."

Destry? "I'm in Bellevue."

"Are you all right?"

"I wouldn't be here if I was all right."

"There's no need to take that tone, sugar. I've been absolutely frantic since I heard. You might have had your Italian Dick Tracy call me."

Smith made her weary. "I'm on my way home now. What did Destry tell you?"

"He said that Chris had had too much to drink and didn't behave like a gentleman, that he got carried away."

"A long way."

"Well, is it true?"

"Smith, Chris punched me in the face and tried to rape me. Did Destry tell you that?"

"Oh my God, sweetie pie, how awful for you. But you're okay, right? He didn't rape you, did he? Destry said you shouldn't press charges."

"And what do you say, Smith?"

"Well, of course I can't make those decisions for you, but—"

"You don't have to. I am."

"You are what? Pressing charges?"

"Yes."

"Sweetie pie, I know you're upset and hurt, but it will pass. You don't want to hold on to it. You'll have to go to court and everything will come out."

"What do you mean everything will come out?"

"Oh, you know, your life . . . it can get *so* personal . . . Besides, Chris has agreed to go into therapy, so you just can't."

"I can't?"

"Yes, you know what I mean. You can't press charges."

"What the fuck are you saying, Smith?" Anger, simmering on the surface, began to do a slow boil.

"You have to give him a chance to get treatment, not make things worse for him."

"Since when do you care about Chris? Up till now you were always putting him down."

"Sweetie, you're not hearing me. You can't press charges. It would be a terrible signal for us to send out."

"What signal?" Wetzon heard her voice rise.

"Just calm down for a minute and let me speak. It will let everyone know that we're women, sugar."

"We *are* women!"

Smith rode over her. "It will call attention to us as women, after all the work I've done to separate us from—"

Wetzon hung up.

FORTY-EIGHT

"I don't know why that surprises you." Carlos handed her a coldpack wrapped in a dish towel. "Keep this on the swelling."

"Will you stop bustling around like a nanny? Settle somewhere and talk to me." She flipped her braid forward over her breast. "Just toss me the afghan. I'm cold." She was curled up on the sofa in her living room, sipping iced tea, which Carlos had prepared after he brought her home.

Her apartment with its wooden blinds, hanging quilts, and country furniture had never looked more beautiful. The colors of the quilts seemed vivid, even though she knew they weren't. She touched the small geometric-patterned hooked rug, which she used as an accent piece on her brown sofa, tenderly, seeing the careful hand stitches someone had long ago sewn. The ice clinked in the tall glass as it melted, and the tea was dark and satiny with lemon.

If she could breathe through her nose, she was certain her sense of smell would be heightened. She'd had a terrifying brush with death, and the world seemed extra special to her.

Carlos dropped the afghan on her legs and studied her. "You're looking better, Birdie. Keep the coldpack on."

"Carlos, I love your dear pointed head."

"And I yours."

"You don't think I should drop the charges, do you?"

"No. I'd like to see Chris Gorham tarred and feathered and ridden out of town on a rail. I think you should give it to the mother in spades."

She dropped the coldpack on her lap and gingerly stretched her legs out in front of her. "In spades . . ." she repeated. It triggered something. Spades . . . cards . . . her dream about the poker game. She shivered.

"If you're thinking about the Barracuda, forget it. She'd sell that kid of hers if the price was right. She's laying a head trip on you." He sat down on the sofa and put her feet in his lap, stroking them. "Listen, Birdie—"

"Uh-oh, he's got that let's-get-serious attitude." She grinned at him crookedly, then winced. Even her teeth ached. The coldpack went back on her cheek. His eyes danced. He didn't look much older than the day they'd met in a dance class. "Fifteen years," she murmured.

"Fifteen years?"

"That's how long we've known each other," she said fondly.

"Well, good. I was worried." He tickled the sole of her bare foot.

"Stop!" She tried to pull her foot away, but he held tight to her ankle.

"I'll stop if you let me talk."

"Speak." She closed her eyes.

"I'm going to choreograph Mort Hornberg's next show."

"Oooooh, how lovely. What's it about? When do you go into rehearsal?"

"No dates yet. Next year some time. Interesting subject, but you know how secretive Mort is. I want to ask you something serious, Birdie."

"Okay, shoot. Whoops." She clapped her hand over her mouth, wincing. "I'm sorry. I'll stop torturing you. I'm a little hysterical, I guess." She giggled, then hiccoughed.

"Mort's all for it. Do you want to come back as my assistant choreographer?"

"Not in this life, dear heart."

"I'm sorry I asked."

He looked so disappointed that she sat up and kissed his cheek. "I love you for asking, though."

"Keep that icepack on," he said sternly. "This would never have happened if you'd stayed in the theater."

"Yeah, because most of the guys are gay."

"That does it. I can take a hint." He stood up.

"I'm kidding, I'm kidding!"

"I accept your apology, but I have to go. I've got a replacement going in tonight, and I'm late for rehearsal. Will you be all right?"

"Yes, Carlos. Thank you. I mean it with all my heart."

"I know, my love. Let me kiss your crooked nose and take my leave."

She followed him to the door. "Where'd you put my chocolate bar?"

"You mean the two-by-four?"

"Yup."

"On the counter in the kitchen."

"Okay, you may leave now."

Hand on his heart, he said, "I'm really crushed."

She pushed him out the door and closed it.

The doorbell rang. The sound seemed to reverberate up and down and around her. She opened the door.

"Almost forgot," Carlos said. "Dwayne said you'd called him, but his machine ate your phone number, so I gave it to him." He fluttered his fingers at her and got on the elevator.

"Thanks, pal." She was feeling groggy. Maybe Dwayne wouldn't call her until tomorrow. She padded into the kitchen and found the chocolate bar, breaking it into pieces before she unwrapped it. Then she placed a small brick of chocolate on her tongue and let it melt. She was going to be strong and not let what happened make her afraid of her own shadow. But her person had been invaded and she felt violated. "If you feel like a victim, old dear," she said out loud, "you become one. Snap out of it."

Her answering machine showed five messages. She pressed the playback mechanism.

Doug Culver. She'd forgotten all about him. She was supposed to have called him last night. Well, by this time he knew why she hadn't.

Smith.

Laura Lee. The party for Anne was Sunday. She'd forgotten about that, too. What a picture she'd make. Even a veil wouldn't help. *How about a nice sequined feedbag with breathing holes, Wetzon?*

Smith again.

Then, "Leslie Wetzon, this is Abby Gorham, Chris's wife. I beg you not to press charges. Chris is terribly ashamed of what he did. He's promised to go into therapy. Please. I have two children who need their father."

God, charitable was just what she didn't need to feel right now. First Smith—with a little push from Destry—now this. Wetzon wondered how Abby had gotten her home number. Maybe Chris had it in his address book. Or had it been Smith?

She sighed and called Laura Lee.

"Don't you feel well? They told me you were out of the office today." Wetzon could hear Laura Lee's other phone buzzing in the background.

"I had a little accident, but I'm all right . . . I think."

"You don't sound all right. What happened?"

"A difference of opinion with someone. I got a little banged up."

"Smith?"

"Oh no." Wetzon laughed. "All of Smith's assaults are emotional, Laura Lee."

"Was it someone in the business?"

"I don't feel much like talking about it now. I'll tell you tomorrow."

"Okay, then we're still on for tomorrow?"

"Well, sure. But can you do the shopping? I look horrible. I'll have to wear a disguise for the party."

"Disguise?"

"I got punched in the face."

She could hear Laura Lee's quick intake of breath. "It was Chris Gorham, wasn't it?"

"Laura Lee, you heard."

"No, I hadn't heard. What I heard was that someone at Luwisher Brothers had been arrested for domestic violence, or whatever the hell the male establishment labels beatin' up women. I didn't know it was you."

"Then how did you guess?"

"I'll tell you tomorrow," Laura Lee said in a tight voice.

FORTY-NINE

"And now, to introduce our honored guest, Ms. Leslie Wetzon."

She rose and floated to the lectern as if she were lighter than air. The band played "What's New, Pussycat."

She looked out at the field of faces on the floor of the Exchange, watching them dip and bend like wheat in the wind. Who was the honored guest, she wondered, panicked. Her hand, clutching a sheet of paper, trembled violently. She unfolded the paper and read the names and numbers from the photocopied list.

Waiters in black tuxedos and surgical masks snaked around and up the platform in a conga line, singing the "What's New, Pussycat" refrain. The lead waiter balanced a Coca-Cola tray, holding a single drink, on his fingertips. Perrier and lime. He offered it to Wetzon, who shook her head and backed away, but the tail of the conga line came around and held her in place, a human barrier.

"Drink!" the lead waiter cried, his voice muffled by the surgical mask.

"Drink it!" Smith called.

"Drink!" Hoffritz shouted.

"Yes, do," Destry said, bringing up the rear.

"You might as well, Wetzon," Dougie Culver said, shrugging and extending his palms. "I like you very much . . . I respect you . . . but you have no option."

"No option, no option," they all chanted.

The waiter thrust the Perrier at her, his eyes like onyx, flat and black. *Help,* she thought. He pressed the edge of the glass to her lips while the others held her, and she swallowed the putrid liquid and gagged. The shafts of wheat closed in around her, raising a choking dust. Her eyes burned and teared. She broke away from her captors and with her last ounce of strength pulled the surgical mask from the lead waiter's face. Charlie Chan.

He stretched his lips and stared at her without blinking. "Ancient ancestors say it is a wise man who can separate smoke from fire."

"But I'm a woman," she cried, feeling herself sinking into the wheat.

"Then trust intuition," the Asian voice said as the closing bell on the day's trading sounded.

And sounded.

She rolled over on her left side, liberating a dull, throbbing pain, and woke herself up. On her back again, she took inventory slowly. She felt as if she'd been pummeled. Which she had. She opened her eyes and let her fingers explore the damage. Wonders of wonders, her left eye was working again. A mere slit, but it was working. A crusty layer of gook clung to her lashes. The scuffed skin on her cheek had formed a scab as thick as a carpet. Her jaw ached. She rotated it warily, opened and closed her mouth, testing. The soft rumble of Silvestri's voice in the next room drifted in, reassuring her. Dozing, the sound of the shower sent her rabbiting back to the night before, and she lay cringing under the light cover until she realized she was safe and the shaking stopped.

Her clock said ten-twelve, and the air conditioner hummed. The closed blinds shut away the outside world—daylight, heat, people—and that was all right with her. She'd had about all she could stand of them right now. Except for Carlos and Silvestri, she wanted to surround herself with women, her friends. Fluffy cotton clouds floated across her mind's eye. *Blue skies smiling at me.* And she slept.

"Good morning." Silvestri woke her by sitting on her side of the bed, making it slope.

The inside of her mouth was dry and crinkly as a fall leaf, and her lips were chapped. She'd been sleeping on her back with her mouth open. Semi-dried drool crept from the right side of her mouth. She opened her eyes. "You're dressed. Are you working today?" Silvestri had his shoulder rig on. She pulled herself slowly into a sitting position and took the glass of orange juice he held out to her. It was fresh and thick with pulp, the way she liked it. She gave him an unintentionally crooked smile. "Take off your clothes," she said.

He studied her with serious eyes, then nodded, satisfied. "I'm going to get a haircut." He brushed his hair back past his receding hairline as if he had a full head of hair. "Then I'm going out to Forest Hills."

"Oh." His mother lived in Forest Hills. She was a lawyer with a reputation in women's issues. She'd been widowed young and had gone to Fordham and gotten a law degree. Wetzon had never met Rita Silvestri, although she had spoken with her on the phone. Silvestri seemed inclined to keep the two women in his life separated, which was okay with Wetzon. If he brought them together, it would mean he wanted a commitment from her.

"The Kim produce market is in Forest Hills." His face was a cipher.

She puckered her brow. "Oh, David Kim. He's still a suspect?"

"We're going to talk to Hoffritz, Bird, Culver, and Munchen, as well, although Hoffritz and Bird claim they were at a bar when Ellie Kaplan was murdered."

"Harry's?"

"Yeah, how do you know?"

"Half of Wall Street heads there for a drink after the close. Harry's—huh, that's a good one. At that hour Harry's is like a sardine tin full of brokers and traders. Who would know whether or not they were really there?" She stared thoughtfully at him. "So they alibi each other. How convenient." She bent her knees. "Let me try to get up."

"Go easy, Les." He stood and took the empty glass from her hand.

"I think one would lie and the other would swear to it." She was wearing one of his tee shirts, which skimmed the top of her thighs.

"Are you going to be all right by yourself today?"

He sounded worried. That was nice. "Laura Lee is coming around twelve. We have the tea for Anne tomorrow. You might want to disappear."

"The task force is on straight time till we crack this. The Mayor doesn't want to read another murder headline while his campaign is gearing up." He put on his tan jacket, fitting it over the shoulder holster.

"What about the list?"

He patted his breast pocket. "I've got it."

"Why do I have this funny feeling that we're the only ones who don't know what it means?" She followed him down the hall slowly, her muscles protesting loudly with every step. The barre was a must today. And soon.

"There's coffee."

"Great!"

"Eat something."

"I thought you love my svelteness."

"Yeah." He patted her ass and kissed her bruised cheek. "But Rita'll say you're too thin." He delivered it like a throwaway. Dum da dum dum.

Her heart pulsed a pirouette in her breast. "Oh?"

He opened the door. "The newspaper's on the chair," he said.

"That's it? That's all you're going to say?"

He looked at her quizzically.

"Okay, forget it, Clint."

He grinned at her and closed the door.

She opened it a crack. "Silvestri, Dwayne—Ellie's assistant—is supposed to call me. I thought I'd ask him about the list. Is he a suspect?"

Silvestri came back to her door. "No, but when did you talk to him?"

"I didn't. Carlos did. A couple of days ago, I guess."

"Well, if he calls, find out where he is, or see if you can get him over here. Call me right away if you hear from him."

"I don't get it."

"I want you to promise me you won't try to handle this yourself." His eyes gave her tough, gray slate.

"Okay, okay, I promise. But what's all this about?"

"Dwayne's gone, cleared out. Someone saw him hot-footing it out of his building Thursday night carrying a suitcase."

FIFTY

Laura Lee interrupted Wetzon's workout about one o'clock.

"Hellooo, anyone home?" Laura Lee pushed the front door with her toe, and dumped two stuffed Zabar's shopping bags and one equally bulging plastic bag from Fairway on the floor.

Wetzon had left the door ajar after the doorman announced that Miss Lorelei was coming up.

"In here, Miss Lorelei." Wetzon was on her exercise mat, feet up in a shoulder stand, something she was certain she should not be doing with packing in her nose. Upside down, Wetzon saw Laura Lee was wearing denim shorts and espadrilles. Her white cotton shirt, collar up, was knotted at her waist. "You look nice." She arched her back and put one leg on the floor, then lowered her other leg slowly until she was in a near backbend.

"Darlin', if you can do that, you—"

"I'm okay." Wetzon lowered herself, one vertebra at a time, until her back was flat on the mat.

"Oh, Lordy," Laura Lee said, standing over her.

"Thank you." Wetzon sat up and crossed her legs yoga-fashion. "It feels disgusting."

"Y'all want to tell me what happened?"

"He wanted career advice and he didn't like what I told him."

"Oh, come on now, Wetzon."

"Okay, he did want career advice, or so he said, and he asked me to have dinner with him. I said okay. I never thought . . . well, he's married, he has kids . . . he said he wanted to change firms."

"And he asked you to wait in his apartment."

Wetzon looked at Laura Lee. "He jumped me, and when I resisted, he gave me this as a gift, from him to me, with love. Don't say it, Laura Lee." She looked down at her knees. It hurt to keep her head tilted up.

Laura Lee crouched down in front of her. "Wetzon, darlin', I'm not about to say anythin' at this point. It's all over, and you don't need salt rubbed in. Let me tell you, though, Chris Gorham has managed to get away with this behavior for years because no one has had him arrested—until now. You're a heroine."

"How do you know about him, Laura Lee?" Wetzon blinked tears away. "Do you know Abby?"

Laura Lee shook her head. "No. I knew someone he did it to, someone who was in my trainin' class at Merrill. It was before he got married. We met him at Harry's. We'd just gotten our Series 7 and we were celebratin'." Laura Lee sighed; she'd lost most of her soft Southern accent for the moment. "He was real slick. She started seein' him and it was true love—at least on her part. One day she didn't show up for work, so I called her. She sounded horrible." Laura Lee got to her feet and held her hand out to Wetzon. "Her apartment was in a brownstone in the West Sixties. I told her I was comin' by on my way home." Wetzon took her hand and stood, leaving her hand in Laura Lee's. "Let me tell you, darlin', she looked a whole lot worse than you do."

"You should have seen me Thursday night. What happened to her?"

"She packed up and went home to Tampa. Never called, never wrote. I guess she just wanted to wipe it all out."

"And Chris got away with it."

"And Chris got away with it."

"Well, he's not getting away with it this time," Wetzon said. Her cotton leotard clung to her damply. "Smith is having a fit that I'm pressing charges."

"Smith!" Laura Lee spat the name. "Your de-ah partner is only interested in the business it might hurt. Am I right?"

"You're right."

"I suppose Hoffritz is putting pressure on."

"No, not Hoffritz. Destry Bird."

"Wetzon, my poor darlin', Destry Bird is a moon."

"A moon?"

"He reflects, that's all he does."

"Let's not talk about it anymore. I want to see what you've bought."

They unloaded the shopping bags of smoked salmon, breads, coffee, and cheese.

"I hope you have watercress. And eggs."

"I do."

"And cucumbers?"

"Yes."

"We're in business, then. I'll make a chocolate pecan torte. We'll do the sandwiches tomorrow just before they get here."

"Here's the flour. Butter's in the fridge. You can use the KitchenAid, and I'll use the hand mixer." Wetzon took a can of pumpkin out of the closet. Using the old recipe from the can, she doctored it with vanilla and almonds and fresh nutmeg. She beat everything together and divided the batter into two buttered loaf pans, and stuck the pans in the preheated oven. She brushed the flour off her hands. "That's the way I like to bake. One, two, three and into the oven." She stood on tiptoe and turned the timing knob. "I'm setting the timer for forty-five minutes."

Having used every available measuring cup and bowl, dusting flour on the quarry tile squares of Wetzon's kitchen floor, Laura Lee poured the chocolate batter into a greased spring-form pan and slid the pan into Wetzon's second oven. "I do love that you own two ovens, and neither one is a microwave."

Wetzon stood on tiptoe to reach the timer again. "How long do you need?"

"Forty minutes."

"Mine has to be in an hour and a half so we'll time it by yours because that timer is not working and I haven't had a chance to get someone over to fix it." Wetzon rinsed off the utensils and loaded the dishwasher.

"What's this?" Laura Lee had her head in the refrigerator.

"What?" Wetzon, who had wiped down her marble counter, now dried her hands and peered over Laura Lee's shoulder. "That's leftover pasta. Silvestri made it last night."

"Mmmmm. Smells luscious." She took a fork from the drawer and scarfed up the leftovers. "All that and he cooks, too. I say, let's not let this man get away." She looked at Wetzon from under her mascara'd lashes.

Wetzon felt herself redden. "I want to show you something, Laura Lee." She took the roll of taped paper from her briefcase and held it out to Laura Lee, who had followed her. "What's this look like to you? Do you want some iced tea? I have a bottle made up already in the fridge cooling."

"Yes. Lots of lemon, please." Laura Lee was studying the paper intently.

As she poured strong tea over ice cubes and lemon slices, Wetzon could hear her in the living room reading off the names out loud.

"You know what this is?" Laura Lee called.

"No, that's why I showed it to you." Wetzon came into the living room carrying two glasses.

Laura Lee flapped the paper at her. "Well, it surely looks a whole lot like a list of brokerage clients with account numbers." She slipped off her espadrilles and curled up on the sofa.

"Those numbers are account numbers?"

"That's the way they look on a print-out. But look-a here, darlin'." Laura Lee was pointing to something on the sheet of paper.

"Wait." Wetzon set the glasses down on the glass top of her coffee table and sat down next to Laura Lee. "Okay. What?" She stared down Laura Lee's long rosy fingernail.

"Don't you see anything odd here?"

"Mmmm." She read over the names. "No. What do you see?"

"Wetzon darlin', two of these names have the same account number. See . . . here."

Wetzon saw at once that Laura Lee was right. Adam Park and Jonathan Young had the same account number.

"What's more, they're both to post office boxes at Knickerbocker Station."

"I saw that, but what does it mean? People have post office boxes."

"Darlin', two people can't have the same account number. It just isn't done. Compliance would pick that up in an instant."

Compliance, Wetzon thought, searching her memory. "Compliance. What if the compliance director in a small firm had an accident—died, or something—"

"He would have to be replaced." Laura Lee took a sip of tea from the sweating glass. Ice water dripped on her lap. "Where are your napkins?"

"In the top drawer, there. Laura Lee, what if an executive with the firm filled in on compliance until a replacement could be found?"

"Okay, but he'd have to know what he was doing." She dropped a napkin in Wetzon's lap, flopped back on the sofa, and tucked one under her drizzling glass.

"And what if this executive didn't notice the two accounts had the same number?"

"I guess that could happen . . . in that situation." She sounded doubtful. "In a real small firm, maybe. But all this is illegal. You can't get away with it forever."

"You can't get away with anything forever." Wetzon took a sip of her tea.

"But you could make a hell of a lot of money while you were gettin' away with it."

Wetzon jumped up, almost spilling the tea. "Oh, Laura Lee, you're terrific," she cried.

"Well, thank you very much. Would you mind tellin' me what this is all about?"

"Carlton Ash. He was killed because when he used the late, departed compliance director's office, he discovered something illegal the compliance director had been working on."

Laura Lee frowned and put her chin on her bent knees. "Then all you have to find out is who the broker is who handles these accounts and you have your murderer."

FIFTY-
ONE

The question was—What broker had these accounts as his clients? And what if it wasn't just one broker involved? She'd put in a call to Midtown North and passed the information on to Metzger.

It would be easy enough to find the broker. Every brokerage account had the name of the financial consultant covering the account stored in its computer systems, and if not the name, the broker's I.D. number. All roads led to . . .

Wetzon folded memo paper into strips and tore the strips on each fold, then wrote *sandwiches* twice, *pumpkin bread, cake, biscuits, scones,* and dropped each onto the serving plate she'd laid out for it.

"There, that's it for today." Laura Lee came down the hall from the bathroom and found Wetzon surveying the living room.

"Does it look all right?" Wetzon felt anxious, unnerved. Her heart fluttered and throbbed, then settled down, then fluttered and throbbed again. "I hope it'll be cool enough." She could feel Laura Lee's worried eyes on her and she avoided them.

"I hate like the devil to leave you."

"Oh, no, Laura Lee. Go. I have moments of mindless panic, but really, I'm solid as a rock." She smiled. "A slightly cracked rock. And, you can't disappoint the general."

Laura Lee laughed. "Can you imagine, li'l ole me with a general? Wouldn't Daddy love it? Too bad he'll never know." Laura Lee delighted in torturing her parents with stories about all the Yankee Jewish liberals she was going out with. Now, standing at the door, she gave Wetzon a hug. "We women have to stick together."

"I know. I love you for this, Laura Lee, but I'd rather be alone. Honest. I'll walk you out, though. I want to get my mail and maybe treat myself to Mexican take-out for dinner. Then I'm going to have a good soak and get into bed with a book." She knew she had Scott Turow's new one somewhere in the apartment.

"Well, put somethin' on for the street, darlin', 'cause I want to get goin'. The general's flyin' up for dinner and the Juilliard String Quartet."

Awkwardly, Wetzon slipped a cotton miniskirt over her leotard and tied the laces on her Keds. "Sounds serious."

Laura Lee rolled her eyes. "Oh, *puh*-leeese. Thinkin' about it gives me hives."

Arranging the straw hat over her forehead and adding the sunglasses, Wetzon said, "That's because you don't really want to get married. I can understand that." They grinned at each other.

Laura Lee inspected her. "No one would ever know. What are you goin' to tell people?"

"That I walked into a door. Or the truth. I don't want anyone to think Silvestri did it."

Outside, the heat was horrific, and Manhattan looked like a cement desert. Laura Lee got into a cab and Wetzon strolled over to Broadway. The air was spongy and dense. The West Side was a ghost town. Traffic was sparse, except for City buses, and the only cab she had seen was the one Laura Lee had gotten into.

Standing at Broadway and Eighty-sixth, Wetzon looked downtown. The deserted streets shimmered in the sun like an optical illusion. It must be her eyes. She took off her sunglasses. It wasn't her eyes. The palm trees on the island between uptown and downtown traffic drooped fronds to the dry earth. Palm trees? Was she mad? She put her glasses on. Another optical illusion.

The Mexican take-out had the air conditioner on frigid, reviving her. She ordered a chimichanga to go, and waiting, she watched the deft hands of the cook lay out the tortilla, fill it, roll it, and lower it into the hot oil. She wondered if he hit his wife or girlfriend with those hands.

Stop that, she thought.

He drained the rolled package and fitted it neatly into a foil container, adding refried beans, rice, and salsa, then rolled the foil rim around the cardboard top with enviable expertise, all the while cleaning off the spill around the sides with a clean white towel.

Out on the street again, the sun beat down through the straw of her hat and streams of perspiration trickled down her face, making her nose a slide for her sunglasses. Overhead the sky was blue and cloudless, and twice as uncaring. She felt as if she were on the grill and wondered at what temperature blood boiled.

Upstairs, she dropped her mail and the chimichanga on the kitchen counter and went into the living room. Parking her hat on one of the finials of the slat-backed chair, she stood in front of the air conditioner, turning, front to back, cooling, back to front, and thought about the pieces of the puzzle. Her bruises throbbed in the temperature change, and she left the chill, aiming her tired body for the bedroom.

At last she lay on her bed, looked at the beams on her ceiling, let her eyes rove over the brass filigree of the ceiling fan, running lazily on low.

"Why," Wetzon had asked Laura Lee, "would a broker have two accounts with the same number?"

"It might be a back office foul-up."

"How could that be, in this age of computers?"

"Oh, my dear, it happens more often than you'd think. We're only as good as the support we get, and with all the cost-cuttin' goin' around, you get help that can't read, write, or comprehend. You get what you pay for."

"Okay, okay, get off your soapbox, y'all." Wetzon laughed. "I get your gist. What else could it mean?"

"Well, darlin', you didn't hear this from me—but look at those names. They could be phony accounts, phony names, all leadin' back to the same broker."

"And that's illegal—"

"Oh, my, is it ever illegal. And if there's a lot of tradin' goin' on, they can trade in and out of a stock without ever payin' for it. That's called kitin', darlin', and that's a no-no. And if it's an options account, there's a ton of money to be made if you don't have to keep the margin requirements."

"I don't get it."

"Darlin', the rule is that if you're playin' options, you must have the money in the account to cover. If you have a whole lot of accounts, you can keep switchin' from one account to the other and never have to put up the whole—"

"It sounds like an awful lot of stress to me."

"Listen, Wetzon darlin', you'd be surprised how many people thrive on stress like this. Put a greedy computer genius with a touch of larceny in his soul into a brokerage situation and, trust me, there's no tellin' the number of ways he can find to feather his nest."

F I F T Y -
T W O

"Barf in a bag!" Laura Lee shrieked. "He wants to be your *intimate* friend but he's in love with his *shrink*?"

Only five of the girls were left. Laura Lee, Wetzon, Anne, Tobie, and Sylvie. They were flaked out on the sofa and the floor, playing can-you-top-this with stories about dating in New York. Ice clinked in glasses; the sandwiches and cakes were mere crumbs on empty plates. And Tobie had just finished telling about her latest relationship.

"Save me from Wasp men," Tobie groaned. "They might as well be made of granite. It's unbelievable how out of touch they are with their feelings. And they love their little drinkies."

"Amen to that," Laura Lee, who had been brought up a Southern Baptist, said. "I much prefer Jewish men. They love good food." She paused until the laughter died down, then said, "And now, Wetzon is goin' to tell us about Italian men."

"Oh, do," the others caroled, all except Anne, who said, "I, for one, am tired of being polite and would like to know if *he* did that to you."

Wetzon's hand flew to her damaged face. "No, he didn't. He wouldn't. I got this from a client, along with an attempt at rape, and I'm feeling—I don't know—I just didn't want to spoil today for you." She swallowed hard.

Laura Lee slipped off the sofa and crouched next to Wetzon, hugging her. "It's okay, darlin', that's what we girls are here for, we're a support group for each other, even though we don't get together that often. Right, girls?"

"Right!"

"Now divert us with stories about Italian men," Sylvie demanded.

They all laughed, and Wetzon, pressing her hand to her bruised cheek, said, "I'm no expert on Italian men. He's the first." She smiled, feeling her smile only on one side of her face. "And he's not the definitive Italian man because he's a detective, so he hides the Mediterranean emotion. But you know it's there, always seething under the surface." Her eyes filled with tears, and she thought, *Why can't I control all this emotion that keeps washing over me?*

"You hear that, girls?" Laura Lee refilled her glass from the pitcher of iced tea on the coffee table. "I think we're about to lose Wetzon. You're goin' to follow Annie into marital bliss."

"The truth is, I'm no more ready to get married than you are, Laura Lee, although I'm practicing right now."

Sylvie held up her hand. "I have a story, does anyone want to hear?"

"Oh, goody."

"Tell."

"Well," Sylvie said, "I meet this really attractive guy at a cocktail party for the UJA, and we have this fantastic flirtation. We head right for the Hilton and he takes a room and we get upstairs and start tearing each other's clothes off, and here I am practically in the buff, and he produces these handcuffs." She paused and got the effect she wanted.

"Oh, God!"

"Sylvie!"

"Kinky!"

"What happened?"

"I said, 'I just remembered I have to make a phone call,' and I grabbed my bag and my clothes and ran. And there I was trying to get dressed and running in the corridor for the elevator, and these two old people are getting off the elevator, and they stare at me like I'm crazy, and I jump on the elevator—and their eyes are popping out and I say, 'The health club is great, they get you in and out like a shot,' and the elevator closes."

"I don't know, girls, datin' in New York is like having a toothache," Laura Lee said, after the laughter had died down.

"The philosopher speaks," Anne said.

"Then there's Howard," Tobie said. "He's sixty-two and very sweet. He sends flowers to my office the day after we see each other. The guys call it my put-out bouquet."

"Is he sexy? Some older men are sexy," Wetzon said, trying to drink iced tea while supine without spilling any down her neck and not succeeding. *Like Alton Pinkus,* she thought. She sat up and blotted the spill with a napkin.

"Do y'hear that?" Laura Lee said.

"Name one besides Paul Newman," Sylvie said.

"Well, one of them died, Bart Giamatti." Wetzon waited for all the negative comments to pass, then said, "Felix Rohatyn."

Groans, laughter.

"I couldn't lock lips with either of them on a bad day. I much prefer Robbie Robertson," Laura Lee said.

"Or Harrison Ford," Anne suggested.

"Not bad." They were all in agreement for once.

"I must admit to a certain attraction to Tom Stoppard," Laura Lee said.

"The playwright?" Tobie, who'd been stretched out on the floor, sat up. "I've met him. He's one of those clever, brainy guys."

"I like brainy guys," Wetzon said. "Prefer them over brawny ones anytime."

"I was having an affair with this brainy Englishman—you could never call him a guy—who was an economist for a big bank with a branch here, and he used to fly in once a month." Anne smiled. "We'd spend the weekend at the Warwick."

"The Warwick? Get a grip!" Laura Lee interrupted.

Tobie choked on her tea and started coughing. Sylvie clapped her on the back.

"Yes, a bit of all that tacky English stuff—are you all right, Tobie?"

Tobie nodded, gasping and laughing.

"Well, it went on for about a year and then I never heard from him again."

"Cameron Kendall," Tobie gasped between coughs and laughter. "What year were you?"

"1988." Anne looked confused.

"I was '87."

"You're kidding!"

"Now isn't that just what you'd expect in New York?" Laura Lee said.

"I once was fixed up with a guy," Wetzon said, "who looked okay and took me out to dinner at the Rainbow Room after the show I was in—I can't remember which one. Anyway, he kept sending the food back, and I was so ravenous—I never ate before a show—I kept saying, 'Please, it's fine, it's fine, just let me get a bite out of it before you send it back,' and he kept snapping his fingers at the waiter—with the hand that wasn't holding the big fat cigar."

"L.D.C.," Laura Lee said knowingly.

"L.D.C.?" they all asked.

"Little dick complex."

"Then there's this thing I've noticed," Wetzon said, "on Wall Street, the shorter the man, the bigger the ego."

"The truth is," Laura Lee said, "men are really a whole other race. They don't even talk the same language we do."

"Hold on there, girls, I'm not sorry to give up the toothache." Anne spoke suddenly, breaking through the laughter.

"I think we should drink to that," Wetzon said. "Does anyone want champagne?" She rolled herself into a standing position and went into the kitchen. Anne followed her.

"Tell the truth, Wetzon, is your guy battering you?"

"Oh, no. Really." Wetzon pulled the champagne from the fridge. "I told you the truth; it was a client."

"Wetzon, I recognize it. Don't kid me. Charlie did that to me for years. I don't talk about it, but I got out with the help of people who know how to deal with battered women, and now I've got Ed, who's such a sweetheart. But, Wetzon, listen to me, you don't have to take it."

"It's okay, honest, Anne. Silvestri has been wonderful, and I'm pressing charges against my client."

Anne patted her back doubtfully and twisted the cork of the champagne. It opened with a loud pop, and the cork shot to the ceiling and dropped back to the floor, leaving a small indentation in the ceiling.

"Come on," Wetzon said, putting glasses on a tray and carrying them into the living room.

They drank to Anne and each other and called it a day.

"I can't imagine being married," Laura Lee said after everyone had gone. "It's so . . . I don't know . . . permanent. You never can have any privacy, there's always someone around."

"You have to include someone in all your plans, your decisions."

"You can't come and go as you wish."

"That's why you like your long-distance relationship with the general."

"And that's why you're livin' with a man who works funny hours."

They looked at each other and laughed. "I love my apartment when nobody else is here," Wetzon said. "I admit that. But it's really nice to have someone who cares about you."

"Watch it, darlin', you're waverin'." Laura Lee wagged her finger at Wetzon.

At seven o'clock, everyone was gone and the apartment was hers again. Wetzon went through the living room, picked up a napkin and Dustbusted the crumbs from floor, table, and sofa. She took the empty champagne bottle from the coffee table and brought it into the kitchen. It made a loud thump when she dropped it in the trash bag.

The downstairs intercom buzzed.

"Yes?"

"Package came for you yesterday, Ms. Wetzon. Arlo forgot to tell you."

"Okay, I'll come down."

"It's too heavy for you to carry. I'll bring it up."

"Okay." She took her finger off the intercom button. What could it be? Since the explosion in the garden, she was leery of packages.

When the doorbell rang, Wetzon opened her door and Sammy, the Sunday handyman, lugging a case of wine, said, "Where do you want it?"

"Right here is fine." She eyed the package warily. It was a liquor carton and looked harmless enough. "Thanks, Sammy." She closed the door and probed the envelope on the top of the case. Nothing but a card. No funny wires or strange instruments. The card read, *With best wishes, Douglas Culver.*

A fury of major proportions took control of her. She literally saw red and kicked the case of wine, jamming her toes. "Dammit, dammit!" She hopped around massaging her foot. She was incensed. Did he think this would make up to her for what had happened? She had half a mind to send it back to—she bent to look at the label—Liberty Liquors.

Clawing at the corrugated cardboard of the case, she tore a fingernail and swore, roundly cursing out Dougie Culver and Luwisher

Brothers. How dare they try to bribe her! She pried the top of the case open with her bread knife, plucked one bottle out and was staring at the label of a really fine California cabernet, William Hill Reserve, 1987, when the phone rang.

Still holding the neck of the bottle, she snapped, "Hello."

"Wetzon!"

"Who is this?"

"Dwayne."

"Dwayne?" She'd forgotten all about Ellie's assistant. Hadn't he run away, left town? "Where are you? I have to talk to you."

"I'm at Penn Station. I've been hiding out on Fire Island for the last few days, but I can't do it anymore. I want everything to be like it was. And it's so hot I can't stand it. Carlos said to call you, that you—I'm really scared—"

"Dwayne, slow down. Get in a cab and come up here now." He knew something about the murders, she was sure of that now. He sounded terrified. She decided to be smart, for once, and not tell him that the police were looking for him. "Come on. I'm on West Eighty-sixth Street."

"Wetzon, I'm getting on the first train to Baltimore. I'm not hanging around here."

"Please, Dwayne. We need your help. I have something I want you to look at."

"No way. I'm not leaving here. My train is at nine."

She made up her mind quickly. "Then I'll come to you." Penn Station on a Sunday night was probably full of people coming back from weekends at the shore. It would be safe.

"Weeell, okay," he said, reluctance hanging on his words.

"Where shall I meet you?" She could hear breathing, but he didn't respond. "Dwayne?"

"There's this bagel place, you know—underground, near the Long Island Railroad."

"I'll find it. Stay there. I'll be down in about fifteen minutes."

"Wetzon, don't look for me. I'll find you."

She hung up the phone and called Silvestri at Midtown North. Mo answered. "You just missed him," she said. "How are you feeling?"

"Mo, Dwayne—I'm okay—but Dwayne called me about a minute ago. He's been hiding out on Fire Island. I didn't tell him you're looking for him. I'm going down to Penn Station to meet him now. He's running away."

"Stay where you are, Leslie. I'll try to get Silvestri."

"Mo, I can't. We'll lose him. Tell Silvestri I'm meeting Dwayne at a bagel shop on the concourse near the Long Island Railroad." She rested the wine bottle on her hipbone.

"No, Leslie, let us handle it. I'll get Silvestri—"

"Just tell me one thing, Mo—Dwayne is still not a suspect, that hasn't changed, has it?"

"I can't—"

"It's okay. I know he's not. He can't be." She hung up. She was not afraid of Dwayne. He hadn't killed Ellie and he wasn't at the dinner and he wasn't even at Luwisher Brothers the morning Carlton Ash was killed. A stab of pain stung her palm. She looked down at the bottle she was strangling. Her nails were digging into her palm. *Relax, dummy,* she thought. She lifted the bottle again and read the label, turned it to put it back in the case, took it out again and reread the label. Near the bottom it said in large block letters:

CONTAINS SULFITES.

FIFTY-THREE

Daylight was just beginning to fade, and without the intense heat of the sun, it actually seemed a fraction cooler. Was that a breeze she felt ruffling the tiny hairs on the back of her neck? She stood out on Eighty-sixth Street for a minute and saw there were no cabs.

With so little time, she should probably just take the IRT at Eighty-sixth and Broadway, which went right to Penn Station. If she didn't have to wait for a train, she could make it in ten minutes, fifteen at the most.

The low roar from the subway entrance told her that a train was approaching. If it was a local, which made the stop there, she was in luck. She fumbled in her purse for a token, feeling all thumbs, and raced down the stairs, barely avoiding a derelict who had set up shop with a Styrofoam cup on a cardboard box at the foot of the stairs.

A local was slowly pulling into the station, and there was a line at the token booth. She'd never make it. She knew one of the turnstiles was contrary. Sometimes it let you through without a token. Closing her eyes, she said a prayer and nudged the turnstile with her hip. It gave, and she pressed through and onto the train just as the bing-bong chime announced the doors were closing.

It was one of the new trains—no graffiti, not much track noise, and loads of air-conditioning—and it was crowded. She joined the people clustered around a pole, holding on . . . one potato, two potato, three potato, four . . . letting her thoughts drift. Dwayne knew . . .

"I need another dollar for a soda, y'hear?" a woman yelled from the back end of the car. Her voice carried over the conversations and rumble of the train.

Wetzon looked around, but couldn't see anybody doing the talking. A young man with shoulder-length hair looked up from his paperback and frowned. "What?" he asked. When no one responded, he went back to his book.

"Just a dollar," the woman said. "I'd like a soda."

"So would I," someone called.

Laughter flitted over the car.

The woman's voice was coming closer. "Just a dollar," she repeated. "Just a dollar." She had not developed a slick line of patter, so she wasn't having much success.

"Just a dollar? Yo, she wants a dollar. Give her a dollar, man." Three teenagers, two black, one white, were poking each other and roaring.

Wetzon kept her eyes averted, looking out the windowed door into the darkness of the subway tunnels. Now and then red and yellow lights flashed, and then they'd pull into a station for a minute, disgorging passengers, taking more on, then they'd pull out into the dark tunnel again. The train was making good time.

The begging woman said again, from somewhere behind Wetzon, "Just a dollar." She was at the near end of the car now, and Wetzon heard the connecting door to the next car open. "You cheap mutha-fuckas," the woman screamed, leaving the car just as Wetzon looked up and saw her, an emaciated black woman in a filthy raincoat and rubber thongs.

A pall of uneasy silence fell on the car, then a door opened and a voice from the far end of the car said, "My name is Robert, ladies and gentlemen, and this is new for me. I'm a Viet Nam veteran. I'm a victim of Agent Orange, I have cancer, I lost my job when I got sick, my apartment burned down, and my wife died in the fire. Me and my two little kids, Robert Junior and Nancy Lou, are living in a city shelter with drug addicts and weirdos. Can you help me get out of the shelter so I can get back on my feet?" He made coins in a cup jingle. "Anything you can give me would be wonderful. God bless you."

Wetzon sighed. He had the whole litany down, buzz words and all. Change hit metal all through the car. People were emptying their pockets for him. Guilt, perhaps, because they hadn't helped the previous beggar. Were New Yorkers so jaded, she wondered, that even their panhandlers had to have a glitzy presentation? They didn't cough up money for amateurs. And then, what if it were all a scam and the two panhandlers were in cahoots? They could be sharing at the end of the line at South Ferry. Sharing at the end of the line. She thought, this was the reason for the murders at Luwisher Brothers. There was a kitty—illegally gotten—that someone just didn't want to share. It always came back to greed.

The train pulled into Penn Station as the cold began to raise goosebumps on Wetzon's arms. The ride had taken less than twenty minutes.

She got off into the brain-numbing heat on the platform and took the down stairway marked PENN STATION, LONG ISLAND RAILROAD, skimming past people coming up, dodging around the slowpokes going down.

The air was foul with perspiration and urine. When she pushed through the turnstile and came out on the well-lit concourse, mall-like, with the cheap eateries on either side, the stale, rancid smell of buttered popcorn blocked out all previous odors.

The bagel place . . . where was it? She slowed to a walk. This area under Penn Station was honky-tonk and tacky as an amusement park, with fast-food stands and gimmicky souvenir shops, news and magazine stands, even two bookstores. Something for every traveler. AMTRAK, the LIRR, the Path Trains to New Jersey, and the Seventh and Eighth Avenue subways all converged here.

There it was. The Bagel Bar, open 24 hours, spelled out in neon and blinking on and off like a goddam roadside tavern sign. No tables, of course. Just a long counter with barstools on the left and a ledge on the right, where you could eat your bagel with a schmear standing up, a phenomenon particular to New Yorkers, who were always on the run.

A maintenance man in blue overalls and an AMTRAK cap stood at the ledge working *The Sunday Times* crossword puzzle with a ballpoint pen. He was devouring a huge onion bagel with an inch of cream cheese topped with raw purple onions. *An adventure in cholesterol,* she thought as she squeezed by, quickly taking in all the other occupants. Dwayne was not one of them.

Two women sat next to one another at the counter; they were not together, Wetzon reasoned, because the one had her back turned slightly to the other and was smoking and studying the classified pages in a folded-up *Newsday,* a mug of coffee on her left. She spilled out of gray painter's pants, in the rear and over the waist, breasts flopping low and loose under a tee shirt that said FREE THE NEW YORK YANKEES.

The other, much younger, wore Porsche sunglasses and had long curly red hair and a nice pale-gold suntan. She was wearing tight stone-washed jeans and a crisp white cotton blouse, its collar straight up, and gold chains; a bright shawl was tied around her waist like a sarong. She snuffled a Coke noisily through the straw and flirted with the Hispanic counterman for all she was worth.

Wetzon chose the seat at the counter farthest in and sat down, keeping her concentration on the entryway. No Dwayne. Was this going to be a wild-goose chase? It was almost ten after eight. Dwayne mentioned a nine o'clock train to Baltimore. He had to be here. She put her elbows on the counter and stuck. Damn. She pulled back, wet a tissue with saliva and wiped the sticky smudges off her elbows.

The fat woman got off the stool, took her Macy's shopping bag, and waited. The cash register rang. The counterman gave her change, winked broadly at the redhead, and sauntered over to Wetzon.

"What'll you have, girlie?" he asked. He looked her over and she could see him decide she didn't hold a candle to the redhead.

"Diet Coke, please."

"Is that all?"

"Could you wipe the counter here? It's sticky."

He mumbled something under his breath that sounded unpleasant and tapped her a Diet Coke, slid it in front of her, stuck a wrapped straw into it, then wiped the counter around the glass with a dirty rag.

Wetzon unwrapped the straw and discarded the wet paper onto the counter. Well, that explained the stickiness, she thought. He was a real prize. She reached for a paper napkin from the metal trap on the wall at the end of the counter and wiped up the mess. Silvestri should be getting here any minute.

Someone sat down on the stool next to her. It was the redhead. Frowning, Wetzon said, "I'm afraid I'm saving that seat for someone."

"Yes," the redhead said, giving her a nervous smile with shiny Paloma-red lips. "Me."

FIFTY-FOUR

"Dwayne?" Wetzon gaped at the attractive redhead.

Naked curiosity crept over the face of the counterman, and only the arrival of a customer stopped him from sidling toward them.

"Shsh. Don't let on." Dwayne fluffed his curls and fiddled with one of the long chains that lay across his pert bosom.

It was astonishing, Wetzon thought—but then, she had known some of the dancers in *La Cage aux Folles,* and they were equally astonishing. "You're beautiful , but why—?" She stopped. Maybe he was a transvestite away from the office, and she didn't want to insult him.

Dwayne shook his head. "I dress like this sometimes, but right now I just don't want anybody to recognize me."

"Anybody? Give me a for instance."

"I'm leaving town. Don't try to stop me." His hands, with their gaudy red nails, trembled. "Are you drinking your soda?"

"No. You can have it." She pushed it to him. "What are you afraid of, Dwayne?" Where the hell was Silvestri? She pulled the pieced-together list from her purse and unfolded it flat in front of him. Moisture leached onto the mounting paper from the counter. "Damn." She snatched it up and wiped the back of the paper and the counter with a paper napkin, then spread it out again.

"Oh, God," Dwayne said in a tiny voice, when he saw the list. "You know."

Bingo, Wetzon thought. "Is this why Ellie was killed?"

"Oh, God, what am I going to do?" He got off the stool and picked up a bulging red backpack which Wetzon had not noticed before. "Does everybody know?"

She ignored his question. Better to pretend she knew what he meant. "What about your job, Dwayne?"

"My job? That's a joke." He stared at her from behind the dark glasses. His voice broke. "I'm outa here, I'm outa there. It's not safe."

Wetzon took the paper off the counter and stuck it under Dwayne's pretty nose. "I'm not interested in whether you go or stay. Just tell me what this list means."

"I can't . . . I'll be dead."

"Dammit, Dwayne, you'll be dead if you don't."

Dwayne ducked his head. "It's a list of accounts," he said in a hoarse whisper, placing his heavy pack on the stool.

"Whose accounts? What broker?"

Dwayne stared at the list until she thought he'd gone into a trance. Finally, he said, "Ellie."

"Ellie? I can't—" Wetzon stopped short of saying she couldn't believe it of Ellie. He looked down at his feet and she saw he was wearing black patent spike heels. When she looked up, Silvestri came into view on the concourse. "Wait a minute, Dwayne. Are these legitimate accounts?"

As Silvestri clapped his hand like a vise on Dwayne's shoulder, Dwayne let out a small squeal. The counterman and the customer looked over at them.

"Dwayne, have you met Lieutenant Silvestri?" She folded up the list and put it in her purse.

"We've met," Silvestri said. "But stop me if I'm wrong—you had a different hairdo."

Dwayne smiled nervously at Silvestri, but he spoke to Wetzon. "How could you do this to me? Carlos said—"

Wetzon felt her cheeks get hot. She'd betrayed him.

"Come off it, the woman probably just saved your life. We would have found you, but it may have been too late. Let's get out of here."

Silvestri took Dwayne's elbow and Dwayne squealed again. The counterman stared.

Wetzon put two dollar bills on the counter and followed the odd couple out and up the moving stairs to the renovated Penn Station waiting room. Departing trains were being announced, the digital board was clicking with changes on incoming trains, and people milled around, even at eight forty-five on a Sunday night, waiting for trains home.

Dwayne's heels tapped rat-a-tat-tat on the marble floor. They took another escalator up and exited at the cab station, where Silvestri's black Toyota was waiting for them, Mo at the wheel. A long line of exhausted, bedraggled travelers stretched out toward Thirty-third Street waiting for cabs that didn't come.

"Les, slide in front with Mo," Silvestri ordered, opening the door.

Wetzon climbed in. "Hi." Silvestri slammed her door shut and opened the back door, pushing Dwayne in first, hand on his curly red head, then following him.

"Hi." Mo's eyes were on Dwayne. "Lovely," she said.

"Pull up near Thirty-second," Silvestri said. A driver behind them leaned on his horn. "And stick up the light."

Mo started the car and they rolled a few yards forward, then she stopped, took the bubble light from the seat, reached a long arm out the window and up, planting it on the roof. The amber light roiled from the roof of the car, making mad reflections on the cement surroundings.

"Am I under arrest?" Dwayne's voice was ragged.

"Not yet. Take off those goddam glasses."

"Oh, God." He took off his glasses and buried his face in his hands. "What am I going to do?"

"You're going to tell the truth. You have that list, Les?"

Dwayne sat up. His eyelids were caked with gray eye shadow and black mascara all run together. Wetzon handed Silvestri the list and Silvestri unfolded it and thrust it at Dwayne. "Let's have it all, Dwayne. Come on. You're a target. We know you didn't kill anybody, but you were in on the scam, weren't you?"

"No. I wasn't. I didn't. Wetzon—"

"Don't look to her for help, man. Let's have it."

"I told Wetzon. They're clients."

"Whose clients?"

"Ellie's, but—"

"What about these accounts? Why did Ellie tear up the list? Cough it up or I'll haul your ass down to the House of Detention."

"Oh, no, please."

"You're being a little hard on him, Silvestri," Mo said. "Come on, Dwayne. Tell him."

"She was upset. I don't know. Dr. Ash sent the list to her and said he was going to tell everything unless she cut him in. She didn't know what he was talking about, but when she checked, they were all under her AE number."

"But you knew what he was talking about, didn't you, Dwayne?"

"I didn't know anything, honest to God," Dwayne blubbered.

"Who knew?"

"Chris Gorham. I mean, we found out afterward that he got the same letter from the fat fuck, but it was the day of the dinner for Goldie, and no one had time to check it out. Then Goldie died and everything began to get crazy."

"Who called the early meeting last Saturday?"

Dwayne scrunched up his face and sniffled. His mascara gave him black eyes. "The fat—Dr. Ash. I wasn't there. I don't know what happened. Please—"

"Was Gorham in on whatever was going on?" Silvestri asked. Wetzon knew he'd love to nail Chris on a murder charge.

"I don't know. I guess he was going to have to cough up some money, too."

"Wait a minute," Silvestri said. "I'm not following you. Gorham and Ellie were being blackmailed? By Ash? Why?"

Dwayne stared at Silvestri, then at Wetzon. "I thought you knew." He licked his lips, then pressed them shut. "I'd like to talk to a lawyer."

"Dwayne," Mo said. "We can hold you as a material witness."

"I want a lawyer."

"Dwayne, come on," Wetzon said. "Didn't you tell me you were scared of someone?"

Dwayne nodded.

"Who are you afraid of?" Silvestri leaned in on him. "Who killed Ellie? Better tell us because he's sure to come after you if you know who he is. He's killed three, maybe four people already."

Dwayne choked. "I didn't know at first. I didn't understand. Ellie figured it out after she saw the list, but she didn't believe it. She was going to talk to him, have him explain."

"Him? What didn't she believe?"

"The trades. Ellie did the spreads and picked the stocks—she didn't know the good trades would go into the phony accounts and the bad ones went into the clients' accounts."

"Jesus," Wetzon said.

"How long had this been going on?"

"I don't know . . . a year, maybe. Clients were complaining about losing money."

"But it wasn't Ellie. She couldn't have known about it," Wetzon said.

Silvestri gave her a warning look.

"She didn't."

"Then who did? Say it, man. Say it and you're safe."

Dwayne's Adam's apple bobbed twice. He said: "It was David Kim."

FIFTY-
FIVE

"Do you want some coffee?" Mo asked. Her voice was flat as the dead air in the windowless room. Through the open doors of the offices that fed into this room, the window air conditioners sang a medley of moans and drones and power surges, but the anteroom remained stifling.

Dwayne shook his head. "Could I have a Diet Coke with lemon and lots of ice?" His hand was hot and moist in Wetzon's. He'd been holding on to her for dear life since they'd gotten to the Midtown North precinct house.

Mo smirked at him and raised an eyebrow at Wetzon. "How about you, Leslie?"

"Thanks, no. I'm fine." It wasn't true, though. She wasn't fine. She was feverish and tired. A dull, throbbing ache banded the crown of her head. She was feeling roundly guilty about Dwayne's misery. And his pointing the finger at David Kim had rattled her. She was having a hard time dealing with it. The David Kim she knew—*thought* she knew—wasn't—*couldn't* be—hadn't seemed like a murderer.

Mo left the room briefly and returned with a can of Tab. She snapped it open and set it down in front of Dwayne on the scratched and gouged metal table.

"Oh," Dwayne said. He let go of Wetzon's hand to take the can. Sweat reeked from every pore—flop sweat, made fetid by fear.

Silvestri and Weiss were holed up in another office with an assistant D.A. and Arthur Margolies, Carlos's attorney friend, whom Wetzon had called on Dwayne's behalf.

Dwayne's red curly wig lay on the table like a hairy dead creature. He fingered the curls. "This girl must look a sight," he murmured, sipping the Tab. In fact, with his slim body and small features, short hair and feminine makeup, he looked androgynous. His backpack had been confiscated. "Do you have a mirror?" He looked at Wetzon.

"I don't know." Wetzon opened her purse and found a mirror in the zipper compartment. She held it out to Dwayne.

"Don't!" Mo leaned over and grabbed the mirror, handing it back to Wetzon. "Just hold it up for him, don't give it to him."

God, Wetzon thought, were they worried Dwayne was suicidal?

"Precautions," Mo said, answering her thought.

Wetzon held the mirror up for Dwayne, and he took one look at himself and dissolved, sobbing childlike, head in his arms on the table. She patted him on the back. "Come on, Dwayne. It'll be all right. And you know they'll protect you from David." She exchanged glances with Mo.

The door opened, wafting a brief draft of cool air toward them, and Arthur emerged, followed by Silvestri, Weiss, and Rachel Konstantin, the assistant D.A. Konstantin carried a loose-leaf notebook in black leather. They all looked pleased with themselves.

"Dwayne," Arthur said, putting his hand on Dwayne's shoulder. "I want to talk to my client privately for a few minutes and then we'll come back to you." Arthur looked so reasonable and calm with his neat gray beard and horn-rimmed glasses that Dwayne stopped crying. A clarion blast sounded as he blew his nose into the tissue Wetzon handed him, then he meekly retired with Arthur to the room that had just been vacated.

"What's the story?" Mo asked.

"We have a deal," Silvestri said. "He's got immunity and we get to tape his story, so let's get it set up." Mo rose and left the room.

Wetzon had seen pictures of Rachel Konstantin in *The Times* because she'd been getting some really big cases, but the pictures had not been flattering. The assistant district attorney had red hair, the same color as Dwayne's wig, but she wore hers cropped close to her head. Her face was a little too broad and a little too pink and freckled to look attractive on television, but nevertheless, in the flesh, she had a glint in her eyes and crackling electricity in her manner. She drew attention like a magnet.

Silvestri said, "Stay put, Les. We're going to need you to fill in the blanks."

Konstantin picked up the phone, punched one key, waited, then turned her back and began talking at top speed into the phone, gesturing all the while. She was wearing a yellow-and-white shirt and a black stretch skirt that stopped about three inches above her knees. She had the wrong knees for the skirt.

Weiss stood with Silvestri near the door to the hall. Weiss shook a cigarette out of a pack and lit it with a high-flame lighter. He said something to Silvestri about a search warrant, but she couldn't quite catch it.

When Weiss left, Silvestri pulled a chair out of the way and sat on the edge of the table facing Wetzon. Konstantin kept her back to them. Silvestri traced the line of her cheekbone to her lips with a gentle finger.

"Search warrant?" she asked. She kissed his finger, took his hand in hers.

"We're looking for sulfites."

"Where?"

He brought her hand to his lips. "The Kim produce market."

She felt dizzy, collected her hand. "Then you think David Kim did it?"

"He had the best motive." His voice was husky.

"Can you arrest him on motive?"

"No, but we sure as hell can bring him in and try to get a confession."

"Is he a citizen?"

"Don't know. Metzger is working on Immigration."

Konstantin hung up and turned around. "We're in business." She looked at Wetzon and folded her arms.

"You might try to find out what happened to the head of compliance at Luwisher Brothers, the one who had the accident in the subway. I don't even know when it was—seven or eight months ago."

"Yeah." Konstantin nodded. "He jumped, fell, or was pushed, October, November last year. Angelo La Rocca."

"I figure he caught on and must have let David know. Then he had a convenient accident."

"I find it hard to believe that Kaplan didn't know what was going on right under her nose."

"Ellie was in love with him, Ms. Konstantin. If she'd had even an inkling of doubt early on, I think she would have brushed it away. People do uncharacteristic things when they're in love."

Konstantin nodded.

"I think," Wetzon continued, "it wasn't until Dr. Ash tried to blackmail her—he wasn't content with just taking from David—that she began to suspect something . . . Oh, my God!"

"What, Les?"

"Ms. Wetzon?"

"I'm sorry. I just realized how terrible this is going to be for Luwisher Brothers. They could go under when this gets out. Clients will lose faith in the firm. It'll be horrible for the whole Street. Public confidence in Wall Street will be damaged again. One bad apple and the party is over."

"More than one, Les. Why wasn't this monitored internally? Someone was in on it—or maybe looked the other way."

She thought immediately of Doug Culver. He should have been handling this. Who had told her he was in charge of compliance until they found someone . . . ? Did Dougie have his own agenda? What had he been doing meeting with Janet and Twoey Barnes? She said, "The SEC has people who watch for things like this, but they don't always have enough manpower, and it comes down to a spot check. The firms have to learn how to police themselves, the industry has to."

"They'll never do it," Konstantin said.

"Why would David kill Goldie? That doesn't make sense. Unless it really was an accident."

"We're going to find out," Silvestri said, looking at Konstantin. "We haven't got Kim placed at the banquet yet. No one seems to remember if he was there. He wasn't on the guest list. Did you see him, Les?"

"No." Wetzon scanned through her memory of that evening, heard bits of the angry words in the men's room, which now, with hindsight, she realized had more to do with salarying brokers than . . . she saw Goldie and Neil on one side, Hoffritz and Bird on the other. And Culver leaning toward Hoffritz and Bird. Gorham . . . she couldn't think about Chris without feeling a flutter of panic. She saw the investment community in their finery . . . Jack Donahue, Smith, Ellie . . . the table. Wait. Roll back to Smith.

Clear as a bell she heard Smith say, "Wall Street is getting to be a regular grubby United Nations with brown, black, and yellow faces, though I did see Ellie Kaplan talking to a rather attractive Chinaman at the bar. . . ."

FIFTY-SIX

Wetzon came out of Bellevue Hospital and took a cab to the office. Monday. No let-up in the heat wave. *The Times* had another op-ed article by a scientist predicting global warming unless the ozone layer was protected. Her knee was healing nicely; and having had the packing removed, she could breathe through her nose again, although it felt really strange, as if she had to relearn how.

What she really needed was an oxygen mask or—she remembered the runner in the breathing mask, making the turn from Ellie's street and running down West End Avenue. He'd had dark hair and long legs. Had that been David Kim? Had he killed Ellie and left the rose because they'd been lovers?

It was early, only eight-thirty. She hadn't been able to reach Smith last night, and she'd tried her again at seven-thirty this morning before she left for the hospital. Still no answer. Smith hadn't come home last night. Actually, now that she thought about it, she hadn't heard from Smith since they'd argued on Friday about Wetzon's decision to file a complaint against Chris. This was most unlike Smith.

Uptown traffic on First Avenue wasn't bad this morning, but the City and its people had lost their usual up-'n-at-'em Monday morning killer New York energy. She didn't have it herself. Even the cab driver was just driving, not talking. It was an effort to make conversation. The perfect climate for a headhunter whose lifeblood was talk. She smiled and didn't feel the stiffness as much. At least her face was returning to normal.

She started to unlock the outside door, but it was already unlocked. Had B.B. or Harold gotten there early? She stood in the cool reception room. Coffee was dripping in the Bunnamatic. "Hello?" B.B.'s desk was unoccupied.

"Wetzon!" Smith shrieked. "Where have you been? I called you last night and you weren't home." Smith stood in the door to their private office, wearing the white linen dress. Her eyes were glinty and manic.

"You didn't leave a message."

"I hung up after the fourth ring. I hate your answering machine. I have so much to tell you, sugar. Get right in here and sit down. Wait'll you hear." She pulled Wetzon into the office and sat her down in her chair.

"I have to talk with you, too, Smith. When are we due down at Luwisher Brothers?" When, she wondered angrily, was Smith going to acknowledge her bruised face?

"That's just it, sweetie, we're not going. Twoey is keeping our appointment."

As angry as she was with Smith, curiosity overcame her. "Twoey?"

"Yes—your face really looks dreadful, dear—Twoey. He's—"

"Excuse me," Wetzon interrupted. "That's all you're going to say about what happened to me?"

Smith stared at her, hand over her breast. "Sugar, we've been all over this. Your face will heal, and it's better not to make a big deal out of it."

"My face will heal." Wetzon heard her voice rise into screechy registers. Damn, she sounded like an hysteric. She breathed herself calm. "I'm pressing charges," she said defiantly, "whether you like it or not."

Smith looked hurt. "I'm on your side, sweetie pie. You do whatever you have to do, but of course it will send out all the wrong signals. We can't be seen as whiners."

"Whiners? My God, Smith, get your priorities straight."

Smith beamed at her. "Doll baby, let's just agree to disagree here, okay? Now let me tell you my news."

Why was she in partnership with this woman, Wetzon wondered. They would never agree on important things. She ought to have her head examined. "Be my guest."

"There was an emergency board meeting on Saturday and they voted to sell if Twoey got more than fifty percent of the shares, and he did. He's taking over Luwisher Brothers—or rather, L.L. Rosenkind is buying it, and Twoey will run it as a division of Rosenkind." She clapped her hands gleefully. "There now, what do you think of that?"

"I'm amazed. What happens to Destry Bird and John Hoffritz?" It was pointless to try to get Smith to see it her way. A waste of time. The best she could hope for was—

"They're out. One of them is a murderer anyway, so who cares. They were probably in it together. They got rid of Goldie, but they couldn't get the voting shares on their side. Isn't it exciting?"

"Who else at Luwisher Brothers was in on this takeover? They had to have a major insider besides Twoey and his mother."

"Well, let's see . . . how about Doug Culver?"

"How about him? Are you telling me Doug sold out his cohorts?"

Smith nodded. She flipped through the pages of *The Journal*. "I don't see anything, except—look, it says 'rumors continue re the possibility of a large trading loss at Luwisher Brothers. John Hoffritz, president, refused to comment.' Ha!"

"What does Doug Culver get for his disloyalty, may I ask?"

"Wetzon, there you go again. He wasn't disloyal. He was entrepreneurial."

"Oh, so now entrepreneurial is a synonym for ratfink betrayer."

Smith smiled benignly. "I know you're being bitchy because you're mad you weren't in on all the politics of it."

"I couldn't care less."

"Oh God, it was lovely, just lovely." Smith danced around the room. She was ecstatic.

"What's Dougie getting as his reward?"

"He's going to run the capital markets division."

"What about Neil? Is he in or out?"

"He's head of retail."

"And salaries for brokers?"

"A good idea whose time has not yet come."

Wetzon couldn't squelch a broad grin. "Now that, I like." She rose and filled her coffee mug. The windows had all been replaced. The office looked as it had before the explosion, except for the disordered stack of suspect sheets on her desk that screamed out to be sorted. "The office looks good."

"The boys and I did some cleaning. We'll have to replant the garden."

"A small thing." She looked at Smith and could tell there was more; Smith was just bursting with it. "So it's you and Twoey now?"

"Uh-huh."

"And poor dear Jake Donahue?"

Smith blew a kiss and waved bye-bye.

Wetzon laughed. Jake Donahue deserved it. "I tried you last night and this morning. I wish you'd get an answering machine."

Smith smiled indulgently and ruffled her curls. "If it's important, people will call again." She opened a drawer and took out a new pair of pantyhose.

"Well, it was important."

Smith broke the plastic wrap and pulled the new hose out of the package. "Oh?"

"Are you listening?"

Smith wriggled out of her old pantyhose. "Of course I'm listening."

"Didn't you say something to me at the banquet about how Wall Street was looking like the UN?"

Smith pulled the new pantyhose on. "Yes. Blacks, Japs . . ." She slipped her feet back into her shoes and threw away the old pantyhose in her wastebasket.

"And didn't you say one of the Asians was good-looking?"

"Yes, the one at the bar with Ellie."

"Would you recognize him again if you saw him?"

"I don't know. Why?"

"Would you try? Let me call Silvestri and see if you can identify him as having been there that night."

"Who is this he?"

"Maybe David Kim."

"Well, finally I'm being invited to contribute to this investigation."

"Oh, Smith. You've been so involved with Twoey, you haven't even noticed anything else. I'm going to call Silvestri and find out when he wants us." She picked up the phone and tapped out the numbers with the head of her pen.

The outside door opened and Harold appeared, carrying the mail and wearing another new suit. "Good morning," he said. He seemed surprised to see them both in their office. "Gee, what happened to you, Wetzon?"

Wetzon listened to the ringing of the phone in her ear. "Metzger."

"Hi, Artie, it's Les."

"Hello, Les. How ya doing? When Mo brought you in—"

"I'm okay, Artie. I'm tough." She flexed her knee where the stitches had been. The healed cut was tight and vaguely itchy under her hose.

"You are. You coming in with your partner to make an I.D.?"

"Yes. When do you want us?"

"He's going through booking now. How about ten-thirty?"

"Hold on, Artie." She spoke to Smith. "Ten-thirty, Smith?"

"Yes, fine."

"Ten-thirty, Artie." She hung up.

The outside door opened and B.B. came in carrying a duffel bag. "Hi."

"Nice weekend?" Wetzon asked, looking up. Now both Harold and B.B. were staring at her. "Oh, this?" She touched her face. "Didn't Smith tell you?" She looked at Smith, who shrugged. "It looks worse than it is."

"Okay, enough of this lollygagging. Isn't it time we started dialing for dollars, team?" Smith said. "But stay out of Luwisher Brothers and L.L. Rosenkind. They're merging and they'll be *our* client." She closed the door. "A *very* good client."

"Doug Culver sent me a case of wine," Wetzon said. "I'm going to see if I can catch him."

"He's too busy to talk to you right now, Wetzon. Why not wait till tomorrow?"

Wetzon ignored her and punched out Dougie's direct number.

"Douglas Culver's office."

"Hi, this is Leslie Wetzon. Is Doug available?"

"He's in a meeting, Ms. Wetzon. May I help you—oh, wait—hold on. He wants to talk to you."

Doug came on the line with an explosive, "Wetzon!"

"Doug. I hear you've been very busy."

"Rather."

"Well, I guess congratulations are in order, then. I'm really calling to thank you for the wine. It was a very nice thought, but it isn't going to do you any good. I'm not dropping the charges against Chris."

"Wetzon, you do what you have to do, but we pink-slipped Chris this mornin'. He's history."

"You fired him?" She felt sick. "You didn't have to—"

"Oh, we didn't do it for you, Wetzon," Doug drawled. "He's just not one of us, he doesn't fit here."

What had made her think they'd done it for her? She was really losing it. Actually, even if Chris were to be convicted of assault, it wouldn't keep him off the Street. She sighed. "Tell me, Doug, since we're talking so honestly here, didn't you spot something not kosher going on with Ellie's accounts when you took over compliance?"

"Not until very recently. David was good at coverin' his tracks and I was a little busy carryin' two loads."

Why didn't she believe him? Because he was so glib about it. If he was thinking of taking out the firm, this was a perfect situation to make it vulnerable.

"Wetzon, you've been very helpful and I'd like you to know we're grateful. If there's ever anythin' we can do . . ."

Gee, thanks, she thought. "You can do one small thing for me."

"What is it?" He sounded doubtful, as if he'd never expected her to call in her marker.

"Dwayne, Ellie's assistant. I'd like you to keep him on, find a job for him with someone there."

Irony colored Doug's response. "But I intended to do that all along, Wetzon. I owe the little bugger."

"You owe him?"

"I was the one who clobbered him with the vase that night at Ellie's."

Wetzon inhaled and almost choked. "God, Doug, you could have killed him. What the hell were you doing there anyway?"

"Why should I tell you, Wetzon?"

"Why not, Doug? Let me admire your Machiavellian thought process."

"Funny, Wetzon. Okay, since what I say to you is confidential, and you still work for us, I don't mind hypothesizin'." He sounded amused. "Now, what if both Melissa and Ellie had votin' shares—not much, but enough? And what if Ellie was givin' me their proxy? And what if I found Ellie lyin' there with her head in the fishpond, dead? Christ."

"So *you* put her on the chaise and gave her the rose."

"I couldn't very well leave her in the fishpond."

"Touching, Doug. Why didn't you call the police so they could try to—"

"She was dead. There wasn't anythin' I could do. Grow up, Wetzon. This is the real world. When the ball's in play, you either run with it or you're out of the game."

"Is that what this is, Doug? A game?"

"That's exactly what it is, and losin' is no option."

"Too bad you weren't able to get the proxies."

"Ah, but I did," Doug drawled. "They were just lyin' on the kitchen counter, signed. That's when Dwayne walked in on me. As it turned out, we didn't need them. We got the votes elsewhere."

"Oh, really? From whom?"

"Gail Munchen. She's a Luwisher."

FIFTY-
SEVEN

Midtown North was housed on Forty-second Street between Eighth and Ninth Avenues, a half block from the Manhattan Plaza complex. This had been an old-time ethnic neighborhood, mostly Italian, and still was, only now the butcher shops, bakeries, and grocery stores catered to the diverse population that had settled in this area near the Lincoln Tunnel passage to New Jersey.

In the early seventies the boom in building new residential high rises burst with New York City's fiscal crisis, and Manhattan Plaza, which had been built as luxury housing, sat empty until someone had the bright idea that it might be a boon to theater people, performers, musicians, and production people. A compromise was reached: the rent rolls were quickly filled with subsidized tenants, one-third entertainment people, one-third elderly, and one-third local residents. For theater people, it had been a miracle in affordable housing near the theater district. For a derelict, even dangerous, neighborhood, it had been heaven-sent. Charming little bistros sprang up everywhere, and thriving non-profit, Off-Broadway theater groups surrounded Midtown North, which had moved into the old McGraw-Hill Building.

Smith and Wetzon waited in an anteroom, where an oversized

window air conditioner expulsed cold air with the maximum amount of noise.

"Humpf," Smith said, looking at her watch. "We've been here a half hour already. Don't they know we have a business to run?" She crossed one long leg over the other. "What are we waiting for?"

Wetzon wondered herself. The facility was a corporation of controlled energy, with both uniformed police and detectives going about their business. She'd picked up something subliminal, though, from a distracted Mo, who had brought them in hurriedly and left them there. "Maybe we're waiting for the A.D.A. It's Rachel Konstantin."

"Am I supposed to know who that is?" Smith asked irritably.

"She was on the cover of *New York* magazine this past winter. Don't you remember? She was prosecuting that murder at Madison Square Garden."

"Rachel Konstantin . . . fat and ugly . . ."

"No, not really. She's quite nice-looking in person. Alex Konstantin is her brother." She knew Smith would know Alex Konstantin because he was an M&A genius who had just left Shearson to form his own firm.

"Reeeally?" Smith perked up and the petulant frown left her face just as Mo reappeared without an apology.

"Will you come this way, please." Mo led the way out of the room and down a wide corridor.

Smith gave Wetzon an exaggerated poke in the ribs as they followed. She pointed with her chin at Mo's rear. Mo was wearing tight cotton leggings and a loose shirt that barely covered her attractive round butt. A gun belt settled on her hip, protruding from under the shirt. Her long auburn hair hung below her shoulders. There was something overripe and sultry about her. "Silvestri must love that," Smith stage-whispered.

Mo squared her shoulders. "Shut up, Smith," Wetzon hissed, but of course it was too late. The dead could have heard Smith's loud whisper.

"Leslie." Metzger, his gun in his waistband, was waiting for them at the end of the corridor. He brought them into a room with two rows of folding chairs facing a large dark picture window. An immense floor fan, scaly with dust, rustled hot air from here to there. Metzger studied her face. "How are you? You gave us a bad scare."

"I'm okay, thanks, Artie."

"I'm Xenia Smith," Smith said, offering her hand to Rachel Konstantin, whose wardrobe seemed to consist of too-short skirts. A matching red jacket was hooked on the back of one of the folding chairs.

Seated in the last seat in the first row was a man in his early thirties wearing a rumpled brown suit; a worn leather briefcase sat open at his feet. He took off metal-rimmed glasses and wiped the sweat from his face with a handkerchief, then wiped his lenses and put his glasses back on. The ends of a sparse brown mustache met an equally sparse beard.

"Richard Fuchs, Legal Aid," he said, introducing himself. Wetzon shook his damp hand; Smith ignored him.

"Let's get going," Weiss said. He lit a cigarette.

"Can we not have that." Konstantin frowned. "There's no air in here as it is." Weiss flicked his eyes over her, then dropped the cigarette and ground it into the floor with the sole of his Bally loafer.

When Silvestri appeared, Wetzon saw immediately that there was trouble. His face was dark, almost sullen. "Are we ready?" he asked abruptly, avoiding her eyes.

"Why don't you two ladies sit here," Weiss said, indicating the front row.

Smith smiled at him. Wetzon could see she was adding up what he must have paid for his expensive suit and shoes. "Of course, just tell me what you want me to do." It came out like a sexy invitation as Smith batted her eyelashes at him.

"Jesus," Wetzon said, rolling her eyes.

"We're going to bring out a group of people. They can't see or hear us. All we want you to do is see if you can pick out the individual you saw at the dinner for Goldie Barnes, if he is one of these men." Weiss's eyes never left Smith.

"Take your time, Ms. Smith," Konstantin said. "We want a positive I.D."

Silvestri picked up a receiver on the wall. "Go," he said.

A light went on outside the picture window. A voice said, "Move forward and step up to the line, face front."

A line of six Asian men came out and faced them. Three were tall, two were average, and one was very short. Wetzon let her eyes run from one to the other. The tall one on the end was nervous; his chin was on his chest.

"Heads up," the voice said.

The end man's head came up. *Was this some kind of joke?* Wetzon thought.

"They all look pretty much alike to me," Smith said.

"Turn to your right," the voice ordered.

"I—" Wetzon felt a firm hand on her shoulder. It was Silvestri. He shook his head at her. What the hell was going on?

"Turn to your left."

"I don't know," Smith said. "The one I saw had a sexy smile and beautiful teeth." She looked up at Weiss and smiled.

Silvestri went back to the phone. "Ask them to smile."

"Face front. Smile."

It was like a stand-up act that went bad. Wetzon shivered. Death's-head smiles.

"I'm sorry," Smith said. She shook her head at Weiss.

"Face right," the voice said. "You can stop smiling."

"What do you think, Les?" Silvestri prompted her, giving her leave to speak.

She turned in her chair. He was leaning against the back wall, hands in his pockets. She looked out the window at the six men. Were they serious? Was this some kind of setup?

"Well, Ms. Wetzon?" Konstantin said, impatiently.

"I don't get it," Wetzon said. "None of these men is David Kim."

FIFTY-EIGHT

"You might explain what this is all about," Smith complained as they threaded their way past the shoppers at Manganaro's into the back of the Italian fancy grocery where there was a small restaurant. Neither snow, nor heat, nor anything kept New Yorkers from eating. The place was crowded, with only one or two tables available. They were seated immediately next to an oversized gentleman in a business suit reading *Ad Age,* a napkin tucked into his collar. He was eating garlic-scented spaghetti with red clam sauce from a large soup bowl.

"Let's order first. Do you want to share pasta with ricotta?"

"Yes, fine." Smith took a mirror out of her handbag and redid her lipstick.

"Pasta with ricotta." Wetzon gave their order to a matronly woman in a black dress. "We're going to share."

"To drink?"

"A bottle of Pellegrino, okay, Smith?"

"Fine, fine." Smith's voice had gone steely.

"David Kim gave them the slip."

"Not New York's Finest," Smith said sarcastically.

Wetzon ignored her. "Number six in the lineup, they arrested him because he told them he was David Kim, and I guess they're like you, all Asians look alike."

"Spare me, Mother Teresa." Smith looked at their neighbor with distaste. He was ingesting his spaghetti with loud slurping noises, his napkin bloody with red sauce.

"Besides, his name really is David Kim. It was the wrong one, that's all."

"How is that possible?"

"Because Kim is as common in Korea as Smith is here."

"Go on, Wetzon, have your little joke. I'm not paying any attention."

The woman brought the bottle of Pellegrino, opened it, and poured the mildly carbonated water into their glasses.

"The whole fiasco bought the real David Kim time to make his getaway."

"You're starting to talk like them."

"Them?"

"The cops. Slangy."

"Regardless. In all likelihood he's on his way back to Korea, where he'll live like a king with his ill-gotten gains."

She didn't tell Smith what Silvestri had warned. "Don't go off by yourself anywhere. Don't open any strange packages. Stay with the crowds until we get him."

"After killing three people and trying to kill us. I'd like to get the money it cost to replace the windows, and I can't even imagine what the garden will come to."

"The hell with that. It's only money, and we make plenty of it. We're alive. That's what counts."

"Oh, puh-leeese."

"And I think he actually killed four people. The compliance director was the first. He pushed him in front of a subway train, and got away with it. Then when Dr. Ash began blackmailing him, he thought getting rid of Ash would be easy because Ash had severe asthma and let everyone know he was allergic to sulfites. David's family's produce market still had cans of sulfite powder in their basement from when they used to sprinkle it on the salad bar contents."

"Ugh."

"Silvestri said it's such a fine powder, you wouldn't know it was there, unless you had an allergy. David spiked the bourbon Ash was drinking, but he had no idea Goldie was also allergic to sulfites, was also drinking bourbon, and would pick up Ash's drink by mistake."

The pasta arrived, already divided into two portions. The ricotta had melted into a thick cream over the hot pasta. The waitress ground fresh pepper over each and left them with a bowl of grated cheese.

Smith sprinkled cheese over her pasta. "This is heaven." She twirled her fork full of fettuccine and put it into her mouth.

"So where do you think Hoffritz and Bird will surface? They're not going to retire." Wetzon broke off a piece of bread and dipped it into the sauce. "God, this was a good idea."

"Their shares have to be bought out. They won't feel any pain."

"Not in their wallets, perhaps, but definitely in their egos."

Smith laughed. "This David Kim. Such an unimportant person turns out to be the murderer . . ."

"I don't think they'll get him either." Wetzon ate the last of her pasta and poured more Pellegrino into her glass.

"You mean he'll get away? And with all that money?"

"No, I mean I don't think he'll risk being taken alive. I think Asians have a strong sense of family and face. I don't know. I still can't quite accept the fact that that nice, bright, eager kid could have murdered people."

"Whatever." Smith airily dismissed her with a wave of her hand. "Let's get back to the office. Twoey is going to call me when it's a done deal."

"I thought it already was."

"In principle, but you know lawyers. They have to knock out the details elaborately so their fee looks worth it. Pay the bill, will you, Wetzon. I don't have any change." She walked past the cashier and stared into the deli counter at the various hams and prosciuttos.

One day, Wetzon thought, she'd like to see Smith grab the bill for something, but it was just too hot to argue about right now.

When they came out on Ninth Avenue, it was one-thirty and the sun was blazing like a hot ball of fire, the sky brilliantly cloudless. Smith stepped into the street, snapped her fingers, and a cab pulled over to the curb. The driver rolled down his window. "Upper West Side only," he said. "I'm going off duty."

"Okay with us." Smith crawled into the narrow backseat and motioned for Wetzon to follow.

"Smith! You can't."

"Would you get in here." When Wetzon climbed in and closed the door, Smith said, "Forty-ninth between First and Second."

The cab, which had started rolling forward just before Smith spoke, screeched to a stop. "I told you Upper West Side only. Get outta my cab, lady."

Smith didn't move. She wasn't even intimidated. Wetzon took the handle of the door. "Don't touch that door, Wetzon. Take this man's name and number. We'll report him."

"Oh, fuck this shit. You'll get yours, bitch." He started the cab and gave them a wild ride back to the office. Smith put six singles in the drawer, flipped the drawer closed, and they both got out into the choking heat.

"I thought you didn't have any change," Wetzon grumbled, not even bothering to keep the irritation out of her voice.

"I found some in my bag. And as far as that cab driver is concerned, they're supposed to take us wherever we want to go. We should report him for his language. Did you get his name?"

"No I didn't. Some day someone is going to whack you for your attitude."

"Oh, for pitysakes."

They found the market was off over fifty points when they sat down at their desks, and that's the way the rest of the week went—down, down, down. Down fifty-one Monday, up twenty Tuesday, down forty-two Wednesday, down another thirty Thursday. The gurus were predicting doom and gloom again, advising everyone to go to cash.

Wetzon hadn't seen much of Silvestri, who was under tremendous pressure to arrest David Kim and close the books on the Wall Street murders. The whole City was alerted. The headlines screamed for blood in the *Post* and *News*.

And the intense heat continued unabated. Tempers were raw. A weatherman on one of the local TV stations was set upon by a hostile crowd, roughed up and left nearly naked in front of TKTS, the discount theater ticket booth on Forty-seventh and Broadway, even though he'd promised a break in the weather.

By the time Wetzon got to the office on Friday, she felt she'd put in a full day, and it was only nine-thirty. She'd stopped using public transportation. Descending into the pit was like going willingly into an inferno; the heat was so intense on subway platforms that lipsticks melted in their cases. People talked to themselves, and it was hard to tell the sane from the crazies.

"Hi, Wetzon." Harold was standing in the open door to his small office, talking to B.B.

"Harold, B.B." She opened the door to her office. The air conditioner was doing its job splendidly. Smith wasn't there. "Any calls?"

"Yes." B.B. handed her two messages: one from Smith saying she'd be late, and the other from Marty Rosen.

What was that about, she wondered. "Do we have anybody interviewing with Marty Rosen at Loeb Dawkins?"

"No," B.B. said.

"You, Harold?"

"Uh-uh."

She closed the door and sat down at her desk, thumbing through her Rolodex for Marty's number, then punched it out.

"Marty Rosen's office. Marcia speaking."

"Hi, Marcia. This is Wetzon. Marty wanted me."

"Hold on."

"Wetzon!"

"What's up, Marty?"

"Sharon Murphy. She's at Loeb Dawkins."

"Sharon Murphy? She's with you?"

"No. She went to Ron Mitchell's office."

"I don't believe it. How could that have happened? She was interviewing with you. She met department heads through you. She never told me she was talking to anyone else at Loeb Dawkins."

"Believe it. She's there."

"I'm going to talk to her and I'll call you right back."

"Wait a minute. You didn't do it?"

"Jesus, Marty, I don't show brokers to two different managers in the same firm without clearing it with both managers. What do you think I am? Don't answer that." He could well have said, *you're a headhunter*, with all the scorn the word sometimes provoked. Maybe other headhunters acted like whores, did unethical things, but she did not. She hung up, outraged, figuring twenty-one thousand dollars down the toilet. She called Ron Mitchell's office and asked for Sharon Murphy. Sharon was there all right because they were putting her through, dammit. Wetzon was so angry she didn't see Smith had come into the room.

"Sharon Murphy."

"Sharon, it's Wetzon."

"Oh, it's you."

"Yes. What are you doing in Ron's office?"

"Well, he made me a better deal than Marty did."

"He couldn't have. The deals are all the same. Didn't you tell him you were talking to Marty? It's not ethical to play one manager against the other."

"I don't know what you're making such a big deal about. I got thirty percent up front from Ron, and Marty told me he could only give me twenty-five. That's seventeen five more in my pocket."

"I don't know how Ron got it past regional. Did you work with another headhunter?" Smith made a strangled sound and Wetzon looked up and nodded at her.

"I'd rather not say, but Ron put the deal through as a package with two other brokers he hired."

"Let me guess. It was Tom Keegen, wasn't it?" She curled her lip at Smith, who made a hissing noise through her teeth.

"Yes."

"Yes, she says." Wetzon hung up the phone. "You heard it. Keegen just took twenty-one thousand dollars from us."

Smith screamed.

FIFTY-NINE

The market was off seventy-five moving into the final hour of trading and still on a downward slide. Sell programs had kicked in and there were fewer and fewer buyers.

Anxiety did an erratic time-step in Wetzon's chest. She felt down, oppressed by the relentless heat and humidity, depressed by the events of the last weeks, and worse, disconnected from Silvestri.

David Kim a murderer. Could she have been so wrong in her judgment? Chris Gorham was the one most capable of violence, was he not? Not David—brilliant, charming David—with the world in his hands.

Automatically, she cleaned off the scattered notes and pink phone message slips from her desk and set up her calendar for Tuesday, after the long Fourth of July weekend.

"Damn it all." Smith slammed down the phone. "I'm sick to death of four months of the-check-is-in-the-mail excuses. We have bills to pay."

"Um." Mind adrift, Wetzon was only vaguely aware of Smith's grumbling comments as she went over operating expenses for the first half of the year.

"Is that all you have to say?"

"Um," Wetzon responded, dumping the contents of her briefcase onto her clean desk and methodically picking through the accumulation of papers, suspect sheets, invitations to museum and gallery openings, dance concerts—all having passed without her presence—and a sale notice from Barney's. She tossed everything into her wastebasket but the suspect sheets; those went into her update file.

"And here's the estimate for redoing the garden," Smith mumbled. "Would you believe, three thousand dollars. Are we made of money here?"

"Um." Hidden among the suspect sheets was the baggie with the rolledup list she had pieced together from Ellie's torn scraps, the copy of the whole one she'd found on Chris Gorham's desk. She took it out of the baggie and rerolled it in the opposite direction to smooth it out. The names and addresses meant nothing to her . . . or did they? She picked up the phone and called Silvestri. She was put on hold.

A knock on the door.

"Yes?" Smith called.

B.B., casually dressed in khakis and running shoes, shirt sleeves turned up, opened the door. "Okay if I take off now?"

"Of course, sweetie pie." Full of good will, Smith beamed at him.

Wetzon smiled, shifting the phone to her other ear. B.B. looked like a Yalie going off on a yachting weekend. "Have a good time." She was still on hold.

The door closed behind his thank-yous.

"Where's he going?" Smith sighed and began punching numbers into her calculator.

"East Hampton. Where else do the young and unattached in New York go on a summer weekend?" The phone was giving her an earache.

"Humpf. I've forgotten what it's like to be young and unattached. What's Harold up to?" Smith got up and opened the door.

"Damnation," Wetzon said. She put the receiver down on her desk and rubbed her ear. Returning the receiver to her ear, she had a dial tone. She hung up and studied the names again.

Smith called, "Harold!" Then she returned to her desk.

Harold appeared in the doorway. "What's up?"

"You might as well call it quits, too, sugar bun. No one's going to be around to talk to." Smith gave him a brilliant smile.

"Oh . . . okay." He took off his glasses and rubbed his eyes. "I'm just going to get myself organized for next week."

To Wetzon he sounded mellow. As if he were on something. When he left them, she said, "What's with Harold?"

"What do you mean?"

"I don't know. He sounds high—as if he's been smoking funny cigarettes."

"You've got it all wrong, sweetie. He just needed to be beaten up, and we did it. He loves it." She turned back to the work on her desk. "I'm almost finished here. Do you want to go for a drink?"

"Um." Wetzon was staring at the list of names, smoothing the paper so it wouldn't roll. She fiddled with a strand of hair that had come out of her topknot, then called Silvestri again.

"Silvestri."

"Hi, it's me."

"Make it quick, Les." He was irritatingly brusque.

"Okay. Did you check all the addresses on that list of names I gave you? Maybe David—"

He brushed her off with a sharp, "Mo did. Go home and cool out, Les."

"Wait, Silvestri. Isn't it possible that David is dead, too—murdered?"

She heard a commotion, cheering. Then, "I'll take it. Les, get off the line. Tell Weiss."

"Wait—" But she was listening again to a dial tone. "Damn." He hadn't even heard her. She replaced the receiver with a loud thunk.

"Do you mind, Wetzon? You are mumbling and grumbling. I'm trying to finish up here. It's distracting."

"Um." Wetzon rose and pulled open the filing cabinet, trying to remember how she'd first met David Kim. Had someone referred him? There had to have been a resume. The resume file might yield something. She pulled out the file and flicked through it. God, there were resumes here from the year one. "Worthless," she muttered, sorting through and dumping those. "Ah, here it is." David Kim's resume with a letter attached. Standard letter. But the home address was not Forest Hills, it was 2904B Mott Street. "Eureka!" she cried, and flapping the resume in her hand, she sent the file drawer home with a thud.

"That does it!" Smith threw down her pencil and turned. "What's with you, Wetzon? You're mumbling to yourself, slamming down phones, tearing up papers, and punishing innocent filing cabinets."

"Look at this." Wetzon dropped the resume down in front of Smith. "And—" She bounced back to her desk, grabbed the list of names. "Now look at this." She set it down next to the resume. "What do you see?"

"Is this that list of phony accounts?" Smith's eyes took in both the resume and the list, swinging back and forth from one to the other. She chewed on the eraser end of her pencil, then she ran a bright coral fingernail down the list of names and stopped at one address. 2904B Mott Street, the address of one Collin Lee. It was also the address David Kim had used on his resume.

They stared at each other.

"What—" Wetzon began.

"The police know about the list," Smith interrupted.

"And supposedly, checked it out and came up with zip." Wetzon put her hand on Smith's shoulder. "Smith, listen to me a minute. What if David didn't do it? What if he was set up by someone else at Luwisher Brothers. Hoffritz, maybe—or Destry Bird."

"Or Doug Culver?"

"Yes. What if he's lying hurt or dead somewhere?"

"Like 2904B Mott Street?" Smith's smile was dazzling.

"Thank you." Wetzon snatched the resume and list from Smith's desk and, folding them, packed them into her handbag. She pulled out her wallet. "Forty dollars. Good." She had enough money.

"And what, may I ask, are you doing now?"

"I am going down to Chinatown to see what's at 2904B Mott Street."

"But what about our drink?"

"It's not as if we're never going to see each other again."

Smith slipped her feet back into her spectators and opened the door. "Harold, Wetzon and I are leaving now. Be sure the lights are all out when you leave, and lock up after yourself."

"Okay," Harold called, cheerfully. "I'm almost done here."

"What are you up to, Smith?" Wetzon slung her bag over her shoulder and headed for the door.

Smith was right at her heels. "You don't really think I'm going to let you solve this by yourself?"

SIXTY

Canal Street, which really had been a canal and a promenade in the early eighteen hundreds, was now a merchandise mart where peddlers hawked everything from batteries and socks to fish and vegetables. It also served as the portal to another world—Chinatown, a maze of dark, winding, densely populated streets in Lower Manhattan, a perfect place to hide, particularly if you were Asian.

Bound on the north by Canal Street, by Lafayette on the west and the Bowery on the east, it teemed with immigrants, legal and illegal. Vicious street gangs sold protection to small businesses, which were mainly restaurants in storefronts one after the other on Mott, Pell, Bayard, Baxter, Division, and Chatham Square. Even more restaurants cluttered second floors and cellars. Barbecued ducks dangled glistening in the storefront windows alongside other assorted fare. Disregarding the heat, shoppers—mostly Asian—were haggling loudly with vendors, watching, veil-eyed, the two white women in business clothing.

No way, Wetzon thought, could she and Smith not be conspicuous, particularly Smith, whose height was exaggerated by her high heels. They turned right off the Bowery onto Pell Street, the raw underbelly of Chinatown, edging around people clustered on the narrow sidewalks. Everyone seemed to be shouting. Where Pell ran into Mott, they stopped. They had not spoken since getting out of the cab.

Lined on both sides with run-down tenements that appeared to lean toward each other, these cramped streets, not made for auto traffic, were snarled with trucks and cars. Exotic odors mixed with garbage rot; a bakery in yet another storefront sold rice cakes and almond cookies, and the dead air floated sugary.

"2904B Mott Street," Wetzon murmured. "Here we are."

Smith's eyes searched. "Of course, they're never around when you need them."

"Who?" Wetzon was jostled by two elderly Chinese men, who made no apology as they kept up their dialogue as if the women were not there.

"The cops." Smith considered the tenement with narrowed eyes. "No. We're not going in there by ourselves."

The storefront of the building housed yet another restaurant—the Blue Flamingo Tea House. Peering through the steamy windows, they saw a luncheonette counter with a few people sitting, smoking, bowls in front of them. On the side were Formica-topped tables where an old Chinese man sat reading a newspaper.

To the right of the restaurant and up a step, grooved out by generations of footsteps, was a door with a big grimy window. Wetzon held the door open for the reluctant Smith. They entered a dank, dirty vestibule; the mud-brown linoleumed floor was cracked and threadbare. The stench of urine and mildew pervaded. Six mailboxes with names missing or crossed out and written over were in a horizontal row on the right wall. Each was marked with a letter.

"I'm going up." Wetzon's voice sounded hollow.

"Listen to me," Smith spoke in a throaty whisper. "I'm not going up there and neither are you. We could be kidnapped by white slavers and never seen again."

Wetzon guffawed. "You have to be kidding."

The door to the stairwell hung crookedly ajar from a broken upper hinge, which squeaked in protest when Wetzon pulled it open and peered in. A bare ceiling bulb dangled from a dirt-encrusted wire, its wattage so low, its exterior so caked with dirt and grease, that it gave off little light.

Smith leaned over Wetzon's shoulder, taking in the dim stairwell and the dirt, and shivered in spite of the smothering heat. "It's disgusting up there. You can't—" She pushed Wetzon aside and blocked the doorway.

"I'm not asking you to come with me. In fact, it's better that you don't. And I'm not going to stand here and argue. I'll be right back. Move."

Smith shrugged and stepped aside, careful not to brush against the filthy wall. "I'm not waiting here. It stinks to high heaven."

"Then wait outside." Wetzon smirked, thinking of tall, willowy Smith, in go-to-business clothes, hanging out on the street in front of the Blue Flamingo Tea House, like a hooker.

The steep, narrow steps were covered by a ragged rubber runner, and the whole cramped building seemed to tilt to the right. Voices and the muffled sound of china and pots clattering filtered through the cracked and chipped walls.

At the top of the stairs she found a short hall, two doors, and another set of stairs going up. Somewhere above her, a child began to cry, bunched and bleating. Footsteps shook the building and the child's crying stopped.

Wetzon listened at the first door, trying not to touch anything. Chicken soup permeated the landing, mingling with roasting meat, cabbage, all smells accumulated from those who had lived, died, or moved on from here. She knocked on the door. There was no response. Sweat dripped from her forehead, her upper lip. She licked her lips and tasted salt. *God,* she thought, and knocked on the second door.

"Hurry it up, will you." Smith called up from the floor below, skittery.

Wetzon raised her hand to knock again, but the door opened slightly, just enough for her to see David Kim looking just as shocked to see her as she was to see him. His face, even in the bleak yellowish light from the hall, looked white, skin drawn taut over his cheekbones; his dark eyes were sunken. A death's-head.

"My God, David."

He backed into the room, and she pushed the door open the rest of the way, following him into a warren of small, boxy rooms. A railroad flat. A sofa and a leather easy chair. A cream-and-blue nappy carpet. Track lighting. And a very complex stereo system hooked up to a television and a VCR. A fan whirled, but it was stiflingly hot. An odd humming sound seemed to come from the sofa.

"David—thank God you're all right." Why wasn't she afraid? In her heart of hearts, she knew he was innocent.

He sank into the chair and leaned his head back, closing his eyes. He looked as if he hadn't slept in days, weeks.

"David," she said again. "What's happened to you? What is this about?"

He opened his eyes and she saw agony. He said, "I didn't do it. They set me up."

"I knew it," she cried triumphantly. She sat down on the edge of the sofa and leaned toward him. "Who did it?" When he didn't answer her, she said, "David, come in with me and tell them you didn't."

He shook his head bleakly. "I can't. They'll never believe me. I have no money. You have to be rich to defend yourself."

"David, do you know who killed Ellie?"

"I'm scared." His hands trembled. Wetzon took them in hers; they were dry and cool.

"I'll go with you. It'll be all right. Come on." She stood and moved to help him up, and from that position, she saw the new Vuitton suitcase parked behind the still open door. Turning back to David, she said, "You were running away."

He nodded, mute.

An old, black AT&T telephone lay doggo under a newspaper, off the hook, humming. She knelt, threw off the paper, replaced the receiver, and punched out Silvestri's number at Midtown North.

"O'Connor."

"Lieutenant Silvestri, please."

"Not here."

"Is anyone else there?"

"Yeah, I'm here. Waddaya want, lady?"

"This is Leslie Wetzon. Tell Silvestri I'm at 2904B Mott Street with David Kim. He's going to—" A mighty sledgehammer hit her, glancing off her head, slamming into her shoulder, and she felt herself go down, sprawling across the telephone.

The suitcase, she thought. He'd bashed her with the suitcase. She lay gasping, trying to catch her breath, heard O'Connor from a distance, crackling from the receiver, heard David's thudding footsteps down the stairs. *Wetzon, you fool,* she thought, scrambling to her feet. She got to the door and collected enough breath to scream, "Smith!"

Then she came clattering down the stairs, heard brakes squeal, a terrifying shriek, as she threw open first one door then the other onto the street. Paper was flying from everywhere, scraps. Smith was rubbing her ankle, looking pleased with herself. A yellow cab. A crowd was dancing, jabbering in Chinese, in English, grabbing at the floating paper. It was money . . . bills. The cab driver, a small Pakistani with a pencil-thin mustache, was standing beside the cab, wringing his hands, crying, "He ran in front of me . . . did you see? . . . You saw, he ran in front of me. . . ."

"I tripped him." Smith grabbed her in a smothering hug. "Thank God, you're all right. I tripped him and he went flying into the street."

Where was David? Wetzon broke away from Smith. "David!" A siren wailed in the distance. A fifty-dollar bill floated past her nose and Smith clutched at it.

Wetzon pushed her way through the crowd. David lay on the street on his back, twisted among the orange rinds, bits of torn newspaper, and chicken bones, as people snatched at the explosion of bills, fifties and hundreds, that spilled from the split-open suitcase on the hood of the cab.

"David." His eyes were open. His mouth moved. Wetzon knelt on the filthy street. She touched his face, felt his wrist. There was a pulse, faint but steady. "Oh, David," she said. "Why? You had it made. Ellie loved you."

He moaned. "She was going to spoil it. She would have told."

"Dear God, was it worth it, David? The money"—She waved her hand around—"look, it's all gone."

His eyes were wet black marbles. He said, "I can't feel my legs."
Wetzon stroked his hand.
He looked at her and said, "I'm sorry, Father."
The sirens filled the vacuum.

SIXTY-ONE

They'd found a cab quickly on Chatham Square, Smith chattering, Wetzon silent.

"Altogether, I think it was a very profitable afternoon," Smith was saying. She patted her bulging pockets.

"You can't keep that money."

"Why not? What would it matter, and who would know, anyway?"

"Smith!"

"Well, all those people on the street got theirs, why not us?" She tapped on the Plexiglas divider. "Driver, please drop me at Forty-ninth and First."

"You're going back to the office?"

"It's early. I want to finish the budget, and besides, I left my watch on the desk. We can have that drink now, though, if you want. I could really use one."

"No. I've had it. I'm going home."

But she didn't, at least not right away. She couldn't. She was wound up, and having a drink with Smith was not her favorite way of unwinding. She had the driver drop her at Zabar's. She'd buy food. A pound of lobster salad, Eli Zabar's ultraskinny sourdough bread, a sharp chevre from Vermont, decaf espresso for iced coffee. She'd buy vegetables for a white gazpacho and fruit for a tart. Do domestic things.

Silvestri was probably at Bellevue right now, getting a statement from David Kim. He would clean up the case and come home, and everything would be the same as before. Or would it? She felt a dread that bordered on premonition.

Zabar's turned out to be civilized, without the usual crowds at cheese and deli counters. Probably because the heat had driven people from the City early.

The sky was overcast when she came out of Zabar's with her shopping bag. At long last, it was going to rain. It might break the long heat spell. A breeze blew up Broadway from the south and cooled the back of her neck.

She stopped at an Asian produce market and bought three boxes of raspberries for the tart, a cucumber, tomatoes, peppers. She had enough white wine to last for months, thanks to Doug Culver.

Inside the market, down the center, was an extensive salad bar with hot and cold food. She would never be able to look at one without remembering David Kim. He had caught the contagious disease of Wall Street—greed. Surely, as a mathematician in academia, there was no motivation or opportunity for the kind of money that could be made on the Street. But could you take someone with good morals, an honest person, and drop him down in the middle of unmitigated greed and think he wouldn't be tainted? Yes. An individual would have to have a streak of avarice and dishonesty already. Opportunity didn't change David Kim; it just made it easier for him. But what made him think he could get away with his scam forever? He wasn't even very smart about hiding it. They never were. He could have stopped after the first killing—the compliance director. But by that time he liked all the money he was making, and he couldn't stop. He thought he was invincible. So when Dr. Ash began blackmailing him, he killed again.

Thunder rolled faintly in the distance. It was raining somewhere— maybe Washington Heights, maybe New Jersey. She turned toward her building on Eighty-sixth Street. Lichtman's, the wonderful Austro-Hungarian bakery that used to be on the corner of Eighty-sixth and Amsterdam, was gone now, the victim of rising rents, and in its place was an antique gallery featuring art glass and furniture of the Arts and Crafts Movement. She wondered if she would ever find a bakery that made the perfect chocolate babka that Lichtman's had.

Lightning flashed behind a purplish cloud, giving it a glittery edge, and rain hovered so close she could almost feel the dampness on her face.

Her apartment was hot and claustrophobic as a tomb. She left the mail on the counter with the raspberries and vegetables, put everything else into the fridge, and turned on all the air conditioners. After a long, cool shower, she dressed in black cotton leggings and a loose pink tee shirt, and put on Channel 13's business report. The market had dropped almost three hundred points. *Disaster, darling,* Carlos would say. Well, that would be next week's drama. This weekend, she was going to give herself time off.

Having rinsed the berries and left them to drain, she measured the ingredients for the tart shell into her Cuisinart and processed it not quite into a ball, then emptied the contents onto the marble counter. When the phone rang she was fitting the dough into the pan carefully so as not to break the circle she had rolled out, and she was not about to stop, clean her hands of the sticky dough, and grab the phone. She'd never make it anyway and would leave a messy film of floury gook on everything she touched. And to this Carlos would say, that's why God made answering machines. She laughed out loud and felt better. The crust fit neatly into the pan. Her answering machine picked up in the middle of the fifth ring and clicked a few times. Concentrating, she tucked the extra dough smoothly under and flattened the sides.

She was putting the tart shell in the fridge when she heard a frustrated scream. "Wetzon! Where *are* you?" Smith was literally howling. "Call me at the office *at once.* Harold's gone and he's taken *everything* with him."

Damnation. The little shit. Wetzon stuck her hands under the hot-water faucet, got them half scoured, and grabbed the phone, but Smith had hung up. She dried her hands, dried the phone. *Calm down,* she told herself. How could Smith be sure Harold was gone? It was a holiday weekend. He'd probably just neatened up his desk.

She took a beer from the fridge and went into the dining room to check her answering machine. It was blinking two messages. One was from Smith, obviously, but the other must have come in while she was in the shower. Silvestri, maybe, telling her she'd done good—you wish—and he'd be home for dinner.

She called Smith first, before checking the other message, and found her in a frenzy.

"The *snake*. After all we've *done* for him, do you *believe* it? He's *japped* us."

"Wait, how do you know that? You're making a judgment without knowing—" She looked at her barre. It was inviting her to stretch and unwind, and how she needed it.

"Babycakes, trust me. He left a note. I'll kill the little dirtbag."

"Calm down. What does the note say?"

"Just that he's resigning as of today and he has enjoyed working with us."

"That's it? That's all?"

"What else do you want? He did it sneaky, too. When we weren't here." Wetzon could hear her opening and closing drawers and cabinets. "He cleaned out his desk, and God knows what." A howl and another slam. "I don't *believe* it. The little *rat* took our copy of his contract."

"It wasn't worth anything anyway."

"And maybe you'd like to know where he's gone?"

"How would we know that—uh-oh, don't tell me." Wetzon sat down on the floor, stretched her legs out, and folded herself over her knees.

"Yes. I called Tom Keegen's office, said I was with Merrill Lynch, and asked for Harold. They said he was away from his desk and would call back. Do you *believe* it?"

"Smith, let's calm down and think this through rationally. If brokers want to deal with him, they'll deal with him. It works the same way as brokers' clients. Isn't that the chance we take?"

"Logic is not what I need right now, Wetzon. I am having the locks changed as we speak. I'll talk to you later." She hung up.

Wetzon rose, weary, and replaced the receiver with a sigh. What a day this had been. First David. Now Harold. She was sorry to see Harold go. He was a pain sometimes, with all his airs, but he'd been a good competitive worker. Perhaps they could move B.B. up now and hire a new cold caller.

Idly, she pressed the playback button and the machine clicked several times and rewound the tape, clicked again. Then she heard Chris Gorham say in an intimate whisper, "Now I'm going to kill myself, Wetzon, and you're going to have to live with it forever."

SIXTY-
TWO

She played the tape back. Chris was going to kill himself. *Don't overreact*, she told herself. *Panic won't help.* She found his home number in her client book, and with shaking hands, called it. It rang three times, then, "Gorham residence."

"Oh, thank God—" Someone was there.

"No one is here to answer your call right now. Kindly leave your name and number and a brief message after the beep and your call will be returned."

She hung up before the beep, and called Silvestri at Midtown North. The line was busy. Chris couldn't have called more than a half hour ago, maybe less. She paced the apartment, tried again. Still busy. Lightning twitched through the sky and thunder cracked right overhead; then came the rain, slapping down hard on her windows, smacking the air conditioner. She felt trapped. She ran into the bedroom and slipped on her Keds, grabbed an umbrella and her handbag.

She skidded to a stop at her front door, came back, and dialed Smith in the office. It rang and rang. *Pick up, damn you, Smith, pick up.* Finally, "Smith and Wetzon." Smith sounded rotten.

"Smith, listen, we'll deal with Harold. We can handle it, don't forget, we're terrific. Just say okay."

Smith sniffed. "Okay."

"Smith, I want you to do something for me. It's very important."

"What?" She sounded suspicious.

"I can't get through to Silvestri." She was breathing hard and couldn't seem to get enough air. "I want you to keep trying him. Chris just called me. He's going to kill himself. I've got to stop him."

Smith sucked in her breath and said sharply, "You'll do no such thing."

"Don't tell me what to do. I've got to get out of here." She gave Smith Silvestri's number and Chris's address and hung up on her, hoping she'd gotten it all down.

In the elevator she wondered what the hell she was getting herself into. Why was she making herself responsible for Chris Gorham after what he'd done to her? He wanted to make her responsible. Her fingers played on the buttons. The minute she got to the lobby she would hit 12 and go right back up. Let the creep kill himself.

But when the door opened to the lobby, she stepped out, greeting tenants just coming home, dripping umbrellas, faces she recognized, names she didn't know. She had wanted him dead, had wanted to kill him herself, but her anger had ebbed. He had two children. She didn't want him to kill himself. How could kids live with that? How could she? What was she waiting for? She raised her umbrella and stepped out of her building into a monsoon of sweeping rain and wind.

With daylight entirely obscured, the world had a yellowed, sulphurous aura. Headlights beamed hazily on wet streets, where oil slicks formed patches in rainbow streams.

No cabs. Her best bet was to go over to Columbus and try to get one coming downtown. Choking the umbrella on its stem, she staggered against the wind to the corner of Eighty-sixth and Columbus. The cool rain smelled sweet and fresh, like wild honeysuckle. The wind buffeted her umbrella as she struggled to hold on to it, blowing it inside out, and when she lowered it, perversely, blowing it whole again.

People were hurrying by, holding newspapers or briefcases over their heads; others didn't even bother to protect themselves, it felt that good. Smiling faces everywhere. Comradery. The heat wave was over—at least for now. Look, we've come through.

The rain had soaked her in spite of the umbrella, which she fought to keep upright. Her Keds had gone squishy as she darted out on

Columbus and flagged a cab down only minutes later, just as a bolt of lightning seared the sky and a sharp clap of thunder followed.

"Twenty-ninth and Madison." She slammed the door closed.

"What a storm," the driver said. "Yeh, yeh. We sure need it." Abe Kravitz. A heavy man in his sixties, a crown of gray, kinky hair. Over his radio a voice crackled and faded out, came back and gave an address in Greenwich Village. Kravitz picked up his speaker and said, "I'll be at Twenty-ninth and Madison in ten minutes. I can get down to Tenth Street from there, if they'll wait."

A moment later, the radio sputtered, "Mrs. Goldsmith, six ten West Tenth. She's all yours, Abie-lla."

They sped on the transverse through the Park to Sixty-fifth Street, to Park Avenue, then a right and downtown.

"Didja hear, they got the Jap?"

Wetzon looked up, confused. "I'm sorry?"

"You know, the Jap that killed the Wall Street people."

"He isn't Japanese, he's Korean."

"Same thing."

Wetzon grunted. *Just shut up and drive,* she thought.

"Sit back, lady, or you'll get hurt."

She sighed and had just sat back when the cab was side-swiped by another cab making a turn from the wrong lane in the blinding rain. She fell over on the seat, sat up slowly, listening to her body. She wasn't hurt, but dammit, she had to get to Chris before he did it. Both drivers jumped out and screamed at each other, shaking fists.

Wetzon rolled down her window. "Are we going or not?"

Kravitz got back in his seat and said to the front window, "Sorry, lady." He turned off his meter. "You can pay me and go or you can wait till the cops come." Horns began to honk all around them. The noise was deafening. Wetzon wiped the steam from the window and saw they were blocking the turn on Thirty-fourth Street. It wasn't that far, then.

"I can't wait." She gave him seven dollars and got out into the downpour, put up her umbrella and squinted to get her bearings. Then she began a steady jog down Park Avenue. Only five blocks. She heard a siren in the distance above the car horns—either for the accident, or just possibly Smith had done her job and gotten through to Silvestri.

In fact, why did she think she had to be there at all? Because Chris had directed the call to her. It was a spiteful, hostile act. Blame the victim. *And you're letting yourself be victimized again. Don't get involved. Turn around and go home. You've done enough.*

Leave me be, she told herself. *Let me do it my way.*

Drenched, she jogged west on Twenty-ninth Street one block to Madison. Around her, everywhere, fragments of umbrellas, mangled skeletons, lay on the sidewalk and in crosswalks, sticking out of trashbaskets, blown to shreds. A New York ritual. How many umbrellas did she go through in a year—five, six, more?

The rain had eased, and steam was coming from manhole covers, drifting skyward like lazy smoke.

She ducked under the awning of Chris's building and shook the water out of the umbrella, folding it up under the Velcro tape. What was she going to say to the doorman, she was thinking, as he opened the door for her.

"Yes, miss?" He recognized her, she thought.

"Um, I'm here to see Mr. Gorham. He's not feeling well. . . ."

"Your name?"

She felt uncomfortable, fidgeted in her wet Keds, pulled her damp tee shirt away from her breasts, looked around. A woman carrying a briefcase and a D'Agostino's bag passed her en route to the elevator. She had to get into the building, had to get to Chris before—

"Good evening, Mrs. Steinkoller," the doorman said. He looked back at Wetzon and repeated, "Your name?"

"Ms. Wetzon." She shivered. The lobby air-conditioning was cold against her damp clothes.

"Go right up. He's expecting you. Twenty-four L." He handed her an envelope and she saw her name was written on it in longhand. Was this a setup? Was it going to happen again? No. She was a little wiser now. Besides, Silvestri would come, the EMS people would . . . she got on the elevator with the woman and squeezed the envelope. He was expecting her? Yeah. The envelope held a key.

Her heart hammered against her ribcage, making her tee shirt flutter; she squeezed the wet nylon of the umbrella until it was a club.

"Well, at least the heat broke," the woman said. She shifted her briefcase to the other hand and picked up the shopping bag. "Good night." She got off on the fifteenth floor.

"Yes, good night," Wetzon said. It seemed as if everyone wanted to talk . . . and she didn't want to talk to anyone. She got off on the twenty-fourth floor and ran down the hall clutching the umbrella as a weapon. The door to his apartment was closed. What had she expected? She turned the knob. Locked. So maybe he wasn't expecting her. *Ring the bell, dummy.* What if she was too late and he'd done it?

She went back to the elevator and pressed the down button. *Get out of here,* she thought. Wait, what was she doing? She had the key. She tore open the envelope. Yes, it was a key. She walked down the hall to the door again, determined. Heavy rock music came from one of the apartments. She heard a woman yell for someone to turn down the TV. Cooking smells permeated the hall. No sound came from Chris's apartment. She put the key into the lock and opened the door. Back down the hall behind her the elevator door opened and two EMS people were getting off, followed by a uniformed policeman.

"Down here," she called, pushing the door open with the umbrella. The apartment was dim and silent. She walked in tentatively. "Chris?" She walked into the living room toward the terrace. The sky was streaked with pink and blue hues. A blanket, probably blown by the wind from another terrace, hung limply from the terrace above onto Chris's. It swung and turned in the wind.

The EMS men came into the apartment. She turned to look at them and then looked back at the blanket. It was wearing shoes, toes pointed downward.

SIXTY-THREE

Wetzon leaned her forehead against the cool refrigerator door; she was burning up. The door was studded with notes under Hershey bar magnets: a recipe for chicken pot pie from a magazine, a child's crayon drawing of a mother, father, and two children. The father was gigantic in size.

She could hear them working in the living room, on the terrace, trying to get Chris down. Someone had gone upstairs to cut the rope he'd attached to the terrace rail directly above his.

Her stomach heaved. A two-way radio crackled, breaking voices in midsentence. She heard grunts and a shout, then, "Okay, lay him down."

There was nothing to do, nothing to keep her here anymore. She wandered out of the kitchen, stopped briefly to look at the silhouettes of the men working over Chris, and walked out the open door into the corridor. Nothing. Nothing to do. People were standing in the doors to their apartments. Someone called, "Who's sick?" But she couldn't see clearly. *No one is sick,* she answered in her head. They all looked as if they were under thick glass, bulging and shimmying. What were they saying? She couldn't understand.

She stood a little to the side and saw herself press the down button and then get on the elevator. So she followed, staying close to herself, so no one would notice two of them. A woman in shorts with Minnie Mouse legs ending in huge running shoes was stretching her hamstrings against the side of the elevator. The instant the door opened, the woman jogged out of the elevator, and Wetzon followed her out the front entrance past two uniformed policemen coming in.

Sirens, like beads on a string, whined, paused, whined, paused, and lights whirled on the white EMS van, blending blue and yellow with the bands on top of the two police cars in front parked against the traffic.

She let her Keds lead her and they took her across Twenty-ninth Street and toward Fifth Avenue.

The sky was a watercolor wash, and the wet earth of the garden smelled sweet and rich. Huge trees shook their leaves at her in the soft breeze and sprayed her with raindrops. She walked through the gate and under the stone arch, up the curving path to the Little Church Around the Corner.

She opened the heavy oak door and walked past the vestibule and into the church. Ahead, candles flickered in a small altar. To her right was the church itself, with stained-glass windows on the north and south walls, narrowing in perspective to the burnished, gleaming altar. It glowed with light, but was closed.

Veering left, she entered the dimly lit chapel. A woman knelt in the second row of pews, her head down. Otherwise, the chapel was empty.

The gentle calm drew her in, and she let it wrap itself around her. The pews were so narrow her knees almost touched the back of the next pew. Kneeling cushions hung nearby.

He had killed himself and laid the blame on her. Her other self spoke up and said, "It's not your fault." He'd wanted her to find him like that. To get even. To punish her. It was so ugly. She looked up at the mosaic of the ceiling and thought, if she hadn't agreed to have dinner with him, if she hadn't gone to his apartment, he might still be alive. Her judgment was flawed. Hubris. She had too much pride. Would she ever be able to trust herself again?

She closed her eyes and felt the presence of all the people dear to her that she'd lost . . . her mother's sweet face, her father, friends who had died . . . and she cried. For her parents, for missing friends, for poor Ellie, for people who had no one to care about them, for David, even for Chris.

The oak door opened and footsteps thudded behind her as someone came into the chapel, paused, then came and sat down next to her.

"How did I know I'd find you here?" Silvestri said, taking her hand.

"You're a good detective. The best." Tears seeped from under her closed lids.

Silvestri squeezed her hand. "You're pretty good yourself."

"Why did Chris do it?"

"He was sick. Listen to me, Les. It's not your fault." Silvestri put his arm around her and pulled her to him.

"Is David going to live?"

"Yeah, he'll live. If the schmuck hadn't been waiting around for the last check to clear, he would have gotten away clean. Ninety-seven thousand dollars."

"Does being born here do it, do you think? Is it something endemic to this country? Look what he set in motion. Look how many lives—" She stopped. "Ripple on ripple on ripple. Angelo, Goldie, Ash, Ellie—and now Chris. Why do things like this happen? What kind of mean, vicious world is this?"

He blotted up her tears with his handkerchief. "I'd like to protect you from all the crap in the world, but I can't."

She opened her eyes and saw him, steady as a rock, and smiled. "I wouldn't let you anyway," she said.

"No, you wouldn't." He rose and held his hand out to her. They left the church and stood for a moment on the garden path. Silvestri looked down at her. "But that doesn't mean I'm not going to try."

"Okay."

"Okay? You said okay?"

"Yes."

His eyes laughed at her. "Then, take off your clothes."